Rise of The Spring Tide

James Stitt

ISBN:1532912099

ISBN-13:978-1532912092

This is a work of fiction. Names, characters, businesses, places, events and incidents are either the products of the author's imagination or used in a fictitious manner. Any resemblance to actual persons, living or dead, or actual events is purely coincidental.

Contact;

https://jamesrstitt.wordpress.com/

@stittwords on Twitter

Contents

Maps and Travels - The West

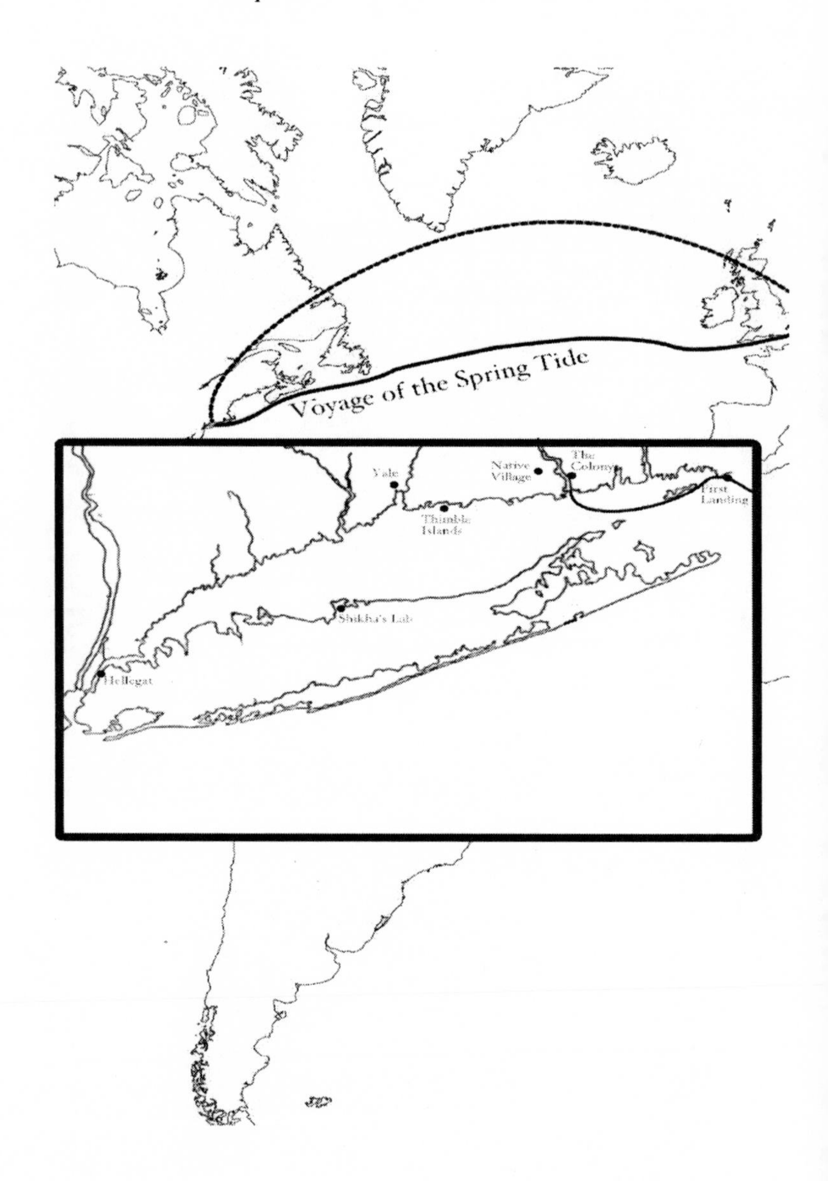

Maps and Travels - The East

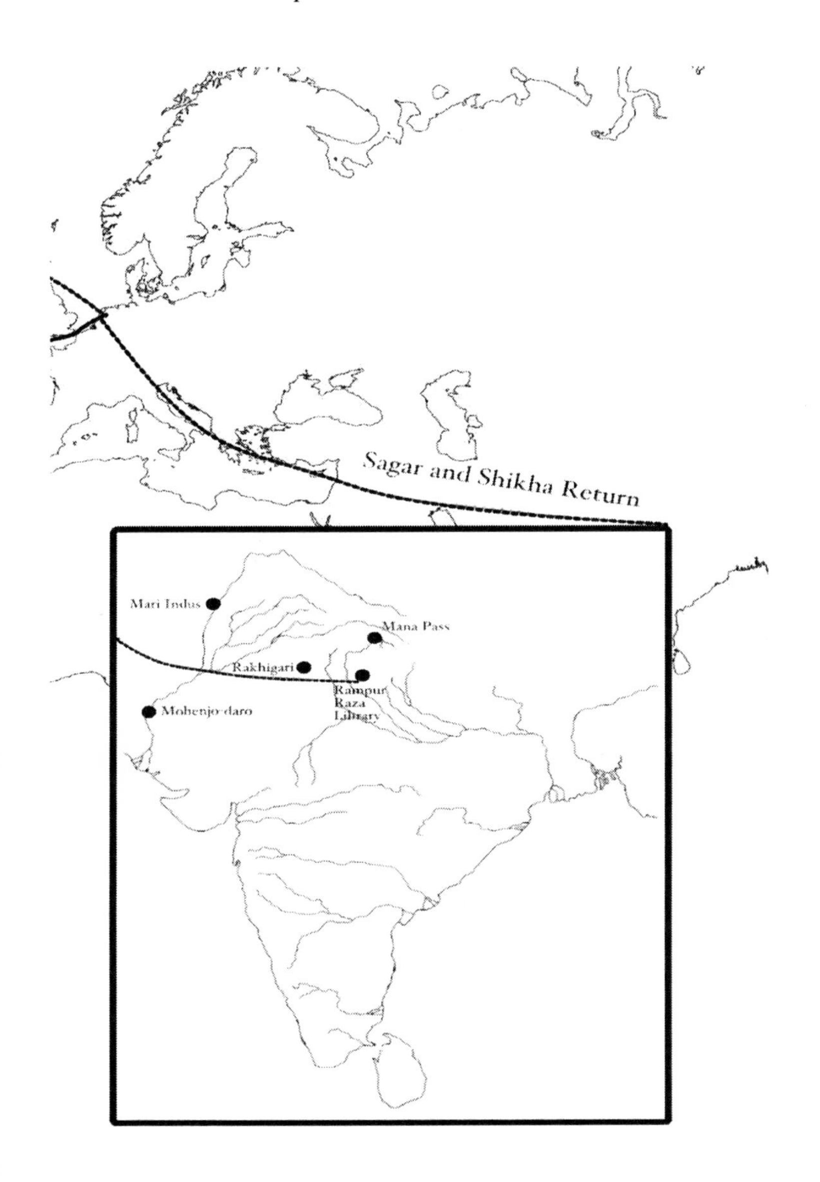

PART ONE

CHAPTER 1 - March 29, 2013

Shikha slumped on a high stool, swiveling slowly back and forth. She gazed out at the white wall of wet snow, isolated from nature by the triple-paned glass and cocooned by modern engineering. How many storms had she endured: at sea, on the New England coast, the winter maelstroms in the foothills of the Himalayas? None in quite such comfortable surroundings as where she found herself today, but Shikha recalled none as lonely. From inside the newly opened protein synthesis lab, save for the occasional wind gust off the Atlantic, the storm's growl could barely compete with the low hum of the environmental control system.

As she did each Saturday night, Shikha waited for any overzealous researchers to filter out so she could work alone. Perhaps due to the weather or because the next day was Easter, only one person, a new PhD candidate from the City named Jordan, remained. Four Saturdays now he had lingered in the lab well past what she considered an appropriate bedtime. Her half-second impression placed him among most of the PhD's and post docs: he was petrified of Shikha, who held a singular position at Stony Brook.

While teaching no classes, having no PhD students of her own and not specifically involved with any project the students could identify, the department chair and the dean herself would consistently seek the young Indian woman's counsel on key scientific questions and organizational decisions. A few times Jordan turned toward her from across the sterile lab, trying to catch her gaze, which she noticed but ignored. A second more of consideration revealed his motives. The poor boy had a crush on her.

Lessons learned, relearned, and rare relapses into love all

ended the same for her. Better to remain detached, observing, than risk the temporary joys of companionship. Others could believe in a happy ending, some even found it, but not her. A blink of five years, maybe ten would be all they could share. Twenty, fifty, a hundred years from now, she would simply have another grave to visit.

Deal with it straightaway, Shikha said to herself. She threw him a concerted scowl, which soured and reddened his face as if he'd eaten raw rhubarb and sent him scurrying to the far side of the lab. In that scowl, her dark eyes had just barely moistened with tears before she turned away.

Enough ruminating. Shikha had little fear of anyone discovering the nature of her work, especially Jordan. If he couldn't ask her out for coffee, how could he possibly steal her research? Besides, Shikha had developed her own encryption toolkit when at Yale and had recently added a failsafe script that ran in the background of her UNIX environment. If her workstation login had no activity for ten minutes, all programs were terminated, connections dropped and files encrypted. For now, with the lab nearly vacant, security was the least of her concerns. She removed six DNA samples from the storage refrigerator, completed their preparation by attaching fluorescent dye and warmed up the massive DNA sequencer.

Questions require answers. She told herself, limit your focus to the work at hand, not the past, not the decades of memories precisely stored within you. They had led nowhere. Shikha sometimes wished her mind would finally fail, easing her into oblivion like a little leaf, slowly pulled underwater by the river's flow. The hundred and fifteen years of separation from her kin had worn away her resolve. Letters, telegrams, calls, now texts, they pricked at her, intensifying her yearning for the touch of a finger, a hand held and the power it evoked.

Faria, her twin sister, now traversed the middle east and the Indian subcontinent while Sagar, their only known relative, rode the waves and winds of the Pacific. Like the doting spinster auntie, Shikha had remained within fifty miles of where the Spring Tide first beached herself in the muddy banks of the Connecticut River in 1603, the three of them aboard. Adopted by Puritans traveling to the new world, each could recall every day and hour of the voyage: the storms, their hammocks, the cramped gun deck where they slept, and always, dearest Abby.

Stretching further back another two hundred years, the edges of their memories had never dulled. Beyond their earliest recollections where the twins subsisted at the base of the great mountains and Sagar in the snows of their peaks, lay a singularity where only consciousness remained. It was as if they stared into a perfectly black sky with no stars to guide them, like the candle on a child's bedside table blown out by a hovering parent. Strange enough was their fate, stranger still what dwelled within the twins.

Shikha's attention was pulled back to the present by the sound of the DNA sequencer completing its first stage. Rather than allowing the standard software to perform the subsequent assembly steps, she immediately transferred the raw data to several binary files. She then shut the sequencer down and destroyed the samples. Despite Shikha's trust in the manufacturer's algorithms, indeed she had contributed to their source code, she prepared the raw data for a custom analysis using her own software routines. After two years of following this line of research, Shikha felt close. Performing the pattern recognition across several servers in parallel was the breakthrough she felt was key to deciphering the somewhat unusual results. These DNA samples were different. They were her own.

Just as Shikha launched the programs that helped control traffic across the multiple computers, the power cut out. Pivoting toward the windows, she saw through the snowy night only her building had lost electricity. She considered the facts: the underground power lines were unaffected by the storm, the building had independent diesel generators that should kick in immediately, and the failover system was tested twice a month. Shikha didn't think it possible that the most technologically advanced building on Long Island could have completely lost power. A menacingly familiar pressure wave began to penetrate her consciousness and the slight awareness of Jordan remaining in her mind evaporated as he fell to the floor, out cold. Her cell phone illuminated the desk.

Picking it up brought a small measure of relief: it was her sister Faria, who, when last they spoke, was somewhere in Utter Pradesh. Before Shikha had a chance to say hello, Faria spoke frantically across the crackling connection: "Shi, are you there, are you okay?"

"I'm here," whispered Shikha. "Did you feel it?"

"Like an earthquake, yeah, but you're okay?"

"Not sure yet. I'm in the lab. The other person here was knocked out, the power just died and there's a Nor'Easter raging outside," Shikha whispered back.

Their conversation, the connection between the twins, jolted awake a slumbering presence shared between them. Since her death in 1637, their adopted mother Abigail's spirit had inhabited their collective consciousness. Under exceptional circumstances, she would manifest her voice, but only when the twins were together. Her words echoed from deep within. "Girls, the storm's just a ruse. Shi, you're in deep danger."

Across the cell phone, her sister Faria begged: "Get out of there, save your work if you can. They found me here in Rampur today, destroyed my research and several volumes I had borrowed from the Raza library."

Shikha was about to respond but instead paused and listened. Finally, she said, more to herself than to her sister, "Someone's coming down the hall."

CHAPTER 2 - January, 15, 1603

Eleven children clustered around a low-burning fire set slightly back from the Niewe Maas river road. A lean man lazily herded them, circling the group as if, left to themselves, they might wander into the darkness of the Rotterdam night. A steady mist coated the odd group's black wool garments in tiny water spheres and a few of the children realized they could use the moisture-soaked wool as a canvas. They inscribed one another's backs in symbols unrecognizable, though unnoticed, by the thrall of humanity moving along the road.

While all the children shared similar physical characteristics, as if born from the same litter, two preadolescent girls stood apart, identical twins who failed to play with the others. Their long black hair, pressed against cheeks the color of lightly roasted coffee, framed sorrowful eyes that scrutinized each passerby on the congested thoroughfare. Brigu, their shepherd, sensed their apprehension. Tonight, they would be claimed, placed with strangers traveling to the new world. Any of the faces the twins glanced at upon could be their future father or mother.

Brigu and his caravan of children, half as large today as when they departed, had traveled over four thousand miles together, yet this journey was only half complete. This meeting with adoptive parents was not the first, but for Brigu, it was the most precarious. He had planted children in cultures across thousands of miles, but the little ones always parted one by one. Tonight, in contention with the principal directive of his mandate, Brigu would place three children together.

The forest of masts lining the water's edge swayed but a little in the eddies spawned by the river's snaking turn around Fijenoord Island. From the North side of the river, the island's lights diffused through the mist into a soft glow. As the hours passed and the temperature dropped, the children huddled closer to the fire, their retreats into the darkness ceasing. Traffic on the river road waned, and beside the more substantial brick warehouses, other fires were lit, attracting sailors from the bellies of their ships.

Brigu scanned the cobbled thoroughfare, trying to pull an unseen target from the damp darkness. He exhaled a long breath when first discerning a gray mass emerge, moving East, upriver, along the road. When passing in front of a sailor's fire some fifty yards off, it resolved into a group of five individuals. The three men and two women anxiously checked in at each fire as they neared, sometimes only to glance at the surrounding crowd before moving on. They had come at last.

Brigu gathered the twin girls and a boy of the same age close. "Patience. There is time enough for the three of you. Stay together for as long as you can. Sagar," he continued, addressing the boy, "this congregation must thrive in the new lands. They are not of one spirit, not of one purpose. This you will see. You must make their way safe for as long as is needed. I could only ask this of you, my strongest. You will not find an easy home, but persist in your labors." Brigu turned to the twin girls. "Shikha, Faria, my sweets, there is one among the approaching group, she with fiery hair, who needs your guidance. Watch her. She is not like us, but still, not like the others. Stay with her until the end. She is your charge, she is your purpose. She must survive."

Smiling upon them as a father might before a child left for war, he stepped back behind the fire and whispered a small prayer to himself. Mirroring his movement, the three children edged to the outskirts of their small group, positioning themselves as first to receive the approaching strangers.

They were led by a well-dressed man, a proud silver buckle bedecking his black hat. He strode briskly in front, tapping an ebony cane upon the cobblestones. Two couples in their 20's, of fair and ruddy complexion, trailed him. With features worn down by lives of outdoor labor, like the children they approached, they wore simple, unadorned clothes. Their leader slowed his gait and pointed his cane at the children's shepherd. "Are you the man known as Brigu?" he barked, and assuming the answer, continued. "You should have chosen an easier place to find. We have been wandering in this rain for nigh two hours." Brigu watched the man's eyes sweep across the children, his kinfolk, the silver buckle reflecting the deep red shades of the fire's dying embers.

Waiting just a moment to allow the sharp words to settle from the air, Brigu replied, "I am known by that name."

"Yes, of course you are. I am Reverend Smith. At the behest of Reverend Williams, we have come from Amsterdam to inspect your orphans and possibly place four within our flock," said Smith.

Brigu mused: Smith, a common name for a common man, it would seem. This reverend was peripheral, but the other four . . . "Williams. We talked of your religion, of predestination and free will. A strange paradox, but a thoughtful man. He now possesses two of my most precious books. I hope in time, they will guide you as they did me. Williams' eyes were brighter than yours, but he came to us in the daylight," replied Brigu, crafting his odd response to befuddle the reverend.

It was as if Smith were working off a formal script, but he did not receive the next line as expected. Whatever Smith's next statement was to be, it had become stuck in his mouth. His jaw opened, closed. He looked away and into the darkness, focused on remembering exactly what color eyes his mentor and spiritual leader, Williams, had. He didn't know. Perhaps now they would hear from the others, Brigu thought.

One of the two women stepped forward, first glancing at Smith, then the children. During their long walk from the boarding house, a few coarse straw-colored hairs had escaped from her black shawl and now wafted across her reddish cheeks. "My name is Mary Tanner. You see, Sir Brigu, my husband James and I seek to follow our Reverend Williams as he founds a colony in the New World. Without children of our own, there will be no one to help us in the toil we face."

Brigu wondered if she intended to address him as Sir Brigu or she started with Sir and realized that she'd heard his name. Mary's humble confusion forced his mouth to crease slightly upwards. He had spent many years in the West, been known by many names, but none as elevated as Sir Brigu. He moved forward, standing directly behind the fire. In turn, he focused on each of the five travelers, gauging their intent. He dwelled on the woman who had yet to speak until she uncomfortably stepped backwards and looked into the embers. Satisfied, he swept his right hand across his body and motioned to the children.

"These three are Sagar, Faria and Shikha. I am their steward, not their keeper. They have already known a full measure of hardship, which should have been meted out over a lifetime, and have subsisted on lean provisions and rough travel for many years. Workers though, all three, and I know they will serve you and respect your wishes."

With Smith still incapable of speaking, Mary's husband James, the most stoutly built of the group, addressed Brigu: "It was our aim to choose four to accompany us, two children for each couple. Our journey will be difficult. From Amsterdam we will sail across the Occidental ocean, following the route of the salt cod fishermen. Only two of our party have any seafaring experience: our ship's captain is Mary here's father, while the first mate Jorge is a Portuguese who shares our faith and has worked the fishing grounds some twenty years. Our route is known to him as the books of Scripture are known to Reverend Williams. With only two seasoned mariners, each member of our colony will man the sails, tar the lines and serve equal watches on deck. Once we reach the land across the ocean, our new life will unfold as only the Lord has predetermined. So you see, while we promise to care for these children as Mordecai did Esther, Ours is a perilous path."

Brigu looked at James' hands, no doubt a blacksmith. Reddened and burnt from exposure. He understood full well the earnest laborer's statement. They sought four children, two for each couple, as a way to insure against the death of one. This need validated the selections he had made during his meal with Reverend Williams some weeks ago. The twins, Faria and Shikha, and Sagar would make their way across the ocean with this congregation, thus serving many purposes. Walking around the fire and placing his hands on the shoulders of Shikha and Faria, he addressed the travelers, but his gaze did not leave the woman who had yet remained silent.

"Twice as many as you see here set out from a mountainous

land years ago. Brothers and sisters separated as paths diverged and providence required. We have lost none and these three will not be lost on your journey. Faria and Shikha can sow and reap barley, sorghum and rice. They know the art of knots and can mend fish nets as well as ship's rigging. Sagar has taken more than one turn at a ship's wheel, although for his size it is best to anchor him to the deck during rough seas. He is more than fair with a hammer and is better than most with a bow. On our journeys, he has shown himself adept at new languages and can write a few lines of English."

At length, Brigu turned to Reverend Smith. "No four can offer you as much as these three. Sagar and the twins are related, while the other children hail from another clan. It would be well to keep them together." The dormant fire sputtered to life as an unburnt log fell into the coals, throwing sparks to their death in the moisture-laden air. During the earlier exchanges, Smith had sufficient time to compose himself but Brigu's odd method of address again confounded him. Brigu remained looking at Smith; his stare alone seemed to part Smith's lipless mouth, forcing forth a few words.

"Yes, children must be kept together, and as our Reverend Williams did not specify a number, we can be satisfied with three." With his gaze, Brigu mined Smith's thoughts, which had regressed twenty-four years to his mother's death; he was too young and his father too infirm to care for his little brother and sister. They were taken in by their aunt in Edinburgh and Smith was left to care for his father in London. Six months later his father succumbed to the cough. Reverend Williams, still a Jesuit Priest, had administered extreme unction. It was the last act Williams performed under the old faith. Smith attached himself to the Reverend from that point forward and willingly followed him down the path of reform.

Mary Tanner spoke again, addressing both Brigu and her husband. "We will welcome Sagar into our family, so long as he will honor our ways. My father will be pleased to have another seasoned hand upon the decks, even if the hands are still a bit small." She haltingly smiled at the boy standing in front of her. Brigu acknowledged Mary's words but followed her thoughts into what she dared not say. Williams and Smith might believe their path was righteous and preordained, but being the daughter of a ship's captain, she knew well enough that the rolling black ocean and its denizens paid no heed to the will of God, or His followers who sought passage upon its surface.

"These twin girls, they will do," said the tallest of the group, George Fielding. A carpenter by trade, he chose his words in the same manner as he worked: methodically and with no wasted effort. Faria and Shikha were therefore paired with George and his freckled wife Abigail.

In him, Brigu and in turn the twins, saw an honest but indifferent man, who would care for them as he would a hammer and plane; they would serve their purpose, nothing more. Abigail could not be so easily read. She had said nothing, rather had observed the others, particularly Brigu. In her, they sensed depths, which, through her silence, she would not betray. Brief glances and nods were the only goodbyes exchanged between the three children and their longtime companions. As Brigu watched them disappear into the darkness, he thought again upon his decision, a betrayal of his mission. The seeds had now been sown and perhaps one day, together, they would grow to see the light.

The party set out for their boardinghouse, following the contours of the Rhine's tributary as it snaked toward open water. Ebb tide and the clearing sky had exposed the river's muddy banks, leaving smaller tenders and fishing vessels, typically not made fast to pilings, lying on their sides, keels stuck into the soft riverbed. Faria and her sister thought this gave the boats a relaxed, lounging look, while Sagar viewed the riverbank like an abandoned cemetery, the barnacle bedecked hulls serving as forgotten gravestones.

The two couples had coolly welcomed the children in words; it would remain to be seen whether their roles would be as accepted members of the family or simply as servants on the mission to the new lands. What the children could recall of their lives before Brigu gathered them was a directionless, lonely existence. They had come to rely on his counsel and purpose, and on each other for strength. Now the twins and Sagar would need to stay wary and alert.

While Sagar knew nothing of Smith's past, he saw through to his weaknesses and insecurities. The man was much like a few ships' captains he had known: the kind who would lead a group astray, fearing the shame of being wrong greater than the inherent danger at hand. He bore marking. Sagar felt anxious to meet Captain Tanner and the Portuguese sailor Mary had mentioned, in whose hands this strange group had placed their lives. He suspected the three of them would bear the hardships of the voyage more heavily than their passengers. Inexperience on board meant slow sail changes and clumsy greenhorns endangering themselves and others aloft in the ship's rigging.

Faria and Shikha had always had one another. Their attachment to the Fieldings, as Brigu had instructed, gave them no pause, indeed it was a relief that they would remain together. In the times before Brigu discovered them in the verdant forests at the base of the great mountains, they had thrived in the wilderness, subsisting off the fruits of the sandy white soil, fed by the annual rains and watchful of both man and beast. In two bodies, yet acting and thinking as one.

At a large bend in the river lay several sooty, wooden boarding houses that seemed to lean away from its salty stench. Smith halted in front of the lowest slung of the three and turned to the group. "We return to Amsterdam and our congregation tomorrow. It is over an hour's walk to reach the carriage, so we must leave just after dawn if we hope to find the carriage driver in good spirits and still willing to complete the journey." Having issued his instructions, Smith disappeared through a freshly painted black door.

James motioned to his companions, who followed him across the threshold into a low-ceilinged room. Sagar noted the dense oak beams running lengthwise abutting a fireplace on the far wall, in which only coals remained. A few sailors lingered in the common room, too drunk or tired to make their way elsewhere. While Mary slipped down a corridor to the left, the other adults ascended a staircase that creaked and moaned under each step. The twins and Sagar paused, not sure who to follow. Sagar shrugged but reckoned their room wouldn't be on the ground floor, so the three children leapt after the adults. To the third story they went, where under the meager light of the small candle George held, James fumbled with a key. At last he released the catch and swung the door wide. George entered first. The dim glow of the candlelight was augmented by the moon reflecting off the river through a window at the far end of the small room. Below the window sat a basic wooden table, flanked by two high double beds.

Mary appeared at the door with a stack of sheets and rough wool blankets and went to work fashioning bedding for the children. Abigail helped by moving two sea chests against the wall, creating more room. Sagar, Faria and Shikha looked on, their wariness melting with the warmth of the gesture. Never once had another human made a bed for them and they were confounded at how to express their gratitude.

"Well now, that should do. James, George, if you would please. Girls, I hope you have something to sleep in besides your coats." The twins unslung their packs and began to search for their sleeping shirts while the men exited, Sagar tailing them. As Abigail removed her shawl, she revealed tightly curled locks of the brightest orange, which she expertly tucked back into a sleeping cap. Even in the light of a single candle, the twins were struck by the brilliance of her hair.

Mary blew out the candle and let out a soft call to the men in the hall, at which point they entered the room lit only by the setting moon. Sagar followed them and burrowed into the covers at the base of the beds, lying perpendicular to the twins. An uneasy sleep crept over everyone in the room, excepting George the carpenter, who, without an anxious bone in his body, could turn off his wakefulness just as easily as he could turn a screw.

CHAPTER 3 - January 1603

Sagar woke before the sunrise, before the others. He peered down from their single window at the ships, which had come up the river with the tide, now unloading cargo in the dawn haze. He need not wait long for the others to rise. The growing shuffle of boots in the hallway ensured the denizens of the first room on the third floor were awake, packed and in the common area well before Smith. In a first-floor suite at the lee side of the boardinghouse, the reverend must have had quieter surroundings, Sagar suspected. He emerged from the dark hallway nearly an hour after the sun's rays broke over the horizon, the son of the landlord close behind, enduring a sharp reprimand from Smith. The boy undoubtedly didn't understand the words themselves, but Sagar knew their tenor was not lost on him.

The party moved outside, where a two-wheeled cart, overloaded with their belongings, waited. A solemn gray horse stood hitched to it, ever ready to move at the single speed the beast knew: slow. The same boy who woke Smith began to lead the horse downriver to where the party hoped to meet their hired ride to Amsterdam. Despite Smith's gesticulations, the boy, and the horse, would move no faster than was their custom. After nearly an hour, the gray nag came to rest in front of a nondescript warehouse a few blocks off the riverbank. A lanky blond man with a shortly cropped beard paced the cobbles. Before the cart had fully stopped he began hoisting the trunks into the back of a four-wheeled wagon. More suitable for delivering farmers' goods to market, it had been bedecked with two long, rough boards running its length, which served as seats. As the landlord's son helped him, the excitable man muttered to himself, mostly unintelligible to his passengers, but Sagar caught something about night and dark.

They soon reached the outskirts of the city where warehouses, granaries and merchant houses gave way to farmland. Penned cows quietly watched laborers cutting peat from the vast low-lying areas and took no notice of the wagon as it rolled by. Sagar and Mary both smelled the salt in the air as they now were only a few miles from the open sea, with no aromas of city detritus clogging their noses. The passengers were all lost in their own thoughts, except Smith, who was still trying to converse with the driver.

Mary remembered sitting high above the cliffs in Plymouth on breezy winter mornings such as this, watching the waves crash against the shore, imagining those same waves breaking against the bow of her father's Ballinger as he plied the shipping routes to Wexford in Ireland, and as far as Brest and Cherbourg in France. His narrow double-ended vessel was best suited for a larger crew of perhaps 10 to 12 who would row when the wind slacked, but he manned the ship with only three or four men, relying instead on his experienced read of the local currents, and her slippery hull riding high and light through the seas to gain an advantage over more recent hull innovations. Her father would often say he could outrun any ship on the southern coast, given a trailing wind and a bit of luck. As he would approach the desolate shores of Ireland, the land itself might have been caught recoiling with long memories of the ancient Viking invaders and their grim deeds, borne on similarly shaped ships. Mary's mother, now dead these 12 years, would always keep a weather eye out for his return, and her reaction when spying the vessel was as if life itself had breathed back into her lungs.

While Mary's mind had drifted into the distant past, Abigail considered the more recent events that had brought her and George here. Despite sitting next to one another, sharing the same view of the low farmlands, even being bumped closer together by the uneven roadway, they couldn't be further apart. Abigail had lost a baby in childbirth just 10 months ago, her fourth failed pregnancy.

The midwives finally admitted defeat and said it was just never to be; when the fires in the local tavern burned low, the villagers' murmurs grew into accursed accusations. Abby could at least depend on mechanical and disinterested George not to listen to them: it's why she attached herself to him years ago. She could not say whether George still loved her because she couldn't say whether he ever did. He now simply found her less useful.

Abigail came from an Irish family that settled outside Bristol. At first, her young mother and father worked the outlying farmlands as day laborers, slowly earning the confidence of one of the largest landowners in western England. They kept to themselves and rarely spent time in town, except on their master's business. Little was known of their origin and little was asked, so when the black-haired couple revealed their only child to the local priest, a baby with intense red hair, who could question why it differed so from its parents?

Abigail grew to be a boisterous young girl and the perennial favorite of the children to play the role of the May Queen at Whitsun-tide. Each spring, she would lead the girls of the village door to door, bedecked in garlands of flowers and carrying sheaves of oats, receiving presents and singing songs to welcome the rebirth of the land. The boys would follow, a few houses behind, toting the May pole, usually a denuded oak tree no more than 12 feet high. At the outskirts of the village, the pole was placed in a roughly dug hole and anchored to the ground with flaxen rope, dyed red and yellow. Abby, as May Queen, would choose a suitable boy for her betrothed. The two would lead the children back into the village, hand in hand.

On a drenching February night just before Abby turned four-teen, a knock shook the door of the cottage they rented from their kind benefactor. The late hour startled her parents and Abby recalled her mother frantically clearing the hearth and the table as her father slowly walked toward the door. Out of the darkness the village priest and their landlord appeared, sour of face and wet with cold rain. Abby's father welcomed them in and arranged seats by the fireplace, as her mother looked on apprehensively. In low tones, the priest, Father Brenton, in-formed her father that while the Church tolerated the innocent peasant rituals among children, "Abby is now entering womanhood, you see, and mustn't be May Queen this year." He spat out the word woman-hood, as if it were distasteful to his delicate mouth. While Abby was kept busy at the far side of the room, her mother overheard the conversation. Few other words were spoken before the two men departed into the gloom.

While her father had little intuition about the effect this might have on his only child, Abby's mother feared how the headstrong girl might react. They did not tell her that night, but waited until morning. As her mother relayed the reasons before dismissing the girl to her duties, Abby sat quietly, staring straight ahead, as if she were trying to burrow a hole through the stone wall of their house with her eyes. Her father took no notice, but her mother, recalling the storms that once brewed within her own head, knew this would weigh heavily on the fiery haired child. But Abby made no mention of it and over the next several weeks, seemed as joyful as always. As Whitsuntide approached, Abby's mother kept close watch on her daughter, only to see no discernible change. The morning of the festivities, Abby busied herself with washing and started on cleaning the hearth. Her parents shortly left for the manor house, where they now had the privilege of working in the stables. As they walked up the broad hill to the square house a half-mile away, Abby readied herself.

On the day after the Priest's visit, Abby had assured her friends that she would once more entertain the honor of May Queen. While her nearest challenger had grown weary of always following behind Abby, she dared not confront the immensely popular girl. When the children assembled, Abby was again in the lead, flowers complementing her grinning face. However, most of the village women had heard of the Priest Brenton's harsh words, so after ensuring they had shown proper respect to the Queen of the season, many started to trail at some distance behind the children as they moved through the village. A casual observer would say that Abby took no notice, playing her part expertly. On the outskirts of the village, where the boys had assembled themselves and their white oak, a large contingent of villagers also ringed the ceremony. As the young girls danced innocently around the pole, red and yellow streamers waving, Abby stepped forth to choose the May King.

"Late this winter Father Brenton and his church decreed it would be foolish for me to participate in our annual Whitsuntide rites, as I am of age. He believes we play children's games for our entertainment, for the amusement of the young and the old. But you all know that it is his beliefs that are folly, not ours. We shall see what comes of spring this year."

With these few words, she paused to scan the gathered crowd, grown quiet and pensive, and walked calmly off the dirt path to town and into the darkening woods. Ten years later Abigail found herself in a foreign land, still seeking to outrun and atone for the curse she brought upon her home that day. Bouncing along in a wooden cart with strangers, two of which were now her adopted daughters, she knew full well that no live child would ever emerge from her womb.

Along the road to Amsterdam, the party stopped briefly just as the sun began to trace its way back to the horizon; the horses received water and hay, the passengers bread and cheese. Smith had given up on conversation with the driver hours ago, but now, more practically, tried to discover how much longer it would be to Amsterdam, where their ship and compatriots awaited their return. Gesturing at the sea and up at the sun, the lean driver, betraying better English than during the first leg of the trip, made Smith to understand that while they could make it to Amsterdam today, it would not be until well after nightfall. With the winds bringing the threat of a storm, depending on the weather, they might need to stay at a tavern along the way and he knew of a dependable local house in Hoofddorp. He hurried to hitch the horses and they were underway again. As it passed midday, the onshore wind had increased in ferocity. Bursts of 20-knot winds shook the carriage and while the horses paid it no mind, the passengers kept their heads low and blankets tight.

Dusk came quickly and as it did, the children moved to sitting on the floorboards of the wagon, escaping the wind. The twins flanked Abigail, sharing a blanket between them, alert but still. Sagar moved to the end of the wagon and crouched low over its tailgate, his body swaying back and forth. Sagar's eyes scanned the low lying farmland

and after a time, his gaze changed from vacant wandering, to a specific stare, as he looked for something just out of his field of vision. The boy overheard the driver tell Smith in a low voice that the weather shouldn't impede their progress to Amsterdam tonight. His small face hardened at this decision, but he said nothing and resigned himself to whatever danger he perceived in a way that seemed routine.

With the full array of starlight augmented by the rising moon, his eyes now became more intensely focused on the fields, and after a time he made a quiet comment to the twins, likely unheard, but certainly unintelligible to the rest of the passengers. They crouched lower into the carriage at his words and just as they had repositioned themselves, the moon cleared a very light cloud, allowing its full luminosity to ignite the pale gray grasses off to the right side of the carriage in brightness; Sagar's gaze met its mark as he caught two pairs of eyes reflecting the moonlight back at him, keeping pace with the carriage through the low grass.

He leaned forward and as he did, Abigail took notice; she glanced over her left shoulder to see what transfixed the boy. Abigail's mouth gaped and she pivoted her whole body toward the fields, nearly jumping to her feet. Her movement so startled Sagar that he broke his focus on the field and stared blankly at Abigail. She looked from the field to Sagar, the color completely flushed from her face, in absolute terror. A nearly infinite stream of possibilities raced through the boy's brain. Surely this was impossible; upon their journeys, Brigu had bestowed upon him the duty to watch for the devilish night spirits, but never before had he encountered a person gifted with the same sight.

The horses had quickened their pace without any prodding from the gaunt driver. This went unnoticed by most of the passengers; if the twins perceived it, they said nothing and made no outward signs of concern from their low position. Sagar returned his gaze to the fields, as Abigail moved closer to him and with her eyes on the field as well, she gripped his arm with her left hand and pointed into the road behind them with her right.

"There, and there away, two Pucas or will-o-wisps give chase!

What have you brought upon us?" she whispered in desperate but low tones.

Noticing his wife's harried state, George swiveled around to the rear of the carriage. His face showed little emotion in the moonlight, but his voice boomed: "Abby, what troubles you, is it the boy?"

This accusation caught even Smith's attention; he turned to Abigail and the others who were now also awaiting her reply. She paused, still crouching next to Sagar. George's words had pulled her mind back into the present world that rarely rewarded curiosity, especially in young women. She knew to be cautious, "I thought I saw two wolves in the field following the carriage, but the boy Sagar spotted them as well and marked that they were just lonely stray dogs wandering through the grass."

As she said wolves, the driver let out a brief yelp of a laugh. To further assuage her husband and the remainder of the party, she forced a smile and reseated herself next to George, pulling a coarse blanket across her legs, and in turn the twins. Sagar took the cue and sat down as well. As their speed increased, confirmed by a few whips from the driver, the carriage jerked and bounced more aggressively. Abigail and Sagar kept their heads bowed, each desperate to speak with the other but knowing this was not the time.

The shape-shifting spirits preferred to remain within the marshes and fields along the water, deriving their power from the strength of the living land and sea. These beings, despite the many names and many curses humanity had thrown upon them, were not wicked or hateful. They would react in defense of the world they protected, the willows, oaks, ashes, fish to fowl to fox. But there were those, as Sagar knew and Abby would soon enough, who could marshal the spirits to fell purpose. Tonight, the Pucas were instinctively attracted to the budding awareness bucking along within the wagon.

The fields gave way to roadside taverns and houses. At first, the buildings seemed randomly scattered, but as the dirt road became cobbled with stone, the structures coalesced into a small town. The driver slowed and beckoned to Smith to lean in for a chat. This time,

Sagar couldn't hear them. After a few quietly exchanged words, the driver again whipped the horses and they sped through the lee end of Hoofddorp. "It will be a few hours further, but the road from here to Amsterdam is well cobbled and we shall likely be among other travelers entering the city," Smith advised the passengers. The damp air hung heavy with the earthy scent of salt marsh mud and indeed the sounds of activity populated the road. Carts laden with goods for sale or trade in the city moved at a leisurely pace, pulled by sad-eyed beasts of burden, their masters walking alongside their loads. Cities, Sagar thought, no different here than any other part of the world.

The abrupt stop of the carriage served to awaken all those who had dozed off. Mary and James threw off their cocoon of blankets, a bit embarrassed perhaps to have entered one of Europe's largest ports wrapped up like swaddled babies. The twins reclaimed their places on the roughly hewn plank that served as a seat, content that the city offered little risk to their adoptive mother Abigail. Smith peered up and down the broad expanse of the wharf, gaining his bearings.

"With the hour so late, we should proceed to the warehouse where our companions, no doubt, are sleeping." Smith pointed to the right and the driver obliged. A few minutes later, Smith motioned to halt in front of an unmarked brick building with two sets of wide wooden doors facing the adjacent wharf. The driver jumped out, tied the horses to a hitching post and began to efficiently unburden his carriage of the travelers' bags. Smith approached the closer of the two sets of doors and rapped it with his cane 3 times.

After some moments, the sound of the doors being unbolted was heard and a tall but bent figure emerged from the warehouse. Smith held out his hand in greeting and it was heartily met with two hands and a vigorous shaking in return. In his prime, Reverend Williams must have stood a full foot taller than Smith, but the years had curved his back and shoulders, so to Sagar, he had the look of a huge man stooped over to hug a child. The doors were swung wide and lantern light from inside bathed the scene in a soft yellow glow, revealing makeshift living quarters for over 70 people.

Williams disappeared inside again, but straightaway, two teenage boys arrived to assist the returning party in getting settled for the night. As they carried the trunks and bags into the structure, at first, the boys took no notice of Faria, Shikha and Sagar, but when the children entered into the light holding their own packs, the lads stopped and gawked. A quick rap from Smith's cane motivated them to finish their job. The carriage driver, having been paid his full amount, hurried into the waiting arms of a local tavern, while the travelers made their way into the warehouse for the night. James and George bolted the doors behind them and led their respective families to their sleeping quarters.

CHAPTER 4 - January 1603

Abigail woke Faria and Shikha with a few quiet words. "Girls, we must help prepare breakfast." Abigail wanted to speak candidly with them, to know whether they saw what Sagar did last night, but there was no time and no safe place. Shaking off their slumber, Faria and Shikha followed behind their adoptive mother to the rear of the warehouse where half a dozen women buzzed around a massive fireplace. Several girls of varying ages helped, carrying pots, water buckets and fetching supplies from unseen, adjacent rooms.

As they entered the kitchen, cold, sour glances struck the newcomers. Abby briefly recoiled, but regaining her composure, she held her arms out to the twins, who willingly grasped her slender and pale hands. She wasn't fourteen anymore, alone and hungry, but the feelings were the same. Abby wanted something more for these two girls than what she endured. No daughters of hers would be treated as she once had been, Abby thought. Giving their dark fingers a soft squeeze, she took a deep breath. Smiling, she laced the twins through the onlookers, making her way to a portly and aged woman commanding the largest cauldron on the hearth. "Mrs. Bray, may I present Shikha and Faria. In the presence of Reverend Smith, George and I have adopted these girls to accompany us to the colony," Abigail said in a formal but deferential tone.

"Presence? In the presence of Reverend Smith you say? It would seem as if the only job that man has is to simply be present. These two, though. They look willing enough to work," Mrs. Bray barked, easing the tension in the room. Most of the onlookers got back to work. "Girls, do you know how to cook barley so it is soft, but still absorbs the cream of cow's milk?" The elderly matron quizzed.

First looking at Abigail, who nodded, Faria said, "Yes ma'am, as long as the barley hasn't been soaked for more than a few hours and no salt has been added to the pot. I'd boil it for half the hour, covered, drain the water and let it set up in milk for another half-hour."

Mrs. Bray very nearly smiled. "That'll do." Motioning to the largest pot hanging over the fire, Mrs. Bray continued. "It will be a rough day for the lot of us. We load that ship straight after breakfast. Girls, our stomachs are in your hands. Abigail, follow me." Already on the move as she spoke her last words, Mrs. Bray marched from the kitchen with Abby following close behind.

Left to themselves, the twins jumped to work. Checking the large cauldron on the fire, Shikha found the water still only warm to the touch. She lowered the pot until it settled into the coals, stirred it with a wooden paddle and looked around for additional fuel. Faria followed her sister's thinking and tracked the movements of a young girl who entered the kitchen overburdened with firewood. Guessing its source, Faria turned a corner and exited the back of the warehouse into a dead-end alley dripping with the moist stench of rotting vegetables.

At one end, aggressive decay was busy transforming kitchen garbage into an indistinct brown mass; at the other lay several cords of wood, neatly stacked. Faria began to fill her arms with the wood when one of the older girls she recognized from the kitchen howled at her. "This is our wood, for our families. It is not for outcasts and heathens. Try the other end of the alley."

Faria looked upon her accuser with a curious compassion, not unlike that a lynx might display before devouring a baby mouse. "Heathen and outcast I may be, but I cook for your families, upon the command of Mrs. Bray. If you wish to help me with the wood, you will be helping your parents and siblings as well. If you choose to loiter in the alley, surely Mrs. Bray will understand." Faria whispered her words, yet spoken so coolly, they captivated a few of the other girls, who now went to the woodpile and loaded their arms as well. They followed Faria back into the kitchen, leaving the bully and two of her friends gawking in the alley.

The twins made quick work of boiling the prodigious amount of barley. As if she had been counting out the minutes, Mrs. Bray returned exactly an hour later, sans Abigail. Without speaking, she surveyed the twins' work, nodded, and moved on to review other kitchen business. After overseeing the assembly of various bowls, utensils, brown bread and copious amounts of hard cheese, she rang a large bell.

The twins watched the congregation assemble for breakfast. While Smith filled his plate and took a seat on one of the long benches adjacent to the kitchen, Williams stood at the head of the food line and greeted the members of the congregation as they passed. They glimpsed Sagar walking alongside James and Mary, accompanied by two strangers: a rotund and jolly fellow with a bushy gray beard and a darker man with leathery skin wearing a curious hat. After most people had taken their seats, Abigail and George appeared and beckoned the girls to join them. Gathering their food, they took the only seats available, closest to the noxious alley.

After all were seated, Reverend Williams rose, gathered himself and bowed his head. While the congregation did the same, Faria looked across the warehouse to Sagar, who returned her gaze as if saying, so this is our task. They both quickly mimicked the rest of the group as Williams began to speak. "Heavenly Father, we are but simple people with a simple purpose. We seek to live our lives in accordance with your divine will. Today, we load our ship and depart soon thereafter. We thank thee for this nourishment, which is only a means to achieve our purpose. Whether or not we succeed means little. It is our act of submitting to your will that means all. Amen." He reseated himself and began to eat. A few bites into the meal, he rose again and made his way over to Abigail and George's table. George stood up, as did Faria and Shikha, but Abigail remained seated, visibly tense.

"So, these are the barley girls that made my breakfast so delicious. Welcome to our congregation, and I trust that your new parents, with the guidance of Reverend Smith, will deliver you from the darkness of your past into the light of the one true faith in Jesus Christ," he said.

George responded, "Thank you, Reverend. We are honored by your belief in us."

Abby nodded her head at her husband's words. Williams moved on to other tables. The girls reseated themselves and Abby leaned in and whispered, "So it seems you have gained a reputation for yourselves. Let us hope, for the sake of us all, this reputation remains in the kitchen alone, please." She did not so much chide the girls as implore them. Abby owed her survival to her husband's simple, unquestioning outlook on life. With no money, little education and only rough skills, few paths lay open to a young woman and most led to ruin. George saw only what was on the surface of this world, like the ripples on a lake, but not that which stirred below. Their marriage had surely been convenient for both of them, but Abby's true self, her curiosity and strength, had gone unnoticed by George, like fish deep under water.

After breakfast, Abigail assisted Mary as she took charge of the kitchen. "How you convinced her to leave the kitchen and let me tend to the packing, Abby, I can't fathom. That Mrs. Bray takes orders from no one, not even Reverend Williams," Mary said as they worked. "You've known her long, haven't you?" she asked while sorting through the array of copper pots.

"I worked for her in Bristol, years ago. It didn't take much convincing, really. She's a proud woman, but pragmatic. Before breakfast, I just asked her if she didn't think it would be easier for you to pack the kitchen while she tallied the food stores. She understood. You're the only one of us with any knowledge of a ship's galley and best suited to determine what to bring and what to leave behind. She has always had a kind heart, although she hides it well," Abby replied, glad to steer the conversation away from her past. With the pots and other kitchen supplies stored into four sea chests, Abby and Mary sought out a means to transport the chests to the ship. Shikha and Faria, who had been assisting with the packing, scurried away just as their adoptive mother stood from her work. They reappeared with a wagon, seconds later, requisitioned from the alley. "Girls, wonderful! You've read my mind," Abby said.

In regional harbor towns across England, two women pulling a wagon full of sea chests, accompanied by the dark and diminutive twins would have garnered stares and questions, but in Amsterdam, where tattooed Pacific islanders mingled with weathered Portuguese fishermen and grim St. Petersburg traders, the city paid them no heed. They waited for a pause in the harbor traffic and pushed their load across to the wharf where their new home, a forty-year-old galleon rechristened the Spring Tide, rested in the gray-green water.

The three-masted ship, built in Lisbon, had worked the northern Atlantic shipping routes for decades, earning a reputation as a slow, but dependable craft, able to withstand the ice of German and Russian ports, and the winds of the Solent. She was 300 tons in total and 90 feet long, but was deceptively roomy below the waterline, which had added to her utility. For her size, few ships could match her storage capacity, and this added to her reputation as a comfortable ship to manage and live aboard.

Sagar worked high up in the rigging alongside the weathered man from breakfast, Jorge, the first mate. From afar their movements looked effortless, almost lazy, but it was a fluidity of motion borne of experience that allowed deckhands to maintain their balance and poise in the rollicking environment of a ship at sea. The two teenage boys who had helped unload the bags the night before were taking instruction from Jorge, and in turn from Sagar, but each clung furiously to the running lines, standing upright, knees locked. As the ship was loaded with water casks, the slightest movement, imperceptible on the deck below, would sway the mainmast two feet or more from side to side, upsetting the boys' stance again and again. They were useless, but would have to steadily improve over the next few days.

Captain Tanner surveyed from the aft deck, trying to instruct confused farmhands, carpenters and blacksmiths where to store the water casks, and other essentials piling up on the deck of the Spring Tide. He hailed Mary when the wagon reached the gangplank: "Do you bring us chests of gold, Mary? There is hardly room for treasure onboard."

"Or in Heaven," murmured Revered Smith, who had taken to slowly walking the deck, trying to look aloof yet busy.

"No, father, only chests of copper and tin. That is, I bring the kitchen aboard. Will you send some of your able-bodied men to cart these chests up the plank?" Mary replied, her face flushed with color from pushing the wagon. At her words, her father bounded across the deck and in three long hops, was on the pier.

"Able-bodied indeed, Mary. This lot will serve as ballast, but not much more. That boy you brought from Rotterdam, he is Iberian, no? He's a salty one. Jorge has been chatting him up all morning, eager to speak freely in Portuguese, and not in his stunted English. I get along well enough in their native tongue, but the speed at which they chomp their words, I can't keep up," her father said, leaning in a bit as to hide what was obvious to any sailing man within half a mile.

"But father, he's from Inde, as far as we could discern. I didn't realize he knew Portuguese. He speaks English with only a slight foreign intonation," Mary responded, looking surprised. Her father, however, had stopped listening as he saw a solution to his previous problem.

"Sagar, boy, make haste and meet me at the fore hatch. Jorge can well enough manage with those two greenhorns," captain Tanner yelled up to the tops of the mast. Sagar threw a quick glance and a few words at Jorge, who just shrugged, which sent the boy sliding down a series of ropes in a controlled fall. He landed, crouched low on his feet and skipped over to the broad opening in the deck at the base of the foremost mast. The Captain met him presently. They spoke for no more than a minute or so, with Sagar nodding and giving brief responses as Tanner talked and gesticulated. Sagar then disappeared into the hold of the ship, while the Captain returned to his band of farmhands on the aft deck. He arranged them into two groups, the first went below decks with Sagar, while the second, under the Captain's direction, began to organize the supplies on deck and feed them into the ship through the fore hatch. Thoughtfully, he also sent two men to unload the kitchen chests from Mary and Abby's wagon.

Below decks, as supplies came down the ramps deep into the hold, Sagar instructed the men where to position each cask, chest and box, some closer to the ladders, others as far aft as possible, depending on if and when they would be needed during the voyage. He also sought to balance the loading to equalize the weight, port to starboard.

"Sir, yes, push that one farther aft, if you would. Roll them down nicely and stand the casks on their heads, so they won't roll, please. Let's have a look in here before we stow this chest away. We wouldn't want the sugar far from reach." Sagar spoke in such a smooth manner as to put the men at ease with taking directions from a child. While many in the congregation had labored on the estates of English nobles, where young sons might have the run of the stables, issuing whimsical commands, this felt altogether different. What he was doing actually made sense and he soon gained the men's trust as he explained each action.

While the congregation labored in earnest, their efforts were not terribly efficient. More than one chest fell off the boarding plank and despite Sagar's guidance, deep in the hold, boxes became crushed under the weight of stacking. The line to ask Mary questions was four deep and the inquiries ranged from "are there chamberpots on a boat?" from one of the little girls, to "Will the men sleep on a different deck?" from an older mother. Ships were just not built to accommodate seagoing families. Most crews in galleon-sized ships slept where they could find a dry spot, usually forward of the mainmast, in hammocks, behind and on top of ropes and supplies. On what had originally been the primary gun deck, Mary instructed the women to fashion sleeping quarters, similar to the arrangements in the Amsterdam warehouse. She reminded the women that each of them would have a room with a view, if they so chose to open the cannon ports.

Shikha had managed to stack the chicken crates against the port side railing and organized the goose pen directly below the galley. She had a calming effect on the animals, who, like most of the congregation, were anxious of their new surroundings. Abby noted that Shikha was more comfortable working alone, tending to and chatting politely with the geese and pigs in a foreign tongue, while Faria took instructions from Mary and requisitioned a gaggle of young girls to execute her orders. Two days ago, Abby couldn't tell them apart, now the differences were becoming more evident.

Around two, the congregation ate their first of many meals aboard the Spring Tide, albeit one that had been hastily assembled on land. Mrs. Bray had been surprisingly absent from sight most of the day, but at about one she appeared at the gangplank and hesitantly boarded the ship. She took her bearings, ducked below decks into the galley, and briefly consulted with the Captain, departing with Abby and Shikha in tow. An hour later, the three of them returned with loaves of dark bread and a massive cauldron of stew from a nearby public house. Mary and the other women arranged bowls and utensils in each of the makeshift sleeping quarters, so that the congregation could eat one last meal together, prior to eating in shifts while at sea. Bellies full, but coffers empty, they would spend their last night in Europe.

The men working deep in the hold had been unaware of the pending meal, so when Captain Tanner bellowed down to them that supper was served, a shout all around was heard, and they raucously piled onto the gun deck. For many of the congregation, this was the first time in their life they labored on their own behalf, working to secure the future of their families and the colony. The specifics of religious freedom were but curious ideals, best left to Reverend Williams and Smith, but the ability to set their own future was electrifying. Indeed, what Reverend Williams had truly sold them on was not a set of unique Christian tenets or practices, but on destiny itself, couched within the blanket of God's Will.

With soup bowl in hand, Captain Tanner walked the gun deck checking in at each family, asking after bruises and bumped heads, but more critically, he assuaged the congregants' unfamiliarity with the ship and its quality. "Ahh, she's a fine ship, so beamy and strong. Say, boy, look out that porthole, you see those slight dents in the planks? If 20-pound cannon shot can't pierce her sides, a leisurely trip across the Occidental will seem like a holiday; she'll take good care of us, this beauty. George, when you were down in the hold, did you mark any bilge water? Dry and tight you say? Dry as Reverend Williams' liquor cabinet? Well, she must be quite a ship." He bantered in his easygoing manner while weaving through the crowded ship.

When he came to Mary, Sagar and James, his appearance changed. His eyes became heavy and the corners of his mouth turned downwards, highlighting deep wrinkles. Tanner inquired of his daughter: what was left to be done, and if there were sufficient space for the congregants.

"The galley, ship's stores and sleeping quarters are all in decent order, father. We probably need a few more hours to prepare permanent enclosures for the livestock, and could run through our manifest once again to ensure we have all we need. Most families have their belongings on board and a place to sleep. We could all manage to fit on this deck, but if the older boys move into the forecastle, we'd have a bit more space," she reported.

"It will be done. The lads will appreciate having a space to themselves, even if it does get a bit damp in rough seas." Looking at Sagar, Captain Tanner motioned upwards and said, "Boy, walk with me." Sagar popped up from his cross-legged position and followed the captain up the ladder and into the open air. As the two of them traversed the empty deck and headed to the Captain's quarters, Tanner looked skyward. "Looks like rain, wouldn't you say?"

Sagar glanced offshore to the northwest, replying: "Perhaps, but these clouds are as of yet unready to release their heavy burden, Captain, and the clearing, onshore breeze may shepherd them away by nightfall." This forced a smile to Tanner's face as he opened the door to his personal quarters, in the aft of the ship.

"Good lad, but we shall see." Sagar followed him into the cramped room, which held a roughly hewn table bolted to the floor. Another door led to the Captain's bedroom. A large brass oil lamp hung from the ceiling, but Tanner did not light the lamp, rather, seated himself closest to the door. Sagar took the bench across from him. The two sat in the relative darkness of the room, and while Sagar's face was illuminated only by the gray light filtering through a high round window, Tanner's hulking body rested in shadow. He opened his mouth to address the strange boy, only to think through his words and after hesitating once more, began to speak.

"Boy, we haven't much time so I will go straight at it. You have an uncanny way around the rigging, and can pull men together, as if they're in a trance, better than many first mates I've shipped with. Where you hail from and what manner of vessels and crew you're accustomed to is not my business and I'm not a man who asks questions. But this motley congregation has entrusted me, and this hunk of a ship with their faith, their dreams and their lives. When we are 1,000 miles from land in the blackness of the cold northern sea, will those icy waves be crashing over my bow to pull you back to your maker in retribution for some dark deeds you are running from, or can I trust you to stand at that wheel next to me, with me, and will this ship to its mark, like an arrow toward its target?"

Sagar paused while digesting Tanner's words. "Captain Tanner", he began, "I have slaved aboard vessels destined to break upon hidden shoals, I've seen ships twice the size of the Spring Tide dismasted and devoured by the same waves of which you speak, and I have shared the forecastle with inhuman shipmates, forever trolling the sea for prey, yes. But on this voyage, when the ocean rises up to test our vessel and our crew, I will be like oil upon the waves; when the frigid spray reaches up to knock me over the rail and into the depths, I will anchor myself to the timbers to maintain our course. Captain Tanner, you will be dearly tested, but not by me. I am here to serve."

At this surprising statement of fidelity, the captain held out his hand, which Sagar willingly took. "You are no boy, but you are no man, either, that much is true. A few hours of daylight remain and we as of yet have much to do: back to work for the both of us." Tanner stood, easing off the bench with clear tightness in his back, and exited his quarters with Sagar close behind.

By nightfall, Mary, Abigail and the twins had the families settled on board and the livestock prepared for the journey. Lanterns illuminated the gun deck, where children tumbled about, "visiting" one another's makeshift nests, while the women gathered aft near the galley, trading experiences from the day. Those who had some idea what lay ahead remained quiet, while the others, with little exposure to the realities of life at sea, bubbled with a naïve excitement. Abigail set herself apart from the group, alone with her thoughts, while Mary listened in to the buoyant conversation, saying little.

Since their experience on the way to Amsterdam, Sagar had avoided Abby. She had chosen to defuse any suspicions when it would have been just as easy to feign ignorance or protect herself. That was enough to convince the boy that she might have things to hide too, just like him. Outright association with her would likely be scrutinized, if only on the grounds that a young boy befriending a married woman would not be proper behavior for either of them.

After supper, however, Sagar saw his first chance to talk with Abby privately. He watched her edge farther and farther from the crowd of women in the galley, back to the ladder leading to the lower deck, until only a thin outline remained standing in the narrow hallway. When her shadow slipped into the hold below, Sagar casually threaded through the chatterers, and followed Abby into the ship's belly.

His movements evoked no notice from the elder matron, her eyes briefly flicked to the right, following his path as he disappeared deep into the ship. She had been Abby's protectress more than once before, and hoped the little fiery haired girl, now all grown up, knew what approached.

Descending the angled ladder, over his shoulder, Sagar spotted Abby sitting atop a larger barrel. He made sure to be obviously loud as he set foot on the lower level, announcing his presence as he jumped down the last two rungs.

"Miss Abby?"

"Yes… who is there?" she replied, at first not seeing him among the barrels and boxes.

"Sagar, ma'am. Am I disturbing you?"

"No, no. It's just so loud up there. They all talk as if we are going on a holiday. I don't know what awaits us, but I feel . . ." she trailed off. "Is there something you need down here?"

"I thought, perhaps we could talk. Talk about the trip to Amsterdam. And other things," Sagar said. He looked up at Abby, trying to see her face in the darkness, trying to gauge how she would respond. She remained silent, so he continued. "Miss Abby, in the moonlit darkness of that wagon ride, you saw creatures and called them by name. Shikha, Faria and I also see these things. Even now as I pass time at the helm, others of their kind lie just below the surface of the water. I suspect they follow the ship, sensing in us, the four of us, a place where their world and our's coexist. Can I please ask, who has bestowed you with this gift of second sight?"

Abby had only spoken about it with one other, and never the full truth. She put her hand on his shoulder, and letting her fingers run down the length of his thin arm she looked fondly at the wide eyed boy and replied, "when I was very young, and like all children, I thought I saw shadows in the darkness, monsters in old barns, spirits dancing in the woods. As I grew, whereas other children's visions grew hazy, mine became more acute. I never thought of it as a gift really, more as a consequence. I wish I didn't see them." Her eyes dropped to the floor. He waited several seconds, hoping she would continue, hoping she would tell him more. "My mother, she may have known, but I left home," she stopped short and he knew Abby wouldn't continue.

"I am sorry, Miss Abby, but I only risked asking because my sight of the other world and its very real denizens has always been with me. I know you will find this fantastic, but my mind swims with decades of experiences, yet none betray my origins. I can't grasp whether the memories of long sea voyages are things I myself have done, or visions of others' lives. To me, the past is a churning, roiling maelstrom, utterly orderless. My earliest memories, the ones I somehow know are truly mine, are of mountains, bitingly cold air, and the whitest snow. No people, just the silent, frigid air. Everyone on this ship seeks a new future, including you, yes? The twins and I, we seek our past, our identity. To me, the future unfolds with ease, as I have witnessed it happen again and again. Similar people, similar patterns. It is never new."

Sagar caught his breath, glanced at the deck above and smiling, returned his gaze to Abby. "Faria and Shikha, they are my spear kin—we are related through our fathers. At least this is what Brigu told us when we met in Istanbul. The twins were already traveling west with him when he shepherded his flock aboard the leaky ship where I was cabin boy." He couldn't help but grimace, recalling the brutal crew of that tired vessel.

"As I learned from the other children, Brigu just knew where to collect us, weaving a path across deserts, jungles, seas and wastelands. The twins he discovered living alone in the East. Faria was always curious about people, and would sometimes venture into the local villages perched at the edge of the great mountains. I suspect that's how Brigu heard of their whereabouts, but Shikha, she was always perfectly content in the woods. We're related anyway, I know that much. They tell me how kind you are to them; you are their first real family. If not in me, confide in them. Not today perhaps, or even on this voyage, but someday. You must."

"Thank you for trusting me on the wagon. If you see any Pishachas, or what did you say, Pucas, onboard ship, come find me. I reckon together, we'll be just fine," he finished awkwardly.

Abby took his hand in both of hers and held it. She looked at the strange boy who had just revealed a lifetime's worth of secrets and said, "When I was very young, I remember sitting in front of the fireplace, nestled in my mother's arms, staring into the flames. I asked her what fire was, and for a while, she just stared into the coursing orange embers. At length, she said 'my dear little Abby, there are things in this world that can be seen and heard and touched, and things that are unseen, that cannot be held, and cannot be heard. Fire, fire is both. You see it, but then it's gone. You can feel its heat, but not the fire itself, and you can hear the logs crackle, the embers hiss, but the fire itself, it is silent. Never believe that because you can't hold something, or keep it in a jar, that it doesn't exist, because fire exists.' Sagar, I just wonder what else remains hidden to us."

"Much, I suspect," he said.

Abby returned to the gun deck, where only Mrs. Bray had noticed her absence. Sagar, by way of the forecastle, climbed out of the hold and into the moonlit night. The clouds, as he predicted, had moved offshore. He espied Jorge lounging high in the rigging and the first mate hailed him "Ola, se aqui." Sagar smiled up at his fast friend and quickly joined him.

The men of the congregation still loitered on deck, exhausted from the day's accomplishments but too anxious for sleep. For them, the sun could not rise soon enough. Years of planning and saving, now they had sold most of their possessions for supplies. In England, their farewells to astonished relatives and employers were a month ago. Still, tonight, the ship remained tethered to land. They could just walk off and return to their past. Tomorrow, the gangplank would be pulled away, and with it, their lifeline and their prior lives would evaporate like the clouds moving offshore.

The men huddled in twos and threes, talking nervously. From below, they could see Jorge and Sagar pointing into the night, but the two either did not speak, or spoke too softly for anyone to discern their words. Jorge and Sagar sat high up on the horizontal yardarm of the mainmast, legs dangling 30 feet above.

Henry, a short bearded man gestured up at the mate and boy. Turning to George Fielding he said, "George, what do you make of those two? By their color, they could be father and son. Curious circumstances brought them on board, is the way I hear it."

"Sagar is now Mary and James' boy, just as the twins belong to Abby and me. All three proved their worth today. Isn't that enough? If not for Sagar, we'd still be down in the belly of this ship, breaking boxes." George, not one given to idle chatter, added, "as for Jorge, the Captain trusts him, but I'll mark him a spell before doing the same. A man with no wife, no kin and no family lives for one thing: himself."

As the night wore on, the men trickled back to the gun deck, and like a light mist finds its way to the ground, they found sleep in their new home. Sagar and Jorge waited in the rigging for the Captain to return. At length, a dark stumbling figure appeared on the dock carrying a wooden case. Sagar looked to Jorge, knowing how the liquid vices of men often expose what lies beneath.

"No, no, our Captain, he will sing and stomp, but is kind through and through. We help him," Jorge said, descending two lines onto the deck. Sagar followed. Flanking their captain, they directed him up the gangplank and onto the empty deck. His rosy nose and glistening eyes were all the proof they needed that he had been making merry and probably reminiscing on his last day in port, his last day in civilization.

"My lads, we set off for destiny at dawn! Where be the right Reverend? A prayer to Wotan who will turn the wind our way, surely Williams could forgive us that," he wailed as they maneuvered him into his quarters. Unburdening him of his crate of brandy, Tanner grew solemn, now under roof. "It'll be the three of us. Tis a heavy load, this Congregation, but we must carry it." Sagar and Jorge stared back at him, their silence all the acknowledgment they could muster. The captain threw his wool cap in the corner and fell into bed. Sagar and Jorge soon did the same, leaving the ship's deck empty for what was to be the last time until they, God willing, reached land again.

CHAPTER 5 - January 1603

The morning the congregants untethered from their old lives began in glimmery, dewy sunlight. They assembled on the gun deck, and peering up through the open hatches or out the ports, found it had rained overnight, leaving the air crisp, with little traces of the haze and stench that often hung low over the great cities of the time. Willed together over years by the elderly reverend, they now awaited their shepherd and their destiny in the cramped space that once housed 20 cannons but now served as their nave. Williams stood beside Captain Tanner, leaning on a rough cane. An open hatch above them flooded the area with the early morning's promise. Squinting, neither could make out the faces of the congregants. The Captain took one step forward, into the shadows.

"Right. A few tactical words before Reverend Williams will address us. For the next few months, this ship is our home, our floating cork bobbing along on the waves. At all times, one of three watches will man the deck, led by myself, Jorge, or Sagar. This is no man-o-war, and we are all equals here, but if your watch-master tells you to do something, step up and do it right quick, as all our lives may depend on it. Families will eat and work at the same times as their men on watch, excepting during the night watch. We have no greedy merchants waiting for us in a distant port, and no kin anxiously awaiting our return. As such, we won't press any wind advantage, and we'll keep our sails set as to avoid making many changes. Within the hour, the harbor master will come calling to pull us out of port, otherwise, we owe him another week's dock fees, which we don't have. So, we set off."

As he spoke, Captain Tanner scanned the room to gauge the reaction to naming his watch-masters, that is, the officers of his crew. He was surprised to see more of the men balk at Jorge's name than at Sagar's; this, he would watch closely. Tanner took a seat next to Reverend Smith, as the elderly Williams tried to straighten his bent frame before speaking, still standing in the bright light.

"Ahh, my flock. So long have we labored for this moment. Nigh two years ago we had only an inkling of what the heavenly father had planned for our lives. The gracious Lord has now made clear the path for our deliverance. We have only to walk along that path, his path, in accordance to the divine plan. As we look to scripture, however, we know that the chosen path is never the easy one." Captain Tanner's attention failed him. Israelites, John the Baptist, deliverance and salvation intermingled with his daydreams of the open sea.

Briefly surprised when he realized William's had completed his blessing, Tanner called for all able men, and boys older than 7, to meet on the aft deck for watch assignment. He realized the delicacy of this decision. After they had assembled, he went man by man, boy by boy, asking them questions, particularly if he wasn't familiar with their histories. "Excited for the trip, Billy? Did you work stables or in the fields, John? Butchered meat, you say? Worked as a smith?" trying to align experiences with shipboard duties. Strong hands, unafraid of heights, a rare one that could even swim, these were part of his considerations. With the men, he recalled their earlier reactions, placing the most seemingly opposed to either Sagar or Jorge in their respective watches, but first taking each man aside. "Henry, I've known Jorge for twenty years. You'd think he could have learned better English in that long a time, eh? He's a good one, and you'll see that soon enough," he confided in one man; to another he noted, "The boy Sagar knows his way around a ship, but he's never had a father until now. You've got three boys of your own, Gordon, keep an eye on him for me." Just as he reached the last man, he noticed three salty characters approaching the ship.

Tanner called out, "Harbor master, we'll be with you straightaway." The captain turned to the assembled: "We'll only be raising the main sail until we reach the open water. Jorge, you'll take the first watch, then it'll be my turn, afterwards Sagar. While I pay these blasted docking fees and arrange the tow, take the men through their stations. James, you're with me, please."

It was no easy feat to tow a galleon by oar, but it was a daily, even hourly occurrence in Amsterdam. The experienced local crews had built broad backs and deep bank accounts pulling ships from their berths. Having safely cleared the last ships moored outside of the city, the harbor pilot collected his handsome fee and approached a rope ladder draped over the port side of the ship. It fell into a stout launch where his crew awaited him. Four more jobs like this today would earn them as much money as some of the Congregants had seen in a month. As he began descending, he faced the deck. Repeat customers, these were not, he mused. This lot would never see civilization again, and even if they did, none would be fool enough to attempt another venture like this. None of his business anyway. Even before he dropped into the launch, the men aboard it had pulled their first stroke away from the Spring Tide.

Among the piers and pylons of Amsterdam, a dark serpent had circled the ship, just feet below the surface. Not quite black inasmuch as it was an iridescent absence of light, the 20- foot Makara had sovereign reign over the ocean's swells and depths. Unlike its distant relatives the Pucas, which Sagar and Abby had espied days earlier, it had not grown weak through mankind's dominance of the land. Men only cautiously traversed the edge of its domain but had not, and would never, fully conquer it. Also unlike the curious Pucas, this creature bore a grim purpose. But it could wait.

Jorge and his watch managed well enough raising the mainsail, and the ship glided smoothly through the gray morning chop at a stately but metered pace. As Captain Tanner had hoped, the winds remained moderate but steady and late morning uneventfully passed into late afternoon. When the captain's watch took the deck, he called for the raising of the fore and mizzen sails. Jorge and Sagar led the men through the process and after some confusion on which lines did what, and a brief chorus of loud canvas flapping aimlessly in the breeze, the sails were set. The Spring Tide took her first full breadth of the North Sea wind, bounding forward toward the setting sun, allowing Sagar and Jorge to return below deck for warmth and food.

On his way to the galley, Sagar passed Shikha, planted directly under one of the lanterns hanging from the ceiling. She deftly worked with several ropes, tying them into a pattern that had yet to emerge. Every few minutes she would make a quiet exclamation, seeming to recall some dusty bit of knowledge, undo a knot or two, and furiously continue. After laboring for about a half-hour, she held up what looked to be a rectangular net with six loops, one trailing off of each corner, and two midway across the longer end. Shikha fastened each of the loops to hooks in the ceiling of the gun deck, revealing the nature of her work: she had constructed a large hammock.

Soon enough, Faria appeared with the other girls of the ship trailing her, all now wanting to construct their own. After requisitioning additional rope from Sagar, the girls arranged themselves in a rough circle under the light. Shikha moved from child to child, personally fixing mistakes in their work herself, while Faria stood in the center of the circle, providing general instruction. Three distinct hammock versions emerged, a double, a square single, and a double-ended single. Each used an asymmetric knot pattern that had a consistent density of overlapping ropes, but not in a simple grid.

The laughter of the girls drew Abby away from loitering near the women in the galley. As she approached, the twins grinned up at her. Small interactions she had observed throughout the day, an extra effort with the animals, or a thank you to a stranger, had given her greater confidence in their decision to adopt them. They were hard workers, each in her own way. Seeing all the children together made her yearn to be their age again, so she could just plop down on the floor and lose herself.

"So, girls, you've set up quite an operation here. Soon this deck will be dripping with your creations. Next the lads in the forecastle will be asking for your handiwork, and what will the captain think when he sees his precious Spring Tide bedecked with hooks and hammocks?"

Faria took her words in stride and fired back at the woman who was, ostensibly, her mother now. "Oh, Miss Abby, but have you ever slept on a cloud? Been cradled by the wind itself, and lulled to sleep by the quiet roll of a ship at sea? Surely we do right by the Congregation and the Captain by providing restful nights?"

Shikha couldn't help but let out a squeak of a giggle, knowing her sister's line of reasoning before the words came out. Abigail had a similar response, but held in her laughter, if only to play her part in the charade.

"I suggest we request approval, at least, from the newly appointed Captain of the gun deck for these activities," Abigail said. "Sarah," addressing one of the smallest girls in the circle, "can you please go fetch your aunt Mary from the galley. She as still looks unoccupied." The blond-haired Sarah nodded and scampered away, shortly returning, leading Mary by the hand.

"What's all this then? Cargo nets for people? Is that what you think of our ship, delivering cargo across the Occidental? And what if your knot work unravels in a midnight gale, children tumbling onto their parents, rolling out the cannon doors into the sea?" Mary said sternly, but with just a slight twinkle in her eye. "Faria, before these human cargo nets are made fast to the ceiling, you are responsible for checking every knot and every bend. Demand that Sagar assist with the ceiling hooks. Altering the ship is not our business, so let's make it his. But really, girls, these hammocks are quite ingenious. Well done, doubling our already limited space."

The night brought an uneventful change of the watch, with little for Sagar's crew to attend to, except idly staring into the darkness from the lee side of the main cabin. If they spoke at all, it was in low tones to avoid waking the captain, Jorge and the reverends, who slept in their spacious quarters directly below the helm.

Sagar and James stood at the ship's wheel, above the men on the main deck. Sagar whispered, "Watch the mizzen, just above us, as I turn the wheel and fall off the wind a bit. It will begin to flap. And as I turn back, it fills with wind again. Turn too far," he waited for the change to take effect, "and feel the ship pulling quicker, stronger, but off course."

The two of them shared the quiet of the aft deck, with only

the occasional creaking of the ship breaking the silence of the cold night. As they moved farther from land, the waves broadened out from frothy chop into deep groundswells, giving the ship a slow but persistent loping motion. Sagar hoped there would be many more nights such as this one: a fresh breeze, the ocean sleeping as soundly as the congregants in the deck below, breathing free and light. He knew better, though.

Most of the congregants had little experience with such a period of inactivity, so accustomed to working most hours of their lives on someone else's behalf. The exceptions, however, included a large farming family of more than modest means. Through adept marriages among relatives and to prosperous neighbors, this family had increased their land holdings over several generations. While occasionally working the land themselves, they could also afford to employ men to work for them and women to manage the more irksome household chores. In sum, the Gaithers totaled 13, led by two brothers in their late forties, the patriarchs of the clan, who shared many physical features, but none as pronounced as their massive heads. Asymmetric and mottled with acne scars and protuberances, the geographic diversity of their skulls mimicked the bulbous shape and irregular pattern of a common turnip. Herbert, the eldest, had married a cousin, while Harold, two years his junior, wed the daughter of a wealthy local landowner. Siring 7 offspring between them, all on board, each also had seen the birth of a grandchild. Ann, the child who had accosted the twins over their use of firewood a few days prior, was one of these grandchildren.

Why they had chosen to uproot their entire families and accompany Reverend Williams to found the colony remained a question within the congregation. They had done more than their share to finance the voyage, freely given and openly appreciated, yet had never seemed particularly interested in religious freedom or religion at all. Both ambitious, as had been their father, perhaps they saw the limited upside for their family line if they remained in southern England, where they could only remain turnip-headed farmers, albeit successful ones.

Another unusual addition to the voyage was a young schoolteacher and his family. Tom Robbin and his wife Susan had been cut from a finer cloth than the Gaithers. Delicate of frame, almost feminine, Tom was well educated, and well financed by his family, the third born son to a wealthy London merchant banker. Over seven years junior to his two brothers, who now co-ran the family business, Tom's blustery father had insisted he enter politics, by first stopping at Eton and Oxford. At 19, he married the daughter of one of his father's business associates, a girl named Susan who also had been pressured into the arrangement. Surprising to both of them, they fell deeply in love. Having shared many of the same rough experiences, as children of hard men who cared little for others, and much for money, Tom and Susan's values had aligned perfectly.

When, after completing University, Tom indicated that he wished to leave London and educate in southwestern England, Susan not only supported him, but was overjoyed. Always with a soft spot for her youngest son, Tom's mother made sure the young couple was well provided for to the amount of several thousand pounds. While both their fathers denounced the couple's foolish actions, Susan's grandparents also took great care to support the young couple.

Tom had first attended Reverend Williams' church just after settling in Plymouth and immediately gravitated to the elderly figure. So firm in belief but gentle in words, when approached by Williams about the voyage, Tom saw a way to provide meaning to his life beyond the height of a stack of coins. Tom used his and Susan's modest fortune to purchase the Spring Tide for the congregation, yet, he insisted on laboring alongside the congregants. Whether Tom believed in the notion of an everlasting and all-powerful Creator, original sin through abandonment of God's direction, and salvation through Christ's sacrifice, he was fascinated by the idea of religion and the power belief itself had over the actions of men.

CHAPTER 6 - March 29, 2013

Shikha remained motionless beneath her desk. She closed her eyes, concentrating on what caused the power outage and what now approached the DNA sequencing lab's door. Her body pleaded for more air, but she suppressed its urge, taking only shallow silent breaths. Sliding her phone into her sweatshirt pocket, she slipped from her seat and wedged herself under the desk. This room had only one door, and something had reached the other side of it now. Shikha's mind couldn't reconcile the sudden wave of feelings crashing over her. She felt at once comforted and fearful; allowing the emotions to drop from her mind like October leaves, she centered herself by gazing out at the snowy maelstrom pounding against the floor-to-ceiling windows.

The lab door was secured by an electronic lock, and she listened as the mechanism was methodically circumvented. The door swung open and a voice from the hallway whispered "Shikha? Of the mountain valleys, voyager across the ocean, sister of Faria, daughter of Abigail, please, we must leave." Its intonations were both familiar and distant and she now understood what she had sensed.

Sagar stepped into the lab, tall and thin, but looking strong like a whip. He wore a white anorak and snow pants, making him stand out in the darkness of the lab, but rendering him invisible outside. "They've conjured this storm. The Asuras have dropped power to the building to destroy your research and perhaps you. Shi, you must be damn close to something."

"I was just about to perform the sequencing routines on my DNA," she replied. Shikha unfolded herself from under the desk. She hadn't seen him in twenty-three years and only that one time since they had agreed to maintain a safe distance from one another a century ago.

"When was your last encounter?" he paused "Let's go. To the roof." Sagar motioned to the hall as he slipped out of the room.

She followed him out the door and, jogging alongside, she shot responses and questions back at him.

"Encounter? Many times, I've marked their contrails in the sky and on the sea, but an attack? Not since we three were together. Sagar, how did you know to find me?" she asked.

"Thirteen hours ago, I was on the south shore of Kauai when I received a cryptic message: To the twins, Sagar Sur Sa. That's it. I reckoned I knew where you'd be, unlike," he trailed off and Shikha knew why. Beginning again he said, "and your, your sister, any surprises befall her recently?" Sagar stuttered. He eased open the door to a darkened stairwell and held a single finger close to his mouth, implying two things at once: be silent, and we are going upwards. They edged up the concrete stairs and at the top lay a white duffel bag, from which Sagar pulled a puffy white down parka. He handed it to Shikha. "She's very angry tonight."

"She has every reason," Shikha quipped back at him. They both smiled until interrupted by the cacophony reverberating up the staircase. "That'll be your lab getting destroyed," Sagar said. He waited for her to zip up the parka and pushed the exterior door open. The wind drove them back but gaining their footing and crouching low, they succeeded in trudging through the drifting snow on the rooftop to the eastern edge of the building.

Shikha knew better than to doubt Sagar's planning, but she couldn't help but wonder how they would extricate themselves from the top of the six-story building. Sagar, however, pulled an awkward gun with a spool of wire on its side from the duffel bag and shot it into the darkness. He attached a pulley to the trailing wire feeding out, grabbed the bag, and held his arm out to Shikha.

She held close to Sagar, clutching him with both arms, but added, "I thought you would have outgrown playing with toys by now. Some people, I guess, never grow up." Sagar pretended not to hear, focusing on where his dart had found purchase. They stepped onto the ledge of the roof and jumped together, sliding down the wire. The snow cut at their faces as they zipped through the night air.

Just before smacking the building into which Sagar's grappling dart had buried itself, they simultaneously let go, landing in a puffy snowbank. As her movement stalled, the warm feeling of safety washing over her was arrested by the spring snow invading the space beneath her parka. Thousands of miles away, Faria felt her sister now out of immediate danger. Sagar leapt to his feet and began jogging through the darkness. Shikha was quick to do the same, knowing they were headed to a parking lot off of Circle Road. A solitary vehicle sat in the lot, illuminated by the snow's reflection in the yellow glow of the sodium lamps. Sagar remotely started the beast, a six-wheeled Mercedes AMG G63. As it growled to life, the brilliance of its fog lights seemed to melt a path through the blizzard itself.

Once inside, Sagar spun the vehicle around and crossing over Circle Road, he aimed the truck directly at the woods. Plowing through the piled snow, they charged up an embankment, landing on Long Island's deserted Highway 97, heading southbound. They drove in silence, watching the thick, early spring snow swirl over the car like a bursting down blanket. Their minds and thoughts, deliberately apart for so many years, began to harmonize again.

For a quarter millennia, they had searched for their origins, only to find that whenever they felt some critical clue neared, they were passively thwarted. Manuscripts disappeared. Ships to remote destinations left without them, or if they made a journey, their contacts would either remember nothing, or not show up. It would seem they were allowed to live, but not to know why. As the long dawn of adulthood cast its light upon them, their collective consciousness awakened and they found it difficult to avoid scrutiny. Even in humanity's state of detached perception, their presence itself would react with those around them, amplifying base emotions seated deep in the primitive minds of modern humans. Apart, the effect was harmless enough that most people felt their emotional state mildly intensified. When the twentieth century neared, they agreed to live separately and pursue the question of their existence more subtly, under the guise of scientific research. They had been too obvious in their quest. Now, and for over a hundred years, they pretended to have given up.

Well, Shikha mused, she and Faria remained on that path. Sagar chose to pursue something altogether different. Inheriting his first clipper ship from a kind captain whose life he had saved off the coast of Sumatra, Sagar's bulk carrier empire now spanned the Pacific Rim and included vast land holdings in Indonesia, Japan, and several western states, so named Brigu Trust. He had always been a creature of action rather than reflection, and his contribution to their effort came in the form of material support.

In the rare circumstance where Shikha couldn't get access to a lab or machinery, Sagar would provide a grant for a research chair for which only she was qualified. Faria had equally benefited over the decades. Sagar made little personal use of his fortune, preferring to hitchhike his way across the world's oceans as a simple crew member rather than use his private jet. At a voyage's termination, Sagar was just as likely to hop to another vessel as he was to disappear from port into the Indonesian jungle or the deserts of North Africa for a month, or a year, as it suited him. No one who worked for Brigu Trust knew Sagar as their ultimate employer, but Sagar knew every employee like family. His screening process was simple. Sagar hired those with the most need and ensured that their future, for generations, improved substantially. In 92 years, he had never lost an employee, either overboard, in port, or to another company.

Shikha perceived Sagar's discomfort: ashamed of the pride he felt in his works and his wealth, as the half-million-dollar truck hurtled through the storm, six-wheel drive engaged. Something else still lingered in his mind. It soon surfaced.

"You still love her, don't you?" Shikha whispered. He didn't reply. He didn't need to. "She feels the same. You know this," she added. Silence still. Shikha tried another tack. "You're cousins, Sagar!" She laughed and for the first time in over a hundred years, Sagar blushed.

"Brigu never said that, directly. He claimed we were from the same clan. We both know he told us many things that weren't true, or were partially true," replied Sagar, almost pleading with her. Shikha's longstanding frustration with the topic began to simmer when he added, "But isn't that what your research seeks to uncover?"

"Yes, Sagar, I've dedicated my recent life, science's entire modern era, to the study of genetics so I could verify it wouldn't be awkward for you to hook up with my sister. It's taken seventy years, but I'm close." She sliced open a deep wound, which in a century had never healed. And she knew it.

"I'm sorry, you get what I mean, Shi. It's possible to know though, isn't it? We have no idea what would happen, what children would be produced, what the consequences would be, who, or what, would take notice," he pleaded. Unlike the eruptive passion Shikha had felt many times, the slow burn of Sagar's feelings for Faria, and hers for him, had been imperceptible at first. It grew so slowly, just as they did. Through adolescence into their early adulthood in the eighteenth century, their love was like a trickle of water smoothing a rock face until it was defined by the water itself. In the nineteenth century, it had driven the three of them apart.

They both let it drop and minutes later, Shikha replied to the question now churning in Sagar's mind. Where to go next. "I think my data is safe but to continue my sequencing, assuming the Stony Brook servers have been destroyed, we'll need to go to . . ."

"Yale," Sagar interjected, completing her sentence. "You still have all the access you need?" he continued.

"We all do, and always will. It's written in the charter. The original, anyway. Nathan made sure of that," she said, gazing out the side window. "I maintain an office in one of the oldest administrative buildings, but, as you know, have found it impractical to remain on the faculty for more than a blink at a time." She had learned to follow the rule of five: five years unchanged was easy to pass off as healthy living, ten became nigh impossible without modifying her appearance. "Surely you remember how dreadful my hair looked when I dyed it grey. So, yes, back to New Haven."

"I have a jet ready at MacArthur airport. We'll be on the tarmac in ten minutes, in the air in twenty, and at Tweed New Haven airport within a half hour," replied Sagar.

"And then? After I get my listeners running on the servers and can begin the sequence assembly steps? My research may continue for a time, but how long until the next 2am power outage, or worse?" She replied. Shikha began to lead his mind to the conclusion she and Faria had reached late the prior year.

Shikha had resided within a few miles of Long Island Sound since they split apart, whereas the place Faria called home swung like a pendulum across Anatolia, the Levant, Persia, and the British Indian Empire. She had never held a formal university position, unlike her sister who bounced from Yale to Columbia to Stony Brook, and she published no research. Yet no other could rival her contributions to twentieth century archaeology. Faria had been a translator at the Koldewey digs in Babylon at the turn of the century; she managed all the laborers on Marshall's Mohenjo Daro excavation in 1922; she assisted Virolleaud and Bauer in the deciphering of Ugaritic during the early 30's excavations of that Canaanite city. The pendulum swung back to Anatolia during the 60's where she surveyed the Neolithic site Göbekli Tepe, only to see her return to the subcontinent. For the last half-century, Faria skirted the edges of the vast Thar desert: an unlikely nomad among both the Indus River villages clinging to the life-giving Himalayan waters and the northern Rajasthan subsistence farms standing in defiance of the scorching winds and sand dunes of the Thar.

It had been during the Mohenjo Daro dig in what was now southern Pakistan during the 1920's that tales of Faria, now told across a thousand-mile stretch of desert, could trace their roots. Three workers became pinned under a ten-ton stone block when the crude, wooden retaining wall holding it at bay collapsed. Their young sons frantically looked on, helpless to extract their fathers when the black haired angel with fathomless eyes descended in aid. Decade to decade and hamlet to hamlet the tale evolved, but the last living son, who still resides in Mohenjo Daro, would state the facts as such: the sand itself on one side of the block evacuated as if repelled by force, upending the block, and their fathers emerged unharmed from underneath.

By the mid 1990's, each hamlet had its own unique tale of subtle kindness, dispute mediation, or act of guiding premonition linked to the willowy Faria, her hair as wild as the desert winds. While Shikha found solace in solitude, Faria found it among those on the fringes of human existence, who manifested their reverence by never questioning her age or motivations, but seating her in the place of honor at village festivals. In time, she came to be known as 'young Grandmother,' and her auspicious appearance in a dusty town, one she hadn't visited for perhaps ten years, was cause for celebration and storytelling. Faria catalogued the village myths and family histories, however humble their origins.

A tireless listener, Faria thought she had heard all the permutations of the Indus River Valley mythology, local religious customs and oral histories, which stretched back into time by eons. That was, until one morning in 2009 when she was summoned to the bedside of an elderly Pakistani woman in the town of Mari Indus. She had known the family for many years, recalling fondly the woman's grandfather, a schoolteacher who reminded her of Tom Robbin. During the partition of the Punjab, when rioting tore many towns apart, his cool temper and humble speeches saved many lives. While he could not remove the blackness growing in men's hearts, he could keep them from acting upon it. The woman's skin, rather than being roughened by the desert, had become soft as tissue paper, and just as wrinkled. She was dying. Rather than fearing her fate, she sat propped upright in the corner of her mud-brick house smiling like a child awakened to a new day.

"Is it you, young grandmother?" she asked, her eyesight having failed in its purpose the prior year.

"Yes, yes, how can I aid you, Asha?" replied Faria. Her elderly friend held out a trembling hand, which Faria delicately grasped.

"Please, sit close. My words are few. I have waited for your return to our village. Little life remains in these limbs of mine, but it is time enough. You have wandered long, yes? I remember your visits from my childhood, always searching, digging and asking," she began, looking through the darkness of her sight, but still beaming, a serene smile crossing her face. "When I was very young, my grandfather told us legends of a great migration, of the early peoples, long before Islam came to this land. Our ancestors abandoned their grand city of the East, near Rakhigarhi, when the River Sarasvati flowed less and less until it was no more. They searched, they wandered, just as you, but settled along the Indus."

She paused, uncertain how to continue as her face grew troubled. "Grandfather was fond of you. You once dwelled at the base of the mountains in the North?" Asha finally whispered, to which a surprised Faria, rarely astonished, squeezed her hand in agreement and replied yes in a trembling voice. "He thought so. I am old, and have forgotten much of what my grandfather said. But I recall the riots of 1947, when many fell under the spell of hatred, Hindu and Muslim alike." Asha took a heaving breath, and continued. "I returned to the house for a shawl. It was late in the year, perhaps even early 1948, and I found grandfather, eyes reddened, gazing out the window into the setting sun. His concentration fixed on an ancient ruined Hindu temple. You know the one." Faria nodded, although Asha could not see it.

"I asked what troubled him; I was fifteen at the time. He held a yellowed newspaper that had made its way upriver. It spoke of a land called Palestine that was also in conflict much like ours. He said to me, Asha dear, what you and I believe, what is practiced in the Mosque, what we perceive in this world, is only the surface of existence. The distinctions we draw between peoples and religions are like tiny ripples on the river. We create them for our own fancy, but there is a deeper undercurrent, now neglected, that once bound all humans, indeed all life together in an earlier age. It is right in front of us flowing through time, he said, but we can no longer see it." Asha stopped for a moment, caught between the joy of recalling her grandfather and the sadness of his memory. She turned to the young woman she had known for seventy years, her smoky and unseeing eyes piercing the veil of Faria's mind.

Asha continued in a firm but soft voice. "We humans now only glimpse that earlier age in our most base fears, when we are alone in the desert, when we dream, and within the myths that thread through all our contrived religions. But you, Faria, you are of that age, bound to it for eternity, each day becoming more detached from those that live but a brief time." She squeezed Faria's hand, more intensely than one might think possible. "You were a great comfort to my grandfather. He mused on long unspoken stories, lost endings to the tales we all know. He said you were part of those untold stories. Rakhigarhi, grandfather would say, Faria must dig there and stop her wandering." Asha leaned back and released Faria's hand.

Faria's experiences among humanity had often fed Shikha's need for human companionship, even intimacy. She felt the same joy, loss and frustration as her twin who traversed the globe village by village. On Long Island, Sagar remained focused on the road ahead, staring down the intensity of the storm for nearly a minute before Shikha began to sense the concussive response to her thoughts building in his mind. He had no doubt perceived most aspects of her recollections. When he spoke, it was as if issuing a challenge to the gods themselves. "The three of us, we will find if this river meets the sea. I have served destiny for six hundred years, along paths that were not of my choosing. Enough. After New Haven, to Moradabad we fly, to Faria and to recast our fate."

They hurtled past a bright orange snowplow, the only other vehicle on the road. It had paused in its duty and the driver stood hammering away with a shovel at the sanding mechanism attached to the back. Sagar's black Mercedes flew by so quickly the snowplow driver thought it a particularly strong gust of wind. Five minutes later Sagar slowed, turning into the back entrance of MacArthur airport. A stout,hooded figure met them at the chain link fence gate. He forced it open through the wet snow, bending the gate in the process, but created an opening large enough for the truck to pass. Sagar rolled down his window and spoke to the man. Shikha didn't recognize the language, but discerned that Sagar was thanking him, and asking if the plane was ready. The man hopped in the back seat.

"This is Hehu. He is Maori. Hehu, this is Shikha, one of my kinfolk." Hehu held out his thick hand, which Shikha shook; he didn't shake her hand back, for fear of crushing it, but just left his meaty paw dangling in the air. He had the look of a young boy who found himself in the most curious of circumstances, thousands of miles from anything familiar, but excited to be along for the adventure nonetheless. Hehu put his hand back in his lap and gazed out the window at the falling snow. The big islander reminded Shikha of a Fijian shipmate Sagar had introduced her to in the 1870's. Love, she had discovered, is not a solvable problem. After he left because she refused to commit herself to him for life, Shikha lost herself in despair, in a way she had only known from Abigail's memories.

Sagar fishtailed the truck to the left, heading for a series of hangars hugging the runway. The truck skipped onto the recently plowed tarmac, and Sagar continued to add speed. Shikha felt him enjoying the sensation of hurrying, as if time were a quantity they had too little of now that they acted with purpose. A single gray jet stood before them, lights on, boarding stairs down. Its seven windows illuminated the falling snow like a little submarine casting light into the depths of the ocean. Sagar eased the truck to a stop and said to Shikha, "Ready?"

Glancing at the plane, she mockingly furrowed her brow. "We're not taking a log raft across the Sound?" Sagar shrugged and replied, "the conveniences of modern life cannot be avoided." Hehu was already halfway up the boarding stairs, burdened with several duffle bags but unfazed by their weight. Shikha followed him onto the plane: several desks held electronic equipment on the port side, as well as a large aluminum cabinet built to fit the curve of the plane, a single row of seats and a couch covered the starboard side and two sets of bunk beds were aft. An executive jet for the most unusual executive, she mused. Sagar soon appeared, but ducked into the cockpit before pulling the stairs up and closing the jet door. The engines fired and they were off.

The three of them exchanged no words for the brief flight. Hehu snacked on dried fish, Sagar slumped, eyes closed, lost not in sleep but in thought. Shikha watched a monitor that displayed airspeed and elevation; the plane never rose above two thousand feet, just skimming below the maelstrom until across the Sound where the haze of light that was New Haven harbor came into view. They flew over the oil storage tanks and the Q bridge, which had been under constant construction for the past 20 years, and touched down at Tweed airport. As the plane taxied to a lonely hangar, Shikha texted her sister "With Sagar in NH. Hope to be in Moradabad by Monday." This drew an immediate response: "Get Abby's book-the black one. We need it." That might prove problematic, Shikha thought. While it technically belonged to all of them, along with about 300 other texts in the Beinecke Rare Book and Manuscript Library, evidencing that claim, and finding someone on Easter Sunday to listen, was another matter entirely.

CHAPTER 7 - February 1, 1603

During the first few days aboard the Spring Tide, most adapted quickly to the schedule of the watches. Never did the gun deck fall completely silent. Some slept while others ate. Children played constantly, taking advantage of their parents' wakefulness, no matter the hour. To those who had worked the land, it was reminiscent of harvest time, when work progressed nonstop. Overnight, hatches remained closed to keep the warmth in and the wind out, giving the impression that the congregants were indeed not on a ship at all, but living prehistorically, inhabiting a deep but narrow cave. Rather than a foreboding atmosphere, the ceaseless chattering of children and constant activity imparted a warm and comforting feeling to their floating home.

Abby had taken to teaching all the girls to knit, dipping into their stores of spun wool for the purpose. A few were already quite proficient, having been taught by their own mothers, elder sisters, or aunts, but in particular, Abby's twins excelled. They had never used the western needles but had an intuitive grasp of the yarn, how it wanted to turn, and how to achieve certain patterns. Abby busied herself helping one of the smallest girls, Sarah, while Susan Robbin looked on with interest. She had always wanted a daughter, but instead found herself with three rollicking boys, so much like her elder brothers. She watched Faria weave the needles through the air, her hands retracing the same movements, but occasionally introducing a slight variation.

Abby stood up, arching her back after being hunched over her student for several minutes. Softly, Susan addressed her. "Abby, what do you make of that pattern in Faria's scarf? Did you teach it to her? It's something I think I've seen before, but I can't recall where."

Abby narrowed her focus, and as she twisted her head to the side, she slowly responded, "No, I've only showed them the technique itself, Faria must have incorporated that on her own. I do say, it looks

… I'm not sure really. Faria, dear, what is it you have incorporated into your scarf? It's a lovely pattern."

"It's just something that is in my head. It repeats every so often, but I haven't quite got through the entire sequence. Do you really like it?" Abby smiled back and nodded approvingly, returning to help little Sarah. Faria realized this was not the place to test her new mother, but soon enough. All of the girls had made some progress in their knitting that afternoon, and in a few days' time, would be able to warm themselves with their creations, or gift them to family members.

Abby marked the time and, with a nod, she and the twins returned to the galley to prepare the evening meal. When George and his watch-mates descended into the ship that evening, they were buffeted by a sharper cold than previous days, as if the ship gasped a frigid breath. The line for warm comestibles formed quickly, while the next watch lingered below, trying to absorb as much warmth as possible before heading on deck.

"Hallo, the captain stands alone on deck! Where be my men? If I catch a few winks at the wheel, why, we could end up back in the Hebrides! Tumble out men and be quick!" Tanner called down into the hold. He spoke in a jolly and harmless manner, but he also knew how a ship could be undone due to an unchecked mistake by one deckhand, a mate or the captain himself. The men were spirited by the captain's light words and headed up onto the frosty deck.

After supper, Abigail and George, who had never spent much time talking, called the twins to bed. Abigail knew with bitter certainty that she could never be open with her simple husband. He was as predictable as the sun, but understood little of the gray shades of the world. In him, she knew she had a man who would defend and support her, as he had on the carriage to Amsterdam, but in him she could not confide. They silently readied their thick layer of blankets, which served as a bed. The girls slept directly above them in one of the double hammocks. Sleep found George at once, as always, but Abby lay awake, ruminating on the day's events.

Her eyes remained open in the darkness of the gun deck; occasionally a swaying lantern would throw shadows onto the hammock above her, where her twins nestled in a dark wool blanket. The contrast of the black blanket against the hammock ropes highlighted the structure of knots, which, Abby realized, resembled the pattern in the scarf Faria was knitting. Like a wave slowly building in form and momentum as it approached the shore, disparate subconscious thoughts, suspicions and experiences crashed into her conscious mind, overwhelming her. She suddenly felt as if the ship had disappeared from under her and she was falling through space: her stomach convulsed, her pulse exploded as Abby's mind raced to the conclusion her instincts had drawn. She now knew this pattern to be a written language, one she had not seen since she was 14, since she cursed her entire village on May Day.

Abby's realization pulled her back to the events of ten years ago, the day she walked away from the stunned crowd of May Day celebrators. For weeks prior to Whitsuntide, she had scoured the woods outside their village, trying to discover the cave she had once visited with her mother. She couldn't recall her exact age when her mom half-dragged, half-carried her through the ancient forest that night, probably 4 or 5 years old. She knew it had been close to her birthday, and that her mother, even in the moonless darkness of winter, had no problems finding her way. The images of those haggard crones who inhabited their destination were branded into her mind and became part of a series of recurring dreams throughout her childhood. After that visit, the lives of her family changed and whatever bargain her mother struck with those creatures, she aimed to strike a similar one.

After searching for the cave several times during the daylight to no avail, she determined to venture out into the woods after her parents had fallen asleep. Young Abby wrapped herself in her thickest green shawl and crept out the front door. The wind through the leafless trees whispered in deep silky tones as she defiantly strode through the woods. Somehow, Abby came across a path she hadn't seen before, and struck out along it. Soon she caught a glimpse of a flickering deep orange light in the distance at the foot of a small hill. As she drew nearer, the light grew in radiance and she knew she had found it.

Hesitating at the mouth of the cave, a high voice beckoned to her from within: "So, you have returned, child." Before Abby could act or respond, another voice echoed back: "Who has returned, sister?", to which the first and stronger voice replied, "You will smell her fiery locks soon enough."

This exchange emboldened Abby enough to take a few steps forward and speak. "My name is Abigail Kelly; I once came here with my mother, long ago. I come now to ask for wrongs to be righted."

"There's much in your statement, young Abigail. Yes, your mother visited us five and ten and then ten again years past. To be so fortunate as to think ten years was long ago. Child, each spring comes to us as quickly as the sunrise comes to you," the weaker of the two voices said.

"The years have blinked by; your mother had hoped to care for a beautiful girl, and indeed, you are that. But you are also stubborn and vindictive. To think that the fruits of her selfless wish now return to us asking for vengeance against a subtle slight, it is as if the spirits mock our craft. Enough of history, speak your desire, Abigail Kelly," intoned the stronger voice.

The aged sisters' words gave Abby pause. She hadn't known what to expect, but the mockery of her motivations and the intimacy with which they addressed her angered the girl. She tried to compose herself, but she felt her face reddening in the chilly darkness. Deep in the cavern, the sisters smiled at her passions, their words sticking like deftly placed barbs in Abby's mind.

Finally, Abigail burst forth, "I have been wronged by the Christian father Brenton and in turn, father Brenton and the Church have wronged us both. He belittles the customs and ceremonies of our ancestors with utter disbelief in the faith that brought my mother to you, but if you feel no slight, stay in your cave and watch the springs pass you by until you are altogether forgotten." Her chest heaving, Abby waited for a reply.

At length, and in a quiet tone, a response came. "Please, child, warm yourself by our fire, and tell us what you would have us do."

Somewhat cooled and urged on by her icy toes, Abby stepped through the mouth of the cave, revealing a broad, circular room with a fireplace at the far end, in front of which sat a low stone slab. The walls consisted of carefully stacked stones in concentric circles of decreasing size, giving the impression of being inside a beehive. Roots pierced the crevices in the walls, some as thick as a man's arm. Abby now realized that what she remembered as a cave was an ancient stone structure that over hundreds of years had found its place in the natural landscape. To her left sat a massive wooden table cluttered with objects: unfamiliar contraptions, scrolls, small boxes of dried earth, and what looked to her like a tiny, living tree. Two hooded figures slid forward to greet her, clothed in dark woolen garments. With the firelight at their backs she couldn't see their faces, only their frail outlines.

"So, Abigail Kelly, we have three questions: Do you come to see the sisters out of desperation or faith?" said one figure.

"Do you come to see the sisters because you want revenge?" said the other.

"Are you willing to suffer the same fate as those you seek to injure?" said the first.

Abby again felt herself on the defensive as her face reddened further. She knew her responses would dictate not only if the sisters would aid her, but also the manner of their aid. "I share the same faith as my mother; I believe in the power of the trees, the grasses, and the flowing water. I do not seek personal revenge, but I wish for a reminder to those who would so easily dismiss what was once sacred. I will pay whatever price you ask."

The sisters turned to one another and back to Abigail. Reaching out their withered hands, they led her to the stone altar, where they achingly sat down, beckoning her to do the same. Abigail hesitated, but finally sat on the rough but warm slab of granite.

"On Whitsuntide, visit the villagers' houses, gather your garlands and ribbons, but when all eyes are upon you and it is your time to choose, choose not. Spring unconsummated, an unrequited Imbolc, even if the blackthorn has bloomed and your mother has prayed to her Brigid. Find your way back to us before the sun sets, and we will complete our work. Know this, though. Just as the fields will suffer for an entire year, with crops sprouting with promise, only to wither in the burnt soil, so you will remain as the land for your entire life. This is a heavy price, but it must be paid." In alternating phrases, the sisters spoke with compassion and sadness, knowing that Abigail would acquiesce. Despite her intentions, and true enough to her harsh words, the two of them, and the faith which bound them to nature, would in time, be forgotten.

"I, I will do as you instruct," Abby replied. Of her own accord, she rose from the warm stone and departed into the windy night, marking the way in her mind so as to be certain of the path upon her return.

What Abby couldn't know is that these crones, relics of a distant age, were bound by nature to fulfill her request. Time had bent their bodies low, their limbs gnarled like the branches of a long dead tree. Yet, nearly 600 years separated these sisters' births and so 600 years of knowledge the older possessed that the younger did not. "We should not hasten to action if it spells our doom. She is but a human girl, and there is risk in what she asks," the younger warned.

"It is not haste that compels me but something deeper, you felt it too, sister, nigh ten years ago," the older mused in her soft tone.

Searching her memories, the younger shook her head dismissively and paced into the darkness of the cave. "There is but a trace in her, a droplet, nothing more."

"A trace! As if the blood of the gods grows diluted with time. Is a drop of the sacred river any less pure, less potent than the river itself? Oh Aibhlinn." It had been dozens of years since she had spoken her sister's name, Aibhlinn, and it awoke in her images of their mother, whom her younger sister had never known. "We, the elder race from before the cataclysms, the Watchers heralded in the books of Daniel and Enoch, do not possess what dwells within this Abigail. Aye, we live through the centuries, perfected first in form but mortal in our suffering still." The older crone's voice first rose as she spoke, booming, then ebbed back to a whisper.

"We suffer mortality, but our folk remain free at great peril, unlike those who returned to the mountains and now chained, unknowingly do the bidding of the gods," Aibhlinn replied.

"Recall the words of our father: do not heap praise upon yourself for what our kin did. Their reason for abandoning the call of the gods was lost long ago. We all must do the bidding of destiny. Whether chained to the gods, servants on earth or free here in our cave, there is no escape from the path of time." She spoke so softly in response, her words competed with the hissing fire.

Aibhlinn knew her words to be wise, and the younger returned to her older sister's side and asked, "Should we tell her? There is much we have to teach. Much this Abigail Kelly could learn."

"We will grant her request, nothing more. Destiny works along her own paths. This Abigail, not Kelly but De Danann, has the right to find her own way."

Abby recalled her flight from the May Day ceremonies, and how, despite her fears, she strode boldly through the woods. Approaching the witches' abode during daylight, she realized why it had been so difficult to find those many times she had searched. When viewed head-on during the day, the entrance was nearly invisible: three massive white oak trees grew staggered just in front of the opening to the stone enclosure. From the left, center or right, one would need to look precisely through the narrow openings between the trees to see the entrance; otherwise, it was as if these fathers of the forest were growing in front of a small, steep hill. At night, with the firelight glowing from deep inside, it was easier to discern its location.

As she entered, the sisters silently beckoned her to again sit at the altar. Only coals remained in the massive hearth, but the rough slab of granite still possessed a warmth that unnerved Abby. The two withered creatures drew close, and the younger cut copious handfuls of Abby's tightly curled red hair. This, she affixed to slender oak sticks and, reaching deep into a dark velvet bag, spread a fine white sand around the altar. In the sand, they drew rings of text in a fluid, roiling script. Abby sat transfixed as their aged hands deftly wielded the sharp oak branches. The two circled the seated girl, moving in opposite directions around the slab until their writing had woven a pattern several lines thick. Once finished, they threw the sticks onto the coals, where the wood slowly smoldered and the burning hair released an acrid sulfuric smoke into the room. As the sisters stood back from the hearth, Abby glimpsed tears in their silvery eyes.

"Arise, child, it is done. Return now to your family. Speak not to anyone about what has transpired. Your mother will guess soon enough," said the kinder and older of the two. Abby left the warmth of the cave and as she walked home in the dying light, an unseasonably bitter wind swept through the woods.

That beautiful script, buried in her memories of who she once was, now chained that past to this very uncertain future, but she didn't quite know how. Yet. Abby lay awake for some time, eyes open, staring at the patterns in the hammock above her, body listing back and forth with the movement of the Spring Tide as she rolled through the Northern seas.

CHAPTER 8 - February 1603

Overnight, a few lonely snowflakes, at first met with curiosity by the night watch, gathered into a dense, wet snowfall, muting the sound of the ship slipping through the cold sea. The black ocean spirit, which had tailed the Spring Tide since Sagar and the twins had boarded her, saw its chance. Able to whip the waves and wind into a fury, the creature knew it had the entire voyage to plan its strike but on this day, it chose to intensify the storm and reap its victims.

By daybreak, three inches of snow covered most of the deck, with small drifts accumulating in the scuppers on the lee side. Even with all the hatches to the gun deck snugly closed, its denizens could hear Captain Tanner bellowing to the men: "From the top of the mainmast downwards, clear this damned snow from the ship. She must stay light on her feet to weather this storm." His feet could be heard pounding the deck, fore to aft as he checked the men's work. Back near the helm, he approached his young second mate, instructing, "Sagar, boy, rouse the younger lads from the forecastle. We may need their spryness up in the rigging if she really starts to break on us. Jorge, fall off the wind a bit here, but keep us moving forward."

Below deck, the thick timbers of the ship did little to insulate the inhabitants from the cacophony outside. With each rise and fall of the sea, the Spring Tide creaked and groaned, her seams, so far, were holding tight, keeping the hold dry. Occasionally a child would open one of the cannon ports, leading to a unified chorus of "CLOSE THAT PORT." Just a few seconds was all it took to flood the gun deck with frigid air, dissipating the warmth that it may have taken the fire in the galley hours to build.

Throughout the morning, the snowfall hardened into a driving, icy hammer of sharp crystals, which railed against the ship with each burst of wind. The men on deck buried their faces in their jackets as they tried to keep the deck clear of snow. The captain had taken the helm and called Sagar to his side. After a brief exchange, Sagar ducked into the Captain's cabin, emerging with some modest burden, and disappeared below decks. A few minutes later, he and Mary opened the forward hatch to the gun deck and brought forth several steaming pitchers of delicious grog. Mary had added a generous helping of molasses to the hot spiced rum concoction, a hearty fortifier for the chilled souls who had spent the morning trudging the deck. Despite their religious convictions, not one of the men turned away a first or second cup of the brew. Its warming capacity reddened their faces and brought forth a few laughs as well.

During the dispensation of grog, Tanner remained at the helm; Jorge thought to bring his Captain a measure of the mixture and as he traversed the deck, the ship rode up the back of a larger swell, pushed on by the fierce wind. Sagar felt the ship propelled by another force beyond the wind itself. Scrutinizing the first mate's actions and anticipating the movement of the ship, Sagar began to edge closer to the railing where he clung to a mess of unused ropes. As the Spring Tide reached the crest of the massive wave and began the sleigh ride down the face, for a brief second, it felt as if the ship were no longer anchored to the ocean.

In this moment, Jorge slipped on the icy stairs that led up to the aft deck and instantly disappeared overboard into the black sea. Only Sagar and Tanner saw the first mate fall and before the Captain could call out, Sagar dove headlong into the maelstrom, over the railing, rope in hand. Just as Sagar's lean body met the water's surface, Abby found herself pushed into a lee side porthole on the gun deck by a powerful force: her daughters.

"Man Overboard!" bellowed Captain Tanner, pointing over the aft starboard railing. His call echoed throughout the ship, bringing the entire Congregation to sharp attention; men from other watches spilled onto the deck, unprepared for the biting wind, which almost froze them where they stood. Tanner backed off the helm, directing men to scan the surface of the water for his first mate and the foolhardy young boy who jumped in after him. His maneuver slackened the pace of the ship, giving Sagar and Jorge a chance to catch up, but it also exposed the vessel to the dangerous waves, which could now crash freely against her broadsides. Where Sagar jumped in, James traced the rope the boy carried with him into the darkness. He had tied it to the railing.

Below decks, hatches opened and faces young and old peered into the blizzard, praying it was not their son, father or husband tossed in the frothing seas. Scanning the water, the twins muttered in hushed tones only Abby could hear, "There, see the rope cutting the crest of that wave," Faria said. "Yes, and our Sagar at the end of it," her sister replied.

Sagar surfaced about ten yards off but disappeared so abruptly that Abby was sure he wasn't just struggling with the waves but was forced under. "Miss Abby, you must help us. A great sea spirit will drown them both if we can't repulse it."

"Both? Who else is in the water? What should I do?" Abby desperately whispered.

"Sagar jumped in after the first mate. When you see something shiny, iridescent, but black all the same, concentrate on it. Push it away," Faria replied, her eyes still transfixed on the waves. Sagar resurfaced and this time he had something gray in a net with him. He dragged it toward the ship when an oily streak began fiercely fighting him for his catch. The more Abby stared, the sharper its form became, as if her concentration gave it shape: a shiny serpent whose scales stood in deep contrast to the churned water and white snow. "That's it Miss Abby, we have it trapped, now away with it, back to the depths!" Abby shuddered and fell to the floor, unnoticed by the throng still peering out the portholes.

"Captain," James called to his father-in-law, pointing to and holding the line in his hand, "shall I, shall I pull him in?" Tanner was astonished at the speed at which Sagar must have worked, and he seemed to hesitate at first, but the captain was actually counting to himself. After about ten seconds, Tanner responded forcefully.

"Haul them in!" James pulled in the slack on the line, and after retrieving about 20 yards of rope, he felt a heavy resistance. Something was attached to the other end and judging by the weight, it couldn't possibly be just Sagar. More men joined him and they swiftly pulled in yard after yard of line until James, closest to the railing, discerned a bobbing bundle of rope, boy and man entangled in a web of knots but holding fast.

As the bundle approached the broad side of the ship, it became clear that Sagar had retrieved Jorge by using one of the twin's hammocks as a net; in a loud but rasping voice, he called out for another line, which James threw down with haste. He tied off the second rope to Jorge's feet while keeping the first mate's head above water. Jorge was hauled on board and before being carried below decks, Tom Robbin declared the first mate unconscious but possessing a slow and steady heartbeat. Tanner himself pulled Sagar up, and when the lad was safely on deck, he commanded Tom to take the helm and maintain a heading generally downwind. Tanner busied Sagar into his quarters, half-carrying the boy.

Before the door was shut behind them, Sagar collapsed onto one of the built-in benches around the Captain's table. Tanner picked him up and placed him in his own bed, weighing the boy down with a generous helping of wool blankets. Sagar remained lucid but shivering. Before Tanner had a chance to speak, Sagar motioned to the captain to come closer.

"Jorge, he's alive, isn't he?" said the boy.

"Yes, son, thanks to you and your damn . . ." said Tanner.

"And how goes the storm, Captain?" interrupted Sagar.

The captain paused, just now realizing that from the moment Sagar left the water, the storm had moderated, the snow subsided and the strong winds tapered to a steady 15-knot breeze. The ship had not received any heavy waves over her side as Tanner had feared and she now rolled on through a steady 4-6 foot swell. Tanner frowned quizzically. Sagar looked back at the grizzled man, reading his thoughts, and for the first time in a very long while, the dark and thin boy smiled.

"Please, go check on your first mate, Captain, but return

with any news, good or ill," said Sagar, his eyes closing. Tanner nodded, stood up from the side of his bed, and went below. Alone, Sagar allowed exhaustion to overwhelm his small frame. Visions of the mighty Makara, as Brigu would have called the serpent, stung his mind as the pain of her touch still lingered upon his legs and body.

The captain emerged from his cabin and gave Tom Robbin a short report. As he traversed the steps down to the main deck, Tom called out to him. "Strange, don't you think, Captain, how the boy could move so quickly to Jorge's rescue, and survive the frigid waters? Reverend Williams might call it a miracle."

The captain paused, bluffing. "Oh, he's a brave young boy to be sure, but at sea, feats such as this are not uncommon, and are forgotten soon enough. The sea takes when she wishes, and today she did not. Dwelling on our good fortune will hurt all the worse when it turns ill."

This answer clearly did not satisfy Tom, but he said no more. The captain made his way below deck to find Jorge in the galley, surrounded by Mary and Mrs. Bray. He had regained consciousness, and was propped up in a chair sipping on a cup of brandy. He smiled meekly and offered his hand to the captain. Tanner turned the wrinkled hand aside, only to deeply embrace the man. Behind them, Abigail crept closer, pale as a shade and looking disoriented.

"Ah, Capitan, a sorte protégé os audazes, eh?" whispered Jorge into Tanner's ear.

"Yes, luck favored the boy this day," the captain softly replied, in a louder voice, "And you, how do you fare after your leisurely swim? You've thought to clean up in preparation for Sunday dinner, have you? I say, you smell a mite better. Do you recommend we all take a dip?"

Mary looked disapprovingly at her father. "His left arm is broken, as you can see. He is still shivering, and two of his toes are blackened," she said, fussing over the first mate.

"Just two blackened toes and a broken arm? All the same, an old man who's just had a cool bath needs to rest, and we, all of us, should let Jorge rest, don't you think?" Replied Captain Tanner, careful to eye each of the hovering ladies. Jorge had resumed pretending to sleep. "Mary, your boy Sagar rests in my cabin. Could you see that he is brought some warm food and drink?"

"Hot food and hot words are what that boy will be served. Jumping off the ship in the middle of a winter gale." Mary's voice trailed off, just now noticing that the storm had subsided. Abby followed Mary to the galley, hoping simple tasks might clear her mind.

While the snow had stopped falling, it still littered the deck, and ice clung to the rigging. The captain organized a team of boys to clear the snow and to knock as much ice off the masts and lines as they safely could. Tom remained at the helm for the next few hours and as night fell, the favorable wind held them on course. Among the men, few words were exchanged in the dying light, but the boys chattered incessantly about Sagar's deeds. One little lad still beaming after being called on deck for the first time exclaimed, "I saw the whole thing from right here. Sagar caught the first mate like a frozen fish in a net, and they hauled them both back in over the railing. What a swimmer Sagar must be!"

Others didn't share his praise. A freckled boy with tiny piercing eyes, the son of Henry Mason chided, "Luck, that's all it was. Bad luck for us. Those two have much sway over the captain, and I'd as soon be rid of them as I would be of all this ice. A first mate that falls overboard and a second mate that jumps after him. One clumsy, one crazy." Henry Jr. no doubt passed along his father's beliefs as it was clear the deep vein of ignorance that ran through their family had not passed over the son. For two generations, the Masons had labored for the Gaithers, initially as seasonal farmhands during the harvest, eventually becoming full-time employees of the Gaither clan. Indeed, they may have joined the congregation at Herbert Gaither's command.

Billy Gaither, whose blustery voice was not just an odd family trait but a requirement if one meant to be heard among his kin agreed. "My older brother says the dark boy must be some kind of mer-man. Have any of you seen his feet? I reckon they are flippers or fins. He does keep his own company, talking only to the captain and Jorge when it suits him. As you said, Hen" motioning to Henry Jr., "that castoff may have fooled some people, but not us." If one expected to be heard among the Gaithers, one needed to shout.

Nathan Robbin dismissed these tales. "Your brother's head must be full of turnips. Mer-men only exist in the befuddled minds of foolish farmers." As the eldest son of a schoolteacher, thankfully for his health, he had inherited an athleticism and physical presence from his mother's side of the family to match his father's bookish wit. The first few days in the forecastle had seen many attempts to bring his words in check with thick fists, and each challenger had seen the worse of the encounter. While Billy Gaither did not understand about a third of the words thrown back at him, he knew an insult when he heard it. Just as he began to respond, Nathan continued "And as for bad luck, Jorge is the only man aboard this ship able to navigate to the new lands; in saving Jorge, Sagar saved all of us too." Nathan's last comment quieted the open discord, but Billy Gaither and Henry Jr. still fumed.

Throughout the now-cloudless night, reports returned of Sagar sleeping well, but Jorge struggling with a fever. His arm had purpled at the point where it broke, and having bedded down next to the galley stove, he was sweating and shivering simultaneously. At midnight, Mary came on deck to ask her father what, if anything, should be done for the first mate. The captain indicated that Jorge was to be continually pressured to drink hot water imbued with a bit of molasses and brandy. Mary was to keep forcing the concoction on him to the point of annoying the grizzled Portuguese. He thought for a moment and suggested to Mary that Abigail's twins, Faria and Shikha, tend to Jorge, so as not to burden Mary, who needed to keep the entire congregation fed. Mary stared back at her father, letting the silence between them be her words: what are these children we have invited to live among us?

CHAPTER 9 - February 1603

The ship coasted along in the soft night breeze, the full moon brightening the sky and imbuing the sea foam with a milky glimmer as it rushed down the face of the waves. Well over a month had passed since the congregation departed Amsterdam. By the captain's reckoning, the Spring Tide had traveled nearly 2,500 miles, and he wasn't far off in his measure. Having initially set a westerly course, the deep ocean swell that ceaselessly battered the port side of the vessel had pushed them far to the North. With such an inexperienced crew, the tactical changes required to maintain a more consistent direction were impossible.

Before the storm had broken, Jorge and the captain had met to reconcile their progress with the first mate's memories of previous fishing journeys. He had confided that it was only a matter of days before the currents would slack and they would be able to make headway to the southwest; this, in hopes of approaching the broad fishing grounds, which extended hundreds of miles out from the coastline. Three weeks more, two if they were favored, and the ocean floor would rise up to less than five hundred feet. It was here, upon an ocean mount known by many names where Jorge's father lay, and Jorge, in his weakened state, sought to join him.

The bright morning sunrise brought no change to the light winds and calm seas. The captain had spent nearly twenty-four hours on deck but before retiring to his quarters, he knocked on the door to Williams and Smith's room. A weary eyed Smith opened the door, still in his bedclothes. The reverends had scarcely been seen on deck since the Spring Tide left Amsterdam, and even less so in the past week. Both would occasionally make their way to the gun deck to greet the congregants, yet they would dine in their own room. Smith wore several days' stubble on his face and a weariness lingered in his eyes as he blinked back the brightness of the morning.

"Yes, Captain Tanner. What can I do for you at this early hour?" said Smith.

"I wish to speak with Reverend Williams if you please. We have seen little of him as of late, and I hope, this being Sunday, to request, to suggest that is, that the reverend preside over dinner for the congregation today. I also must inform him of the condition of our first and second mates, and apprise him of our progress," replied Tanner. His voice fluctuated between deference, as a member of the religious congregation, and command, as the captain of the vessel.

"Reverend Williams is not awake yet. He has not been well this past week, and is suffering from a cough. I will tell him you inquired of him. As for our progress, I should like to hear more of that myself. Please let me get dressed, and I will come to your quarters shortly," responded Reverend Smith. Before Tanner could respond, Smith shut the door. Exhausted, Tanner returned to his rooms, where he found his bed empty and three blankets folded neatly at the foot. Sagar must have slipped out of the cabin sometime just before dawn. A knock came to the door. That'll be Smith, Tanner thought. As he opened it, the captain was surprised to see both Smith and Williams standing outside. Tanner retreated a step upon seeing Williams, only to bump his head on the lantern above the table. Smoothing his ruffled coat, Tanner greeted the men: "Reverends, please come in"

"Yes, thank you captain," said Williams, with a rasp in his voice. Smith had been in front of him in the doorway, but stepped aside to let Williams enter first.

As the men settled in to the benches surrounding the broad table, Tanner noted the difficulty with which Williams moved, as if he were protecting a fragility of his bones. He slowly lowered himself to a seated position, and seemed to be gathering his strength, taking in a deep breath, so that when he spoke, it was with the power and authority he had used to establish and command his congregation. "Captain," Williams began, "what news of our progress can you report? We are over six weeks out from Amsterdam, and have seen only dark seas, snow and ice."

"Yes, as far as we can reckon, the wind and waves have carried us along a northerly route. Jorge, whose life was nearly lost yesterday, and by whose mental charts we navigate, believes that within weeks, the currents will turn, allowing us to make headway to the southwest. For now, Jorge recovers, but if we lose him, we lose our way. We have only the boy Sagar to thank for fishing the tired Portuguese from the sea," replied Tanner.

"We have God to thank, Captain Tanner," inserted Smith quickly. The two men shared an uncomfortable stare until Williams had a chance to interpret the Captain's comments and respond.

"God's will was done through the boy Sagar. That is all. Captain, what is your estimate for how long we have remaining in our journey? The congregation, as you know, are not sailors, they are men of the land. I sense they grow restless."

"Reverend, your presence alone calms the flock. When we left Amsterdam, we were of one mind, of one purpose. Over time, men have begun to keep to themselves, and keep to their kin. They whisper, as if others in the congregation were strangers, not brethren. I hope, given that today is Sunday, we can all eat supper below decks, where you can address the full congregation. There are many reasons to rejoice together, not least of which is Sagar's actions during the storm yesterday."

Williams replied, "Yes, Captain, I share your observations, and have seen much that concerns me. While life aboard this ship has required us to fracture into three watches, living separately from one another, it is time to bring those pieces back into one." He waited, expecting Tanner to continue.

"Well, we have nearly exhausted our fresh provisions and as you say, our crew consists of farmers, not sailors. Aye, they have eaten like farmers so far. We'd best not ration the remaining fresh food, which will spoil in a matter of days. I suggest we feast tonight, as soon enough our victuals will be dried beef and sea biscuits. Our only surplus is water, spared spoilage by the frigid weather, but if it sours, we can only rely on bitter beer for drink. As for how long remains in our journey, I must consult with Jorge. It could be as short as two weeks, or we may remain another month at sea." As he finished speaking, Tanner's gaze lingered on Reverend Williams. In the few minutes they had been talking, the captain had come to realize how sick their shepherd was.

After looking to Reverend Smith, Williams continued, "Smith, my son, could you please let the captain and I speak privately?" This surprised Smith, but he nodded in acquiescence and left the cabin.

After the graying wooden door to the captain's quarters creaked shut, Reverend Williams waited a few seconds: "Captain Tanner, my health fails, and I feel the Lord is calling me away. I had hoped that the fresh sea air would aid my condition, but the past two weeks have seen me worsen. I cough blood and struggle to breathe. I could easily fall asleep, never to wake again, but I aim to see my people to our new home. I pray to the Lord for more time, more time to see his will be done, but however long I have, it will be too little."

Williams stopped to take a breath, a sigh really, but forced himself to continue: "Years ago, when I first met Reverend Smith, he was a shy and fearful young man. Hardship and loss found him early in life and they injured his heart. Over time, he has learned to hide his fear through arrogance, and gird his fragile heart in a cloak of detachment. Yes, he is a dedicated servant of God, but not of Man. He looks to himself first and rarely to others. Captain, there is no denying that I have failed him; he is a bitter, compassionless man."

Williams was interrupted by a fit of coughing that shook his thinned frame like a loose sail flapping in a strong wind. From across the table, Tanner handed him a handkerchief, and watched as the aged reverend slowly recovered. Wiping blood from his lower lip, Williams forced a smile and began again: "I realize now that this congregation was, selfishly, assembled by my hand, and by my efforts it has stayed as one; it is not self-sustaining. Smith cannot lead. After I am gone, yes, some may follow him, just from the habits of our old life, but those who hunger for a new beginning, or pressed by their own desires, will take their own path. Captain, please, help me by holding this congregation together after I pass on."

Tanner stared blankly back at Williams, whose gentle blue eyes implored the ship's captain to consider his request. As Tanner was about to speak, a jarring knock came to the door.
"Captain, there's been an incident in the forecastle," yelled a young man.

"You see, Captain Tanner, in times of distress, they already turn to you," Williams reflected.

Tanner rose from the table and barreled through the cabin door. Crossing the deck, and noticing it deserted excepting Sagar, his vigilant adopted grandson at the helm, he heard heated voices rebounding up from deep in the bow of the ship, where the boys quartered. As he descended the ladder into the forecastle, he saw men and boys aligned on either side of the dim enclosure. The girth of the foremast ran squarely through the roughly triangular enclosure, which had built-in bunks lining the outside walls. Unlike the gun deck, kept tidy by its inhabitants, the forecastle was a nest of wet clothes, blankets and sea chests, scattered indiscriminately across the cramped space. As the captain turned to face the crowd, he sought an unbiased face to explain what events brought him away from his cabin. Buying himself some time, and to announce his presence to those who hadn't noticed his descent, he boomed, "Whatever this is about, after it's resolved, you boys will spend the rest of your Sunday cleaning this mess up. This pit is not fit for hogs to live in." He saw James standing alone, observing the cacophony, and called to his son-in-law, "James, how do things stand here?"

Before James could answer, Herb Gaither interrupted. "See here, Tanner, that Robbin boy has been after my Billy since . . ."

"Belay yourself, Mr. Gaither, you'll get your turn" said the Captain. "Okay then, James."

"Well Cap'n, as near I can tell from where I was on the foredeck, young Robbin drops down the ladder there all free and easy, but straightaway I hear a fracas, poke my head in to see what's what, and Robbin, Billy and Henry Jr. are brawling. From the looks of it, Henry Jr. got the worst. That's all," replied James. Henry Mason stood with his hand on his son's shoulder; the boy, face swollen and bruised, was holding his left wrist with his right.

"Everyone, clear out, back on deck, except you three and your fathers," said the captain, motioning to the fighting boys. The Gaithers and Masons stood side by side, with Nathan Robbin and his spectacled dad across the forecastle. As the crowd waited their turn to ascend the ladder, Tanner pulled aside a young boy and whispered something to him, to which the boy nodded and made his way onto the deck.

After the crowd dispersed, the captain began, "Boys, I can't stop you from disliking one another. That's your business; but inasmuch as you are part of the crew, and inasmuch as you are part of my crew, I won't have fighting aboard my ship. Billy's wrist looks all twisted up, and he'll be unable to perform his duties, which is what concerns me. This just means more work for the rest of his watch. We can ill afford to lose a single hand, and with yesterday's storm nearly swallowing our first and second mates, this comes too soon."

"Dark fiends," murmured Herb Gaither, glancing up at the deck.

"Is there something you wish to say, Mr. Gaither?" said Tom Robbin, who perceived the man's words had gone unnoticed by the Captain.

"I have a right, don't I, and more right than most," began the rotund but fiery Herb. "Tanner, you may not see it, living in your stately quarters, but those two mates of yours are like little ticks, burrowing under the skin of the rest of us, sickening the congregation with their heathen ways. Mark me well, Tanner, these troubles are only beginning."

The captain had begun to face Herb directly as he spoke, but hearing the elder Gaither brother's bitter words, Tanner swiveled on his heel and looked skyward to the deck. Keeping his back turned, he replied to the angry man, "Herb, do you know who is at the helm presently?"

"I'm none too interested in that and changing the subject," started Herb, but the captain interrupted.

"It's Sagar. And do you know what heading he maintains?" said Tanner, almost in a whisper.

"Captain Tanner, don't toy with me. I care little for who steers your boat," Herb responded, eyes narrowing, smiling at his jab.

The captain turned back to Herb, but the broad and weathered Tanner, shaggy beard more gray than black, was not smiling. He took two steps closer to his antagonist, where their proximity revealed the contrast in shape between the men. While from afar, Tanner might have been described as portly, rather, he was simply thick with brutish strength. Aboard his own ship, his beefy and calloused hands had been forced to do the work of several men. It was upon his back alone that the ship's cargo was loaded and unloaded for the better part of twenty years. Herb Gaither, standing six inches shorter than Tanner, could best be compared to a pear, asymmetric head teetering on a twig like neck, narrow shoulders widening to a lazy belly. Herb was many years removed from the labors that had brought his family wealth.

"At the helm, Sagar steers a course known only to my trusted first mate, Jorge. This course consists not of lines on a chart, or the degrees of a compass. It is a feel for how the waves strike the ship, the way the sea curves and undulates with the currents, and is only known to Jorge by way of the many trips he has made with his family across this great sea. You, sir, curse the ways and means of your providence. We will reach the new lands not due to your efforts but due to theirs. It seems like the tick burrowing is more in your mind than in my crew." Captain Tanner paused a moment after finishing with Herb, awaiting his reply. Herb could be volatile at times, but he was also very cunning. He knew, with land perhaps a month away, open confrontation with the captain now could do nothing but harm his interests.

"Billy boy, make good, eh?" said Herb to his son, pushing him forward. Surprised, the pasty boy grudgingly held his hand out to Nathan Robbin, who shook it, realizing the hollowness of the gesture.

The captain addressed the boys. "The three of you will spend your afternoon cleaning this mess. If any of you feel hard done, by me or each other, speak up. I'll make doubly sure this business gets settled."

Pausing to wait for a response, the captain scanned across the room, "No takers, eh?"

Tanner ascended the ladder to the deck, it and his joints creaking at each step. His conversation with Reverend Williams earlier had somehow hardened the man. He strode across the empty deck, looked up to Sagar at the wheel, throwing the boy a nod, willingly returned, and entered his cabin to find it empty. Williams had left and the captain stood alone.

CHAPTER 10 - March 1, 1603

Below deck, word had spread about the boys fighting and Reverend Williams' pending address to the congregation at dinner; naturally, many thought the events were related. Being Sunday, with only a sparse crew on deck, the gun deck buzzed with chatter. Some relished the idle speculation, while others sought a refuge from the noise. Abigail had spent the morning lost in her own thoughts, oblivious to the gossiping, trying to understand the import of her memories and the twins' actions the day before. Overwhelmed and uncertain, she wished she could confide in someone, the way her mother had once confided in her when she was a young girl.

Next to George and Abigail Fielding, the Robbin family made their temporary home. Separated by only a stack of boxes, Abby had come to know Susan through their proximity and collective work in the galley. At first Abby had been wary of the energetic, educated young lady and the way in which she attacked her duties. Unlike most of the women aboard, who had spent their lives serving others, Susan took orders from Mrs. Bray and Mary with grace. Abby's natural caution soon melted away as she realized that Susan's motives were genuine; she just wanted to do her part.

Since the beginning of the voyage, Abby had overheard Susan and Tom chattering about the school he planned to establish in the new lands: what he would teach, the breadth of the knowledge available to the children of the congregation, and the library of books he had insisted on bringing with them. Tom's voice would rise as he described his chance to create a new way of learning, a universal system of education. To Abby, this seemed curious at the least, but she wondered how the fields would be harvested, the cows milked and the firewood chopped and stacked if their children were in school all day. She smiled at Tom's enthusiasm, nevertheless.

That afternoon, while everyone around her bleated about her son, Susan sat alone, trying to keep busy in her six-by-eight-foot home. Abby loitered outside the Robbin enclosure for about a minute until Susan finally caught sight of her. Abby threw her a wide and welcoming smile.

"May I come in, ma'am?" said Abby, mocking the crudeness of their shared surroundings.

"Why of course, please do, and won't you join me in the sitting room here," Susan replied.

Abby sat on the crate next to Susan, and while she desperately wanted to open her heart to this woman, she dared not say more than was necessary. "Susan, all this nonsense about boys fighting shouldn't worry you. Boys fight. If it weren't this, we'd all be talking about something else. People love to hear their own voices."

"Thank you for that, Abby. How fare you and the girls?" said Susan, eager to change the topic of conversation, being that they sat in such a public place. Abby could tell that Susan had deeper thoughts to share, but not here, not now.

"Yes, the girls, well, you've seen their hammock handiwork; they take their responsibilities so seriously, there's an intensity about them which isn't apparent on the surface. They are a constant help with the other girls and in the galley," Abby began, and like Susan, she only revealed what was harmless in the company of others. "I hear it has warmed slightly and I wonder if you would like to take a turn about the deck?"

Susan scanned the adjacent area. In turn, she responded, "Why, yes, some fresh air might do me some good. How about we meet on the stern in 5 minutes or so?" Susan's suggestion allowed the women to depart the gun deck separately, under less suspicion. Abby got up and fetched her warmest shawl, her mind turning over the words she wished to say to Susan. Somehow, she knew she could trust this daughter of wealth, the schoolteacher's wife.

On deck, the women stood against the stern railing, a good 15 feet behind Sagar, the diminutive stoic still steering the ship, making no notice of the two. Susan glanced back to Sagar, frowning, but Abby nodded, implying either she felt the boy could not hear them, or that she trusted him to hear what she wished to say.

"Susan, I must admit that I have heard you and Tom talking about the school he plans to establish, and the library of books he has brought with you. I wonder, are you familiar with these books?" Abby began.

Whatever Susan expected to talk about on deck, it had not been books. After a moment, she said, "Why, yes, many of the books in Tom's collection originally belonged to my grandfather." Susan remembered how her aging maternal grandfather looked kindly upon her and Tom at a time when their parents did not; when he passed on, he left them the entire lot. "I know many of the titles myself, but what is this about books?" she continued, still recalling where many of them had sat upon the shelves in his study.

"Have you ever looked closely at the hammocks Faria and Shikha have woven? The other night I was lying awake, staring up at the pattern of the knots for hours." Abby lowered her voice and moved closer to her friend. "Susan, I think, well, it may be a script, a written language. I dare not mention it to George or anyone else, for fear they either think I am just a foolish farm girl or worse. George can be, well, very narrow-minded. At times, it is convenient." Abby hesitated, fearing she may have gone too far already, but eventually continued. "Even hearing my thoughts spoken out loud makes me feel silly, but I was hoping that you might be able to help me understand what it means." Abby took the chance to be as honest as she could be and hoped that Susan would understand her predicament.

"You are not a foolish farm girl, Abby. I feel there is something at play aboard this ship. Tom says it's like a pressure building. My son Nathan was ambushed by those cretins because he defended Sagar's actions in the storm. Whosoever is angry at the bravery of others will burn their own souls, needing no devil to aid them. The more we learn about your twins, and the boy, the safer I believe we will be. Look around at this congregation, who among us really seeks religious freedom? A few, perhaps, but the rest seek something else. I can't see the entire tapestry, but I do see many threads. And as for your script, we are in luck, as my grandfather was a linguist, and Tom stowed away several volumes on the subject of primitive languages in the hopes they would assist us in communicating with native populations we encounter."

Abby was both comforted and frightened of Susan's words. She had only been thinking of herself, her experiences and the script, unaware of really anything else aboard the Spring Tide. "Can we access these books?" Abby said.

"We can try. Follow me, Abby," replied Susan, smiling.

"Wait a spell if you would. There's something else." With the greatest of care, Abby said "did you, well, see anything in the water when Sagar and Jorge struggled in the sea?"

Susan thought, replying, "No, dear, just the waves, why?"

"Oh, it's nothing really." Abby dropped the topic. Susan didn't press her, but casually started toward the stairs down to the main deck, first finishing a laconic round along the outer railing. Abby followed her down the stairs and into the hold.

Abby and Susan reentered the warmth of the ship by way of the stairway adjacent to the galley. They snuck behind a group of women, whose backs faced them, backsides to the fire. Just aft of the large hearth lay a narrow stairwell, more like an angled ladder, really, which descended into the lower levels of the ship. The level directly below the gun deck contained an array of items, for literal or figurative consumption during the voyage: food, kitchen necessities and general stores such as spun wool, light ropes, and firewood were organized for easy access, but not easy passage across the length of the ship.

The creaking flooring just inches above their heads was a constant reminder of the tightness with which they all were packed into the ship. More than once, the two of them jumped at a dropped box above them, or the noise of a child bounding off a chair or table, landing hard on the floor. Normally, these everyday sounds were a comfort while alone in the hold but today each noise accosted their senses, as they were both attuned to any movement or noises not of their own making.

While the women knew their way through the dense maze of boxes, they needed a lantern or candle if they were to descend farther. Susan dug up a few tallow candles from an open box, and pulling a flint from her apron, soon had the ladder to the deepest levels of the ship bathed in a soft light. Neither had descended this deep since Amsterdam, when they double-checked that their families' belongings, had been safely stowed for the duration of the voyage. The din of the ship's inhabitants died away as they took cautious steps down the ladder, while the rush of the frigid ocean against the hull rhythmically washed out any other sounds.

"This way, Abby, I just hope the trunk is on the top, and not underneath some immovable load," Susan whispered. "Tom surely wouldn't mind us digging about in his books." Susan smiled faintly. "He'd be rather amused, but if Reverend Williams or Smith knew what we pursued down here, well, I must tell you, I have little experience lying."

Abby's life had been one of deceit and concealment. Susan, a young woman of privilege, was of a protected class; she probably could have become quite adept at lying, but she had no need. Whatever trouble she found herself in, or however annoyed she had made her father, a broad net of aunts, uncles and grandparents invisibly followed her all her days. Abby had survived on a diet of fabrications, some her own, some thrust upon her, and she hated herself for it.

"Oh, there it is, over behind that row of casks. We're in luck, it's on top!" Susan spryly slid across the top of a large water cask to address the four-foot-wide chest. It was not locked, and the bronze clasp moved freely. Susan opened the lid, revealing a trove of hardbound books.

Abby hesitated to climb over the tun. "Susan, I am sorry, you don't have to help me. Perhaps we should just go back up to the galley before anyone notices our absence. Please, don't put yourself at risk for my sake."

Susan looked up from the chest of books, frowning. "Abby, dear, we've both been at risk since we stepped on board this ship, nay, even before that. We are just now discovering the full extent of our peril. If we go back up to the gun deck now, that won't change, we will simply know less. Ignorance is never a solution, so come over to this side and help me look through this chest. Books are wondrous things, and we are . . ." Susan stopped as she heard movement on the level immediately above them.

Abby crouched as low as she could, hopefully hidden enough by the double-stacked crates in front of her. Susan peered over the top of the water tun, candle now extinguished. She saw a light swaying with the movement of the ship, a lantern. It stopped at the ladder, and was slowly lowered. A wide and familiar face appeared in the glow of the lantern light as Mrs. Bray squinted into the darkness. After pausing a few more seconds, she stood up and walked out of sight. Both women surmised that she had been on the level above gathering foodstuffs and had heard talking, or at least a sound. They waited a few minutes, listening to the ship. Satisfied that Mrs. Bray had returned to the galley, Abby jumped across the large water cask and Susan relit their candles.

"Okay, we are looking for a few red-bound books with gold lettering. Abby, um, can you read?" Said Susan.

"Yes, my mother started me and I picked up bits and pieces in the manor kitchens I worked in. I don't know about these kinds of books though. I will try," replied Abby. She looked about the lowest level of the ship, squinting, distracted not by a sound or movement, but by the feeling of another presence, as if the noise of rushing water unnaturally reverberated against an unseen entity.

Abby watched Susan to see if the schoolteacher's wife discerned it too, but Susan was busy sorting through the books. Perhaps it was nothing, perhaps the events of Jorge's rescue still reverberated in her mind. Abby desperately wanted to confide fully in Susan but let it pass and returned her attention to the chest. Her intuition was not misplaced, however. Just a few feet away, on the other side of the ship's planks swam that same slippery black Makara, the serpent now defeated was drawn to her, as it was to its masters.

They continued pulling books out, stacking them on top

of smaller barrels close by. Abby pulled out three thick books fitting Susan's description. Realizing they hadn't thought what they would do once they found them, Susan suggested they light two more candles, under cover of the largest water casks, and begin to look through the volumes.

"These are the collected works of a good friend of my grandfather. They contain many wood blocks, both primitive and modern alphabets. I remember when I was a girl, sitting in his study, trying to make up my own language, but mostly I just copied the interesting characters," Susan said, recalling her younger years.

They started flipping through the tomes in no particular order, first trying to find engravings and illuminated pages. Susan would point images out to Abby, always with the same negative result. A half-hour passed before Susan came upon an engraving that seemed to be a reproduction of a long, narrow stone with markings carved into it lengthwise. The following page was a categorization of sorts for each of the glyphs found on the stone.

"This is curious, isn't it, Abby? Says this stone was found on the Isle of Man," Susan murmured.

Abby glanced over as she had already perhaps a dozen times, and was transfixed. She ripped the book from Susan's hands and turned it sideways, upside down, and sideways again, inspecting the two pages, flipping them back and forth and back again. "My god, that is the crones' script," she whispered, so quietly under her breath that Susan failed to discern her words.

The subsequent pages supposed the symbols were associated with trees: yew, rowan, oak, birch, but also listed were posited English letters. Many of these had question marks next to them, as the author was uncertain of their true nature. "Susan, what does this mean? Can you please read this section?" said Abby.

Susan began, squinting at the text in the relative darkness: "The language of the ancients, so named Ogham in honor of their pagan god, who helped deliver the islands to the earliest human inhabitants. While the origins of the symbology are indeed uncertain, having been discovered at dozens of sites from Wales to the Hebrides, it bears a keen resemblance to Norse runes and to a lesser extent, the cuneiform of the Sumerians. As with many primitive scripts, it no doubt was used for liturgical purposes, each symbol being imbued with the pagans' worship of their natural surroundings." Susan paused for a moment. "Abby, we can't allow Reverend Smith or Williams to see this. If the twins are knowingly reproducing this language, it's blasphemy. The text indicates further that there is no clear or even suggested translation." Paging back and forth through the relevant sections, Susan closed the book. "I suspect we can learn little more from this volume. Let's pack up the collection, this one at the bottom of the chest, and return to the gun deck. We can continue our research another day. Ogma, Ogmios …" Susan trailed off, brow furrowed.

Abby nodded her head in agreement, putting the books back in haste while trying to place these new pieces of information in order. She felt numb and exhausted, while Susan was just the opposite, giddy with excitement. They put out all but one candle, left the stubs at the base of the chest and ascended the ladder. As Abby took her last step, she turned her body and peered into the darkness of the deep hold, again searching for something unseen. Only blackness gazed back. Prior to returning to the galley, the women thought to fill their arms with firewood, as if to imply that their absence had been due to their diligence in maintaining the hearth fire.

CHAPTER 11 - March 1603

Susan remained in the galley, striking up a casual conversation with Mary, who was just now considering how to feed the entire congregation, in one sitting, in one spot. Abby walked back to her family's berth, to find George and the twins awaiting her. "No longer misplaced, the wife returns," said George as Abby neared. "We were about to count you lost, and ask Sagar to jump in after you too." George would on rare occasions make statements approaching the humorous, but they never achieved the desired effect.

"I was in the galley, George, helping with supper," replied Abby who couldn't stop herself from glancing at the twins when she spoke.

"That so? I sent Shikha after you, and she came back empty handed," George murmured. He paused, considering how hard to press his advantage, and thought better of it.

"What did you need, dear?" Abby sat down on the box across from George. The twins were leaning against the hull of the ship, where they had piled several woolen blankets into a nest.

"I hear they'll be some sort of announcement from the captain at supper. Most are saying it has to do with that little fight in the forecastle, but I'll wager we're nearing land. Does Mary say the same? I don't mind the quarters, or the food, but I'm all thumbs on deck, except when things need mending," said George. Abby knew shipboard life was eating away at his confidence. Since a young age, he had been learning his trade, slow to understand a task, but once mastered, he filed it away, each lesson, each experience, into his own mental toolbox. George could tell if the angle of a chisel would cause it to bind or cut crisply in walnut, oak or maple. He could see where wood would give, and where it would fight him; he saw the patterns of its natural strength, and how to apply that strength with the least material.

George learned through repetition, slow, steady trial and error, not through the dynamism of interpreting an ever-changing environment, like life on deck where each situation was different than the last. He had never been good with words and on deck, it was as if he didn't speak the same language as the rest of the crew. Most had started out confused at the barrage of commands, stations, sails, masts and lines, but George had never caught on. He was as green as the day they left Amsterdam.

"I'm sorry George, but I feel I know less than you do. Mary hasn't said a word, but I do recall before we left that Captain Tanner said it could take us more than 2 months to reach the new lands," Abby whispered, bending forward and placing her hand on top of his. While George hadn't come out and said it, he wanted off this ship.

"Ahh, well," said George. He gave her hand a slight tap. After they sat in silence for a minute, the lean man stood and bumped his head on the floor timbers to which the deck was fastened. That one bruised spot had become swollen from the daily pounding. He walked away, ascending the companionway leading to the main deck. Abby was needed in the galley, but she delayed, realizing the twins had been listening to her brief exchange with George.

"Miss Abby, Sagar has searched for a quiet moment to convey his gratitude for what you did during the storm," Faria said.

"I, I did nothing. I fainted, that is all. I did less than nothing," Abby replied, herself unsure of the truth.

"But you did. Without you, Sagar might have saved himself, but never Jorge. What troubles you? Sagar reckons we have less than a month until we find our new home and that it may only be a few weeks before we sight land," said Faria, encouraging her adoptive mother. The twins had come to call her Miss Abby, adopting the form of address from Mrs. Bray, who still referred to the now-married woman in this manner. It made Abby smile every time she heard it, which is probably why they continued.

"Girls," began Abby, sliding off the box where she sat, inserting herself snugly between them. "I hope, over the short time we have been together, you have come to realize that I care deeply for the both of you. And for Sagar. You have trusted in me, and for my part, I am proud to call you family. However, there are those aboard this vessel who are not as welcoming and who look to differences as a weakness rather than a strength. You see, the more I can know of you, and the more I can confide in you, the better I can watch out for all our safety." Abby stopped to gauge their response.

Nestled betwixt them in the mess of blankets, she had to look at each girl individually. Faria sat cross-legged, back erect, attentive. Usually the first to speak, she betrayed no emotions. Shikha was wedged between one of the large boxes separating their area from the Robbins' and the inner planks of the hull. The lanterns, hung at intervals along the center of the gun deck, failed to cast their light into her corner, only managing to throw deep shadows across her face. She did not lean forward into the light, but spoke from the darkness. "You are afraid, Miss Abby, and we share your fear. But we are not on this voyage for our own benefit, we are here to help protect you. Sagar told us what you can see, and you now know we all share this vision. Further, we can glimpse backwards, revealing hazy images and deep-set emotions from your past. Just as in your history, there is nothing that we do not accept, there is nothing in ours that should cause you concern."

Shikha leaned into the lantern light, exposing her round face, and as she did, Faria continued, "Please understand: while, in time, Sagar may stray from his adoptive family, we will never stray from you."

Abby sat motionless, allowing the comfort and sagacity of the young girl's words to filter through her mind and into her heart. She wished to speak more, to learn more, but her words failed. With her eyes tearing up, she reached her arms around both girls and hugged them. As they returned the gesture, a wave of familiarity washed over her body. In their thin arms, Abby felt the embrace of someone else, her mother perhaps. Slowly releasing them, Abby stood and smiled. "Girls, we mustn't shirk our duties. It's time we help prepare supper. Mary will be needing us, and only a few hours remain until the entire famished congregation descends upon us."

The three of them marched off to the galley, where Mary and Mrs. Bray were debating what of the fresh foodstuffs they should serve and what should be saved. "Really, we can scrape the dark rind off the cheese wheel, and cook it up with some beef fat. Onions and turnips will give the stew some body," Mrs. Bray argued. The round kitchen sergeant fought daily battles with Mary over what meals to serve. It was mostly a good-natured compromise, which saw the congregation eating progressively less fresh food as the voyage wore on.

"Your frugality serves us well, but today, I feel we must celebrate. If we make haste, roast goose and duck can be had," Mary replied. As she spoke the words roast goose, Mary's voice intentionally rose, garnering glances and grins from those closest to the galley. Birds sacrificed their lives for the good of the congregants, precious spices were retrieved from the lower deck, and within an hour, two geese turned on the galley spit, while the largest black cauldron bubbled with a thick and savory duck stew. The tightness of the gun deck intensified the warm, smoky aromas emanating from the galley.

At dusk, the congregants assembled on the gun deck. The sky had cleared and with a mild breeze blowing from the direction of the setting sun, the ship was just able to make northwesterly progress. Only three men remained on deck. But taken aside, they had been promised grog by the captain and the first serving of goose by Mary, so neither minded missing the affair. While a wide table was set up adjacent to the galley, most prepared to eat in their families' makeshift enclosures. The table had been set for the captain, Jorge, the reverends and Mrs. Bray, who along with several other women, busied herself transferring the duck stew into smaller pots to be carried around the deck.

Few knew that the gun deck could be accessed through a small stairwell in the captain's quarters that led to a storage area aft of the galley, but Reverend Williams made use of it that evening, so as not to draw attention to his arrival. A few congregants were surprised therefore, when anxiously circling the galley, they spied the bowed, bald head of their spiritual leader. Williams moved somewhat awkwardly, and from afar, appeared stoic. To those closest to the aged man, a faint smile was barely visible. The corners of his mouth turned upward, in contention with his drawn and heavy eyes, which sagged at the edges. He wore two deep emotions on his face; at least for now they were in perfect balance.

The younger girls completed dishing out generous helpings of stew and bread, and a bit of goose for each plate. As they traversed the deck with the deep pots of stew, their narrow frames ebbed and flowed with the regular rhythms of the Spring Tide as she cut through the evening swells. In their own right, they had become little seafaring sprites, adapting to the weeks at sea in a way their parents never could. Dismissed by Mrs. Bray and returning to their families they settled in with the rest of the denizens of the gun deck. All eyes were now on Reverend Williams.

Removing his tall black hat, their spiritual leader rose to his feet, bones creaking like the wood floors of an old house; careful of the low beams, he stepped forward to avoid hitting his head on the heavy oak timbers. In the swaying lantern light, Reverend Williams' skin bore a faint yellow hue, and as he stood, at first he had trouble keeping his balance, but steadied himself by leaning back upon the edge of the table. "I am sorry that you have seen too little of me of late, but more than sixty years on land has not prepared me for these six weeks at sea. I have kept to my cabin, but my thoughts have always been with you," Williams began.

"The captain and I met this morning, and he informs me that our progress has been providential. God willing, we may sight land within weeks. Our first mate Jorge, lost overboard but saved by His hand, will help us navigate these unknown waters. We must give thanks for his rescue, and to his rescuer." This statement drew murmurs from the congregants. "By the accounts of the few others who have trod this same path, we should find more fertile ground and temperate climates by keeping a southerly course for some time, as much as a month. We may make temporary camps on land to refresh provisions, but mustn't be hasty in selecting our future home." Williams paused for a few seconds, holding back a smoldering fit of coughing that just now had chosen to erupt deep in his chest. He brought his handkerchief to his mouth and appeased the fit with a single heavy and hoarse cough, swallowed and continued.

"While in this life, godly persons make take pleasant comfort in our election in Christ, we have little respite from the wear of the physical world. I am thankful for the years the Lord has provided me on this earth, but selfishly, I fear my time with all of you draws near. God calls the elect to Him in accordance with His divine plan. We have no choice but to humbly submit."

"Be not sad at my words. When I look about you," began Williams again, glancing back to the captain and Reverend Smith, "I see the collective strength and experience to guide the congregation forward, physically and spiritually. After I pass on, Captain Tanner will lead our colony, deferring to our beloved Reverend Smith in matters of faith. As I believe our Lord has, I put my full faith in these two men. Please, pray with me now, before we partake in this celebratory feast."

"All glory be to thee, O Lord, our God, for that thou didst create heaven and earth, and dist make us in thine own image; and, of thy tender mercy, didst give thine own Son Jesus Christ to take our nature upon him, and to suffer death upon the cross for our redemption. Lord God, whose Son our Savior Jesus Christ triumphed over the powers of death and prepared for us our place in new Jerusalem: Grant that we, who have this day given thanks for his resurrection, may praise thee in that City of which he is the light; and where he liveth and reigneth for ever and ever. Amen," concluded Reverend Williams. Rather than sitting down, he began to make his way among his flock. At his first uncertain step, Nathan Robbin, whose family sat beside the galley, sprang to his feet and leapt two boxes to assist the aged reverend in his rounds.

For now, those threatened by Tanner's growing influence kept mum. He was hired to pilot the ship, they thought. Steely glances between colluding families said enough. Besides, questioning their founder's decision now would irreparably ostracize them from the people they would soon need. When Williams and Nathan Robbin reached the Gaithers, a respectful exchange ensued, with no mention of the boys' fight, or of the earlier encounter in the forecastle between Herb and Tanner. But just as Williams was moving on to the next family, Harold, the less subtle of the two patriarchal brothers, asked, "So, how long do you think you can hang on?" not with sympathy, but seemingly as a challenge.

Williams turned, acknowledging the question, and said, "Only the Lord knows, my son, as the Lord knows and sees all." Whether he realized its true intent, he didn't let on, but Nathan saw the obvious motivations, and glared at Harold Gaither, stunned by his impudence. The pasty man grinned back at the boy, proud of himself and apparently proud to display his deeply yellowed teeth. When returning to his family, Nathan whispered the details of the exchange to his father, who nodded and told the boy to eat his supper for strength, which, he thought to himself, they would all need.

***

The next morning dawned crisp and blustery, but cloudless. The Spring Tide forged through the waves with determined purpose, seemingly running from the rising sun. The first full watch fell to Captain Tanner, during which he called for a gam with Jorge, Sagar, and a few of the other men. Jorge's condition had stabilized somewhat, but he was in no shape to spend any time outside, much less hours on deck or in the rigging. Mary's husband James had stepped in to lead Jorge's watch. At the Captain's behest, James and Tom Robbin now joined the strange officers' meeting in Tanner's quarters, where Jorge and Sagar were already chatting.

"No, no, es analogo, eh, the coast off Sao Jorge de Mina Castile, you know it? Or, el banco de Galicia. Sim, yes, yes," said Jorge, keeping his words between himself and Sagar, but gesturing as best he could with one arm. "Muito maior, though, much bigger." Sagar nodded as the injured Portuguese spoke. The captain entered briskly from the deck and took his place at the table, leaving little time for the others to continue wondering what the mates had been agreeing on.

"Feels different out there, doesn't it, lads? More like a cold spring day, than a warm winter one. We're positively on a downhill run through those swells," bellowed Tanner. A pewter pitcher sat in the center of the table, joined by several cups, which had gone untouched until the captain started pouring drinks for everyone. A hot, light brown liquid steamed out into the cups. "So, Jorge, you're ready? Won't be too much for you?"

"No, Capitan, we talk now. It is good now, and the more the better," replied Jorge, glancing and smiling at the addition of Tom and James. Holding his cup high, he gave a salute to everyone. "Saude!"

"Cheers," replied the captain. "So, let me help you two along. Since leaving Amsterdam, we've been putting as much distance between us and our old home as possible, with less regard for precise course, and more interest in letting the winds and currents take us where they may. This has likely put us much farther north than our destination may be, but as Jorge explains it, this is the only way to make headway unless we wanted to contend with the damned Spanish, by having gone south by southwest."

"The western ocean swirls like a clock, we sit at seven bells, trying to skirt the hour hand as it sweeps across the evening," said Sagar, to Jorge's surprise.

"Yes, it is so. The Spanish, they take the three to eight in the evening way. It is easy for them. We, though, we go against the time, from two to one, to twelve, and so on, to about nine. How is this?" Jorge said, smiling a bit. "Ah, this is my father's way, and it is not as easy, even as Capitan says it is. After passing the bank, as I said to you, boy, like Galicia Bank but much, much bigger and only 20 fathoms to the sea floor, we go west at all costs for three days perhaps, until the colder waters turn us southwest. South too soon, and we get pushed back into the hour hand, swept back to England!" Jorge accentuated his last statement by swinging his bandaged arm in a rough circle, wincing with pain, but smiling all the same.

Sitting back down, the first mate took a deep swig of his warming drink, and began again. "So, if tomorrow is like today, and so on with the wind, this week … this week the waves will change. Shorten from long swords into short daggers. Fish will nearly jump into the ship.

Three days further to the colder waters, where we turn southwest until, hmm. Quem Sabe, Capitan?"

Before Tanner could reply, Tom interjected "So, you're saying we are perhaps only a week from land? Is this possible?"

Jorge weighed the schoolteacher's words carefully, and responded in turn, "Land, maybe, maybe no. But it is no good. Rocky, cold, cold winters, the sea freezes. Too, eh, perigoso, dificil now. And in the summer, it is full of my people, fishing, drying fish. So, we go southwest with the current. How far, that is not for me." While Jorge had been eager to explain their route, even this modest exertion tired him. He now leaned back, sliding low on the bench, and in the shadows, his once dark olive skin looked terribly pale.

The others followed suit, relaxing into the benches, and Tanner addressed them all again. "Within ten days, we'll need to start making our way southwest with a purpose, beating against the winds if necessary. At the first sight of the coast, you can bet we'll have a ship full of lubbers saying they've seen paradise. So orders are, keep a weather eye out for signs of land, and stay any feelings you might have for a closer glimpse. We need a home that'll sustain us year-round and as far north as we are, as Jorge said, we've got no chance unless we head hundreds of miles farther south. Only then can we start searching for a home. Sagar, mind that you spend more hours in the rigging or even up in the crow's nest, so that this group and this group alone knows when we might be nearing the coastline." Getting nods from those gathered, Tanner added, "I'm trusting in each of you to help me keep this ship and its inhabitants safe. Out in the middle of the ocean, there's nothing to decide, so nothing to question. From here on in, every day we'll struggle to keep them focused on the greater goal of finding a permanent home and believing in the decisions we make." Waiting for his message to sink in, the Captain raised his cup, and toasted, "To The New World," which the men heartily echoed.

Dismissing the men, Tanner retired to his personal quarters. With the help of Sagar, Jorge made his way back to his own bed, where once entombed in the heavy woolen blankets, he immediately fell into a deep sleep. Dreaming of long voyages past, fishing with his uncle and father and filleting fish on the windy shores of the new lands. His broken and swollen arm throbbed with a deep pulsing pain that, in his dreams, was brought on by the grueling hours of cutting the heavy white bacalhau fresco, the codfish.

Elsewhere, the congregants warmed themselves on deck during the spell of mild weather. Men and women stood at the aft railing, watching the frothy eddies spun by the advancing ship's progress. Children ran from port to starboard and back again, in an endless race, chasing one another. There was one unobserved exception. It would be days until the action became necessary, but strictly following the captain's orders, Sagar had climbed the rigging to the top of the mainmast, where he sat bundled in silence, glad his coat was dark gray, all the better for absorbing the late winter sun.

Since that rainy January night in Rotterdam when he first met Mary and James, Sagar had tried to balance his longing for a permanent family, the first in his life, with his knowledge that it would not be long before he must leave them. He couldn't fully see the path, but the threads coalesced into inevitable fate. As he gathered these delicate strings, he knew that Faria and Shikha would remain with the congregants for a longer spell, and longer still with Abigail, perhaps till the end. Each time Mary encouraged or smiled at Sagar, he wanted to embrace and be embraced by his foster mother, like any child would. Yet he resisted, knowing that giving in would make his departure harder for him and harder for her. So, he would smile back. He sometimes overheard her talking to others about how highly her father thought of her boy Sagar, of how he was a true son, fit for their family. If he could indeed love, he knew that his feelings for Captain Tanner and Mary were as close as he had ever been.

Still, he wished the captain hadn't appointed him second mate; it made it impossible to go unnoticed. It was only a matter of time until the questions a few people now muttered in muted voices about him and the twins became accusations. Wherever he went people whispered, they gawked. He had to give orders to men who outright hated him. He felt it in their stares and it took all his energy to will them to follow orders so he could keep the ship sailing steady. After each watch he would collapse, exhausted from the effort.

The twins, for their part, had done a better job assimilating into the congregation. Working in the galley, they had earned the respect of many of the women and had made friends among the girls. Just now, as Sagar peered down on the deck, he glimpsed them playing alongside the other kids, giggling away. Their happiness elicited an unseen smile, yet overwhelming isolation filled his small body. During the voyage, Sagar had intentionally distanced himself from his kin, for all their sakes.

He was a boy, he glanced at his hands, his arms; he knew if he fell from the mast, he would die upon the deck. Yet from this height he almost felt that he could see the next few years unfolding before him, and decades of tumultuous memories trailing in the frothy wake of the ship. In both directions, however, he was alone.

CHAPTER 12 - March 30, 2013

Sagar, Shikha and Hehu slept on the plane, waking on the final Sunday in March to brilliant sunshine and a slushy mess. The snow had subsided just before dawn. The last of winter's might hurled upon the land, the storm slipped offshore in the dying night, consumed in the warmth of the gulf stream. Hehu and the pilot still lay sleeping when Sagar and Shikha departed the jet. A car and driver Sagar had called sat waiting for them. They wound through the neighborhood of modestly painted split-level houses, around the oil tanks lining the harbor, and across the Quinnipiac River into the city. "165 Prospect," Shikha intoned to the driver. He nodded and plotted his course north. Doors locked, the black Lincoln Town Car cruised past pedestrians on the streets of one of America's most dangerous cities as if they stood frozen in time. In the plush pleather backseat, Shikha could hardly discern their lowered faces at such speed, but as they cruised by New Haven's graveyards, she recalled with bitterness each friend and lover buried in the rocky soil. Like the pedestrians on Easter Sunday, she had sped by their lives and soon enough, they were gone.

"Bulldog-O is on the West campus," Shikha mentioned, referring to Yale's newest supercomputer, "but we need not drive that far. We'll head to an office I still keep in the Osborn Memorial labs complex. It's in the basement, but there's a terminal where I can recompile my pattern recognition algorithms and download the binary files for processing."

The town car stopped in front of the Osborn building on Prospect Street, where Shikha led Sagar through the front entrance and down a ramp to the elevator. She pulled a massive ring of keys from her bag and tried two before finding the firefighters' key that opened the elevator and gave them access to all floors. Once in the basement, they traversed a musty corridor to a hundred-year-old oak door, which required an electronic key-card for entry.

"I've had this space since 1913 when the building opened. You can't imagine the fight I gave them to keep it unchanged the first time the building was remodeled," Shikha said, chuckling. "During the second remodel, when most of the basement was gutted, they didn't even bother to contact me. They just avoided this side of the building completely, excepting one thing: modern security. I received this pass in the mail," she continued, revealing an electronic key card.

Shikha pressed the pass to the reader, which responded with a soft beep, and unlocked the door with a heavy bronze key, pushing it open with both hands. As it creaked open, the yellow glare from the fluorescent hall lights sliced through the expansive room's darkness. Near the door, Sagar could make out a sturdy wooden desk, upon which sat three new black flat-screen monitors. A derelict fume hood stood vigil over abandoned chemistry experiments, while against the far wall Sagar discerned a series of bookshelves which extended to the ceiling, accessed by a sliding ladder.

Shikha was already in her lab and peered back at him as if to say, "Well, are you coming in?" He padded into the space, feeling a soft layer of dust cushion his step. Shikha pulled the chain on a lamp sitting next to the computer, filling the room with the warmth of two antique incandescent light bulbs shining through a green shade. "I'll need a few hours," Shikha said, settling in at the desk and pulling an encrypted ferroelectric drive of her own design from her pocket. Without looking up she added, "There's a couch in the corner." Sagar nodded, knowing Shikha was now lost in her work and wouldn't even notice if he began jumping on the couch like a monkey.

Sagar wandered the room like a museum visitor at a history of science exhibit, looking over the various beakers, bulky centrifuges and rubber tubing. The deeper he ventured into the room, the more disarrayed he found it and he suspected Shikha had pushed older work, papers and experiments into the background over the decades. A high, soapstone table stacked with papers blocked him from reaching the couch. As he passed it, the slightest touch sent a paper flying to the ground, which he instinctively picked up and gingerly returned to its proper pile. Embossed with a shield, underneath which read Sancte et Sapienter, the paper was a handwritten note from one Rosalind Franklin. With Holiness and Wisdom indeed, thought Sagar.

He dusted off the leather couch by sweeping it clean with a curiously smelling Turkish pillow. Sagar reclined, finding the couch quite comfortable. He wondered how many years it had been since anyone had sat on it, if Faria had sat on it. Sagar blinked slower and heavier until his eyes remained closed. Fall of 1823, he had just returned from a whaling voyage in the Pacific, his last before buying his first ship. He wandered down from New Bedford, past where the colony had been, past where his native friends had lived, and met the twins just three blocks from where he sat now. Six years and three voyages had separated him from his kin. He longed to see them, to see her. In their collective embrace, he pecked Shikha on the cheek, but as he turned to Faria, their eyes locked. Their heads tilted, lips delicately approached, quivering for the kiss they had waited decades to experience when a magnetic repulsion threw Faria backwards onto the wet street, littered with the decaying leaves of autumn. Sagar's anger spiked and bottomed just as quickly when he realized it was not Shikha who had separated them but their kiss itself. The force they commanded to repel Asuras and others in the spirit world had deprived them of that first touch.

Sagar opened his eyes again and glanced about the dim room. Shikha's desk lamp threw just enough light to the far side for him to make out most of the titles on the high bookshelves. Sagar, however, found no interest in biochemistry journals, heavy bound treatises and research notes. One hundred years of scientific progress lay before him on those shelves, the history of the greatest puzzle ever solved by humankind: life's genetic code. Yet he sat motionless, eyes tracing the intricately carved detail of the bookcase's three sections. Separated by two thick, black walnut tree trunks carved in relief, the shelves from left to right became more disarrayed, with the lower sections on the far right no more organized than the papers on the adjacent stone table. The walnut trunks seemed to grow directly out of the floor, anchoring each twelve-foot section of the case. Branches departed the trunks and intermingled under each shelf, with their delicate leaflets extending into the two-foot entablature above.

More than an hour had passed since they entered Shikha's lab and Sagar could almost hear the dust resettling. Just the occasional quiet clicking of a keyboard broke the silence. Something continued to pull his gaze back to the walnut tree limbs inscribed into the bookcase; even in the darkness he perceived a slight asymmetry between one tree trunk and the other. He stood and edged nearer to the shelves, trying to clear his mind so that Shikha wouldn't discern his thoughts. His fingers ran along a high shelf on the left-hand side, where they found their mark. He smiled, and instantly knew his thoughts had betrayed him.

Across the room, Shikha shouted, "It took you an hour and a half? You're aging." Resigned to her abuse, he twisted the branch where his fingers rested. With the most muted click, the walnut tree trunk to his right swung open, revealing a narrow passage leading down a crude stone staircase. Sagar surmised that the building itself must have been built around the passageway. Thoughts from Shikha confirmed his suspicion as he reached into the darkness for an oil lamp he knew hung before him. He lit it with a modern butane torch from his pocket and its warm flickering glow illuminated roughly cut granite slabs.

Crouching, he entered the passage, left arm holding the lamp near the ceiling. Just like the floor, the walls and ceiling were also granite, likely from the quarry in Stony Creek, east of New Haven. During the gradual descent down the worn slabs, the walls widened until Sagar found himself in a circular dead-end enclosure. In the center of the room lay a raised slab, above it an iron hook where Sagar hung the lamp. He slowly turned full circle, digesting what surrounded him. A mural flowed across the walls, the colors shimmering in the lamplight like stained glass: forest greens, orange, silver and crimson. Sagar knelt next to the cold stone slab that served as Abigail's coffin and closed his eyes. He had relived the events portrayed in the mural so many times that the scene was just as etched in his mind as it was on the walls of the underground sanctuary. The lamp flickered, burned low and at length, the room fell dark, yet Sagar did not notice. His eyes remained closed, and his mind deep in the past.

The twins had memorialized the scene of Abigail's act of sacrifice on the walls of the granite catacomb in which Sagar now sat. His mind still anchored in the past, he did not notice Shikha's approach. She knelt next to him, her warmth stirring Sagar into the present. "It's time to go. If we linger, we may be pursued, as on Long Island," she whispered. They both rose and looking about the room for just a moment, Shikha smiled as one might when looking at faded photographs of someone who died all too early.

CHAPTER 13 - March 7, 1603

Jorge's condition worsened. Over the next week, he was seen on deck only a few minutes a day and when he did appear, he hid his arm from view underneath a heavy wool coat. The wrinkled Portuguese would emerge from his cabin late morning and glance up at Sagar, stationed at the top of the mainmast. They would exchange a nod, a frown, a wave of a hand, at which point the first mate would return to his quarters, head low.

On the seventh day after their meeting around the Captain's table, Jorge did not appear all morning. The ship's deck was littered with nearly the entire congregation. Winter had begun to lose its battle against longer days and warmer weather. Sagar thought to himself that Jorge might have just peered out onto the crowded deck and gone back to bed. The day waxed and waned while the ship pursued the orange horizon. Sagar gazed out across the sea, occasionally scanning the deck for movement as the ebbing sunset dispersed the crowd, which now sought supper below. Opaque waves mildly broke against the bow of the Spring Tide, greeting the aged wooden hull, just a few waves per minute.

In the distance, perhaps a half a mile off, the green-black ocean became milkier. At first, Sagar thought the light from the setting sun was just reflecting oddly through the cloud cover but as the ship pressed on, he discerned a long arc of lighter water stretching beyond his vision. The helmsman took little notice, but the waves no longer rhythmically peppered the ship transforming instead into a chaotic but light chop, as if two powerful currents had paused their relentless contention for dominance of this stretch of sea. Sagar knew that under less-perfect conditions, areas of the sea like this could be whipped into a frothy maelstrom, from which no ship could emerge. However on this day, the Spring Tide passed the threshold with no complaint. Daylight near gone, Sagar descended to the deck to check in on Jorge.

As he hit the deck, the door to the captain's quarter's swung open and Tanner himself strode out. Walking straight to the port railing, he peered over into the sea. Looking forward into the declining daylight, his eyes met Sagar's. He gave the boy a puzzled look and closed the distance between them.

"What do you make of it, boy? Seems harmless enough at the present, anyway. Let's see if we can take a sounding; fetch the lead and line, would you, Mr. Sagar?" Captain Tanner would refer to him as Mr. only when he was feeling particularly jovial or when he had been taking a nip of wine or brandy, which typically induced the former.

Sagar ran off to fetch the long thin line and the lead weights used to take depth measurements. He jumped down the ladder into the forecastle, ignoring the piercing looks of the boys lounging in their hammocks, rummaged through several chests, slung the heavy coil of 1/4" rope over his shoulder and heaved it up onto the deck. A few of the lads followed him up the ladder, curious as to what the quiet, dark mystery boy was up to.

He lugged the rope over to the captain, who motioned to the man at the helm to fall off the wind, slackening the ship's pace. The Spring Tide's momentum carried her forward for a spell, but soon she lay at rest. Tanner unwound the narrow rope and, ensuring the multiplicity of coils were clear of one another, he threw the lead weight attached to the end of the rope overboard. The line dove into the depths with purpose and both Tanner and Sagar counted out the fathom marks on the line as it disappeared. Tanner fed more rope over the port railing, twenty, thirty, fifty fathoms. Two thirds of the line had disappeared over the side when it finally went slack.

"Oh ho! Down at last, and with little to spare. Sagar, what was your count?"

"Less than eighty fathoms minus the height of the ship. I reckon seventy-five. Just about four-hundred feet, sir."

"Aye, I counted about the same." Glancing around at the audience of older boys, Tanner suddenly looked distracted. "You lads, haul the line back in, coil it up and stow it below. Sagar, you're with me," commanded the captain. As he walked back to his cabin, he motioned to the helmsman to return to his previous course.

Sagar followed him through the cabin door into Jorge's quarters. A single lamp illuminated the bare room, sitting next to the narrow bed where the first mate lay. They approached with care, not sure if the Portuguese was sleeping, but heard him call to them, which quickened their step. Jorge was sweating from under a mountain of blankets, but shivering all the same. "Seventy-five fathoms, Jorge, and by my reckoning at noon, we're close to Brest Latitude." Looking closer at the small man in bed, Tanner continued, "Have you been eating?"

Jorge's features brightened and a wide smile stretched the weathered skin of his face almost to the breaking point. He had been waiting days for this news, hoping to fulfill his promise to the captain and the congregants.

"We are here, Capitan. I am sure. Sagar, and the water?" rasped Jorge, sitting up in bed. As he did, the wool blankets fell away, revealing his bent and swollen arm. All the color had drained from his body except where it concentrated in his snapped forearm. Ignoring the injury, Sagar replied, "As you described, my friend. We have been favored this day, as the currents do not fight. A wide arc stretches north to south, but more powerfully south." Addressing both men, Sagar said, "what course now?"

Jorge thought for a moment and said, "Capitan, how good your reckoning?" Which Sagar understood to mean, how sure are you that you measured our latitude, as being similar to Brest, on the French coast, accurately?

They all knew Jorge needed two facts to identify their position: the change in currents and depth, cross-referenced against their latitude. On any given day, the sun at noon would always be the same height above the horizon for two points of the same latitude. No doubt Tanner had recorded measurements of the sun's angle above the horizon for various days on his trips along the English and French coasts, so with his eyes darting left and right as he did some recalculations, the captain nodded. "Yes, I could be off, but by no more than, say, twenty miles."

"Good, and good enough. We go west southwest until we catch the cold currents. Take your soundings, yes, and Sagar, boy, stay on her mast. Nearly there. Look west for land," said Jorge, and with his last sentence, he closed his eyes, but remained sitting up in bed, with the same smile on his face as when the captain and Sagar burst into his room.

Sagar put his hand on Jorge's burning forehead, knowing the first mate would die that night. Not because he was weak or could not fight the fever that raged in his veins, but because the Portuguese sailor, who had lived more of his life at sea than on land, had chosen the time and place of his passing. It was here and now, in the fishing grounds that had sustained his family for generations. He was home. In Sagar's mind, life was a mess of uncertainty and pain; no greater satisfaction could exist than being able to choose the means of one's own passing into the next life. Strangely, he envied Jorge.

Tanner gazed down at Jorge and comforted his bedridden mate. "You have delivered us, my friend. Sleep deeply with your mind at ease." Sagar squeezed Jorge's good hand and left him alone with his capitan, slipping from between them and down the back stairway into the galley.

Sagar was surprised to find himself accosted by questions from everyone he passed as soon as he emerged from the galley. The depth soundings were far from his mind, and he failed to realize the effect the common shipboard action would have on the congregants.

"Have you sighted land? Will we run aground overnight? Should we begin to pack up our belongings?" These were the questions he heard most clearly but there were others shouted as well. Sagar allowed the crowd to gather around him so he could address all at once. "While we stand here, Captain Tanner takes counsel from our first mate, as we have crossed into the fishing grounds known to him. The depth soundings and the captain's observations confirm our position. While I cannot say when we will approach land, we are on course and all should be comforted by our progress." When he stopped speaking, the crowd remained silent, waiting for more details, but none were forthcoming.

Finally a man in Sagar's watch called out from across the room "How deep is the water, hereabouts, Sagar?" Being addressed in front of so many of the congregants by a trusted watch mate filled the boy with confidence.

"About four hundred feet, Michael."

"Why do you sit at long length at the top of the mast?" asked another voice.

Sagar had not realized anyone noticed his recent daily ritual. "Upon Captain Tanner's orders, I have been watching for changes in the sea, which could help discern our location."

"Have you had any dinner, or anything at all to eat since early this morning?" asked a familiar voice. The question drew laughter from the arranged crowd, which now started to disperse.

Mary looked down proudly at her adopted son and motioned to the galley. "It's no wonder you never seem to grow, working on deck through the night, in the rigging during the day, and little food at all crossing your lips. You, boy, need fattening up!" Mary seated him at the table adjacent to the hearth. She ladled out a generous portion of dried beef now boiled into submission, churning the kettle for choice pieces of meat.

Settling in on both sides of him, Faria and Shikha appeared from nowhere. So careful to avoid him since their voyage began, Sagar understood why they had chosen this point to break their silence. Mary joined the three of them. Faria began, "How fares Jorge? We have seen little of him these past few days." Sagar hadn't realized how familiar Mary and the twins had become; his adoptive mother, nodding at the young girl's words, acted as if the question stemmed from all their minds simultaneously.

"We heard that after taking the depth soundings, you and father raced to inform Jorge of the news. He takes no food, and won't let even the twins visit him in spite of his need." Mary continued on behalf of all three of them. "Sagar, you must implore him to allow their visits." At this point she lowered her voice to a near-imperceptible whisper, "They saved him once and may yet do it again." Mary didn't realize how true her words were.

Sagar looked at each of them and said, "Jorge is at peace. His intent in joining our voyage was to return to this place of great importance to his people. He does not spurn your assistance from spite or vanity, but because he wishes to move on. We can do no more." He looked back down at his plate, pushing the remaining soggy beef around with his fork.

Mary had known Jorge since she was a young girl. He had wandered in and out of their house like a wayward uncle, always welcomed by her mother, who had begun to refer to their storeroom as Jorge's room after he bedded down on the dirt floor for the fourth or fifth time. Mary thought about how he could throw her an expression, a wink, roll his eyes, or mock a stern look and convey much more than what others could say in English. She never understood, until now, his reasoning for coming, but she recalled him talking fondly of his father and brothers, only to trail off into sadness and remorse when asked to recount his separation from his family.

What Jorge had confided was that he and his brother had fallen in love with the same woman. Jorge chose to leave Sesimbra, the fishing village south of Lisbon where he was born, rather than suffer the constant reminder of his unrequited love, which only grew as his brother's family swelled with children. In their younger years, Mary had had an adolescent crush on the man who was her first introduction to the solitary seafarer archetype that littered her hometown. It soon passed, but she could still recall anxiously awaiting her father's return from his voyages, in the hope that Jorge would accompany him home.

The four of them sat in silence as Sagar finished his supper. Finally Mary stood and asked the twins if they would like to pay their respects to Jorge. They fell in line behind her. Mary bent down and hugged Sagar. "Thank you."

After ascending the narrow staircase, Mary looked into her

father's quarters. The captain was nowhere to be seen, so she and the twins pressed on to the first mate's room. Knocking quietly, she did not wait for a response. Her father was sitting next to Jorge's bed. Tanner stood and approached in mild protest, but with great exhaustion, Jorge waved them in, keeping his infected arm well-hidden under the covers. He motioned for them to sit on the end of the bed, eager to speak.

"Mary, girl. You come in time. I have a gift for you. Return a gift, the little ones will know, ha!" Jorge laughed, but his body shook as he spoke. "Long ago, I was young, but troubled under the olive trees. My brother Abilio and I. We loved the same girl. But it is still with me, here," he said, pointing to his chest. Jorge went on to tell of his heartache. Late summer, he and his brother had just returned from sword fishing in a day boat off the coast. Their father had taken ill on their last voyage to the fishing grounds, and so the brothers had remained behind as he convalesced. It was not a physical ailment, but as Jorge recounted the best he could, it was a sickness of the mind.

Celia was her name. Her family had only settled in Sesimbra that year, moving north from Sines in late winter. By October, her choice was clear. By December, Celia and Abilio were betrothed. Avoiding the wedding, Jorge explained, he left for the fishing grounds with his uncle as soon as he could.

Returning nine months later, he found much change had come to his family. His father's condition had worsened. If not supervised, the still physically strong fisherman would wander the village, finding his way into the hills beyond. There, he would sing in a language unfamiliar to his family. The village elders claimed he spoke to the Mouros, or little people who lived underground. Once a favorite son of the village, Abilio now stayed indoors during the day, only to venture out to fish very early in the morning or late at night.

Abilio accused Jorge of abandoning the family and, despite his protestations, the elder brother would not be convinced. "You left me here to care for the old man, like some grandmother!" he yelled, rambling. "Uncle Vicinte must take father to the fishing grounds on the next season. And you, Jorge, you are no good for us. Make your own way in the world. Out of our house!"

Unable to rise to anger in response, young Jorge sought out his father. Finding him in the small courtyard behind their house sitting on an oak stump among the chickens, Jorge tried to explain that he was leaving. His father seemed to understand his young son and without protest, he stood and hurried into the house, leaving Jorge alone in the backyard. Returning in an excited state, the shamed family head carried a leather bag. He handed it to Jorge.

Looking inside, he spied a delicate silver horn. His father implored, "Take it away from me. Please, I have had enough of it! If you leave by land, yes, do that, leave by land, and on to Setubal, into the rocky hills northwest of the city. This is where I was given the horn. At dawn, blow it to call the Moura Encantadas from their barrow homes. They should want this back, but do not give it so willingly, or they will know you mean to be rid of it. Bargain, ha ha, bargain it away!" His father sat back down on the stump repeating the word bargain again and again.

Puzzled, but not wishing to disobey his excitable father, Jorge told him he would set off for Setubal that day. Jorge knew if he were to find work on the larger fishing ships, it was to Setubal or Lisbon he must go. He spent his first night in a troubled sleep, in and out of dreams of his brother chasing him, and of his brother's wife smiling wickedly as the scene unfolded.

By noon he had reached the village of Azeitao; luncheoning on dried fish and bread his mother had packed, Jorge thought back on when his father began to act strangely, and he realized it was about two years ago, after returning from Setubal to purchase several coils of rope in the large port city. In his haste he may have taken an overnight shortcut through the low coastal mountains. It was on that subsequent fishing voyage where his father's mind fell into disarray. Jorge determined he would carry out his father's instructions to seek out the Moura Encantadas, the enchanted maidens who guard the treasures of the Mouros.

Nearing nightfall, he left the road and turned north to climb the gentle slopes of the hills. Navigating through the aged Carob trees and careful to avoid the sharp leaves of the Kermes scrub oaks, Jorge sighted a wide earthen berm, some six feet high and twenty feet wide. As Jorge approached it he felt compelled to stop for the night. No vegetation grew on the barrow, but as Jorge glanced from end to end, he marked that two large trees anchored each side.

Collecting sticks and dry grasses from the surrounding area, he built a small fire for warmth and sat staring into the flames, not sure why his life had abruptly fallen apart. Angry at himself and a bit scared, he unfurled the cord binding the leather bag and exposed the literal instrument of his folly: the silver horn. He pulled it from the bag and held it aloft, letting it gleam in the firelight. He brought the smooth and cold horn to his lips and blew. An unmelodious but familiar noise emanated from the instrument, startling Jorge, who was taken aback by the high pitch and grating sound. Resembling a young woman's scream, the noise carried down into the valley, dispersing into the low forest. He was about to raise the horn again, when he heard muffled whispers rising behind him.

Jorge turned away from the fire, searching for the voices but at first he could only squint into the blackness as his eyes adjusted to the dark. He stood, still holding the instrument, trying to pinpoint their location. Before he could react, two silver streaks glided down the barrow, laughing. Dripping with jewelry, the milk-skinned young women wore flowing dresses of what looked to Jorge to be intricately woven chainmail.

"And what right do you have to call us up to your transient world?" spoke the taller of the two, as she swirled around him. He turned to respond, at which point she returned to the side of her companion. "Fear not, for my boisterous sister likes to scare young men. You'd think her looks would be enough for that," said the other maiden, sweetly smiling. Jorge, for his part, had no idea what she meant. These were by far the fairest maidens his eyes had ever gazed upon. "So, you did summon us, didn't you? What is it that you seek? The treasure we guard, no doubt."

Recalling what his father said, that he must be rid of the horn, yet not make it seem as if he wanted it gone, Jorge blurted out the honest truth. "I have lost my family, and lost my only love. If I could have them back, I would trade you this horn, never to summon you again."

"Indeed, yes, I see it through your eyes. Poor boy, take comfort, but truly, she was not your love but your brother's," whispered the taller being, while the second continued, "and you cannot have both. But in barter, take this golden comb. If in despair, wish upon the jewel inside: love, salvation, even fortune shall be yours. If your heart never finds another, never yearns for peace, and is never blackened by greed, gift the comb to one you deem worthy and you will be reunited with your father and father's father." Jorge found himself reaching out to take hold of a jewel-encrusted comb embedded with dozens of rubies. As he did, he held out the horn as if compelled, which slipped from his grasp into the waiting hands of the two sisters. The two Moura Encantadas turned and rose over the barrow, disappearing into the night.

Faria and Shikha sat close, holding on to his right arm as he spoke, caressing it when he paused, or as he halted to cough or recall a detail. When Jorge finished, Shikha thought to speak, knowing the creatures he described. She went as far as a first few words, 'Kind Asuras," but her sister's frown impelled her mouth shut. The first mate noticed the interplay between them and gravely whispered, "You little ones, these worlds, they do not easy mix. Seja cuidadoso. Be careful how you play with us."

Mary still sat bolt upright in the simple wooden chair next to his bed, hands clasped together in her lap. She wasn't sure if Jorge was recounting a story from his homeland, or if his fever had made him delusional, but she wanted to believe him. Slowly, he pulled his good arm away from the twins, and reached behind his bed, digging his hand into a gray rucksack. The twins sensed what he was doing before Mary, but they gasped louder than she when the bright red ruby in the handle of the comb Jorge grasped shimmered in the lamplight. It was as if it projected its own light, rather than simply reflecting that around it.

Jorge took Mary's hands, placed them side-by-side and pressed the comb into her palms. "For you, for him." With great difficulty Jorge spoke, also glancing at Captain Tanner. He closed her fingers, and closed his eyes. Sinking back into his bed, his breathing came easily for a few moments, then ceased.

***

As it was customary for the ship's captain to preside over burials at sea, there was no small amount of confusion the next morning when Reverend Smith emerged from his cabin and stood next to the first mate's bound body as the congregation assembled on deck for Jorge's funeral. Smith's haughty exterior looked ground thin by days of sleeplessness or contemplation, revealing an honest confusion, an almost uncomfortable humility. Captain Tanner made clear that he would begin and if Smith felt anything, religious-wise, was lacking, the right reverend was free to continue afterwards. Mary and James, the twins and Sagar stood closest to the plank where Jorge lay. Abby and her husband, Mrs. Bray, and many of Jorge's watch stood directly behind them. The remainder of the congregants were scattered about the deck, some to pay their respects, others curious, and a few families to observe with silent derision.

"Most of you are aware I had known Jorge for many years. We sailed in the coastal trade and made it as far as Morocco on a few occasions. Over many lean years, we grew from brash sailors into men, men of God, and of family. While he had no wife, nor children, Jorge was as much a younger brother to me as an older brother to my dear Mary. Few of you will mourn him as we will, it is true, but all of us should thank the Lord God that Jorge traveled among us. He delivered us to this spot, some two weeks from the coast of the new world. Upon fertile grounds we will step, and it will be our home but not Jorge's. He will rest here."

He nodded to James and George, who prepared to deliver Jorge to where his father and uncle rested. Reverend Smith haltingly helped the three men position the plank on which Jorge lay. Before tipping the plain wooden plank upward, Tanner motioned to Tom Robbin at the bow of the vessel, who lit the ship's single cannon in salute. The assembled crowd hadn't realized the cannon fire was impending, most didn't know the ship had one at all. The loud report rang across the open ocean like a valley of air burst open, shaking the masts to their tips and the congregants to their toes. Captain Tanner angled the plank upwards and Jorge slid into the awaiting ocean.

PART TWO

CHAPTER 14 - March 1603

The Spring Tide first dropped anchor some two weeks and 1,500 miles after Jorge's funeral. The voyage had hardened the minds of some on board, whose selfish purpose would soon contend with the good of the Congregation. For others, as the waves and wind pressed them farther from their home, the sea air itself fed their minds, awakening a greater consciousness of who they were, and would be. Abigail no longer clung to her contrived identity, cast by others, but searched the sea of possibilities for her true self. Even Reverend Smith found himself reflecting on the life he had lived, his choices and his calling. For Sagar and the twins, the voyage had brought grim clarity to Brigu's reminder: this congregation would fracture, and without their unseen aid, could not survive in the new world.

Captain Tanner, with the assistance of Tom, James and Sagar at the masthead, had been careful to keep the ship out of sight of land until assured they were well south of the fertile cod fishing grounds frequented by the Portuguese. But with fresh water stores running low, he called for a subtle course correction.

Casually striding toward the bow where several men lounged, the captain struck some idle conversation with the amiable farmhands turned sailors. He looked not at the men sitting among the coils of rope but always at the horizon, as they spoke of food they all missed and the color of barley in the fall and if that same color would emerge from the earthy loam of the new lands. The men had become darker as the sun took its effect on their skin through the early spring and Tanner wondered how they would compare to the natives they would surely encounter.

Tanner watched a slight bubble of quicksilver emerge and spread along the line of the horizon. Over the next few minutes it transformed into a sandy, dune-laden coastline.

"So, George, do you care to sit the rest of the day, or would you like to take a stroll and stretch those lanky legs of yours?" the captain asked.

"Well, sir, as you say, these lanky legs of mine get little from wandering to and fro on the deck of this floating cork," responded George, who more than most, was eager to set his feet on firm ground once again.

"How does a stroll on the beach sit with you," said Tanner. This elicited a few laughs from the gathered men, to which Tanner gestured at the emerging coastline and said, "Suit yourselves, but I mean to feel the sand in my shoes this day or the next."

The men turned and craned their necks over the ship's railing, suddenly in disbelief as Tanner walked back to his quarters. Within seconds, the ship erupted in hoots and shouts of Land! that brought most of the congregants boiling out onto the deck. Minutes later, Tanner emerged from his stateroom and stood by the helm, ready to address the growing crowd.

"Friends! We've made it across the sea and are now safe from her cold fury, but uncertainty still lies ahead. We will try to set foot on land to find fresh water and replenish supplies if we can. The safety of our floating home is our first priority. Know that if suitable anchorage cannot be found, we will beat down the coast, keeping sight of the shore until we may land. We'll break out three boats, two to search for fresh water, and one, well, one to give the ladies and children a chance to stretch a bit. My watch, un-stow the launches. Sagar's watch, you're on the bow readying the anchor. Keep a sharp eye out for rocks and sandbars. Better get a few men in the rigging for a better view. Tom's watch, roll as many of the smaller empty water barrels on to the deck from below. I'll inform Reverend Williams of our preparations." Tanner spoke with authority despite the unease he felt.

This was no landing at Brest or Guernsey. For all he knew, there were no safe anchorages within fifty miles. Further, a barrage of arrows or a split skull might await the man who first stepped on land.

These thoughts hung heavy with Tanner as he knocked on Smith and Williams' door. Smith, who had not been seen on deck since Jorge's funeral, opened the cabin door, asking what Tanner wanted and why the ship was in such a commotion. Tanner replied with a single word, land, at which point Smith walked onto the deck and Tanner promptly walked into the reverends' quarters. The captain moved through the small dining area to the stateroom beyond. Knocking at the door, he heard Williams reply, "Enter".

He found Reverend Williams still in bed, propped up by several blankets. When the aged reverend saw it was not Smith, he said, "Oh, hello, Captain Tanner. I was curious as to why Smith would have knocked before entering our room, but this explains it. What brings you to visit us and how, may I ask, did you get by my trusty guard dog?"

Surprised by Williams' light words, Tanner stopped for a moment and realizing his chance to talk candidly with him, he sat on the chair next to the bed. "We've reached land. Smith, like nearly everyone else, is on deck dreaming of what awaits us once we drop anchor and row to shore."

"Ahh, but we both can see what awaits us. For me, like Jorge, it is death, and captain, I am sorry I could not attend the service for your dear friend. For those who remain, it is toil, hardship, and dissolution into insignificance. As my time here diminishes, my mind is awash with clarity. To think I once believed I knew God's will and was fulfilling His plan. That a speck of dust reflecting in the moonlight can know why the stars shine." Williams trailed off, and Tanner wasn't sure if the man had come to his senses, or lost them, but it was clear why Smith was keeping him here in the bedroom. "One thing more, captain, I would like to set foot on land again. Please do let me know when it is appropriate."

"Yes, of course, Reverend. It may not be for a few days, but I will return when it is time," replied Tanner. The captain remained seated for a moment as he scrutinized the old man. Williams, whose attention was now fixed on the window, gazed outside with a smile creasing his ancient face. To Tanner, he looked like a child patiently awaiting a present, hands clasped together in his lap.

On deck, the only person not moving was Sagar, who now stood resolutely at the helm. Tanner ascended the stairs to the upper tier where the boy gripped the wheel with one hand. "Well, boy, what do you make of it?" said Tanner, referring to the coastline ahead.

"Sandy, very shallow, farther west there, though, it turns more rocky. So, on this course is an easy but unprotected landing, but west, we may find an inlet or river," he replied. "Captain, I think it might be best if I go ashore alone, before anyone else. Tonight." Sagar looked up at the captain, expressionless.

Tanner reflected for a moment and reckoned he must trust the boy. Putting his meaty hand on Sagar's shoulder, he said, "Aye, fall off the wind a hair, and let's make sure we reach that sandy area at nightfall, but no sooner." Looking circumspectly at the sky, Tanner said, "I think we will have a quiet night. Let's drop anchor a furlong from shore. That should give you an easy swim, eh?" Sagar simply nodded at his captain's words and turned the wheel slightly, slowing the ship to a more leisurely pace.

By dusk, the deck was littered with barrels, two small boats and a mess of chain and heavy rope. The captain knew this crew had never dropped or set an anchor, so he took them through the process point by point. After two hours laboring in the waning light, they had the anchor nestled in the sand and sufficient line paid out to allow the ship to swing broadly if the gentle winds changed overnight. A half-hearted call was made by a few to explore the beach by moonlight, but most of the men were either too tired from the day's commotion or afraid of stumbling about in the dark to give the notion much momentum. During an informal dinner, Captain Tanner gave orders. Overnight, three men would remain on deck, one in the rigging, one fore and one aft to maintain a watch over the ship and the shore. The next day, two parties would land after dawn. One would split and search the beach in both directions, while the other group would move inland looking for water. Only if the beach and surrounding area were deemed safe would others set foot on firm ground.

With everyone listening to Tanner on the gun deck, Sagar

slipped up the staircase into the captain's quarters. He pulled a knife from the table beside the bed and opened a small cabin window. Wriggling through it like a weasel, he dropped into the quiet water. Sagar took his time swimming, glad to be in the chilling water, but conserving his energy for the night ahead. The surf was light and unless the weather changed, the boats tomorrow would have little trouble landing on shore. Once on the beach, Sagar noticed that it was near high tide; being overcautious, he shuffled up the beach at a diagonal, creating a very un-human like track until he reached the grasses that grew above the reach of the waves.

Beyond the grassy dunes, a broad marsh stretched for a quarter-mile until it met dense forest with low rolling hills beyond. Despite feeling as if the land swung to and fro, an effect of being on board ship for months, Sagar set off at a light trot as smooth as a little fox bounding along. Sagar knew that marshes usually meant a river was nearby and he aimed to find a fresh water source before dawn. He began searching in a broad circle, heading west. Outwardly, the area looked similar to other coastal regions Sagar had seen, but in the early spring night, with a gentle onshore breeze rustling the grasses, he could feel the strength of the land coursing through him. Here, the tree spirits did not yet fear the iron axe of man.

Sagar followed a narrow but worn track littered with rabbit droppings into the salt marsh and found a small brackish river at the far end. Judging from the grade of the surrounding landscape, he figured it would be another half-mile upstream before the water ran fresh. Careful to avoid getting stuck in the putrid mud lining the riverbanks, he swam across and scurried into the rising adjacent forest, hoping to gain a better perspective of the surrounding area.

The trees, massive white oaks closer to the river and broad maples as he moved to higher ground, noted his presence: something small and unknown walked among them. Sagar kept his mind quiet and empty though; these new lands and the nature spirits guarding them, Asuras in Brigu's tongue, needed no warning from him as to what was to come. As soon as tomorrow this land would begin to sense the motivations of the congregants, just as the sea had. Together, the four of them had parried the attack and quelled the maelstrom but it had been just one Asura, not many. In Abby though, they now had an unlikely ally. Her perception had surprised them but it came at a cost. Hers was not a body meant to wield such power.

A series of progressively larger hills led to a rocky crest and in the half-moon's light, Sagar did not attempt to descend into the valley below, but rather, climb what looked to be the father maple of the hill, still void of leaves but with buds ready to burst forth with the power of spring. Sagar leaped from limb to limb, ascending above the adjacent trees until he could see the breadth of the valley below and back across the salt marsh to the Spring Tide, just a shadow on the glimmering water.

He scanned the landscape, creating mental landmarks degree by degree. Before his eyes spotted the source, his nose filled with the earthy scent of fires burning. Men. At length, he caught the orange flicker of several fires deep in the distance. Smoke rose from what might be a small village. From such a distance, he could not discern much, but he could sense that these natives had lived and died in this valley for many, many years. The soft swirl of their ancestors hovered above the village. Descending the old maple in characteristic fashion, a controlled fall, Sagar took off at a dead run.

He retraced his path through the oaks and maples, over rock after rock, his body thoughtlessly reacting to the firmness of the ground, low branches and undulations in the landscape. All of which caused him to alter his cadence from leaps to small steps and back to a consistent pace, but none slowed his progress. While his body was driven by purpose, his mind was free to wander. Just as the multitude of paths leading to this day had converged to a point of singularity, the paths which spread into the future, significantly narrowed today. Four seasons forward, as spring emerged once again, he must ensure the congregants had a tenuous foothold in this rocky land.

CHAPTER 15 - March 1603

Reaching the beach just as the predawn sun illuminated the clear eastern horizon, Sagar was relieved to see the Spring Tide resting peacefully at anchor, all boats still onboard. He retraced his steps through the dunes and across the beach. Obscuring his tracks with a loping shuffle through the coarse sand, he settled into a hidden spot in the grass to wait the few hours until the first boats touched land. Sitting in the morning dew, several rabbits came tauntingly close to him, as if they knew the small figure would not attempt to catch them, at least for now. Sagar began dreaming of roasted rabbit stew cooked over driftwood.

After sunrise, the deck of the ship sprang to life and Sagar could hear the bark of Captain Tanner's orders echoing across the water. The first two launches were lowered and haltingly found their way to the still surface. Men filled the boats, scrambling down ropes thrown over the side of the Spring Tide; the solitary boy on the beach smiled at the intrepid congregants, each eager to be the first to set foot in the new lands. He spotted Tom Robbin in the stern of the lead launch, steering as the men of Sagar's watch toiled at the oars. The launches ground ashore and the men piled out into the water and onto the beach, pulling the boats above the high tide mark.

Not given to expressions of joy, many of the men stumbled across the beach as if drunk on the catharsis that overwhelmed their sea-worn bodies. Tom Robbin, however, was all business, and likely on the advice of the captain scanned the dunes and surrounding beach for Sagar. Guessing correctly, Tom walked over the rise of the dunes, and Sagar stood to meet him.

"Captain Tanner mentioned we would not be the first on land. How do you find the new world, boy?" Tom said, grinning.

"Densely forested beyond the marshes, smart rabbits abound, deer in the woods and a brackish river turning fresh as it winds inland.

Mr. Robbin, this land is new to us, but it is very, very old. Time has ground the mountains into hills, smoothed the boulders that stud the land, and allowed the great trees to grow undisturbed, reaching heights heretofore I have never seen. It will resist us," replied Sagar, turning inland and gesturing to the slow rolling hills that stretched across the horizon.

Tom scrutinized the boy, digesting his words. The scholar in him was torn from the present, back to Oxford and his study of the natural world. Sagar's description of the land presented a more logical and intuitive explanation of how nature responds to change than the notion of the world as immutable. The boy's final words, though, stood in conflict with his logical summary.

Tom was soon surrounded by the other men who had made their way up the dunes, forcing him back to the task at hand. "There looks to be a river winding through the marsh and into the forest. From here we split into two parties, as the captain instructed. Sagar, take a group to replenish our water stores. Travel no farther than you must. The rest of us will explore the shoreline. Keep together, keep silent. If you spot game, take what easily presents itself, but do not give chase. If threatened or thwarted in any capacity or by any means, return to the boats with haste. Today, and each day forward, success is survival itself."

Imbuing the men with a healthy dose of sobriety seemed the right approach to Tom. Nodding in agreement at his words, they fell quiet and began unpacking the boats. Before departing, Sagar took Tom aside and whispered just a few words more, but they visibly affected his countenance.

"Natives reside farther inland. Several villages," he said, dropping his eyes to the ground. Despite his lack of sleep and food, Sagar knew he must help the men avoid contact until he, Tom and the captain had discussed when and how best to introduce themselves to the native inhabitants.

Reading the boy's expression, Tom handed him some hard tack and a jug containing a thin but salty broth. Sagar took a toothy bite of the brittle bread and a healthy swig of the broth, which made the bread easier to chew. He nodded and the two separated in silence. Sagar motioned to those of his crew on the beach. They assembled around him, unaware he had spent the last 12 hours on land. He explained their plan and instructed the men to carry one of the boats across the dunes, a short cut to the meandering, brackish river that lay beyond.

On board the ship, Captain Tanner paced the upper deck, watching for the return of Sagar and his crew. Over six hours had elapsed since they passed out of sight. Becoming anxious, Tanner commanded the boys milling about on deck to maintain a watch from the spars and the top of the mainmast, more to keep the lads from pestering him about when they could go ashore. None had spied Sagar or his crew. They likely were not keeping a close eye out but planning the adventures they undoubtedly would have once on land. Tom and the men who had remained within sight, from the looks of it, had done well catching several rabbits and prepared to return to the ship with their small but plentiful spoils.

Tanner scanned the beach in both directions, noting the extent of the high tide mark and the six-plus-foot tidal breadth. Farther west down the coast, a small dot caught his eye and soon he discerned its steady pace toward the ship. Within five minutes, it resolved into the familiar shape of the ship's launch. The men must have followed a river into the sea somewhere down the coast, he reckoned. The launch sat heavy in the sea, laden with barrels full of fresh water. Returning by sea was easier than carting their heft over land. Soon thereafter, two men emerged over the dunes, carrying an animal slung over a tree branch. So these were the spoils of the new world, Tanner thought to himself.

The story of Sagar and the deer, as it came to be known, was tossed up on deck through shouts and exclamations even before the launch had come to rest against the Spring Tide. The men had been making slow progress through a steep, dense wood, skirting a marsh to reach the river on the far side. As they approached a granite outcropping running parallel to their path, Sagar stopped, looking askance at the rocks and somehow beyond, signaling for silence. He clambered up the rock face in an instant, and as one of the young men from the launch told it, he disappeared over the far side. The men had paused on his command, and being honest farmhands, waited for further instruction. When the dark boy vanished from sight, a muted rustling resounded back across the marsh, as if a sharp wind had dropped from the sky, yet the maples surrounding the men stood unmoved. In the distance, a younger member of Sagar's watch called out, "there away, and there," pointing to a herd of deer bounding out of sight. Dropping the barrels and the boat, the men skirted the granite massif, seeking out Sagar.

After a difficult traverse of jumbled and broken but smoothed granite, strewn about as if thrown by an angry giant, the men came upon a small clearing ringed by yet more leafless maples. At the base of the stone mount's far side knelt Sagar, a buck three times his size lying motionless at his feet. The beast rested in a bed of graying maple leaves, a knife thrust to the hilt in its throat. On the voyage, the men of his crew had viewed Sagar with curiosity and in due time, respect. Second mate, savior of Jorge, silent but tireless leader at the helm: but now, breathing in the scene before them, a two hundred pound buck with blackening blood staining its coarse winter coat, he was no boy of ten or eleven, but a predator. Each man, according to his experiences and beliefs, bore this astonishing scene deeply, across a spectrum of fear and pride.

All paused for several long seconds in the cool but bright spring sunlight. Sagar rose as if from a prayer and noting the men's presence, pointed to a fallen maple branch, asking the closest two to truss the buck using the straight wooden castoff from a recent storm. They were to return to the beach with their prize, retracing their steps along the river's edge. The remainder of the watch would move north in search of fresh water.

With both Tom and Sagar's watches back on board, the other congregants spent the rest of the afternoon wandering the beach, keeping within sight of the Spring Tide and casually gathering the wood necessary to roast the enormous stag. In great spirits, if quite frail, even Reverend Williams found his feet on firm ground once again. With

Reverend Smith's help, the aged man haltingly knelt in the sand, and gazing skyward, eyes closed with a broad smile that could have cracked his thin skin, he offered a silent prayer of thanks for their deliverance. Smith looked down at his mentor, afraid of being without him, afraid of being alone.

Tanner, Tom Robbin and Sagar met in the captain's quarters where the boy described the events of the previous evening before falling asleep to the sounds of the captain chiding him for killing the stag. Inwardly, Tanner couldn't be prouder of the boy, but he keenly felt the suspicions Sagar's actions raised among the powerful Gaither faction. Leaving him to rest, Tanner returned to the deck and took a few of the more talkative in Sagar's crew aside and coolly asked them to temper their enthusiasm for the retelling of Sagar's feats in the woods.

The day served to assuage the congregants' first-order fears of a strange, foreign land. They dined on rabbit stew and roasted deer, drinking fresh water from the new world. Other than the size of the trees and the vastness of the forest beyond the marsh, it was not so unlike their home. Merry and stuffed with meat, the deck remained full late into the night but Sagar, who had provided the means of their satisfaction, remained asleep at the captain's table. Mary had come in and put a blanket over him, leaving some food in case he woke. Such a curious boy, she thought, watching him breathe slow and easy. It must have been the dim light throwing shadows but Mary thought she saw wrinkles on his brow.

***

Several rainy days of western progress along the low coastline brought the Spring Tide to the mouth of a broad river, nearly a mile across. Under light sail, Captain Tanner edged the ship north into the silty flow of the estuary, using just enough sail to evince forward progress. Several men maintained lookouts at the bow and in the rigging. The utter opacity of the water made their jobs somewhat cursory rather than as participants in navigation but Tanner could ill afford to run the ship upon a sandbar, or worse, a rock ledge. He could read a river's flow well enough in broad daylight, but today's midday was like winter's dusk.

As the estuary narrowed to about a half-mile across, it focused the river's flow into a strong current, forcing the men to increase sail to counter the effect. Looking to a mild bend ahead creating a quiet eddy near the east bank of the river, Captain Tanner nodded to the men at the bow who readied the anchor. So easy did the Spring Tide come to an affable stop that the splash of the anchor and clattering paying of chain were all that informed the congregants below that the ship had come to rest.

Tanner felt optimistic they had found a suitable location for a permanent settlement, but he needed confirmation. Over the next several days, formal exploratory parties received instructions from the captain each morning, while at night, one small boy surveyed the river's shoreline and the woods far to the East. On the seventh day after dropping anchor, James led two crews of men ashore to clear the trees on a low plain set back from the river. Relieved to be working the land again, the men relished the toil. Three days later, their efforts were quite visible not only from the deck of the ship, but even from the distant western bank of the river.

Early morning, as fog hovered upon the river's glassy surface, Sagar surveyed the onshore progress from an open window in Jorge's old quarters. Someone approached. Two someones. Faria and Shikha, whom he had seen little of for a month, had brought him some breakfast, the last of the hard tack and some hot water flavored with molasses and a few cloves.

They knew he wished to talk, and to listen. Without turning to address the twins, he spoke, gazing out the window at the hirsute stump farm the enthusiastic congregants had created. "These people, they think it a young land, they call it the new lands. No, it's ancient. The trees were unafraid until a few days ago, looking pleasantly to the emerging spring. The landscape, once mountainous like in our homeland, has been worn to soft hills by the seasons. Now it finds itself beset by men from the east. Like an aged general from one of Brigu's fireside tales, its fury will rise, ultimately in vain." The three of them stood for a minute or more until Faria pulled away from the window. Sitting cross-legged, she placed three cups on the floor and filled them with drink.

Faria warmed her hands, smiling while clutching the steaming cup. "It is a long road, Sagar Sur Sa, and what today looks like a great victory is a small battle won. Even you cannot see that far ahead." As she spoke, Faria silently placed her cup just behind Sagar's left foot. As he turned, still peering out the window, he kicked it, spilling the sweet liquid onto the floor. She looked up at the both of them, arms spread, grinning. First confounded, Sagar crumbled to the floor with laughter. "Your sight fails you!" Shikha said, settling in between them.

"Any other lessons you have for me this morning?" Sagar mused.

"Oh, no lessons, but can you please hand me my cup. It seems as if you kicked it in your haste to mourn that which can deeply slumber, but never truly dies," she said. Sagar thought for a moment and nodded back at her as he passed her the cup. As their hands touched, Sagar's fingers slipped over Faria's and he nearly dropped the cup. Shikha frowned, but her sister quickly quelled the new thoughts in both their minds. They all chatted for about twenty minutes, first sharing their collective observations: Sagar, his discussions with the captain and the land he had explored, the twins describing the tenor of the gun deck.

The Gaithers and their kin had begun to eat their meals alone. Their sons had also moved out of the forecastle, into their makeshift encampment in the first third of the gun deck, further crowding everyone else. Those impacted assured themselves that soon enough they would have all the land they needed. Shikha said they were scared and Faria continued, "Abby and Tom Robbin's wife spoke up on behalf of those who lost a bit of space, but were dismissed by the dried-up raisin, Mrs. Gaither. The one without the warts. If they only knew what Abigail was capable of." The Gaither brothers' wives were known to many of the children on board not just for their cruel treatment but also by their singular appearances. One, Hattie, was called 'the raisin,' resembling a dried fruit, thin and rarely seen eating anything. The other, Mildred, consumed her sister-in-law's portions and then some. She was less affectionately referred to as 'the mole'. Mildred's eyes sat so far back in her skull, even on a bright sunny day it was impossible to discern their color. Perhaps they had none.

Shikha added, "Mrs. Bray and Mary have remained quiet. I think they don't want to tell the captain."

Shikha paused but Faria spoke what was in her twin's mind, "There is something else. A distance grows between our adoptive mother and yours. Where once they laughed together, they now avoid each other's company. For some time now, Miss Abby and Mrs. Robbin, we have seen disappear for hours on end and last Thursday, Mary noticed their vacancy. She asked us their location. We replied with shrugs. She looked on deck and in the forecastle. Finally, Mary returned below decks. She stole through the galley and I followed her close enough to see she had not gone up the back staircase. She must have descended into the hold. A few minutes later she emerged, face red and eyes narrow. She made for Mrs. Bray like an arrow. Whispering but heated, her fire would not be quelled by the entreaties of the elderly matron." Faria watched Sagar for his reaction, but he betrayed nothing, knowing the longer he waited, the more likely she was to continue.

Faria took a few long breaths and began again: "She, that is, Miss Abby, she once knew the script of Ogmios, of Herakles, and deep in the hold I think she is trying to relearn it with Mrs. Robbin. She discerned the protection spells woven into our hammocks and now studies them, taking rough notes in a book given to her by Tom's wife. She questions us incessantly about Jorge's rescue and for her sake and our own, we reveal as little as we dare, lest we draw scrutiny from the others, not the least of which, our father. Sagar, she is a woman fascinated, even possessed, and Mrs. Bray, once Abby's protector and confidant, looks on dejected, like as one who has failed in her duty."

"Watching helpless from the shore, as a ship barrels headlong toward an exposed reef," interjected Sagar. "And with Mary, there is no hope of reconciliation?" Both girls shrugged but shook their heads no.

"Brigu made clear to us our charge, as he did all the children.

Faria and I must protect Miss Abby, no matter the cost," Shikha said.

"And I the congregation," Sagar replied. "How long before our missions conflict?"

The three of them sat for a time in thought until Sagar looked up and said, "I must find a way to the river's far shore. There are native settlements nearby that may aid us. It is never good to live in the water if your enemy is the crocodile. With the scale of destruction on land, we will be noticed by more than man. It is possible that Abby's growing awareness strengthens us all just as we need it. I begin to see hints of Brigu's plan."

"Sagar, how well do you know Nathan Robbin?" asked Faria. Surprised by the seemingly out of context question, he soon grasped the direction of her thinking.

"I trust his father and believe he will make the right decision when the time comes. I know little of the son, but will learn," replied Sagar. How differently the twins saw the world, he reflected.

CHAPTER 16 - March 21, 1603

At night, all but a few men would return to the ship, and with the gangplank pulled up, the Spring Tide served as the congregants' block house. Those on shore would guard the animals and the hastily piled belongings, but mostly they sat around a blazing fire in the center of the ever-growing clearing, telling stories and eating copious amounts of rabbit stew. Each had a long matchlock gun, either owned or borrowed from another on board. Among all the men, they had some 15 long guns and a handful of pistols. Only a select few were skilled at shooting, being much more comfortable, and deadly, with an axe or set of hatchets. Shore duty became quite popular, and on their third night since beaching the ship, Captain Tanner began appointing who would stay on shore and who must return to sleep, once again, on the cramped gun deck. There were whispers that Tanner supplied modest amounts of grog to those on shore, helping them through the still-chilly nights.

Abby woke to the soft light of a single lantern in the galley. She had dreamt of the woods near her home; she ran, pursued by an unseen entity. At first her mother was with her, but pulled ahead into the distance and Abby couldn't keep pace. Abby's dream ended just as her mother disappeared from view, but a painful sensation lingered. George lay next to her, arms crossed over his chest exactly as he had left them when he closed his eyes. At least she hadn't woken him with her start. The small waves of the river lapped the hull peacefully, but she found no comfort in the noise. Instead, the anxiety of her dream intensified. Pivoting around, she saw the twins out of their hammocks and peering through the porthole. Hearing Abby turn but without facing her, Faria whispered, "Something approaches the camp. Sagar remains away in the eastern forest."

On shore, the men's fire had burned low to where only coals remained, hissing and popping. Abby now stood between the girls and all three looked into the darkness. She saw nothing; but overlaid onto her sight another sense grew. Like standing next to a hot fire but more targeted, more intense, Abby discerned three shapes on the outskirts of the cleared land now littered with stumps. "What do they want? What madness is this?" She whispered, panicking.

"What do the grasses want?" replied Faria. "Or the trees?" added Shikha.

In 24 years of life, Abby's fears had never stood a chance against her anger. The twins' words lit a fuse that spun and snaked through her mind until reaching its payload, exploding in silence. In the quietest of whispers, she screamed, "Girls, enough riddles! On deck, this instant!" Whether the twins knew she would respond like this, knew they could incite her, she didn't care. Half-threat, half-bluff, it worked. They filed like snakes through the sleeping bodies, up the ramp and onto the deck.

Hurrying the girls to the railing, Abby bent down to their level and said, "What is out there and what do they want?"

"We have heard them called them Yakshis, Dryads or tree spirits. They have been observing the men cutting, chopping and grinding the forest since we landed. Men as they have never seen. Men who do not stop at one or two trees but keep cutting," Faria replied, eager to continue but knowing Abby most wanted answers.

"How do you two know all this?" Abby asked, cooling but only slightly.

"Miss Abby, we don't know any of this. Remember the wagon from Rotterdam. You saw, you guessed. We guess, we suspect, we feel as you did in your dream. You woke just after us, confused and alarmed," Faria said.

"Why do we sense these creatures when others do not?" Abby's angered had ebbed to a low heat. She implored as one maligned rather than accusing her daughters.

"Whatever is in the two of us must flow through you as well. But for our part, it is all we have known. For you, I believe you are re-awakening. Our lineage is," Shikha stopped and with her sister nodding said, "as uncertain as yours."

Just when Shikha stopped, piercing cries rang out from the forest. Abby instinctively covered her ears from the pain of the shrieking cacophony. When it subsided she was surprised to find it had awakened neither the men on shore, nor those who slumbered below. Abby again felt anger but it was not her own. "Nobody else heard the cry," she said to her daughters and herself, adding, "those on shore are in danger. We have to protect them if we can."

At Abby's insistence, she and the twins began looking about the deck for a means to get on shore knowing that extending the plank was not possible. It would make far too much noise.

"From the lowest spar of the mainmast we just might be able to throw a rope down," Faria suggested.

With some difficulty they ascended to the first horizontal spar of the mainmast. Shikha fashioned one end of a rope to it and flung the other end on to shore. It would do. They might get a bit wet and muddy but could reach the riverbank. Shimmying down the rope deposited them in ankle-deep water where they jumped to shore and raced to the clearing's edge. The sleeping men began to turn uneasily on the forest floor but otherwise had no sense of what neared. The twins and Abby skirted the area still lit by the men's fire but passed within 30 feet of them before disappearing into the inky darkness.

"Sagar nears," Faria whispered, navigating through the stumps and piled branches. Shikha followed just behind her sister while Abby walked some paces to the left and about ten yards ahead. Abby felt the heat-like sensation grow and began to grasp the position of the spirits. She concentrated on their locations and soon her vision aligned with her new sense; three female shapes materialized in the darkness. The spirits drifted through the clearing, lingering at each stump before moving on. The Dryad nearest to Abby looked up from her vigil, emerald eyes piercing her like needles. A wry, bitter smile of impending vengeance spread across her face.

A dark streak flashed behind Abby, stopping between her and the twins. It was Sagar. "Lead them farther from the forest so their strength will ebb. See, even now she hesitates." Sagar pointed to the spirit closest to the twins. "It is our only chance to break them and banish their kind from the camp. Miss Abby, they derive their power from the living forest, as its protectors and companions." Sagar and the twins moved into defensive positions around Abby who still stood incredulous at the scene around her. She shook her head.

"No, this isn't right. Any of this. There must be a compromise we can strike. We have little claim to this land." But as Abby spoke, a pulse of warm energy knocked her back several feet onto the muddy ground. Her senses cluttered and for a moment, she couldn't see anything. She haltingly stood, clumps of cold, wet dirt sticking to her hands and forearms.

"We have no claim at all Miss Abby, and no bargain can be struck here. There is no thought in their actions, just as the river beyond is unthinking: it flows, it is. That is all," Faria said. Now Abby understood what her daughter had meant earlier. Shikha crouched beside her sister and pressing her arms forward as if resisting an encroaching invisible wall, succeeded in halting the approach of the woodland spirits. Sagar circled between Abby and the twins and did the same. The spirits took a few steps backward, nearer to the forest. But as they did, their resolve renewed and they entrenched among their fallen kin, the trees. The twins and Sagar began to falter and could do no more.

Abby again found herself sitting on the wet ground, Faria at her side holding her hand. Abby shivered in the early spring night, despite Shikha's shawl draped over her shoulders. Sagar stood on a stump in front of her looking back at the ship. Abby tried to stand but fell back again. "What happened?" She whispered.

"You don't remember?" For the first time, Abby sensed genuine hesitation, even fear, in her daughter's voice. "We reached a stalemate, the farther back we pushed them, the stronger they became. You stepped forward, as if possessed, and spoke in a strange tongue. I heard but a single word. The spirits parted and returned to the forest."

"I don't recall any of that. What did I say?" Abby asked.

"Sisters," Faria said solemnly.

Sagar helped Abby back on board via a rope ladder he kept stashed near the bow. The twins scrambled up behind her and led their stumbling mother by the hand back to their nest on the gun deck. She collapsed into slumber while the twins remained awake until dawn, troubled thoughts intermingling between their minds. Even with Sagar's return, the three of them had stood little chance against the Dryads they confronted. Nature still pulsed with her primordial strength in these lands. Had it not been for Abby's intercession, the camp and even the ship perhaps, would have been overrun. Brigu had trained them to resist, to fight these forces when needed, but never had they seen or heard of one who could command them.

Uncertainties inched into the twins' consciousness. Their adoptive mother wielded a power they did not possess, or even understand. Along the desert tracks, through the mountain villages and humid seaports, the twins' principal fear had been the inevitable day that Brigu would call upon one of them to serve, driving each sister to a solitary fate. Their relief in being placed together, and further with Sagar, had now been superseded by doubt. Was it possible they could fail?

"Did Brigu anticipate the travails awaiting us?" Faria wondered.

"He knew much and said little. These two attacks were like nothing we experienced, nothing he prepared us for. It's as if he set us along a path resisted by destiny itself."

"Destiny, dear sister, has no sense of urgency. We will need to wait a very long time, I suspect, to see this play out," Faria mused.

CHAPTER 17 - March 21, 1603

When the corners of the Spring Tide had been emptied and only the huge water tuns remained below, Sagar went to see his captain. He found Tanner sitting alone in his quarters studying a roughly drawn map. It depicted the congregants' handiwork: the growing clearing surrounded by double lines encompassing the area and notations, family name by family name. To the east, Tanner had scribbled the phrase, "clear of natives." He tapped his quill pensively in the uncharted area. "Boy, what do you make of the land west of us?"

Looking more closely at Tanner's rough drawing of their encampment, Sagar grasped his concern. Natives meant warriors, and Tanner was trying to estimate what fortifications might be needed in case of attack. The double line on his page represented a wall. Sagar had done little fighting in his life, but he knew enough of men to realize that a wall was an uncompromising statement, rarely seen as anything but an aggressive gesture. He also knew that if the natives wished, a wall would not stop them from dispatching the congregants with haste.

"Captain, it looks to rise steeply at first, gouged by the river's flow. From the tops of the trees, I have seen slow rolling hills rising to the North."

"Do you reckon it's fit for habitation? Natives, I mean."

"I don't know, sir, but I think it less prone to flooding than our camp," replied Sagar.

Looking frustrated as he scrutinized the map, Tanner said, "there could be villages, even towns in those hills then." He sat for a spell in a hazy stare.

Seeding the man's thoughts, Sagar whispered, "Sir, I'd need a launch and two strong backs to make it across the river." He waited, finally adding, "but I suspect we'd be better off knowing for sure than guessing."

The captain nodded his head, considering the request as if it had come from his own mind, which turned to the import of the results. Sagar pressed the matter. "With your permission, as the tide ebbs, I will make my way upriver to the narrowing point, cross to the western shore, and learn of any settlements. I think I could do worse than to suggest Tom Robbin and his son as oarsmen, sir."

Looking up at Sagar, Tanner said. "Yes, take the Robbins with you, and within a few days, we shall know what we're up against, eh, boy!" Producing an elaborately inlaid box from underneath the bench, he added, "Equip yourself." Placing the box upon the table, Tanner opened it to reveal two dueling pistols.

Leaning in to inspect the instruments, Sagar detected the obvious scent of alcohol on Tanner's breath and saw a mania in his glassy eyes. "Sir, I will give these to Mr. Robbin."

"No, no, one for each, one for each. Here!" Tanner handed the pistols to Sagar and stood, implying it was time for Sagar to take his leave. Sagar departed to find Tom. He had no intention of bringing the pistols along, or at best, would leave them with the launch. He aimed not to reconnoiter the lands of an enemy, but to openly meet with any inhabitants to the west. Spotting Tom working alone on shore, Sagar approached. Sure Mr. Robbin would grasp the gravity in their captain's thinking, Sagar relayed his recent conversation with Tanner, but also shared much of what the twins had told him of the tensions below deck.

Halfway through Sagar's explanation, Tom needed a seat, and found it on a nearby tree stump. There, the former schoolteacher sat transfixed, listening to Sagar, elbows on his knees, hands cradling his chin. Once the boy finished, Tom put his hand on Sagar's shoulder and said with a melancholy smile, "Son, you know more than you tell, but you tell much. Thank you. We should approach any natives as friends. Let us prepare for an encounter by procuring gifts for them, and I should like to consult a few books before we depart. When is the next favorable tide?"

"In Three hours, and again tomorrow early, but I think it best to depart this afternoon," replied Sagar. "I'll leave these devices with you, sir. I don't think we'll be needing them," handing Tom the pistols, "and if we do, we will have failed in our purpose."

A few hours later, Sagar sat perched in the bow of the launch, as Tom and his son Nathan manned the oars. They kept close to the river's edge, avoiding its still-powerful flow, and made for the narrows farther north. Once beyond, they pulled hard for the west bank and landed in a thicket of bulrush which stopped their progress downriver. Sagar sprang from the boat, pulling it through the grasses lining the bank until they reached firm ground. The reeds served as an ideal spot to hide the boat.

Tom carried a rucksack, from which protruded the spine of a heavily bound book. His son, rather begrudgingly, also carried a similar pack, filled no doubt with supplies as dictated by his father. So different in build, Tom being lanky and thin, his son no doubt would overtake him in height within the year. The rucksack rested rather more easily on the son's broad shoulders than on the father's. While Tom felt quite prepared for any eventuality, as he stepped on shore, he thought he caught a look of bemusement in Sagar's face, which bordered on a smile. The boy carried only a knife, and had tied a heavy coat around his waist.

Sagar led them west through the dense underbrush lining the riverbank, into an endless expanse of the elders of the forest, the oaks. He would run ahead just out sight, periodically circling back to the slower Robbins. Nate wanted to keep up with Sagar, but his heavy pack and his father's caution kept him moving at a steady pace. The light through the trees was so diffuse, the daylight dispersed like snowflakes falling into a fast-moving river. Night approached so slowly, they hardly realized it when the darkness was upon them.

About an hour after the full darkness of night had enveloped them, Sagar returned from one of his forward scoutings and told of a village that lay ahead. "Let us move to the top of the hill beyond and sit for a spell." Tom peppered Sagar with questions, to which Sagar responded with one-word answers or shrugs of his shoulders. Tom was so excited that he walked beside Sagar, eyes wide and smiling like a child.

Sagar slowed and began to wind his way up the slope, careful to stay in the lee of the larger trees. He moved so that the Robbins could follow, and with some difficultly, they began to match his steps, slow or still as the wind ebbed, accelerating from tree to tree as the wind rose.

They approached a granite boulder at the top of the hill, sitting among a few diminutive hemlocks. Sagar slumped back against the rock, thinking for a moment. The Robbins crouched low, and when Sagar rose, so did they. He edged to where the rock sloped lower, where they could all see across it and down the other side of the hill. Sagar pointed into the distance, and at first the Robbins saw nothing. "Look for the flickering of fires, and scan left to right, you will see the huts."

Squinting into the darkness, Nathan replied, "Yes, okay, I see one, now two fires. There's a mess of huts as well, and a man standing with his back to us, I think." Sagar nodded and after about ten more seconds, Tom nodded too.

"Mr. Robbin, I think it best if I go down there alone at first. If something were to happen, or I am taken, you and Nathan can make your way back across the river without me, right?" Taken aback at the boy's suggestion, Tom found the meaning.

"Sagar, son, we will all return together, of that I am sure. If you think it best to approach the village alone, please take your leave, but know we watch from this hill, wishing you luck and waiting for your signal!" Sagar began to make his way down to the fires beyond, and while Nathan moved to the left side of the rock, he stepped on something firm, Sagar's knife. They watched as the boy disappeared and reappeared from sight. For a time, perhaps five minutes, they didn't see Sagar at all, but he eventually became visible. Emerging from behind a tree, he walked with purpose, approaching the nearest fire and a man who faced the woods from which he appeared. From the hilltop, the Robbins could not make out what transpired next.

As the village fires burned low, the Robbins grew fearful. Tom kept watch, but saw nothing. Another hour passed. Tom knew if something had befallen Sagar, he and Nathan's best chance to return to the launch would be under cover of night, yet he refused to abandon the boy. The fire closest to them suddenly grew brighter and Tom now made out a man heartily stoking the flames, illuminating the surrounding area.

Tom and Nathan looked on as several natives emerged from the huts lining a central area around the now-blazing fire. Nathan exclaimed, "There, father, there he is!" as he spied the boy walking from the village. Sagar gestured back to the natives, and walked directly up the hill to the Robbins' redoubt. Relieved, Tom was still fearful to wave or make contact and told Nathan to keep low behind the granite boulder.

When Sagar reached the Robbins, Tom expected a synopsis of the past few hours, but he received much more comforting words. "I hope you are hungry, we have been invited to a feast," Sagar said. Before they returned to the village, though, Sagar asked Tom if he had brought the guns given to them by Tanner.

"No, I left them in the launch. I have several books, mostly with engravings. I should like to present one as a gift," Tom said.

Sagar replied, "Their gift to us will be the food they provide; it would be best to wait until after we have eaten for you to respond in kind. I wonder though, if your rucksack itself might be more appreciated." He continued, "Slowly now." Sagar turned and led the two Robbins back through the woods, to the blazing fire. Through the soggy leaves they trudged, boots still wet from their muddy river landing, and at least for Nathan's part, exhausted. Nathan thought back to much more comfortable environs, nearly a year ago, to when his father had announced around their bountiful Sunday dinner table, with a nod from Mother, that they would all be voyaging across the great ocean on an adventure. Tom explained to the family how they had an obligation to bring education and what he called humanity to the new lands. Nate wasn't sure what his father meant, but he knew that in England, never had he been invited to a feast by strangers. If that was humanity, perhaps they were here to learn, not teach.

The firelight revealed an array of long wooden huts, woven together from small to mid-size branches. Loosely arranged around four open areas in a grove of hemlocks and cedars, the huts formed a village of perhaps sixteen extended families. The visitors' steps were softened by the pine needles littering the forest floor, and while Tom discerned the gentle rush of a stream that lay beyond, the dense canopy seemed to mute all sound, not unlike, he thought, the vaulting in Bristol Cathedral.

Three native men stood facing them as Sagar, Tom and Nathan emerged from the forest darkness. Several others were standing behind the fire, in deference or perhaps curiosity. Sagar slowed his pace, but was sure to keep Tom and Nathan behind him. He kept his arms away from his sides and after closing the distance to about six feet, he stopped, held his hands up, and turned to Tom, saying, "Tom Robbin." He repeated this introduction for Nathan. While Tom looked absolutely elated, Nathan was trembling. Sagar added, "Ohshah, wunámônah, father, son," referring back to Tom.

The eldest of the three men stepped forward, his long hair graying, skin weathered by more than 40 winters. With Sagar moving aside, he walked up to Tom, scrutinizing his clothing, and finally struck his own chest and said, "Quniyôkat", referring to himself. Tom instinctively held out his hand, causing Quniyokat to look askance into the schoolteacher's hand for something small. Sagar quickly stepped in and began to motion to the village chief when Quniyokat discerned the intent and grasped Tom's thin hand with both of his. This gesture caused the men behind Quniyôkat to exhale, relaxing, but not entirely. The elder gestured to the men who had stood beside him, "Cikiyiyô Muksihs, wunámônah," and in turn, "Kutomá Nipôwi." Motioning toward a long hut beyond the fire, he beckoned for them to follow.

Sagar whispered to Tom and Nathan as they walked, "Kutomá Nipôwi is the chief's son in law. I can't figure out what his name means, and Cikiyiyô Muksihs, or Raging Cub, is the chief's son; he remains wary of us and told his father not to let us in the village."

They entered the long hut after Quniyôkat and found it spacious and warm inside, comfortably apportioned with deer hides and furs. Elevated off the dirt floor by wooden planks sat roasted deer meat, a large game bird, and various vegetable porridges. Quniyokat motioned for them to sit, and after they had settled in, he began to speak, slowly at first, extensively using his hands in what Tom and Nathan understood to be a general description of the area. Sagar tried to translate what he could, which amounted to saying a word every so often that he recognized. The chief paused for a moment, which gave Sagar time to recount to Tom and Nathan what happened earlier. Sagar indicated, or tried to, that the three of them were travelers from far away, who had reached these lands by the sea. They did not know the land at all, and so the chief was giving them a verbal tour as it were. He began again, and after a few minutes, stopped, satisfied with his speech.

Sagar glanced at Tom and Nathan, saying, "Tawbut ni, thank you." Tom and Nathan repeated these words, at which point everyone quite informally began eating. Tom was the first to sample the food, and found it both fresh and satisfying; Nathan was more cautious, but after seeing his father and Sagar enjoying some yellow porridge, which turned out to be squash, he heartily partook. The dish was sweetened with something akin to molasses, but much finer. On occasion, the natives spoke among themselves. Tom had become increasingly comfortable and Sagar could see him trying to pick up certain words as the others spoke. When he saw that Quniyokat was done eating, Tom again said, "Tawbut ni, thank you", and gestured as if handing something to the chief. He turned to his rucksack and untying the top, he extracted a series of books and a long but narrow wooden case. Placing the items on the wooden plank separating the natives from the visitors, he opened the largest book, thin with a leather cover, revealing wood cuts of birds, pastoral life, and farm animals. He handed it to the chief, who first scrutinized the paper, then the leather binding, finally interested in the depictions therein. As he turned the pages, Tom would say the English word. Sagar realized now that Tom had planned this as both a tutorial and a means of communication.

Tom pushed the wooden case farther into the center of the plank serving as their dining table. This drew the attention of the chief and his relatives, giving Tom the opportunity to ceremoniously open the case and fashion an elaborate ivory flute inlaid with silver, from the components inside. He handed it to Nathan. Embarrassed yet encouraged by his father, he took the flute gingerly and began to play a slow melody. Midway into the song, Kutomá Nipôwi stood and abruptly left the hut, worrying both Sagar and Tom, but the chief remained jovial and as relaxed as before. As Nathan finished, Kutomá Nipôwi returned, bearing a wooden instrument, along the lines of a large recorder. He resumed his seat, visibly excited, and pointed to Nathan to begin again. As the schoolteacher's son started, Kutomá Nipôwi echoed the song in the deeper tones of his own instrument, interlacing a repetitive series of notes in support of the primary melody.

The two took turns introducing new songs, and as they did, Tom noticed a small crowd had grown outside the hut, onlookers attracted by the new music they heard. He sat, breathing in the scene around him, thinking back to Nathan's first music lessons in their parlor. It took not his father's stern hand, but his mother's sweet words to get the young boy to practice. Tom must remember to tease Nathan about it later. And later it had quickly become, as Sagar reminded him. It was now nearing midnight and Tom and Sagar agreed that they should take their leave, or at least attempt to.

At his father's instruction, Nathan handed the ivory flute to the chief's son in law, who turned it end over end, running his fingers around the inlaid silver. After his inspection, Kutomá Nipôwi tried to return it to Nathan, who, palms open, gestured for him to keep it. Both the chief and Kutomá Nipôwi nodded in understanding. As they stood to leave the hut, Tom caught the eye of the chief's son, who had remained quiet and reserved throughout the night. Raging Cub squinted back at the schoolteacher, sizing up the man's thin arms, his disheveled light brown hair and his sack of books. Tom had no doubt the man weighed the schoolteacher's worth and surmised he was of little consequence.

Tom, Nathan and Sagar departed into the darkness; a waxing half-moon hung high in spring sky, lighting their path through the woods. Nearing the rock where Nate and Tom had waited, Sagar looked over his shoulder and saw Raging Cub watching them, alone. From where he left it on the ground, he picked up his knife, and asking Tom and Nathan to wait a moment, he climbed to the top of the rock. The chief's son's head moved higher, trying to see Sagar more clearly. At this recognition, Sagar slid down the rock, and through the woods like a young stag, he bounded back to the village. His speed took Raging Cub by surprise, but as he neared, he slowed, and hands out, presented the inscrutable man with his knife, a gift he hoped the brave would respect. Raging Cub displayed only the slightest smile and said, "Punitôk", looking over the blade with satisfaction. He nodded to the boy and Sagar disappeared into the woods just as he came.

They reached the river two hours later, made a fireless camp and awaited daylight. Nathan fell asleep quickly, leaving Tom and Sagar to discuss the day's events. They agreed that the encounter had been quite productive, and that they should return within a week if possible. Sagar said there were at least two more small villages beyond the one they visited, but he didn't know if they formed part of a larger community. Tom began to speak, only to falter, and for a time, they sat listening to the river and the wind rustling the reeds. Sagar could still see Tom thinking and the schoolteacher finally found his words.

"Sagar, are you and the twins related? Are they your sisters?" he said. Sagar replied that yes, he believed they all were related, but they weren't his sisters. "So, what do you mean, you believe you are related? Did you not know your parents?" Tom pressed, knowing he might not soon have another chance to speak with Sagar so candidly.

Sagar looked to Nathan, who was unmistakably in a deep slumber. Satisfied, he began, "I don't remember my parents. I recollect so many things, but I wish I could see just a bit further back, Mr. Tom. But, that's not quite it. It's like," he stopped and looked directly at Tom. "What are your first memories?"

Tom thought for a moment and said, brow furrowed, "I'd had a bad dream; there was a long narrow road surrounded by water, a castle lay at the end of it, very far away. I was alone. Somehow, I got my foot stuck in the mud wall holding back the waves. The harder I tried to free myself, the closer I came to falling in the water. I woke up screaming. My mother and father came into my room. Father, still in his work attire, looked at me like I had embarrassed him in front of his business partners. He stormed out. My mother, dressed for bed, stayed with me until I fell back asleep. When I woke in the morning, she was still there holding my hand, dozing next to me. What do you first remember, Sagar?"

"Wait a moment, Mr. Tom. Let me ask: do you remember what happened later in the day you just recounted, or the next day, or a month later?"

"Well, no, of course not. That is the clearest early memory I have. Anything before, I think, it was just feelings mostly. There are a few others from perhaps the same year, but they could have been months and months apart. Why?" Tom replied.

Sagar still looked straight at Tom, "I have heard others tell it that way too, but for me, it's like, there is something missing, and then, fully formed, I recall footsteps crunching through the packed snow, growing distant, ice crystals driven by the wind, unceasing, masking the sound of someone departing, and the sun setting beyond the tops of the far mountains, darkness falling across the deep frozen valley. Mr. Tom, this was no dream, and it was long ago."

"How long?" Tom said quickly.

"Almost two hundred years," Sagar whispered.

Tom slumped down, shaking his head. It just couldn't be, he thought, but somehow it made sense: aboard ship, in their new camp, conversing with the natives, the boy possessed a sagacity matched by few he had ever known. Tom's Socratic training failed him. His innumerable questions became stuck in a rush for the door. Silence prevailed.

For several minutes they again sat, feeling the river gurgling by, when Sagar changed his gaze from the river to the woods. Tom made no notice at first but realized Sagar was not just staring vacantly, he was listening. Not wanting to distract him, Tom remained motionless, but still heard nothing.

Shrugging his shoulders very slightly, Sagar stood up, walked over to the launch, peered under the seats, and made his way to Tom as if wandering aimlessly. With his back to the woods, he crouched down next to the schoolteacher and mouthed the words, "We are being watched." Tom nodded. He understood there was little they could do but wait for the dawn, or for those observing them to attack or move on. Nathan remained asleep while Sagar and Tom kept vigil. "They've gone, Mr. Tom," Sagar finally said. After quickly traversing the surrounding area he return and continued, "There were no more than three of them. I do not believe they meant us harm. Probably sent to keep watch or learn if we traveled alone." Relief washed over Tom, leaving only exhaustion. The eastern sky grew deep blue, then pale and soon enough the morning was upon them. They woke Nathan and after a breakfast of hard brown bread and water they departed for the eastern shore.

CHAPTER 18 - March 1603

They returned to camp just before breakfast and found a quiet commotion on the deck of the ship, which spilled into the camp. No sooner had they pulled up to shore before Tom jumped out to see what was the matter, leaving Nathan and Sagar to unload the launch. Sagar's grave circumspection went unnoticed by Nathan.

"Sagar, what did you make of the natives? Friendly, I thought, and what food!" Nate said casually from the back of the launch while throwing a rucksack to Sagar, who stood on shore. He added, "And you know, you could pass for one of them, how do you pick up their language so quickly?"

Sagar smiled at Nate's observations. Trying not to dampen his enthusiasm, Sagar replied, "I've found, wherever there are men, there are good men. As for their language, a few words is all I know, but mostly, I just watched how they said things and what they pointed to." Catching another rucksack from Nathan, he continued, "Your father enjoyed himself too. He's always trying to teach, isn't he?"

Nathan rolled his eyes at Sagar's last comment. "Try living with him. Asking questions, leading us to some known conclusion. My life is a big lesson plan, but last night, it sure helped us, didn't it? I never imagined those hours spent at music practice would be worth anything. It's like he knew."

"He is a wise man, your father. He knew to prepare you for the unknown. Last night, he knew that strength does not always make the best impression. There are those among us who would do well to learn this lesson," said Sagar. The two of them pulled the launch onto the grass and parted ways. Nathan wondered how Sagar could so easily switch from unassuming adolescent to tiny sage. Passing several visibly upset congregants on the way to the ship, Nathan caught up with his youngest brother, who was looking for their mother. He whispered to

Nathan, "Reverend Williams has passed away." They both continued on to find Susan. Like everyone else, Nathan knew Williams had been sick and had seldom been seen over the past month but Tom's eldest son hadn't contemplated that the reverend would not live on.

Sagar searched for the twins. He felt time compressing; critical events were unfolding in sharp succession as if accelerated through an ever-narrowing pipe. He found Shikha feeding the animals, now kept in a makeshift pen south of the ship. She looked content with the ducks and chickens, whispering affectionately to them. The two horses gazed at her absently. Although he didn't announce his approach, with her back to him she said, "Don't worry so, Sagar." She turned to him now and held out her hand. He readily took it. "You have done well for us, for all of us. Your time is now, and you have stitched the pieces together admirably. You come to tell me that the natives across the river might welcome us, but there is uncertainty which weighs heavy on your brow. There is always uncertainty. Slow your breathing, slow your thinking. The pathways, however difficult, will reveal themselves. I tell you this in hopes that when my time for action comes, you may counsel me the same."

Sagar looked into the woods beyond Shikha. During last night's adventure, he hadn't noticed nature awakening from her winter slumber. But now, standing in the moist air warmed by the rising sun he realized the maples had flowered, the forest canopy grew dense, and the deep green grasses lining the river were over a foot high. Sagar closed his eyes, concentrating on his breathing. A slight sweetness filled his nostrils. Opening his eyes again Sagar whispered, "I don't recognize these maples, the ones with shaggy bark. Next time I visit the natives west of the river, I shall ask about them." He turned to face Shikha more directly and chuckled. "I am like the winds, first a northern tempest, then a southern whisper. You are like the river, smooth, running silent and with purpose. You do not need my counsel, young Shikha."

"Perhaps not today, but it will come," she said. Her effervescence always refreshed Sagar's brooding mind. Turning back to feeding the animals, Shikha left Sagar to his thoughts. He ambled through the camp, eventually reaching the Spring Tide. In the captain's eyes Tom and his son had simply been along as oarsmen, so Sagar felt it was upon him to inform Tanner of their findings. Sagar would state the facts, but avoid recounting their experiences and the length to which they went to foster good relations. Tanner was looking for numbers, an enemy headcount, and Sagar would not try to dissuade him from his course, not directly anyway.

The ship swarmed with congregants and for once Sagar felt unnoticed. He first went below deck to find Mary. Being treated like a boy sometimes made it easier to act like one, but Sagar had always found their relationship somewhat artificial, and when he began living in the officers' quarters, Mary was content to see him assisting her father rather than playing her son. Still, she had always treated him kindly and he was grateful to her. When he and the twins had traveled across the deserts of the Near East many of the other children were placed in caravans with families as little more than indentured servants.

Sagar found Mary talking with a woman he didn't recognize. Mary's back was to him and as he approached, the sour looking woman wrinkled her nose at him as if she smelled something putrid. Mary turned and hesitated at his presence. Throwing an irritated glance to her adopted son, she said to him, "Oh, there you are, boy. Mrs. Gaither and I are talking just now. You best find the captain. He heard you were back from one of your travels." She readdressed Mrs. Gaither and continued as if he wasn't there.

Having been dismissed, Sagar knew he should speak to the captain but wasn't quite ready. He stood at the captain's door, recognizing several voices on the other side. His first reaction was to leave but he heard the meeting inside breaking up. Sagar quickly knocked at the door lest it open and those inside think he was eavesdropping. The door swung wide. A bleary-eyed Reverend Smith, James and, surprisingly, Harold Gaither filed out. Each in turn gazed down at Sagar as they passed, James giving him a nod and a faint smile.

Sagar entered, finding an exhaustedTanner slouching at the table. A bottle of wine sat near his left arm, empty. "Williams is dead, poor fellow. I reckon you heard. Smith is much changed and I'm not sure what to make of it. He kept talking about his, what was it, total depravity? Says he has spiritually awoken. Harold had come to me early this morning to talk about Smith and the running of the camp now that Williams is gone. Gaither is a blustery fellow, but at least he and his kin are for staying. Harold says Smith is bent on stirring everyone up to return to England. They've made good progress on their, well, I guess it's a compound on the far side of camp," Tanner said.

Sagar discounted this path back to England as a possibility, believing it unlikely. Something was askew. Still, Tanner needed support. "Captain, I don't know if we could make it back. Even with Jorge still with us, we would be hard pressed to find our way," he replied.

"I told them as much, my boy. We're staying. You might not know this, but this ship, she belongs to Tom Robbin. So, it would be up to him, at least in large part," the captain said. Sagar knew that after last night's adventure, Tom would never leave this land. His passion for knowledge had been stoked afresh, and burned hot as a blacksmith's forge. Tanner continued, "What can you tell us of natives to the west?"

Sagar measured his thoughts, and began, "Crossing the river posed some difficultly. Mid-river, the current runs at three to four knots. The row exhausted Tom and his son and once we thought we would be swept much farther downriver, possibly into the sea. We spotted no easy landing sites on the west bank, it being guarded by deep thickets of reeds. We traversed the reeds and moved inland. Just before nightfall we came upon a village about three miles from the river. Tom and Nathan remained hidden while I surveyed the lands beyond. Three enclaves clustered around a small stream, one east of the little river, two west. I cannot say if they are part of a single community, but their proximity makes it likely."

At this point Tanner interrupted Sagar, "How many natives did you count?"

Coolly continuing, Sagar said, "In all I saw 18 huts, more like long, squat houses. If they serve as living quarters, as many at 20 natives could fit in one, I estimate. If they are used more for storage, then one hut would serve one family. It was after dark and their fires burned low. Only a few natives remained out in the open. A few children, two women, the rest were men of varying ages. One very old man with skin like ancient sailcloth sat apart, drawing pictures in the dirt. At most, close to 200 natives, Captain, but more likely the number only approaches 100."

"Good lad. And defenses? Or weapons?" Tanner blurted.

"No visible defenses, sir. There may have been lookouts in the trees or on the far side of the villages, but if there were, none saw me and I saw none. As for material weapons, nothing to note," Sagar replied. The captain had his head down but nodded, acknowledging the comment. Sagar waited for about 30 seconds, "Sir, would you suggest I return for more information or remain here until after Reverend Williams' service? There will be a service, won't there?" His words caught Tanner off guard, and the aged seafarer sat whispering to himself.

"Service, hmm. Oh, yes. And it might be best if you made yourself scarce for that. Harold tells me that while he personally thinks the best of you, there are others who are beyond convincing that you, or was it those twins, have cast a spell upon the congregants. I can't remember. Too many thing to remember now." Tanner looked out the porthole. "The simple times are long past, where all I hoped for was the wind in my sails pushing me home to Mary and a loyal crew working as hard as I would."

Sagar leaned in over the table. He slowly slid the bottle away from the captain's hand and spoke, "Captain, sir, you still have one remaining crew member and he is loyal. I will leave camp during Reverend Williams' burial. But you are right. The simple times as you say are past: be wary of those who seek to counsel you. I always trusted your own judgment. You should as well."

Sagar left the captain to his thoughts and the remnants of his wine bottle. As he departed, Reverend Smith stood near the door, returning once again to the captain's quarters and for the first time he was downright courteous to the boy. Nodding his head and standing aside, he said, "Hallo, young Sagar." Sagar looked up at him and saw no trace of the man with fiery eyes he first encountered in Rotterdam. Tanner was right on one point: Smith had changed and as Sagar returned the salutation, he scrutinized the reverend, clearly sensing that Smith wasn't set on leaving. He walked with determination. Harold had lied to the captain and was likely using the change in Smith's attitude as an excuse to consolidate his power in the congregation.

From the deck he spotted Tom in camp. Sagar leisurely covered the distance between them, pausing at the bottom of the gangplank and again in the center of camp. Where once a small watchfire burned only at night, now a continuous smoky blaze fueled by green wood, remnants of clearing land, had carved a black crater in the ground. Next to the raging fire had been placed a sharpening wheel where presently Henry Mason sat honing the edge of an axe dull from felling trees. When Sagar passed him, Henry looked up from his work with an executioner's grim smile, making the boy wonder if it were the trees or Sagar who was the condemned.

Sagar found Tom sorting through a large trunk of books, no doubt considering which volumes to share with Quniyokat, the native chief. "So you spoke with Tanner? What did he make of our encounter?" Tom asked.

"The captain was distracted. I shared only what he sought to hear, the number of natives we observed and the nature of their settlements. He sent me not to make contact but to spy. Mr. Tom, he asked me to leave the village until after Reverend Williams' funeral and I—" Sagar said, before Tom interrupted.

"What? Why? That's absurd. I always felt that Reverend Williams thought kindly of you."

"It was in part my suggestion. Mr. Tom, my path lies west. Captain Tanner had met with Smith and one of the Gaithers just before I spoke with him. He no longer thinks for himself, but is content to take others' opinions as truth," Sagar replied. "He now believes rumors that the Twins and I have cursed the congregation."

"He believes there are rumors, or he believes the rumors are true? There is a big difference," Tom shot back.

"There is little difference. A man either stands for truth or he does not," Sagar whispered. "I will return but this camp is fast becoming a dangerous place for me and those who I am fortunate enough to call friends." Tom began to respond, but Sagar put his hand up and shook his head. He smiled at Tom, recognizing what the schoolteacher was about to say. Sagar headed off into the woods. Tom watched him disappear into the intensifying overgrowth of spring.

Tom was unaware that Faria and Shikha were also watching Sagar as he left. They had observed the brief exchange from the southern edge of camp and without uttering a single word between them, took to unified action. The girls hurried onto the ship and careful to avoid notice took two hammocks they had constructed long ago in the voyage and refashioned them into a long narrow bag with anchor points at each end. Shikha measured the bag's length and returned to the center of camp where the brush pile set for burning grew ever larger. She searched for a narrow but straight branch. Finding the perfect limb, she boldly asked Henry Mason, still at the sharpening wheel, to cut it to length for her, if he would please. He rose slowly, and letting out an ugly laugh, cleaved the maple branch with one blow of his axe. She set the longer branch aside and searched for two smaller branches, each with three prongs at one end. Satisfied with her selections, she dragged the limbs to the animal pen.

Meanwhile, Faria tracked down a few inconsequential supplies from the now-depleted galley. Most families were cooking their own food on shore, and while searching, she reflected on the changes in the congregants since the loss of communal living. Their single clan, bound by the confines of the voyage and by Williams himself, had splintered. The anchor of their community would be interred that evening, with Smith providing a eulogy. Smith had insisted that the gravestone be ready, unaware of the effort it would take to locate, dress and carve a five-foot granite stone. Abby had told the girls they should attend but remain on the periphery with the Robbin boys rather than with her and George.

Only a few hours remained of daylight when the twins met

again at the animal pen. They had assembled quite a menagerie of objects, two of which Faria kept close to her in a fold of her shawl. Shikha had filled the long bag with grass from the riverside and tiny flowers she found growing at the forest's edge. They strung the bag lengthwise on the long branch and ascertained that, with one of them on each end, carrying it required little effort. The twins scurried off to find Miss Abby. As she often did, their adoptive mother greeted them with mock anger, followed by big-sisterly love. "I haven't seen you two all day! Did you do any work at all, or were you cavorting around the forest like pixies?"

"Oh there was some cavorting, but mostly we worked. I cleaned the animal pens and Faria helped Mrs. Bray remove the last of the pots from the ship's galley. It's nearly as bare as when we left Amsterdam," Shikha piped up. Faria solemnly nodded in agreement. George had been so eager to move off the ship that their house, if it could yet be called that, was well in advance of any of the other congregants'. The four of them currently shared the smallest room in what George had planned as a modest three-room home. He had set to work each morning just before dawn and in such an orderly fashion that he and Abby hadn't spoken more than a few words a day in weeks. This suited him just fine, as he found much to be pleased with in his carpentry.

After changing their clothes, the four of them, two and two, departed for Reverend Williams' funeral. They met the Robbins on the way and the children fell to the back, Tom and George next with Abby and Susan leading their procession. Tom, Susan and Abby had become close friends and while George did not mind the three of them chattering about old languages and inscriptions late into the night, he would rather spend his evenings sleeping. One language was enough for him. Susan and Abby conversed in hushed tones but Tom and George remained quiet with Tom occasionally turning to keep his boys in check.

Most of the congregants had assembled and the late arrivals found themselves standing with the children. Since their landing, when not tending to Williams, Reverend Smith busied himself by laying out a meticulous and grandiose church design near the center of camp. In its current state, this consisted of many strings crisscrossing the muddy ground marking the footprint of the house of worship. Adjacent to this cat's cradle Smith stood alone, a four-by-eight-foot hole dug in the ground to his left. He fidgeted for a few moments and then removed his tall black hat, causing all the men to remove theirs in kind.

Composing himself, Smith looked up at the gathered crowd, scanning the expectant eyes now focused on him. "We have gathered to lay our most kind friend and righteous leader, the Reverend Philip Williams, to rest. We, who have emerged from our ship just as Noah after the deluge, may have easy hearts, content in the beautiful truth of his election in Christ. As Paul told the Ephesians, so was Reverend Williams chosen in Him before the foundation of the world, that he should be holy and without blame. Surely, look to yourselves, and to the aged and weary body of our reverend; if any of us were predestined to redemption through His blood according to the riches of His Grace, first among us was Philip Williams." Smith paused and dropped his head for a moment.

Smith returned his gaze to the congregants. His eyes reddened and weary, nevertheless, a strength born of revelation illuminated his face. "Reverend Williams tried to teach me many things during his life. Some came easy for me. Others, as I now realize, such as the scriptures' true meaning, evaded my understanding. My sufferings in this life have been mere trifles in comparison to those of our Lord Christ, yet I bore them not by seeking His comfort but in elevating myself in selfish ignorance. Before God, my mentor Philip Williams, and all of you, I humbly ask forgiveness." Warm tears streamed down Smith's face as he spoke but he grinned in self-reflection, laughing at the man he had been, no doubt realizing that the congregants had laughed at him too. "We have lost the physical presence of our spiritual leader, but the seeds of his teachings have finally found purchase in me as I know they have in many of you. I give thanks to Reverend Philip Williams for his patience with an obstinate pupil, for his compassion toward all he encountered, and his unerring faith in our mission here in the new lands."

Smith took his place beside the simple wooden coffin. With quiet instruction from James, he helped lower it into the first grave of their settlement, using the rough ropes from the ship. As the pine box found the earth, a gentle rain began to fall.

CHAPTER 19 - March 29, 1603

Three days after Reverend Williams' funeral the twins woke early, before George and Abby. Gathering the supplies they had stashed by the animal pens, the girls entered the woods under the eyes of the setting moon and rising sun. After walking a short while they came upon a low clearing where the forest floor was soft and flat. "The belly button of the forest, what better spot could there be? Miss Abby will be so pleased with us. Let's get started, and we can surprise her. Do you suppose she would like Susan to come too?" Shikha said.

"They have become quite close, but this, this is something different. It is up to our mother, not us. She grows so quickly," Faria replied. Dropping her end of the wooden branch to the ground, she emptied the long bag, made from hammocks, piling the fresh green grass of spring. Both girls searched the adjacent groves for flowers, returning again and again, arms full of the reds, blues and yellows of spring. Within an hour the colorful testament to the forest's rebirth rested high upon the bed of fresh grasses. "So who shall it be this year, Parvati or Shiva?" Shikha asked her sister.

With her fingers on her lips, Faria said, "Parvati, I think. I can sing her part so much better." They took positions on opposite sides of the mound and began to sing a slow duet. Shikha began in a lower tone, that of Shiva, to which Faria sung back in reply, as Parvati. Singing as one, their voices grew, softened and finally ebbed from a whisper into silence.

The girls stood, eyes closed in the morning sun, their measured breathing just slightly discernible in the gentle breeze. After a few minutes the girls opened their eyes and set to work on building a tripod across the mound of flowers, using the smaller branches carried from camp.

Once completed, Faria removed two small clay figures from

her dress pocket, handing the one resembling a man to her sister. Shikha gave a deliberate nod in receipt and placed it in a crook of one of the branches. Faria positioned the one she kept next to it and delicately joined their arms with a thin blade of grass. The girls stepped backward from the tripod, still facing it but with heads lowered until they were a few yards away. Turning, they disappeared into the woods. Through the heavily canopied forest, Faria and Shikha joyfully wandered back to camp.

Abby awoke to find the girls gone but marking that their makeshift bed, a nest of blankets, had been tidied, she knew they had chosen to leave the house early rather than in haste. Abby also noticed several eggs had been placed in a bowl for breakfast. One of the many advantages of having a daughter who took care of the congregation's chickens was the steady supply of eggs. George ate a cold breakfast of bread and boiled eggs, wordlessly departing to strip logs in the center of camp. Abby wondered if he even noticed the twins' absence. A knock came at the door, a knock on the wall anyway, for in the house's unfinished state a heavy rug still hung in the doorway. A familiar face peeked in; it was Susan. Abby waved her in.

"My goodness, what luxury! We're still in tents, living as soldiers on campaign," Susan said. It had become her common refrain each time she came over. She plopped down on one of the tree stumps serving as a seat, and untying a burlap package revealed a weathered book. It looked to have been rebound several times. The pages were of different sizes, as if aggregated from several earlier works. "I found this in a small leather chest that Tom had tucked away. He said Reverend Williams placed it in his care just before the voyage. I suppose it belongs to Tom now. Unfortunately, most of the book is in Latin and other languages I don't even recognize. There are, however, some interesting illuminated sections."

Onboard ship, the two had spent hours deep in the hold searching Tom's library for hints as to the origins and meaning of the strange alphabet. Abby slowly remembered more episodes from her youth and together they had reached a few tenuous conclusions. Abby's parents, they knew, had emigrated from Ireland where her mother must have learned the ancient script. Abby now recalled sitting by the hearth before bedtime while her mother inscribed the sharp characters into the thinly spread ashes of the fire. She would sing to her young daughter in an unfamiliar tongue. At times, her mother would grow animated, as if recounting an adventure, and at other times, she would sing in a whisper, clutching her daughter's hand. Abby and Susan surmised that the words were Old Irish or Gaelic. Patient questioning by the schoolteacher's wife allowed Abby to pull more and more from her past. They referenced her memories against what resources they had on Irish mythology and modern languages. One phrase in a few forms, returned in the words of her mother time and again: Danu.

That Abby's mother was retelling her daughter the Celtic epics of the Tuatha Dé Danann, or, the people of Danu, became their working hypothesis. Their most reliable source, a heavily bound red tome published just before they had departed England described Danu as the pagan mother goddess of the Celts and the Tuatha De as her descendants or tribe. It quoted several excerpts from the Lebor na Nuachongbála, a 12th century Irish monastic work, which listed the names of the Tuatha De, their mythical gifts and their deeds.

When Abby and eventually Susan had questioned the twins about the hammocks, they gave truthful, but simple answers. They knitted them for protection; they knew certain patterns and when to use them but not the meaning of any individual character or series of knots. They were just as perplexed and frustrated as Abby and Susan that they could not remember how they came about their knowledge of the Ogham alphabet.

What remained unsaid between Susan and Abby was not due to a lack of trust, but rather sprang from a deep well of empathy and consideration. Each time Susan felt she was pushing Abby too far, she backed off. Each time Abby did not wish to burden Susan with her memories or troubles, she grew silent. They both realized the twins were not like other children, almost not children at all; they both grew troubled by Abby's memories of her mother and father, of the seeming formality of her mother's teaching and her father's distance.

Susan began leafing through the pages of her most recent find, a black-hide book in a small chest of Williams, now Tom's property. Some of the pages Abby reckoned were paper, others animal parchment, and the most weathered were a form of crushed reeds. "One might mistake the ink for still being wet, the colors are so vibrant," Susan mentioned without looking up. A flowing, melodious script accompanied some of the images, but it was unfamiliar to the women. "Look at these fellows, without shirts on, and praying to a blue man with a crown emerging from a giant fish," Susan continued, turning the page, "and again the massive fish leading a boat through a storm."

She kept turning the sheets until they changed from animal parchment to stained and decaying pressed reeds. All in monotone, they discovered page upon page of sharp imprints, arranged in neat lines. The lines were occasionally broken by omissions, as if the text had been copied from an incomplete document. Few images existed, but near the end of the section, they came upon a rough depiction of a man surrounded by several animals in pairs. "Is that Noah?" Abby said, unsure if the man's surroundings were an elongated branch framing the scene or a stylized ship."

"I doubt it. I know a bit of Latin, and thanks to my grandfather's patience, can at least recognize Hebrew, and the language around this image is neither," Susan replied, disappointing Abby. Just then, the room flooded with light, for the blanket door had been pulled back. The twins burst in. Surprised to see Susan, their excitement collapsed into caution.

Unsure how to proceed, they stood stiffly until Abby said, "you two have been up to something this morning, haven't you? You could have at least told me last night that you planned to leave the house early. I needn't have worried." The twins knew her well enough to play along.

"Oh, Miss Abby, we had many things to attend to and didn't wish to wake you at such an early hour," replied Faria.

"And are you prepared to tell us what needed attention in the wee hours of the morning?" Abby volleyed back. Shikha approached

her and, gesturing for her to lean in, whispered into her adoptive mother's ear: "The river swells, the green grass rustles, the forest, she is alive. We must all observe the rights of the season."
Abby stood up and looked down at the dark haired girl. She realized that this was not a request, but an instruction. Shikha stared at Abby. Unblinking, she flicked her eyes toward Susan, and back to her mother. Abby understood. She replied by nodding.

"Susan, the twins wish to share something with us. Something private, something sacred. Can they take you into their confidence?" Abby said.

"Why, yes. Yes, of course, upon your lead, Abby," Susan replied, but all three of them sensed a subtle hesitation in her voice. Susan knew she and Abby had done nothing more than read books and talk. So far. She knew some of the congregants whispered about their friendship and her patrician naiveté led her to conclude that the truth would always triumph over rumors. Yet the way Abby said the word sacred, it became active, participatory.

"Perhaps you better stay here, Susan," Abby said.

"No, I'd like to come," Susan responded. She smiled and said, "I'd like to learn." The rhythmic cadence of axes striking live trunks, slow sawing and men stomping about camp filtered dully through the walls of the cabin, making the dim room feel a great distance away from the activity all around the four of them.

Faria and Shikha walked through the doorway and held the rug back so that Abby and Susan could pass. The four of them left camp together. Usually the twins moved at a gallop, but today they weaved through the trees at a slow, methodical pace, leading the women as though in a procession. The gentle mid-morning light found its way to the forest floor where compressed pine needles cushioned their every step. Susan thought the stand of tall hemlocks they traversed felt most welcoming this day.

Surrounded by the vivid evidence of nature's annual consummation, Abby knew what rites they would practice even before reaching the clearing or speaking with her adopted daughters. Thousands of miles separated the twins' and her birthplace, surely the names and nuances would be different, but it was Whitsuntide, and the May Queen would have her husband. Abby would never ask them to abandon their beliefs or to betray the common lineage humanity shares with nature. Not like Father Brenton forced her to years ago, not like her parents, who acquiesced. Maybe they knew she would fight, maybe they were just trying to protect her; yes, to remain unnoticed is to remain safe. But a life of safety, Abby thought, is no life at all. Not for her. The seed that prematurely germinated in her long ago and had lain dormant for years was reawakened, nourished by the voyage.

The twins guided them into the crisp light of a broad grassy field. Lower in the center than the edges it probably kept the forest at bay by serving as a temporary lake a few months a year. It reminded Susan of a navel. Abby stopped short and turning back to the woods she caught sight of a flickering female presence, but this time, no anxiety, no ill will overcame her. Shikha grasped Abby's right hand, Faria took he left, and also softly clasped Susan's delicate fingers. The twins led the women into the center where their wooden tripod stood, beneath it overflowed the tiny, sweet-smelling flowers and grasses. The two clay figures nestled in the nook of one of the branches as they had left them, bound to one another. Circling the tripod, the twins resumed their duet from earlier that morning, encouraging the women to join them in song. Among the leafy trees along the perimeter of the clearing mingled three tree spirits, Dryads drawn to the melodies of the twins.

After several turns, Faria dropped Abby's hand and Shikha led her mother to the far side of the circle, leaving Faria and Susan together. Facing one another across the circle the twins began a liturgical dialogue in their native language. While neither Susan nor Abby understood the words they found the exchanges between the girls melodic and soothing. They were not the only forest denizens affected by the sounds.

The Dryads drew closer and circled the small ceremony as leaves kicked up by a soft wind. Abby closed her eyes, neither fearful nor on guard, but comforted by their presence. In that moment, she recalled the words that had dispersed the vengeful spirits from the camp: Sisters, forgive this trespass and grant these people, lives so brief, their chance. Abby didn't understand her own words, but the thought dropped easily from her mind. Clutching Shikha's warm hand, she felt her daughter's heart beating very nearly in time with the words the little twins uttered. The twins transitioned their chant into a recessional hymn, which Susan and Abby found themselves singing as well.

Rising from a tempered chorus into a boisterous cheer the twins passionately sang a last decisive word in unison. After which Faria raised her hands and looking up at Susan, her face radiating joy, beamed, "Parvati has proven herself worthy, and is once again reunited with Lord Shiva. In their union, we can be sure of a bountiful year!" She skipped to the tripod and grasping the figures, returned to Susan, placing them in her still open palm. Their departure prompted the spirits to close in on the tripod, making three turns around it before returning to the clearing's edge.

Susan breathed in the grove's majesty. The tall hemlocks lining the near side of the clearing swayed easy, the fatherly oaks on the far side stood resolute but all welcomed her and the others' into in the navel of the forest. Susan's sterile experiences with religion in England had never connected her with those around her the way this day had. She didn't claim to fully perceive what just transpired, yet standing in the warm air she had the strongest conviction in her life of a creator, of a world in which humanity was meant to be but one participant. How difficult it was for some to understand, she reflected, that we exist not to command, but to revere.

On the way back to camp, Faria and Shikha were their normal selves again, running ahead of the women, playing among the rough granite boulders and circling back behind Abby and Susan to try to surprise them. Far beyond earshot of the adults, Faria said to her sister, "Do you suppose either of them knew we were being watched by both spirit and man?" Shikha shook her head, none too concerned with the statement.

"Miss Abby, perhaps, but I think we should remain silent on

the subject. It will surface soon enough. What matters most is that they both shared in the ceremony. Their bond will make the transition much easier for Abby," Shikha replied.

"Yes, there is little left for her within the confines of the congregation," Faria reflected.

When they drew closer to camp, the twins fell in behind the women, allowing them to lead the way across the threshold between forest and cleared land. Several hours had passed and hungry from their walk, they made straight for the house where Abby began laying out a late lunch. Susan unshelled the remaining boiled eggs and the twins went to fetch fresh water. Abby glided about the small house, her mind now clear of so many shadows. She and Susan didn't talk of the woods but returned to chatting lightly about the images in the most recent volume Susan had found. The twins reemerged, out of breath, with two great pails of cold water and they all sat to enjoy their lunch.

Just as they were about to adjourn, George entered, throwing the rug door aside in a broad sweep of his arm. With the bright sun at his back, they couldn't see his face but Abby stood, motioning him to join them. He kept his distance. Never a subtle man, he blurted out, "Mason saw you four in the woods, said you were up to something. He's fetching Smith, the captain and Gaither. Says he's bringing 'em here."

Susan had her back to the door but, still seated, she turned to him and said, "Even from over there in the doorway, surely you can see we don't have enough food for all of them." The sharpness of her voice cut into him as only a woman of the landed gentry could. Deflated, he remained motionless, trying to think of what to say. She gave him little time to respond. "Still, if we are to have company, Faria, could you please invite my husband and my eldest son Nathan to join us as well?" Faria leapt from the table and flew out of the house like a bat escaping a cave.

Abby was still standing and as her eyes adjusted to the light she looked dispassionately at her husband. She felt almost nothing for him, except perhaps pity. For their entire marriage, Abby had convinced herself she wasn't good enough for him, that she was broken. But really,

George didn't deserve someone better, just someone different. When they met, Abby had few alternatives and for years George's lack of curiosity had been convenient.

They waited; Abby began cleaning the table and Shikha helped her. Susan tidied the dark book she had brought over, retying it quite securely in the burlap sack and tucking it behind a chest in the far corner. George paced the room and moments later Tom Robbin entered. "Susan, young Faria fetched me, saying I was to come quickly. Are you okay, is something wrong? Nate will be here straightaway." He noticed George in the darkness and greeted him awkwardly, "Oh, hello, George." George grunted. Instinctively, Susan moved closer to her husband, not unnoticed by Abby. The schoolteacher's wife refused to return Abby's gaze, instead looking at the floor.

Abandonment fears crept into Abby's mind. She just now realized she cared more for Susan's friendship than for her own marriage, and she just might lose both right now. So easy did doubt cloud her thinking. She had trusted Susan like no other and quickly Abby readied herself to be cast aside.

Susan took a breath and gave Abby the subtlest wink, which conveyed more than any words could have. "Tom, we're all fine. Abby and I accompanied her twins into the woods earlier today. They offered to show us a dance from their homeland, and courtesy demanded we accept. Sadly, that brilliant critic of native cultures, Henry Mason, espied us. I can't imagine he came upon our festivities by chance, but once again he has gone telling tales, and is rousing the captain, Reverend Smith and one of the Gaither clan." Tom realized his wife was already on the offensive, and read enough into her word selection to grow concerned. It wasn't her judgment he questioned though, rather the potential reaction of the congregants.

"George, what do you make of all this?" Tom said, turning back to the carpenter.

Since entering the house, George had been holding in many thoughts but finally he burst: "Mason's been talking of witchery for a while and says now he has the proof. His boy's been following 'em. We lost Jorge, then Reverend Williams. And that Sagar. Where's he off to each night? And these twin girls, I never should have taken them in. Cursed, is what they is. And my own Abby, pushing it all. Seen it all right here. I've had enough of it, Tom, and you best look to your wife. She might've been bewitched." George's face reddened as he babbled. It was the most he had ever said in one breath and his mouth looked exhausted from speaking.

Faria entered as he finished, moving beside her sister and Abby on the far side of the table. On her heels trailed Captain Tanner, Henry Mason, Harold Gaither and Reverend Smith, none of whom heard George's diatribe. After they had filed in, Tanner began, "Abigail, Mr. Mason here was out surveying beyond the camp this morning and claims to have observed you and your girls leading a pagan ritual in the woods. Further, he brought evidence that Faria had been preparing for this ritual for days." Smirking, Mason held up the sticks the girls had assembled in the woods. Tanner continued. "These are strange lands. We can't have our women wandering the woods unaccompanied. The influence of the primitive landscape could persuade a woman to actions she normally would not consider. Abigail, see here, your history is against you." Looking for support, Tanner deferred to Harold Gaither, who stepped forward.

"We all have it on good authority that at a young age, you abandoned your parents, refused to repent your blasphemous ways, and have persisted, without remorse, in violating the moral teachings of the Church. Now, we have learned that you and your dark children have tried to recruit an upstanding member of our congregation into your cabal. It is too much. If Reverend Williams were still with us, and I am not the only one to wonder if you and yours had a hand in his death, he would demand action." Herb spat his accusations. Gaither was about to continue when Reverend Smith interrupted him, surprising everyone in the room.

"Let us not be hasty," Smith said from the back of the room. "While it is true that we have lost our dear Reverend Williams, we have not lost his wise counsel. At least I have not. Having nursed and ministered to him through his last days, I can assure you all that our reverend's death was according to His plan, and for Williams' part, he welcomed the sweet release from his mortal body. Now, Miss Abigail, pray, tell us what this is all about. If we are to act, as some would have us, in accordance with Reverend Williams' wishes, let us begin with your words."

The change in Reverend Smith since Williams' death had been so abrupt, so fundamental, that none of them expected him to be Abby's advocate. Yet here he stood, a soft, curious smile on his face, his eyebrows raised as if waiting for someone to explain to him how a clock worked. Abby feared not for herself or the twins but only for Susan. She wasn't sure how to respond, only that she had grown weary of hiding who she was and that whatever she said must not implicate or betray her best friend. With Shikha and Faria gathered close, Abby began to speak by first addressing Smith.

"Reverend Smith, thank you. I don't understand the holy scriptures as you do, so forgive me, please, if I misspeak on their intent." She scanned the room, focusing on Mason and Gaither. "My words cannot quell rumors, and I won't try to disprove the falsehoods spoken about my past. The creator tests us all, some more harshly than others. I believe that through those trials, we learn humility, we learn service. We begin to understand, through our flawed existence, the compassion that the creator has for us so that in small part, we can care for others. Some never learn, they remain unaware and unchanged by the work of a higher power."

"I did run away from home. I was an arrogant and cruel young girl. I struggled and fought when all along, the right path was so clear. When George and I adopted the twins, we did so because I knew I could not bear him any children and that we must contribute to the congregation. I had another reason. I wanted to make the path for a motherless and fatherless child easier than it was for me. In my arrogance, I thought I had more to teach than to learn. It turns out I have learned more from them, these two, than they from me." Abby's calm smile embraced the twins, who clung to her simple dress.

Addressing Captain Tanner, Abby said, "Captain, perhaps you are right that this land is strange. It possesses something that has long faded from our old home. The mark of creation still dwells heavy in the rivers, in the woods and in the marshes of this place. What my daughters and I were doing in the woods, if you all must know, was celebrating the land itself, giving thanks for its rebirth, and praying for its continued bounty. Not so strange, is it? Susan happened to be at our house when we departed, and she politely accompanied us, as one might expect from such a kind woman. If Mr. Mason finds our actions, observed whilst hiding behind a tree like a little boy, objectionable, so be it, but Susan's participation, to be sure, was out of pure courtesy."

"Now, see here!" started Mason, but Abby stopped him.

"It makes little difference, really. We are leaving, the twins and I. Like you said, Captain Tanner, this primitive landscape has persuaded me to actions I normally would never have considered. Call it banishment. Call me a witch. Call me what you like. You're rid of us now," Abby barked at the lot of them. She glided across the room directly to Reverend Smith, twins trailing her like shadows. Taking him by the hand she said in the quietest voice: "Thank you, Father. Please pray for us and I will most certainly pray for you and the congregation."

Abby stormed from the half-finished home, leaving those gathered awestruck and standing in the darkness, the twins in her wake. Susan slumped into a chair but looking out the doorway saw the three of them heading for the woods and realized Abby was leaving straightaway. She nearly jumped to her feet but thought better of it. She needed to speak with Tom first.

A short distance into the woods they met Nathan Robbin lounging against a tree with four overstuffed rucksacks. "I'm sure I forgot something, but there's food, blankets, rope, two hatchets and a lantern full of oil, careful with it. Oh, and I have a tent!" Abby herself had not known they would be leaving, the idea just grew inside her as she spoke, so how could Nate have possibly . . . Faria had known.

"I asked him to meet us here with supplies, instead of coming to the house," Faria said, replying to Abby's thought. "Just in case," she added.

"Ladies, I am at your service. Which direction?" Nate said, shouldering two of the packs. He clearly intended to come with them.

Abby's disordered mind couldn't fully process what just transpired. She was still shaking. She needed time to think. Abby wanted to tell Nathan to return to camp, but instead said, "Whatever way you think best, Nathan."

"Let's follow the river north a spell. Maybe I can catch some fish for supper," he replied, picking up a third pack. He handed the fourth to Abby, who took it from him. Nathan then matter-of-factly set off at a brisk pace. They walked single file for a mile or so and as Abby's mind cleared, she stepped up beside Nathan.

"Nate, the twins and I are leaving the congregation. For good," she said. Nathan shrugged, as much as one can shrug while carrying three rucksacks. Abby continued, "Thank you for helping but you must return to camp before you are missed and others realize you aided us." Nathan was at that unideal age where he was quite capable of taking completely unreasonable risks, yet incapable of understanding their longer-term consequences.

"Return to chop trees and strip logs? No, thank you. And besides, what do you think mother would say?" Nate could endlessly amuse his younger brothers by mimicking their mother. Scrunching his face, he screamed, "You what? You left them in the woods? Alone?" Returning to his normal voice he continued, "If you'd like me to return, I will, Miss Abby, but first let me help you get settled somewhere. And I'll need you to sign some kind of note to prove to my mother that you insisted."

Abby chuckled. His impression of Susan was quite good. Abby wished she had been able to speak with Susan before leaving camp, but it would have put her at further risk. They walked another few miles when Nathan slowed, putting distance between the twins and he and Abby. She could tell he was thinking about something, but she gave him time to gather his words.

"Miss Abby, do you think my father is a smart man?" he started.

"Why, one of the smartest, in fact, the smartest I've met," she replied.

"And do you think he is capable of laying out a cabin, planning its construction, and building it? With the help of me and my brothers."

"Of course, Nathan. I expect he would enjoy the challenge of it," Abby responded. "Is this what you wanted to ask me, about your father's carpentry skills?"

"Not exactly, but yes. Have you noticed that everyone else in camp has made good progress on their home, excepting our family? Despite the lumber my brothers and I have piled, we still live in tents," he said, gazing into the woods.

She was trying to follow the young man's logic but did not grasp his meaning. "It is the first time he has built a house, and from what your mother has told me, the first time he has done such rough work," she said.

"True enough on both fronts, but I think there's something more to it," Nate said. He paused for a moment. "I think he has no intention of staying with the congregation, otherwise he'd be building that house. He's not building it; therefore, he's not staying," he said, trying to convince himself of his own conclusion. Abby waited for him to continue, but his next thought was still gathering momentum. About a minute later, he began again, speaking to himself as much as to Abby. "I reckon he has been thinking about it since just before we crossed the river with Sagar. That trip settled his mind though."

Abby stopped walking. Her mind focused on Nathan's conclusion and she admitted to herself it made sense. She wondered why Susan hadn't mentioned it. Maybe she was unsure how Abby would react. The Robbins were as much outcasts as she and the twins but they could start their own settlement together. She mustn't get too excited. Nathan could be wrong. She caught ahold of her racing mind and slowed her breathing. "Girls!" Abby yelled. The twins swiveled about. "Where is Sagar?" They looked at one another and simultaneously pointed west, across the river. "Nathan, can you take us to where you crossed the river?"

***

Back in camp, word of Abby's departure engulfed the congregation like fire consumes a barn full of dry hay. Decidedly negative, the consensus view was also somewhat inconsistent. The notion that Abby had no right to abandon George did not seem to trouble those who also believed he and the congregants were better off with her gone. Similarly, actions such as searching for her, for she was most certainly a witch, were not palatable to those who also figured she and her dark girls would be dead within a day, if not a week.

Alone in her father's quarters, Mary wept, ashamed she had drifted away from Abby, forcing the modest distance between them into an unbridgeable chasm. She had accused Abby of witchcraft, confronting Mrs. Bray and later letting suspicions slip into conversations with a few of the other women. That day she spied them, Abby and Susan were just talking in the hold. Yet she had poisoned Abby's chance of acceptance. She also knew, whatever the twins were, they had at least helped ease Jorge's pain before his death, and had possibly prolonged his life enough to ensure their path to the new world was clear. She still saw Jorge as the handsome young man her father had brought home years ago, not a sea-worn creature, beaten down like a remote coastline by wind and waves. She had loved him dearly and Sagar had saved his life.

Mary cried for her lost mother, her lost friend, and her now lost son. She knew Sagar would not return, not to her. Unworthy of the gifts God has bestowed, Mary thought, she destroyed them instead, like a jealous child. She heaved in anguish, resting her head on the fixed oak table as her tears dripped into salty pools.

At the edge of the woods where the Robbin homestead, or lack thereof, sat, Susan and Tom spoke in low tones around the fire. A soft darkness crept in while they shared the feeling that several hours of the day had vanished before them. Tom explained to his wife that while he hadn't heard what Faria told Nathan after she came skipping through camp to fetch them, he wasn't surprised to find their eldest son gone. His penchant for adventure and affinity for protecting those in need was a simultaneous source of pride and worry.

Abby's explanation of the morning's events had absolved Susan or at least given her the chance to discount Abby and the twins as foolish, or something worse. It would be a simple task to guide opinions in camp if Susan were so inclined.

A convenient story had even come into her head, which went along the following lines: Susan had been teaching Abby and the twins to read. Abby's shame in not understanding the words led them to perform the lessons in private, even in the hold of the ship. Susan had been troubled by Abby's wandering mind, the fiery woman's misguided beliefs, and her closeness to the strange twin girls she adopted. Susan's only fault, she could convince them, had been to humor Abby rather than chiding the delusional housemaid. It would be easy. For all her cleverness, Susan wondered, if she had been so accused like Abby was today, would she have acted so nobly?

"What now, Tom?" said Susan.

Acknowledging his wife's question, Tom gazed into the fire and answered, "Susan, dear, we will do what we have always done. What our hearts tell us is right." In the warm darkness Susan kissed her husband, as sure of him as she had been the day they married. Their eyes and thoughts met, and together they laughed in a nervous, cathartic release. Most of the congregants stayed awake late into the evening condemning Abigail Fielding but the Robbins retired early and slept well.

The Robbins woke before dawn and did not tarry in packing their tents. Tom knew the captain had taken to drink of late and suspected he would not wake till mid-morning so the schoolteacher waited until the sun reflected upon the river to search for Tanner. After a hug from Susan, Tom walked through camp to the Spring Tide. She sat beached in the river mud like so many derelicts littering the English coast, abandoned except for her captain who seemed determined to go down with his ship. Tom neared the captain's quarters and was surprised when the door swung open upon his approach. Tanner stepped onto the deck, saying, "An empty ship makes it easy enough to know when someone comes calling. Hello, Tom."

Tom wondered if Tanner was expecting him. After Abby's departure, the Fielding's cabin had seen accusations thrown in every direction with only George remaining quiet. Confused, the assembled crowd dispersed while so many bitter words still lingered in the air. The view to which most people ascribed was that Abby had acted rashly and would return once she and the twins became hungry. No search effort was given serious consideration; they didn't know what to do, so ended up doing nothing.

"Hello, Captain Tanner," Tom replied. Tanner spread his arms wide, gesturing to the ship, shrugging.

"Captain of what, Tom? No crew, no passengers, no cargo, no destination. Just an old man, and my name is Robert," Tanner said, walking to the far side of the deck. He leaned on the railing and looked downriver to the sea. Tom joined him. "One last voyage, that's all I wanted. I didn't give us much chance of making it, and to be honest, if Mary weren't on board, I wouldn't have cared either way. The adventure was the thing. Jorge felt the same." Tanner spoke as much to himself as to Tom. He smiled as he spoke, but there was little happiness in his voice. The railing felt smooth to Tanner's touch, and he absently ran his thick fingers along the weathered oak.

"We're leaving," Tom whispered. Tanner continued to squint at the glimmering river and at first said nothing. It wasn't that he didn't care, just, at this point, nothing surprised him. He looked up into the sky and said, "Your own adventure, eh? Good man. By sea or by land?"

"Land."

"And the ship?" Tanner said, continuing to caress the railing, as if trying to soothe the largely abandoned vessel.

"She's yours, the congregation's, but we'll need Millie, the horse. There's many books I just can't part with, too many to carry. Seems like a generous trade," Tom said.

"Aye, it does. She's the weaker of the two horses, and if you aim to track down Abby's twins, I don't know which it is, but Millie only heeds one of 'em. That horse has been useless. Won't listen to anyone but that girl." The captain leaned further forward. Staring absently into the muddy water below, he said, "This is wild country. Tom, are you sure you know what you're doing?"

Tom clapped Tanner on the back and laughed. "No, I have no idea, really. But it's what Susan and I believe is right. Isn't that why we're all here, to live as we wish? Who knows, I'll probably eat a poisonous mushroom and die this afternoon," Tom joked.

Growing serious, he faced Tanner. "Thank you for delivering us, but we must now take our own path. The Spring Tide is in your hands. Salvage her or sail her back to England if you like. I wish you and the congregation well and trust that in times of dire need we may rely on one another." The two men shook hands, parting amicably. Tom returned to his family and Tanner remained on deck for some time, wishing he were going with the Robbins.

CHAPTER 20 - March 30, 2013

Leaving the building, Sagar sensed Shikha's guarded excitement. From her research today he knew she had drawn some conclusion, perhaps definitive, yet she now focused on their next task: procuring the book. Shikha handed the driver an address and gave him a few brief directions; he responded with the discrete nod of a seasoned limo driver, keeping a raised eyebrow in check. The black car merged into light traffic on I-95, heading east. They had driven in silence for about ten minutes when Shikha said, "We're going to Stony Creek—The Thimbles. I know, or once knew, the chair of the Linguistics department quite well. He retired about twenty years ago. A bit of an iconoclast, so we got on swimmingly. If he's still alive and remembers me, he will help."

Sagar recalled the Thimble Islands from his travels up and down Long Island Sound. They consisted of several granite outcroppings beyond the hamlet of Stony Creek, few containing more than ten houses. Tales of buried pirate treasure had earned one of them the name Money Island, tales Sagar knew for certain were untrue. Otherwise, it was a sleepy port full of summer houses handed down generation to generation. Arriving in late March after a blizzard, the place didn't look sleepy, it looked derelict. Shikha, eyeing a sorry fishing vessel about to head out, jumped from the Lincoln, and yelled to its crew, "Can you take us out to Governor Island?" Seizing an opportunity to make the day profitable, the boat's captain took one look at the limo and said, "For $100. Each," as he thought, What the hell would anyone want to go out there for this time of year? It's empty. But he kept his thoughts to himself. They would need a ride back, for which he would charge them double.

Sagar stepped onto the thirty-foot fishing boat. In his presence the crew grew wary, as his eyes scrutinized every poorly stowed line, every sloppy repair in their nets, the smelly green mud lining the scuppers and especially the captain himself. After pushing off from the dock, Sagar had a few words with the captain, who began to argue, but was stopped mid sentence by the pressure of Sagar's hand on his shoulder. He changed his course, as it were, and having been instructed by Shikha as to which dock, dropped them off at Governor Island with grace and humility.

"What was that about?" Shikha asked.

"Nothing serious. His nets are illegal, too fine a mesh, and he's been operating in restricted waters, where that green mud is found. We'll have a free trip back. If we need it," Sagar noted.

They slogged from the private dock through the remnants of sloppy snow and picking up fresh tracks, human tracks, knew at least someone was on the island. Sagar saw eyes peering out an upstairs window of the house they approached. The tracks led up a flight of deeply weathered wooden stairs onto an expansive deck spanning the entire front of the house. As they reached the deck, Shikha was about to knock on the sliding glass door leading inside when a desiccated woman of about fifty yelled at her from the other side window, "This is private property. I'm calling the police right now!"

Emerging from behind the irate woman, a diminutive elderly man shouldered her aside to see what the all the commotion was about. Shikha waved at him, yelling through the glass, "David, it's Shikha!" The man, who couldn't have been more that five-foot-three, approached the glass door and nearly putting his nose to the window exclaimed, "So it is!" He began to fumble with the lock on the door and at his command, the mousy woman inside helped him with it and swung it half-way open. She remained blocking the entrance.

"Deborah, please, this is a very dear friend from the university," implored and reprimanded the old man.

"And him?" the woman named Deborah countered.

"Well, he is, hmm, he is . . ." David searched his mind as one might have searched for an old recipe. It was not there.

"David, please let me introduce my, my friend Sagar. We are both in need of a small favor," Shikha said. "It concerns a very old book." Taking advantage of Deborah's confusion, she stepped inside and embraced her old friend. Sagar remained outside until, over Shikha's shoulder, David said to him, "Come in, please, come in."

The four of them adjourned to the kitchen where a teapot sat on the table, two cups next to it, one empty, one full. David motioned for them to sit down, and the wary Deborah retrieved two more cups. "A book, you say?" said David as they seated themselves.

"Yes. It's in the Beinecke library. Sagar and I, along with my sister Faria are in need of it," Shikha said. "Today. We're trying to solve a family problem and are leaving for India tonight. But it's Sunday, it's Easter Sunday, and the book is terribly rare." At that moment, she had lost any sense of her sister. There was no impending danger, no excitement or trepidation, just blank space where her sister's feelings once resided in her mind. She swayed, and Sagar leaned in to prop her up with his shoulder.

"Still fighting the bureaucrats at the University, are you?" replied David. He brayed like a goat. "We'll see what we can do here in a moment. I still know several of the curators." Turning to Deborah, who was reluctantly pouring the tea, he added, "Remember old Watson, I believe he worked in the Beinecke." Turning to Shikha, the little man added, "He was just here last summer with his family."

Deborah replied, "That was nine years ago, uncle David." She was apparently used to correcting him.

"Ahh, I see," he replied, his brow furrowed, but it quickly returned to a happy state. Sagar could tell that David had reached the age where the distant past remained crisply embedded in his mind, yet the present receded at an ever-growing pace. To him, Shikha appearing at his door just after a spring snowstorm, looking as she did 30 years ago was perfectly natural, indeed comforting to him. Sagar saw that in seeking David's assistance, Shikha was betting on this memory dissonance.

"So tell me of your current research while I finish my tea. We'll then try to interrupt some bigwig's Easter supper and get you your book," David said, sounding starved for academic discussion.

Shikha began relaying the details of her genome sequencing

work in some detail, but Sagar felt her blocking aspects of the work from the conversation and her mind. She glanced at Sagar, and all became clear. Shikha was bursting with excitement from today's discovery, but exerted monumental restraint by shielding it from her consciousness. She had realized, which Sagar had not, that whatever had pursued her on Long Island was accessing her thoughts, or at least emotions.

"Fascinating stuff, dear. And your sister is well?" David asked.

"Quite." Shikha lied. She needed time to think, to concentrate on Faria, but this was not the place. "As you might recall, her work is somewhat more aligned with yours. She is in northern India presently, at the Rampur Raza library. Their early Mughal literature collection is unparalleled," Shikha replied. David sipped his tea, nodding and clearly pleased with the visit. They bantered for a few minutes more, but like a clock, as soon as he finished his tea, David changed his tone, and puffing himself up, he addressed his niece.

"So let's make some phone calls. Deborah, where is that i-thing of yours?" Deborah pulled her phone from her apron, and handed it to him, smirking. He left it on the table and scurried into the other room with surprising speed, returning with a tattered address book. Having slipped an additional set of glasses over the ones he already wore, David's fingers twitched through the book, until he found the name he sought. Pushing altogether too hard on the screen of the phone, when it began to ring, he beamed as if he had just accomplished some Herculean feat. It rang for some time before the line clicked.

"Hello?" spoke a voice from the phone, surrounded by the background noise of laughing children yelling at one another and at least one stern adult yelling back at them.

"Watson, is that you? It's Professor David Goldwasser," said David, referring to Lionel Watson, the curator at the Beinieke museum, by his last name.

"Oh, David, hello, it's been quite some time. Well, ahh, we are just now sitting down to Easter supper. May I call you back tomorrow?" Watson asked.

David either didn't hear him, or ignored his response and

plowed on to the matter at hand. "See here, Watson: remember when you came to my office before your dissertation defense? The comments from that blockhead of a faculty adviser of yours had you fearing that you would fail to get your doctorate?"

"Yes, of course I do, David. And we spent days reviewing my text and arguments together. I was, and will forever be, in your debt," Watson replied.

"Oh, it was just a favor from one scholar to another. Which is why I'm calling," David said. "You see, I am doing a bit of research on," David paused while Shikha scribbled notes to him on a napkin, "historical book-binding techniques." He continued, "It's my understanding that there is an excellent example spanning several centuries in the Beinecke. It's of no historical or literary significance, mind you, but I should like to have a look. Today."

In the background, they could hear an irritated woman say, "Lionel, are you coming to Easter dinner?"

"David, I'd be more than happy to locate the book and share it with you tomorrow, however, as you know, it's Sunday, it's Easter and the library is closed. Please," Watson began to implore, "stop by the library tomorrow and—"

David cut him off. "That just won't do, as I am flying to, to, London tomorrow and was hoping to bring the book with me." David spun an interesting yarn and seemed to be enjoying the ruse. Someone on the other end of the line yelled LIONEL! Caught between his mentor and his wife, Watson sought a quick compromise.

"Look: after supper, I can call the 24-hour security detail at the Beinecke. I can instruct them to let you in so you may review the book at your leisure but without knowing whether it belongs to the University, if it is on loan, its condition, it must remain on the premises."

David looked to Shikha, who nodded, before he replied, "Wonderful. Thank you, Watson, and do come to visit us in the Thimbles this summer, won't you?"

"Oh, yes of course. Goodbye now," Lionel said. He hung up.

On the car ride to New Haven, David and Shikha reminisced about old acquaintances and the library itself, a white brick of a building, which allowed the veiled luster of natural light in through thin marble panels on all four walls. Back in the city and nearing the classically proportioned library's structure, Shikha took advantage of a short silence and said, "David, thank you for helping us. You must know that we intend to take the book with us if possible."

He smiled, feeling as if he were part of some devilish international intrigue. "If you do have the chance to abscond with the manuscript, I will tell Watson that I forgot he said I couldn't take it. A senile but respected faculty member can be forgiven for his lapse of memory," David said, chuckling with a glint in his eye. Deborah had insisted on accompanying her uncle on the trip and now looked on disapprovingly but was resigned to the adventure ahead.

"One other thing, David. The book belongs to us. Sagar, my sister and me."

"Belongs in what sense exactly? There are many kinds of belonging," said David as the car slowed in front of the Beinecke. He believed her words but looked unsure if she meant the book as an object, or that somehow they were the heirs to the knowledge itself.

"It was once the property of a family member. It made its way into the school's collection long ago, but remains ours," Shikha said as the driver opened the door for her and the others. She stepped onto the curb and helped David from the black Lincoln while Sagar jumped out the other side. Deborah followed a few steps behind, as if her hesitation would somehow slow the inevitable. Walking to the main entrance, they spotted a burly, mustached security guard at the main entrance. He opened the door and yelled, "Dr. Goldwasser?" To which David replied, "And associates!"

They entered through glass double doors held open by the stocky guard after which he asked for their IDs. David and Deborah produced them quickly, and Shikha and Sagar followed suit without apprehension. More elaborate document referencing always gave Sagar and Shikha pause, but their passports and driver's licenses were manufactured using the same machinery as used by the Government. However, they were in fact forgeries listing them all at an elderly forty-seven years. The passport numbers had been inserted into global databases, so even at international air terminals, they would have no trouble. A cursory glance by a man who had never left a thirty-mile radius centered on East Haven CT, excepting during the high school state football championship in Hartford twenty years ago, was no cause for alarm. Sagar noted the Guard's ID tag read A. Caballero and he introduced himself as Tony.

Tony escorted them through the darkened library, illuminated only by the sunlight refracting through the marble panels, to the rare book archives. He paused in front of the secure glass door, catching his breadth, and swiped his pass. Hearing a positive click, he opened the door but remained outside the archive enclosure. Tony settled in to maintain a constant vigil over the rest of the books, assuming the four of them would find what they were looking for on their own.

David found the environmentally controlled room quite pleasant and took a seat at one of the research desks as if sitting down to a sidewalk cafe. Shikha began to search for their book, passing a Gutenburg Bible but pausing before the Voynich Manuscript in a stout display case. It was open to a page displaying a series of maidens descending a green waterfall into a pool, surrounded by the strange text, which the tome was famous for. She pressed deeper into the archives. "Sagar?" Shikha called out within a few minutes. "Come over here." She had found it. Sagar pulled himself away from watching the guard and jogged back to Shikha. She grasped the hand-stitched tome tightly and, wrapping it in her scarf, she placed it in his backpack. They returned to the reading area, as if reseating themselves at a table in a casual restaurant. Tony the guard had not turned his back the entire time. Sagar walked to the stacks, pulled out a random book and left it in clear view on the table where David sat.

"Back so soon? I was just getting comfortable," said David. "So, let's have a look, eh?" He began to turn to the book Sagar had placed on the table.

"David, may I suggest we adjourn to another location for

inspection?" replied Sagar, tapping his backpack.

"Quite right, young sir," said David. They returned to the glass door, knocked, and Tony obliged by opening it wide.

"Found what you were looking for, Doctor Goldwasser?" he said.

David looked up at him, turning his head to the left, and replied, "Oh, yes, I believe we have."

The guard escorted them to the main entrance, opened the door and locked it behind them without a word. Returning to the car, Sagar unzipped his pack and handed the book to Shikha. Within her mind flooded Abby's memories of her first experience with the book, in the cabin George had built, confirming that indeed they had found that same text. She sat next to David and together they leafed through the thick tome on the short drive back to Tweed Airport. The elderly linguist's only comment on the drive was, "What other secrets have you been hiding, Shikha?"

CHAPTER 21 - March 30, 1603

Nathan spent the morning pulling sharp-toothed fish from the river until he thought he had enough to last the four of them a week. He had no idea how his catch would taste but at least they wouldn't starve. The twins cleaned the oily fish and smoked most of them across a low-burning fire of maple branches, keeping a few for eating today and tomorrow. This gave Abby time to herself, time to ruminate on her decision. A deep sleep the night before refreshed her, and she woke with crisp memories of her dreams: Abby recalled making her way through a vast, antediluvian pine forest. The dense but cool air surrounding her sat undisturbed against the forest floor. Every so often, the trees would ever so subtly sway and she could catch a glimpse of the black storm crashing in vain against the treetops. Their girth, some as wide as a house, allowed no rain or wind to reach her. Only a gentle mist, like dew suspended in the air, gave any hint of the battle raging between the young tempest and the ancient forest.

Abby crouched next to the fire Nathan had built last night, tending it, turning the coals as she had as a young girl. The twins and Abby slept closest to the river with burlap sacks as pillows on top of heavy wool blankets arranged upon the softest ground they could find. Nathan had stayed awake as long as he could, slumped against a tree to "keep watch." Abby thought to herself, she must keep a record of all the noble deeds Nate had performed so that upon his return to Susan and Tom their anger would be tempered. He and the twins now approached with lunch.

After feasting on the oily fish, Abby determined they should build some kind of temporary structure. She didn't know how long they might stay in this spot, but it did have a lovely view of the river, was reasonably flat and devoid of the rocks that sprang from the ground like weeds. Faria gathered hemlock branches for a roof and Shikha searched for thin but straight sticks to serve as ribs or rafters. Abby and Nate cut larger tree limbs for framing. Within a few hours they had assembled sufficient materials to construct a cozy hut. They worked through the afternoon but it did not feel like work to any of them.

As the sun set over the far bank of the river, Nate found himself hoping it would rain that night so as to test their workmanship. However, Abby had chosen a spot between two sturdy young maples for the location of their abode, which would limit the rain falling on the roof. The hut was tall enough for the twins to stand up in and Abby fit well if she stooped slightly but Nathan had to crouch low and waddle his way about inside.

Faria lined the outside perimeter with rocks and while Nate was bringing their packs and blankets inside they all heard something moving through the woods. They hid in the hut. Peeking through the wall they could make out several shapes approaching. From the outside, they heard a faint, high voice say, "What is it?"

A moment later another voice, deeper, replied, "It does not seem of native design, and the work is amateur at best."

"Amateur!" yelled Nathan. Abruptly standing, he bumped his head on the roof of the hut, which to those outside gave the impression that the hut itself had taken offense and convulsed in response. Without thinking, he bolted through the narrow door, still the impatient schoolboy. The day's last rays of sunlight flooded over his back, illuminating his family in orange and red hues and Nathan's consternation melted into confused joy. "Father, what, why are you here? Why are you all here?"

Tom quipped, "Your mother and I thought the family needed fresh air. We were finding the atmosphere in camp a bit congested. It is well that we join your campout, is it not?" Midway through his comments, the twins and Abby tumbled out of the hut and Abby straightaway hugged Susan and in turn Tom. Within a half hour, all the fish Nate and the twins had stockpiled was gone, consumed by the Robbins, who now sat relaxing around a roaring fire.

"How did you know where we would be?" Abby asked Susan

across the fire.

"We didn't, but Tom reckoned Nathan would cover familiar ground, so we headed upriver," Susan replied, picking a fishbone from her teeth. "What do you suppose we should call these fish?"

"I'll call them supper any day of the week" Tom added, to which he received a smirk from his wife, and continued, "No, I quite see your point, dear. Everything we now encounter is unnamed and completely new. Well, not exactly new, but sufficiently different than in England and in Europe. Take these maples around us, they are similar to those in Essex, but the leaves are more pointed, the bark rougher. And this one here is leaking a prodigious amount of sap. A bit exciting though, discovering and naming new flora and fauna."

Abby took his argument further. "Tom, don't you suspect the trees, the flowers, the fish, they already have names? Meaning, native names? They must. So really, we're not discovering anything, we'd simply be renaming them all. A bit presumptuous, don't you think?" she said.

Tom thought on her words for a short spell and replied, "It's a fair point, Abby, and you're right, too often we presume that because something is new to us, it is somehow unique to our experience, giving us the right to claim discovery and ownership. From a practical standpoint though, I do believe a systematic approach to naming of the natural world would be of great benefit to the scientific community. Names are just words, sounds even. By using multiple names we create a distinction that does not exist. Whether it be for a plant, animal or person."

"Or god," Abby murmured, her gaze fixed on the ebbing embers in front of her. Tom's eyes widened and he repeated her words, "Or god, yes." They sat in satisfied silence, staring into the fire as it hissed and crackled. Nathan gathered more wood, some of the remnants from their hut, reinvigorated the coals with the fresh fuel and joined the adults. Susan, Tom, Abby and even Nate each considered broaching the subject of what they would do next: Settle here? Cross the river, or in time return to camp? But the flames had a way of dispelling their anxieties, providing warmth and a feeling of safety that allowed these thoughts to pass untouched and unspoken through their minds. Their options were best considered in the promise of the morning light, leaving the night to quiet reflection and the comfort of sleep.

The sun's warmth blanketed the sleeping Robbins, waking them to a cloudless day. The heat of the morning dissuaded anyone from starting a campfire anew, and while not oppressive, the air felt heavy in the absence of any wind. Susan unpacked a very modest breakfast, careful to preserve what supplies they had been able to transport. She estimated they could comfortably exist for about 6 days without finding native food sources. The fish were indeed easy to catch and plentiful yesterday, but it tied them to the river, and her son may have just been lucky in his catch. It wasn't today's particular worry about food that dwelled with her, rather it was the dark suspicion that their foreseeable future, years perhaps, would be a constant search for safety and resources. Tom woke to much brighter spirits. He surveyed the trees around their temporary camp, gazing up at each, measuring the trunk's circumference with a bit of rope, before moving on to the next.

Tom didn't explain, but soon returned to where their campfire burned, expecting someone to ask him what he had been up to. Unable to wait for their curiosity to overcome the silence, he blurted, "It solves a few problems at once. We will build a log raft, a ferry!"

"A ferry, dear?" said Susan.

"More logging, at least now can we use the wood, rather than leaving it behind?" Nathan added, half-joking but also still sore from his wasted effort in the congregants' camp.

The twins looked on, feigning disinterest, but Abby nodded encouragingly at an excited Tom, who said, "If we clear the surrounding land to both build a log raft, but also to plant for a late harvest, we would prepare ourselves for wintering here, or for moving on to live with the natives." He paused and added, "If they'll have us."

He looked to Susan and Abby and said in a more subdued voice, "Whether we aim to settle on this shore, we would be well-served in constructing a means of transport that can carry Millie and all of us in the event we must depart, possibly in haste." He left the remainder of his thought unspoken, but the women understood his implication. Their party was unsuited to engage in conflict, and must consider retreat by river if necessary. Growing more confident again, Tom said, "Our one encounter with the native chief of the western shore was fruitful, but we must recognize that a man responsible for his tribe would be wary to burden it with outsiders who can contribute little. Our approach must be a fair trade, considered over the course of a season. If indeed we can remain here until fall, we can hopefully bring our own means of sustenance, and success, with us."

Faria looked at Shikha, and making no movement conveyed a thought to her sister nonetheless. "Sagar works for the same outcome," she spoke, turning to Abby. "He decided to leave before you did."

Nathan spoke up: "That's great news. So he'll be joining us, or should we search him out? Father, do you suspect he is with the natives now?"

"Nate," Tom said while looking at the twins, "we can trust in his intentions, whatever they may be. As to searching for him, if he wished to be found, he'd reveal himself, if not, we would never find him. It is a comfort to know he works with us, albeit apart, but we must focus on our own plans and hope to meet him again soon." Now turning his back to them and gazing into the forest, Tom said, "Right, so, now let's get to work!"

Their first days in the new settlement saw trees fall with reluctance, axes dull and backs ache. Work slowed, for the land was reluctant to yield to their efforts, and progress felt elusive. The twins spent day after day fishing, only to have their harvest dispatched by their hungry families. At the coaxing of Shikha, Millie pulled stumps from the ground, which were used to anchor and mark the temporary enclosure around where they slept. The ground itself seemed already planted, but with rocks. The two younger Robbin boys, Philip and Will, spent long hours digging the stones from the ground. Being a year apart, their natural instincts made the job into a healthy competition. After a week, they each had amassed a pile of rocks as tall as their father, both claiming theirs was tallest. Tom set them to work building a stone wall with the fruits of their labor, and so they began again, challenging each other to see whose wall would be longest.

***

Thirteen days later, having consumed scores of fish, collapsing from exhaustion at each sunset, they had cleared enough land to plant. Overnight a warm spring rain softened the ground and they began their third week together next to the river by sowing barley. For the Robbins, this was their initial experience so close to the land and at first they observed Abby and the twins rhythmically spreading seeds as a thurible spreads the sweet smell of incense during Mass. They soon joined in and by noon the flattest land was covered with barley seeds. Susan had procured turnip and parsnip seeds, which they planted along the edge of the field and closest to their camp.

None had experience hunting but Tom reckoned that once the seeds sprouted, the game would come to them. He had read about catching small animals and set Philip and Will the task of building and testing rabbit and squirrel traps. The boys had grown tired of the oily blue fish sustaining them, so were all-too-eager to help. Meanwhile, Tom and Nate began work on the raft. Their design consisted of two layers of heavy logs aligned perpendicularly and bound together with rope and wooden pegs. Along the edge they built a crude railing and filled the gaps in the deck with smaller tree limbs as best they could.

Their attempt at making pitch to further seal the gaps between the logs was an arduous failure. Boiling the profuse resin from a pine tree they felled only succeeded in destroying one of the pots Susan brought, resulting in nothing more than a black, tarry mess. Tom insisted that he had followed the directions in his seamen's handbook, but clearly something was missed. Nearing completion and however crude, their raft was indeed buoyant, yet looked more like a floating dock than a boat. Nate fashioned two large oars from sweeping oak limbs and at last they were ready to test their craft.

Before pushing off from shore, Tom anchored the raft to a tree with their longest line for safety. If they began to sink, it would at worst leave them a lifeline to pull themselves back to shore. Tom and Nate found, while unable to make good headway against the river's flow, by straining in unison against the oars, they could at least keep pace with the current, preventing their lumbering log pile from being swept downriver. Reaching the end of the tether, father and son rowed their modest success back to the eastern riverbank.

That night, Tom decided it was time enough to pay another visit to the native villages on the western side of the river. What troubled him was the need for someone to help him cross the broad and slippery current, yet he couldn't get comfortable leaving his family and Abby's alone. He found Nathan gathering firewood and took him aside. "Nate, do you still have the pistols that Captain Tanner gave us?"

Nathan thought for a moment and started to nod. "Well, when Sagar and I unpacked the boat, I spotted them under one of the seats. I tucked both in my second rucksack, figuring you'd want to return them yourself, but I guess with all the commotion, they must still be there."

"Let's find out," Tom replied, striding over to the now-covered pile of supplies. It wasn't that he feared leaving for just a day or two. Rather, their small tribe could not afford to lose even one of its members. "Ahh, here they are. Good. Someday, we will return these to the Captain," said Tom. He sat on an adjacent tree stump and motioned to his son to step closer. "We need to cross that river and make contact again with Quniyôkat, but it will take two adults to row." Nate did not catch his meaning, so Tom added, "One of us must stay here, but not both." Tom explained his thinking. It was important to slowly introduce their group to the natives; the two of them could not both risk being lost; and whoever remained behind must be prepared and able to carry on. This time, there would be no Sagar to guide them.

After the younger children settled in for the night, Tom, Susan and Abby sat around the fire, as had become their custom. They had been reluctant at first to allow Nate to join them. However, his boundless optimism became a comfort to them all. After a weary day, the adults found his rambling about the future, always positive, both refreshing and entertaining. That night, cooler than usual with a river fog rolling across their camp, they lounged closer to the flames and to one another. Tom spoke almost in a whisper, "It is time that we trust the raft and make contact with the natives again. We have enough rabbit pelts and dried fish to make a modest gift, along with a few books. So, who will go?"

They looked at one another and before Nate could speak up, Abby said, "I will," following with, "if we are to live among these peoples, I should like to understand them better beforehand. What do they value? Will they trust us? How can we trust them?"

"You're right, Abby, we can't trust them, not yet. But don't forget: what reasons do the natives have to trust us? We haven't given them many. A few hours of limited conversation, a shared meal, that would not be enough for me if I were responsible for an entire village. With your help though, we will learn their values and earn their trust," said Tom. He was relieved Abby volunteered but had no idea how the natives would react to a woman, much less one with fiery locks.. Better to know now though, he mused.

Nate looked downcast, not appreciating the danger in crossing the river, finding the natives and engaging them without Sagar. Tom wondered how many obstacles the young boy had steered them away from on their last trip. How simple he made it seem, just a row across the river in the waning sunlight followed by a walk in the woods and a tasty meal. Recalling his conversation with Sagar late that night as they waited to recross the river, Tom's anxiety swelled. Now so far from the schoolhouse, the schoolteacher wondered who among them was in control of their destiny. Smiling at Susan, who looked back at him with confidence, Tom peered into the fire as if seeking the flickering light's counsel and said, "Perhaps we should ask the twins their opinion."

CHAPTER 22 - April 1603

When Sagar strolled into the compound a month after Tanner not so subtly told him to leave for a spell, he recognized the general layout but much had changed. The Spring Tide had been dismasted and her spars sat stacked next to where Reverend Williams lay at rest. The church, four weeks ago only a web of twine, now dominated the camp. Framed with the timbers of the Spring Tide, the structure stood in challenge to the adjacent trees. The beginnings of the stockade Tanner promised came as no surprise to Sagar. He wondered what it would keep out, excepting perhaps the deer.

The spot the Robbins' had staked out remained unchanged, as if there were an expectation, perhaps even a hope, the family would return. Sagar aimed to find Mary and James first, then Tanner, but the captain spotted him from the center of the nascent village and threw him a hearty wave, causing Sagar to change course. "Hallo!" yelled Tanner, forgetful of the circumstances under which he asked the boy to leave. A few others took notice of the loud greeting and Sagar could feel them slinking away to spread rumors of his return.

"Much progress, sir. The ship is put to use across the camp. She will live on, yes?" said Sagar.

"Aye, that much is true," Tanner replied with a broad smile. "Tell me of your adventures and let us eat!" continued the captain, patting Sagar on the back. The boy glanced backwards to the land cleared for barley and oats, which had yet to be sown.

"Do you have anything in the ground yet?" he said, pointing beyond the stockade.

"The Gaithers have a field planted on the other side of camp where little clearing was necessary, yes," Tanner relayed. He began walking, assuming Sagar would follow. When they approached the door to Mary and James' house,he whispered, "I moved in about a week ago. Sweet Mary told me I wasn't to sleep on board the ship anymore. Said it reminded her of a floating coffin. My coffin." He winked at his last statement and swung the door wide, revealing a dark room with a roughly built stone fireplace at the far end. Mary stooped over the hearth and when the door opened she turned and put her hand to her forehead to shade the bright light flooding in. Recognizing who entered, she bustled over to them and exclaimed, "I thought you'd been lost! James and I gave you up for gone after a week."

"Mary, he's made of stern stuff, this one. Boy, I kept telling them that you'd be back in one piece," Tanner said, to which Mary scoffed at her father and hurried the two of them to the table. She doted over both during lunch but mostly Sagar. It felt to him as if she were trying to make up for her dismissive treatment, and that somehow she felt responsible for his banishment. He revealed little of the last month except that he ventured both across the river and some ways north. Sagar was careful with his questions but a few he had to ask after hearing how most of the men were busy at work on the stockade, building homes and the church.

"How are your supplies? What crops do you have in the ground? What from this land sustains you?" He tried to gather the state of their food sources and preparedness for the coming winter through his simple questions, but Mary's concerned looks at each of her father's assured responses told him more than words would admit. They had exhausted their supply of food from the ship, and the boys who didn't help their fathers build in camp were trapping rabbits with marginal success. Tanner explained that point as gently as possible, knowing it would have been Sagar's job, had he been around, to provide for his family. Each Saturday, the men would hunt deer or whatever else they could scare up, but these were carpenters and farmhands, and Sagar knew well enough how they clomped through the forest as loud as an army.

Communal food storage had not been considered, because there was little to store. The congregants ate what they found day to day. The one step taken, the Gaithers' field of barley, sat in a low clearing south of camp and had gone in just a week ago. The men who accompanied the Gaithers from England, such as Henry Mason, guarded the field each night with guns at the ready. On two occasions this week gunshots rang out across camp, but no report of struck game made it outside what Tanner referred to as Harold's compound. Sagar saw how the Gaithers were using the other congregants to build the stockade and clear land while they and those faithful to them prepared for winter.

Given how late the oak and maple buds appeared, Sagar surmised that the winters on this coast were more severe than from where they departed. Chief Quniyokat of the western shore had explained how the ground could remain hard and covered in snow for three, sometimes four moons and that while the great river did not freeze over every year, when it did, the early spring thaw was a violent affair. Massive ice blocks from upriver would break apart and scour the shore, crushed downstream by the spring melt. The chief made to indicate that in these frigid years, the winter would fight very hard to remain, for it thought it had finally gained a permanent foothold. Eventually, the spring always prevailed but two winters ago, it almost lost.

"Have you tried fishing, Captain?" Sagar asked. Tanner replied that on their first attempt to fish the river, one of the younger boys was swept downriver and nearly drowned. The episode put them off trying. "Sir, if you can let me work with the lads for a day, you'll have food for today, and if you can muster a party to head to the seashore, we can put up fish for later in the year."

"Well, I, that is, if their parents will let them," said Tanner, looking to Mary for support. Sagar understood his hesitation to mean the captain could no longer marshal the congregants to a task, his role diminished despite the counsel of Reverend Williams.

"We'll spread the word tonight and have a right crew for you in the early morning," Mary encouraged. "But why would you want to go to the shore?" she asked.

"Salt, ma'am, and we will need the largest kettles you have," replied Sagar.

Early the next day, a crowd of a dozen boys assembled outside

Mary and James' house. With them stood a few fathers who, either from allegiance to the captain and perhaps to Sagar, or just weary of building the stockade, aimed to assist. When Sagar stepped out the door alongside James, the boys' voices hushed at his reappearance. While those who had come at Mary's request were most curious about his return, scanning the faces, Sagar knew none had shown up just to confirm the rumors. The three men accompanying their sons were all members of Sagar's crew aboard ship. Each gave him an encouraging nod.

Sagar looked back at everyone assembled and said, "Thank you all for agreeing to help. Just like aboard ship, we'll be splitting into three teams. One will head to the shoreline. They'll take the large kettles for boiling seawater into salt and fishing through the shore break. Another crew will work the river by boat using the finest nets left on the ship, and the last will fish from the river's shore. Let's all try to meet at the eastern mouth of the river by midday. It's not easy work, any of it, but from what I've seen in the river and from the beach less than two miles south of here, these waters will yield plenty. Anyone know what a cod looks like?" Hearing a loud "Aye, son" from behind him, Sagar was relieved to know Captain Tanner would be coming along as well.

"Good, if we're lucky enough to catch any cod, then we'll clean them, dry them out on the beach near the fire and salt them down. Otherwise, the oily and bony fish caught in and nearer to the mouth of the river should be smoked over maple and oak. The shoreline is littered with dry driftwood, perfect for heating the seawater and boiling it into salt. Even if it's not used today, smoking and salting any game, especially deer, will make it last three times as long."

Sagar paused, making sure everyone had kept up. All looked to be excited about the day's prospects. Satisfied, he turned around to Tanner, who held a long gun in his right hand. "Right, Captain'll lead the shore party. Anyone who can't swim should go with Captain Tanner. Mr. James and I here will take the launch, and will need three or four to help us with the nets. If you can row, all the better. Everyone else can work southward along the river's edge. The backwaters and spots where the current is less strong will be best," Sagar instructed.

Turning, he addressed only Tanner, "South-east might serve you best, if you don't want to get too wet in the marshes. There's also a small stream due south."

Despite their earnest efforts, it took a nearly an hour to prepare for departure. Nets had to be found and repurposed, poles, lines and hooks improvised, and a means to carry the three heavy kettles constructed all while those who didn't volunteer looked on with curiosity and some with veiled derision. As the three crews dispersed, many mothers gathered to see them off, concerned their boys would not return.

Sagar and James shoved off in a launch with four strong lads and agreed to keep in sight of the two men and three boys fishing from the riverbank. Two sets of brothers, the boys in the boat called James uncle, although he was only a family friend of their fathers. James, John Worthington and Matthew Owen grew up together in the farmlands above Bristol and had labored together from a young age so James had known their sons from birth. The current ensured their ride toward the sea would be an easy one, but their return trip would need to be timed with the changing tide.

Tanner and Michael Jones, one of the most trusted men from Sagar's old watch, led six boys south into the woods, past the Gaithers' compound. As they passed the largest block house in camp, yet unfinished, several men paused in their work to gawk and snicker at the strange sight of two grown men and half a dozen boys entering the woods carrying cauldrons. It was indeed an odd occurrence, but eight hours later, when unabashed singing and laughter could be heard echoing through the woods, the snickering Gaither cronies needed not wait for the smell of smoked fish to reach them to realize the excursion had been an unmitigated success.

The largest cauldron overflowed with three types of smoked fish, smartly arranged, while one of the smaller cauldrons was weighed down with nearly a peck of coarse salt. Also packed full were the bellies of those carrying the bounty, who had feasted on more than their fill already. Relieved mothers and children greeted them in front of the church, where Reverend Smith appeared, enticed from within by the scent. Smith's Scottish mother had served their family smoked haddock on many occasions. The distinct smell permeating the camp brought what few fond memories the reverend had wafting back to him. He approached Tanner saying, "Might I give thanks, a prayer for your catch, Captain Tanner?" Tanner began to step aside, allowing Smith to edge closer to the cauldron, but abruptly stopped and said:

"Reverend, there's still four boys with Sagar and James rowing back up river in the launch. I think it best to belay your blessing until their return."

"Oh, well, Sagar? Hmm, yes, true enough, Captain," replied Smith, caught unaware of the missing party and of Sagar's return to camp. Tanner had lanterns hung along the ship's side to act as beacons and within an hour the launch could be seen, heavily laden, making her way upriver. The four boys tumbled out, glad to be back on shore and able to celebrate with the others. James stepped onto land next and tied the launch off against a tree stump. Tanner approached, casting his gaze into the launch, full to the gunwales with fresh catch.

Most of the smoked fish in the kettle had been caught by Sagar and James on their way downriver, and from the looks of it, they fared equally well on the way back up. James grabbed Tanner into the darkness and said, "Captain, I don't know if we could have caught a quarter of these fish without the boy. He swims like a shark and pulls like an ox. Thankfully, those four lads are too thick to realize what they witnessed, otherwise he'd be in a heap of trouble just like—" James cut his comments short as Sagar approached.

"Abby and the twins?" Sagar finished James' statement. "Do not be concerned. I will spend another day to help as I can, but must depart. You are right, father James. I don't belong among you and staying would only create more trouble." Sagar smiled up at both of them, but it was the melancholy, resigned grin of an old man who neither welcomed nor resented the hard labors of life yet knew their toll. Leaving the two men, he added, "If you don't plant your fields this season, till the fishbones into the soil. It will make the first harvest all the more prosperous." He walked on to Mary's cabin leaving the fresh catch to be partitioned among the congregants. Few noticed the small boy's absence, which was exactly what he wanted.

The camp awoke late the next morning, bellies fattened. When the boys who accompanied Sagar downriver in the launch rolled out of their bunks they found him ready to push off into the river again. Eager to depart without adult supervision, even from their "uncle" James, they jumped aboard and drifted away. While the farm boys didn't realize it, as Sagar worked alongside, he taught them how to read the river, how to cast a net without disturbing the fish and pull it slow and easy. They were just having fun, for all they knew. After an hour, he jumped off on the shore and trotted back to camp. Three hours later, hunger overcame the lads in a way reserved for the day after feasting beyond restraint and they rowed back upriver at a sharp pace.

On land, Sagar set to building a fire next to the riverbank in the sunniest spot he could find. He fetched two small firkin sized barrels from Mary, just right for using as a stool or footrest. The Owens boys were the first to return and he started them sorting the fish into silver-sided and blues, larger with an aggressive underbite. The Worthingtons, last to return, had to clean the blue fish while the Owens set to the silvers. The first Owens boy to find dual red membranes within the fish he cleaned let out a cry, "Wot's this here!" as if he had discovered a silver coin inside his fish. Sagar sent Tad Owens to fetch a pan and a hunk of fat from Mary. He ran off, returning minutes later.

To the other boy's surprise, Sagar delicately fried the red membranes with the fat and began eating it. By this point, the lads had found several more and if not keen to try some they were curious. Sagar shared the last bits of his, cooked to perfection, and soon enough they were each crudely heating their own. Tad Owens' impatience saved him from an exploding roe sack. The other boys were not so lucky and returned to gutting fish after cleaning up in the river. Sagar's laughter startled them more than the exploding fish roe; after spending months with him, or at least observing Sagar aboard ship, none had heard his unique low chortle.

Sagar butterflied the blue fish and staked them on maple branches close to the fire, smoking them. The silver fish he laid out on hot rocks in the sun to dry. Sagar then tightly packed the two barrels in alternating layers of salt and silver fish, also salting the inside cavity of each. While he worked, the lads asked questions and he made sure to elaborate enough that they could perform the same task when required. Satisfied, Sagar fitted the barrel tops loosely and found James to affix the head hoops, which would tighten the seals.

Mary, James and Sagar ate a somber supper that afternoon. Late last night, James had crushed Mary's elation at seeing Sagar, when he shared that their adopted son would be leaving again and for the last time. She held some hope that her husband had misunderstood the boy, yet Mary remained quiet, lest conversation lead to verification of what she already knew to be true. Sagar breached the stillness, "The natives tell me the fish bones in the soil will really help."

"Okay, so, thanks, lad. We have enough of 'em. These silver fish are mighty bony," said James, adding, "but mighty tasty," knowing it was the boy who had provided for them all. Sagar looked at the floor.

"If, in the heart of winter, you hear a knocking at the stockade wall, please look before you shoot. It may be me," Sagar said, standing. While Mary mistook his words as an admission that he might need their help, James knew better. They might need his. "Thank you for taking me in." Awkwardly he said, "If I may admit, I wanted to be a son, your son, every bit as much as you wanted to have one. That was not to be. But I am and always will remain your friend." Sagar approached James to shake his hand. Mary began to cry. She stepped in front of her husband and clenched Sagar till he nearly burst. Hearing a muffled grunt of pain from between her arms, she released him and they all laughed.

"Good luck to you, my boy," James said, putting his hand on Sagar's shoulder. Mary's face grew forlorn and she bent down to his level.

"If you happen to see Abigail again, tell her, please tell her, I am sorry," Mary whispered into his ear, and Sagar promised that he would. Walking out their door into the evening sun, he wasn't surprised to find Captain Tanner waiting for him.

"Miss Mary didn't say why you were missing at supper," Sagar said.

"Can I walk with you?" Tanner asked. The two of them strolled to the edge of camp without saying a word and entered the forest where Tanner did not stop. Out of range of any of the congregants he addressed Sagar, "Jorge and I, we voyaged many places, stood on deck under the stars, feeling smaller than those specks of light in the heavens and never kept a thought from one another worth confiding. After you saved him during the blizzard, he believed you were sent to protect us." Tanner stopped in front of an ox-sized granite boulder. He leaned against it and looked out over the river. Sagar said nothing but let the captain consider his words.

"He called you a clever but kind Duende, a little spirit that would nudge us along the right path. Jorge's superstitions almost had him left in England, you know," Tanner said, eyes glistening. "Last October he told Reverend Williams that the voyage was in danger because the water spirits would resist our quest. He had convinced himself that they would interfere with our plan to cross the sea. Something about his people always returning to where they belonged. I tell you, boy, it took a whole evening and a damn good bottle of wine to convince old Williams that Jorge wasn't serious. But he was, you see. He died thinking the only reason we would make it was because you were on board to calm the sea. And after you pulled him out of the water, I began to believe him."

Tanner glanced into the woods behind him. He waited for the boy to reply, but realized Sagar's patience would outlast his own so continued, "Where will you go now?"

Sagar shrugged. "North for now, then winter across the river with the natives. They are much like you and the Congregants, Captain: curious, kind, fearful, and reactive." Knowing full well that Tanner would not heed his message, he spoke on, "If you sharpen swords, you will wield them. If you stockpile guns, you will shoot and if you build a wall, you will find reason to defend it. Consider what will be lost, even if you win. I am very grateful to you, my captain, and I would do all I can to help you and the others survive, but I cannot help you conquer. And so I must go. Goodbye, Mr. Tanner."

"We all do what we must. Goodbye, boy." As Sagar walked away into the woods, Tanner added, as much to himself as to anyone, "Thank you."

Sagar knew the twins' location was only a few miles north; however, he hesitated to rejoin them and the Robbins just yet. Laden with the obligations of destiny, his small body sometimes strained under his charge. An instrument of fate he might be, but right now Sagar wanted to shut down his mind, shut out all the projections, and just feel his free will resonate in concert with his surroundings. Tonight he would wander, purposely without purpose. Quite unlike the rhythmic plodding of a common man, Sagar's movement though the woods was that of a gazelle, asymmetric explosions of boundless speed.

CHAPTER 23 - April 1603

After testing the raft and their rowing skills once more, Abby and Tom reviewed their plan a final time. They would cross the river at dawn, move into the woods and retrace the path Sagar had led to the camp of Chief Quniyokat. They would reach the settlement before noon if they were lucky. Rabbit pelts, smoked fish and a few additional books were their gifts. A subdued affair, the evening meal saw Susan worried but the twins confident. "Miss Abby, keep your hair covered at first until you have sat down, or been asked to," said Faria, with her sister adding, "Look into their eyes for what lies beyond. If he is what we hope, their chief will do the same. Mark well what you see." Abby filed away their cryptic advice.

Before pushing off from the sandy landing, Tom hugged his wife fondly and addressed Nate, still glum he wasn't going, "Next time, son. Mind that the rabbits don't eat all the crops." Faria and Shikha accompanied Abby down to the shore, carrying her rucksack between them. The tide in their favor, Tom and Abby eased the raft off the shore and into the ebbing flow. Long, slow strokes kept the rough craft moving at an easy but smooth pace across the wide river. While they lost some ground and edged downriver once in its strongest flow, they pulled for the far shore rather than try to maintain level with their camp.

Not wanting to embarrass the schoolteacher, Abby matched her effort to Tom's, who was the weaker rower. In over an hour the raft came to rest on shore, its forward progress impeded by thick reeds. Once on land, Tom pivoted in a circle. He peered down the river's shore and back up, trying to discern where they landed in reference to his first trip across. After a few moments he said with false confidence, "Let's walk north a spell." Abby shouldered her rucksack and followed him through the trees.

Fifteen minutes later Tom stopped and now looked back across the river for landmarks. "The lighting was different, is all. And it was earlier in the year," Tom muttered, confused. He turned to head south again but Abby did not immediately follow. "What is it?" Tom said.

Abby had scrambled up a large boulder and looked down into a hidden inlet, choked with reeds. "Was that your camp?" she said and pointed to an area he couldn't see. Tom dropped his pack and climbed the rock as well. He began to laugh as he reached the top.

"Yes, yes it is. Sagar mentioned we had been watched that night, and I guess it was from up here." Tom pointed down to his feet where small rocks no more than an inch wide were arranged neatly into three piles. One stood smaller than the other two but had a black rock atop the pile. Satisfied as to their location, Tom suggested they head west to which Abby acquiesced.

Off the river the forest grew dense. The full thickness of the trees' summer canopy stood resolute against the sun's rays. Only when their branches swayed in the strengthening winds did Abby notice the sky had begun to darken. The day had dawned clear, but with a light haze dwelling at the horizon; it now felt like dusk. Tom took no notice as he deliberately picked his way through the woods trying to retrace each individual step back to the village rather than heading in its general direction. He looked up, speaking to Abby in a whisper, and realized the gusting wind prevented her from hearing. "How long has the wind been blowing like this?" He yelled.

"Nearly an hour, Tom," she replied, adding, "Should we turn back or press on?". A few thick raindrops began to make their way through to the ground.

"I believe we're over half-way there. We'd never make it across the river in this wind anyway," replied Tom.

The gusts grew ever stronger and despite the trees' best efforts the two of them began to get wet. Tom stuck to pathfinding, while Abby kept close but observed the oaks and maples fighting the storm. In defense, the forest drew strength from thousands of seasons of collective adaptation, ill-placed limbs ripped in winter gales, roots sunk too shallow saw trees toppled to become fodder for mushrooms and moss.

Although anchored to the ground, the trees seemed to close ranks like an immovable wolf pack, certain that where one was struck down, innumerable others would survive the violent but temporary maelstrom. In her homeland, Abby thought, so few places still remained, a redoubt for nature's strength, where men failed to domesticate the land into an obedient dog. Pockets remained, protected by isolation or, Abby wondered, perhaps by guardians.

Every so often, Tom halted and scanned the surrounding rocks. He approached each large boulder they met with suppressed excitement, only to turn away disappointed. Abby realized he was looking for something in particular but did not ask what. She reckoned they had been walking for three hours but the storm's intensity made it difficult to tell. Thunder cracked in the distance like cannon fire, startling both of them from the task of finding the native village into the realization that they were ill prepared for weathering this storm. The dawn's warmth had long since faded and the wind now easily cut through their drenched clothing. Tom didn't realize he was shivering but Abby took note and encouraged him to keep moving each time he paused.

Becoming more frantic, Tom unknowingly began turning in a circle to the south. After a few minutes they came upon a fast moving creek and stopped. "We didn't cross this stream the first time Abby. We must be off course somehow," Tom admitted, but Abby wasn't listening. She stood with her back to him and held her head up in the air, despite the heavy rain, which fell unimpeded.

"Smoke, do you smell it?" She yelled, moving slowly away from the stream. Standing on a rounded rock, she put her hands above her eyes to block the rain and scrutinized the landscape for its source. "There, Tom!" He wandered over and saw nothing. Abby wasn't sure what she espied but began walking to where the sky looked just a bit brighter. Tom followed.

"That's it, or I think it is," Tom said a few moments later. They approached more slowly: the only hint of habitation was a smoldering fire, doused by the storm, which stood a silent vigil over the encampment. Tom neared the fire pit and, still shivering, laughed almost convulsively. The sound triggered a hide flap to open on the adjacent long hut.

A confused face peered out at them, perhaps wondering what strange creatures would venture out in such a storm. The face turned sideways, interrogating Tom, and exclaimed "TomRobbin!" The chief's son-in-law Kutomá Nipôwi emerged from the hut, and beckoned Tom and Abby to enter. Abby remained still. She stared at something Tom could not see, and it stared back.

"Abby, come, let's get out of the rain," Tom implored, stirring her to follow him. They both entered behind Kutomá Nipôwi, and found the hut comfortably dry, the fury of the storm outside muted by the structure's layered walls and thatched roof. Several shadows stirred in the recesses of the long, narrow building, but at first Abby and Tom only discerned Kutomá Nipôwi and a young woman who crouched near the entrance. She looked at Tom and Abby, dripping and cold, and began handing them deer hides for warmth. Kutomá Nipôwi gestured to her using a few introductory phrases, which Abby took to mean she was his wife. The native woman repeated the word, Ásuwanuw, ostensibly her name. Curious extended family members now edged closer from the far side of the hut. As Tom and Abby's eyes adjusted, they counted eight people in all, including two babies.

Tom soon realized how easy Sagar's presence had made communication. Without the boy, their dialogue degenerated into a series of fumbling gestures and slowly spoken words that conveyed no meaning. Still, between them all a few important points were clarified. First, Abby was not Tom's wife. Once realizing the nature of the question, Abby and Tom both blushed and their vehement head shaking convinced the native family. Tom began to logically explain the improbability of his and Abby's union, indicating that Kutomá Nipôwi had met Tom's son Nate, who couldn't be more than ten years younger than Abby. This lost the natives, and drew a strange look from Abby.

Second, Sagar had visited the village as recently as two weeks ago and spent time with the chief and his son. Kutomá Nipôwi drew a hunting scene in the dirt, Abby guessed, showing the smallest figure standing above a large buck. Kutomá Nipôwi became animated when gesturing to the scene, which gave them the impression that Sagar had downed the animal himself.

Finally, Tom and Abby came to understand that most of the tribe's men, including chief Quniyokat, were at the shoreline fishing. Expected back any day, it might be as long as a week before they returned. Abby sensed Tom's disappointment, but she felt relieved at the notion. Becoming more comfortable, Abby removed her wet shawl, eliciting gasps from the natives. The humid air had curled her hair into a bushy red nest sitting atop her head. Ásuwanuw held her hand out to touch it. Abby smiled and leaned in, allowing the native woman to run her fingers through her locks. They both smiled, which served as a signal to the other women in the longhouse, who successively touched Abby's hair in kind.

Tom presented Kutomá Nipôwi with the rabbit pelts and smoked fish, and at first the native knew not what to make of them; only when Tom pushed them closer to him, almost into his lap, did he realize they were a gift. With tact rarely seen among the merchants of London, the native accepted them as a father would accept the roughly fashioned gifts of his youthful son or daughter: appreciative of the gesture, however crude their design. The fish had begun to smell and were a day or two away from an inedible state, while the rabbit pelts left little fur remaining, perhaps enough to create a baby moccasin. Each.

What the storm lost in ferocity through the afternoon, it gained in volume of rain blanketing the land. It fell without wind, without furor, but as if God had let the waterfalls of heaven fall to earth. Kutomá Nipôwi was eager to show Tom around the camp and introduce him to those who had heard of the first encounter, but did not witness it firsthand. The weather made this impossible so they all sat in awkward silence. Every so often someone tried to communicate with little success.

In time, the natives began to chatter, paying Tom and Abby no heed. A graying but strong woman, at first Abby couldn't tell whose relation, stepped forward and began drawing in the dirt, recounting a story to the delight of many others. Only Ásuwanuw remained reserved, looking embarrassed and impatient. Abby guessed that the woman was her mother, and the native maiden had grown weary of the story or her mother's telling of it. Abby turned out to be right.

The woman began by passing both hands over her head in a semicircle, as if tracing the path of the sun. Speaking reverently, she chided all those around the hut, wagging her finger in admonition. She began a slow dance, fingers above her head, wiggling them. Allowing them to drop to the ground again and again, her dance grew stronger and more violent. Alternating between the convulsive fits and a mimicry of fearful people running to and fro, she fell to her knees in supplication and covered her head with her hands, silent. Moving into the darkness at the far end of the longhouse, she began walking in a crouch, paddling as if in a boat. Reentering the center, she looked skyward and opened her arms in praise. Nobody moved until she stood. Wearing a wry smile, she then spoke as herself, pointing at the hide door. Ásuwanuw pushed it aside, revealing a glistening, sunlit world.

Tom looked astounded, but Abby betrayed no emotion. Whether Ásuwanuw's mother had indeed stopped the rain or if she smartly timed her tale with the ebbing of the storm, who could say, but Abby knew the ways of witches well enough to realize that much of their craft drew from simply listening to nature. Stepping outside into the sun, Abby found the woman pulling her aside. She introduced herself as Ayaks and made Abby to understand that she was the chief's wife. Hastened away from the others, Ayaks asked many questions, which Abby could not comprehend. But when she pointed to Tom, then to a younger maiden and showed an open palm, and then pointed to herself and clenched her fist again, Abby realized Ayaks asked if she were with a man.

The question took her so off guard that at first Ayaks reckoned that she didn't understand it, but Abby gathered herself and held out both hands. One, she left open, the other remained closed. Abby wanted nothing more than to be able to explain, but her words fell meaningless from her lips. Abby's eyes reddened, and she turned away only to find Ayaks comforting her with a hand on her shoulder. Together they walked back to where Tom and Kutomá Nipôwi were standing in the sunlight. Two young girls who had been in the long hut during Ayaks' storytelling zipped by giggling, reminding Abby of the twins. She pointed at them and back to her heart, holding up two fingers; Ayaks nodded, grinning.

The late-afternoon sun baked the moisture from the ground, humidifying the air. Abby shed her shawl, drawing more gasps from the curious, who had also just emerged from their huts. Tom looked delighted to be back in the village. He had taken a notebook from his rucksack and scribbled notes while Kutomá Nipôwi spoke slowly. At times, Tom would make a circular motion with his hand to ask his native friend to repeat certain words. Neither realized how late it was, alternatively fascinated or fascinating those around them, so when the daylight waned, Abby and Tom were somewhat surprised to be invited to an evening meal and to stay the night in the village. Given the late hour, Abby and Tom's only alternative would be to camp alone in the woods somewhere between the village and the river. Their decision was easy.

After a supper of orange squash and roasted deer, exhaustion overcame Abby; it felt as if she had lived three full days in one. Tom, however, wanted to stay awake all night talking, that is, listening to the natives. Sorting out their accommodations took several minutes but finally Abby just let Ayaks lead her to the hut adjacent to where Tom, Kutomá Nipôwi's family and Ayaks would sleep. The middle-aged woman spoke in rhythmic intonations as she busied herself creating a place for Abby to sleep in the empty hut. Abby was too tired to ask any questions but she tried to help as much as she could. A nest of deerskins altogether too large for Abby quickly grew at the far side of the hut. Abby thanked her hostess by warmly clasping Ayaks' strong and rough hands. They shared a smile and soon Abby slumbered.

Well after midnight the half-moon lounged in the sky. In the distance, it espied the men of the tribe making their way through the woods, but fast approaching the outskirts where their families and ancestors slumbered. Most shouldered long wooden poles, laden with smoked fish, but one man led them walking alone. The chief's son Cikiyiyô Muksihs strode with his head lowered as if pursuing an injured deer, certain he would overtake it, but not soon enough. The others moved with less purpose but at a similar pace.

They entered the village in silence, most heading directly to their families, but the chief and his son walked the outer perimeter, speaking in low tones. Confident in their survey, they returned to the largest longhouse, the chief's, and the adjacent hut, his son's. The chief wore a sleepy grin into his home, weary from the trip but thankful for the bounty the sea had yielded for his people.

If Cikiyiyô Muksihs were weary, it could not be discerned from his countenance. He entered his hut just as he had the village, in a ready state, striding through the deerskin door. But it would seem that even the most vigilant warrior can be surprised. Abby slept soundly on the floor of his hut, chest rising and falling in an effortless rhythm as her fiery hair spilled over the nest Ayaks had made like a sunset over the sea. Cikiyiyô Muksihs stood transfixed. Any other woman he would undoubtedly awaken with a gruff bark, but this beauty possessed him. He thought longer. His mother, yes, this was her doing.

Leaving his hut, but the image of Abby refusing to leave his mind, he first thought to demand an explanation from his mother, but recalled the recent words of his father "a chief must never be first to anger, never first into battle, but sees time as an ally." Another night on the ground under the watchful eye of the moon would suit Cikiyiyô Muksihs. He made ready his bed next to the fire ring in the center of camp and soon slumbered.

Waking at first light, Cikiyiyô Muksihs lay feigning sleep until the morning drew its full breath and a modest commotion of whispers and giggles made their way across the camp. Eyes squinting, he spotted Abby listening to his mother. Ayaks' flailing arms and slow speech convinced Cikiyiyô Muksihs that the redheaded woman knew not their language. But when his mother's outstretched arm pointed directly at him and the face of the strange woman reddened as her eyes lowered, he understood that some communication was possible. He waited another minute and rose, suddenly more conscious of himself and his movements than ever before.

In the chief's long house, Kutomá Nipôwi and Tom ate breakfast, after which they toured the village. Tom thought he had begun to understand his host and tried to ask as many questions as he could. Now fully appreciating the scale of the settlement and its structure, where extended families shared single long houses, Tom enjoyed being an oddity. He was introduced to each person they met as TomRobbin. News of his custom to shake everyone's hand spread like a brushfire and soon villagers approached him with hands, sometimes left, sometimes right, sometimes both, outstretched. Each long house's proximity to the center of the village indicated the inhabitants' relation to the chief, whose hut sat directly in front of the largest fire pit. Kutomá Nipôwi made Tom to understand that the village's size ebbed and flowed during the spring and summer, but in the fall, it would swell with families returning for the winter.

Tom tried to ask where families went during the spring and summer, but couldn't quite articulate the question, so they continued on, reaching the outskirts of the encampment. A rocky stream, no more than thirty feet across, formed the village's natural boundary. Kutomá Nipôwi frowned as he waved with both hands at the land on the other side of the little river, as if cursing or warning Tom of what lay beyond. To Tom, it looked like it either had been recently inhabited, or used in some fashion by the natives. No structures stood, but the ground had a groomed look to it. Abby would see much more in this place than Tom, but even now he found it curious. They walked back to the center of the village by a more direct route and soon stood in the company of the chief and his son.

The chief made Tom to understand that he was pleased at the schoolteacher's return, but also interested in his traveling companion. They adjourned into the chief's long house, empty excepting his wife and Abby, who sat relaxed on the floor conversing in words and gestures. The red haired woman looked up, becoming flushed at the sight of Cikiyiyô Muksihs, whom she had unknowingly displaced last night. Following the chief's lead, the men sat across from the women, and once all had found their place, the hut fell silent. Chief Quniyokat addressed those assembled in a slow but melodious tone, in turn introducing each to the others. Tom heard his named called, after which the chief, Tom assumed, related the details of his prior visit. When reaching Abby, Quniyokat began but it was his wife who described Abby's appearance during the height of the prior day's storm and her appointment of the redheaded woman's sleeping quarters. Careful not to mention Tom, Abby wondered if this was because he had been discussed, or for some other reason.

When all had been introduced, the chief turned intently to Tom and grew quiet. Tom thought for a moment, looking to each face gathered and decided to broadcast their intentions. He opened his satchel, and looking past several books he pulled a quill, ink and large parchment from the bottom. He laid them in the center of the group and scribbled a picture of his family, and Abby's. The speed of his quill and the result astonished the natives, but they soon grew used to his communication method, and watched intently. Tom counted off the names of his younger children, his wife and, pausing at Nathan, he drew under him a picture of the flute they had presented to the chief on their last visit. Mimicking playing a flute brought the point home. Abby's family resided apart from his on the page, and for clarity, he also drew Sagar alone and some distance away.

Turning over the parchment, Tom tried to draw the river, their camp and the natives' village. This took some time to explain, but Abby caught Tom's direction and began assisting with a few native words she had learned from Ayaks. Once everyone understood, he pointed to himself and Abby, to their camp, and then to the village. Tom paused. He faced chief Quniyokat, folded his hands together and bowed his head for a moment. The chief nodded, unsure of the intent, but recognized his gravity. Tom sighed, raised his eyebrows and picking up the quill again, methodically drew his and Abby's family at the far edge of the native village.

Ayaks comprehended first and whispered to her husband, who betrayed no emotion. Continuing to look at Tom, the chief said a single word, "Sagar?" whom Tom had left off his second drawing. Tom only knew what Kutomá Nipôwi had told him of Sagar's second visit and nothing of the chief's view of the boy. He considered the native words he had learned, and spoke very slowly to the chief, "Sagar—his own way."

Quniyokat nodded, and replied, "Welcome to the tribe."

The chief's son accompanied Abby and Tom back to the river, walking ahead of them at a consistent but easy pace. They weren't sure if he volunteered or was assigned to the task but he didn't seem to mind. As they wound through the trees he paused every so often to explain some aspect of the forest, names of trees and birds, which of course they couldn't understand. About an hour from the village, they reached a grove of massive hemlocks, widely spaced. No undergrowth littered the ground among these giants, and the earth looked packed hard and smooth. However, Cikiyiyô Muksihs slowed and began to traverse through the heavy brush on the outskirts, warily avoiding the site despite the seemingly easy path through. To Tom, the detour held no significance, but Abby peered at the ground; it felt somehow darker than it should be. The trees stood a good distance apart, yet sunlight was unable to penetrate to the forest floor.

Abby tried to keep up with Tom and Cikiyiyô Muksihs, who made their way through the mountain laurel bushes, but her gaze remained fixed on the clearing. Drawn by the unnatural stillness, no birds, no squirrels, no wind, she began to slow and just as she stopped moving she glimpsed a shadowy figure skirt from one tree to another. Abby felt an acute absence of sound as if when she focused on the moving image, it pulled all noise out of the air. For a brief moment it paused in its path and while it had no discernible face, Abby sensed it was looking back at her before disappearing behind the girth of the tallest tree.

Abby wasn't sure how long she remained motionless but in time, she felt a warm hand on her shoulder and turned to see Cikiyiyô Muksihs whispering to her, and motioning for her to follow him up the hillside. She acquiesced and trudged behind him through the thickets to the crest of a small hill where Tom waited. "Are you able to continue, do you need to rest, Abby?" he asked.

She replied, but without looking directly at Tom. "Oh, yes, thank you I, I just stopped to admire the grand trees. Please, let's move on." Abby was sure that Cikiyiyô Muksihs didn't understand her words, but he sensed her meaning. He briskly descended the far side of the hill, from which they could see the expanse of the river unfold before them. Some distance south along the far bank, the sharp lines of the congregants' stockade resisted the soft rolling greenery of the trees and grasses lining the river's edge.

The camp's size did not go unnoticed by Cikiyiyô Muksihs. Yet as they began to push north Tom observed the native taking quick glances across the river, shaking his head in amusement. Tom caught Cikiyiyô Muksihs' attention and in halting native and English words, asked him what he thought of the camp. At first he just shrugged but after looking again at the stout stockage and sensing the contempt Abby directed at their former home, he asked, "Friend?"

Abby retorted, No, while Tom was more reflective, wobbling his hands to mean, "Some yes, many no." Cikiyiyô Muksihs looked into the distance. He took a deep breath and swept his arm north to south along the river's path, speaking simply for their benefit. "Water low," he began, pointing at a nearby steep embankment, which fell away to the river. Cikiyiyô Muksihs strode to its edge and scampered out of sight. Abby and Tom followed and peered over at him. Using a bone knife hanging at his side, he cut a notch four feet up the trunk of a spindly cedar tree. The river's path snaked some distance away but about ten feet vertically below where he stood. "Water here," he said, gravely tracing the route from the notch to the congregants' compound. Abby understood. Not every Spring, but some years, the camp would be underwater.

Cikiyiyô Muksihs said no more and just as quickly as he had jumped down the sandy bank he bounded back up and resumed their march. A few minutes later they approached the raft and Tom thanked

Cikiyiyô Muksihs with a hearty handshake and began readying the rough craft. Abby wanted desperately to convey her gratitude to the chief's son who, without complaint, slept in the open last night, allowing her to remain in his hut. There was just no way, she knew the words would fail her. So she followed Tom's lead and extended her hand to Cikiyiyô Muksihs. He grasped it, holding it gently as if it were a captured butterfly.

"Thank you, Cikiyiyô Muksihs," she said, shaking his thick, calloused hand. He looked back at her with determined but softened eyes.

"Come back," he said. It was not a question.

"I will," Abby replied.

CHAPTER 24 - March 30, 2013

In the hangar, David and Shikha continued their inspection of the book. Shikha texted her sister to confirm they had it, hoping the modern means of communication could get through. She did not hear back and worse, she could not feel any emotion from her, even that of restful sleep. David, however, saw no need for external validation of the tome's worth. He sat fascinated, turning the pages back and forth and staring with a set of reading glasses resting on top of his bifocals. No detail could escape his view.

For some time, he failed to utter an entire sentence, rather interjecting the silence with observations. "Medieval binding, much older papyrus, badly damaged palm leaves, vellum in decent shape," he mumbled. "Ugaritic, hmm, original. Sumerian, expertly copied. Avestan and Sanskrit. Ogham. Very focused subject matter. Seen this, yes, there you are, my friends, Utnapishtim and Manu." Despite the intense magnification he brought to bear on the pages, he began to squint at some older pages, retorting, "That's a curious turn."

The rusty gears in his head had been lubricated by the day's events and now his exceptional mind began to engage the subject matter. His shaky fingers traced the sharp text of the papyrus pages. He came upon a rough depiction of a man floating on a wide reed boat, the same that Abby had pointed out to Susan so many years ago. Sagar watched his fingers cover the same text two and three times, as if he were uncertain of his translation. He looked up at Shikha and Sagar, and back down at the pages.

Taking off his second pair of glasses but still squinting, David seemed ready to render a verdict on the tome but thought better of it. "Fascinating book. And you said it belongs to you? What is its provenance?"

"Yes, to all three of us. In the seventeenth century, it was bequeathed to our family, but lent to the Reverend Abraham Pierson Jr. How the original owner, one Tom Robbin came by it, we can only guess," replied Shikha.

David didn't quite grasp the true weight of her words. "You mean to say this has been in the Beinecke, hell, in the collection, since the founding of the school? How did it remain hidden from me all these years?" While Shikha's statements did not bring further interrogation, David's response rang in her mind, "remain hidden, remain hidden." Her own thoughts mixed fluidly with the present and became subsumed by old memories, some hers, some her adoptive mother's.

As David looked back at the pages, Shikha tried to make sense of Abby's commingled memories. Stalling for time so she could order the four-hundred-year-old recollections from Rotterdam and the colony, she asked him, "I admit, it's really my sister's area of expertise, not mine. What do you make of it, David?"

Pulling his bifocals off and now holding a pair of glasses in each hand, David mused, "It's a compilation of myths. One myth, actually. The Deluge. Utnapishtim of the Sumerians, adopted by the Hebrews as Noah. Atrahasis of the Akkadians. Manu. There are many manifestations of the same story. But," David looked out the window, "where did you say your sister was?"

Shikha wasn't listening. She muttered to herself. "It's Brigu's book. He compiled it. It's been waiting for us. He's been waiting for us."

"Where again?" David asked her as Sagar stepped closer, placing his hand on Shikha's back.

Returning to his question, Shikha said, "in Northern India, at the Rampur Raza library. Are they related? The book and my sister's location?"

"Perhaps. Never been to Rampur Raza myself but would have loved to go. It's too late for me," David said. , eyes glittering. "But for you and Sagar, for the young, you have all the time in the world, don't you? Deborah, I'm getting a bit peckish but I don't suppose much is open in New Haven. Shall we depart for our lonely island before the dark sets in?" He stood, an awkward smile creasing his face, and made his way to the door of the airplane. Sagar helped him down the narrow stairs, offering up the use of the waiting town car.

Shikha followed behind, and after Deborah had gotten in the black Lincoln, she said to the wrinkled man. "What is the matter? Are you all right, David?"

Admitting nothing, he looked up at her and said, "My birthday is in two weeks. I'll be ninety-one. Old enough for my kind. My mother thought I would be born during Passover but I was late. I think she never forgave me." He hugged her and gazing out the hangar said, "But for you and Sagar, ninety-one is but a blink, isn't it? By the decree of the wakeful ones is the matter and by the word of the holy ones is the edict. When is your birthday, Watcher of Daniel?"

"I don't know, David. I, we are all orphans," she said. Shikha reckoned she owed him the honesty.

"Do let me know what you find out. And safe travels to you both," he replied, slowly getting into the car. Sagar shut the door gently behind him. They drove away onto the vacant tarmac and disappeared into the emerging twilight.

Sagar's crew prepped the plane for takeoff while he and Shikha ruminated on David's last words and the book. "He knew more than he said. This isn't just a book of myths, I think it is a book of history, our history." She waited for Sagar to respond. He didn't. "And its Brigu's," Shikha repeated. She was sure. Without Faria nearby it was difficult for Abby's persona to manifest itself, but something in Shikha just knew that Abby agreed with her.

"Perhaps. It must have been in the small chest that he gave to Reverend Williams, who in turn left it in Tom's charge, but that is a circuitous route," Sagar said. Why had Brigu not just given the book to him, or the twins? he thought.

Shikha mentally replied: you weren't ready. None of us were. "What would the three of us have done with it in 1603, or even a hundred or two hundred years later? It has chosen to reappear at this moment, but we need Faria to understand why. Together, we can finally discover our origins, what we are, Sagar. Isn't that our right?" He acknowledged her but didn't respond. He was thinking about Faria, her lips, unkissable, his right to happiness. "I believe Brigu knew we just might have a chance, but only together. Destiny has slumbered these many years, but our actions have reawakened her, and she will not stop her pursuit, so we must not stop ours."

Sagar dwelled on his meager contribution to their collective quest, money, before departing for the cockpit, where he remained for the first few hours of the flight. Shikha continued to review their book. She knew the tales of Manu, of Atrahasis, of Noah, even the natives in America had flood myths, she recalled from Ayaks. Struggling to fall asleep in one of the bunk beds, Shikha tried to dream, hoping to find her sister. She had to believe that soon enough they would be united. She was jolted awake by the plane landing as dawn spread her diffuse light over the clear skies of Amsterdam. A few hours, not even an entire night's sleep, found them back where the Spring Tide had departed 400 years before on her long journey.

Hehu greeted her with a pot of coffee and selection of teas; Shikha picked some Orange Pekoe, which pleased the Maori more than she would have expected. Sagar paced the small plane. She knew he hadn't slept in many days. During the mandatory but cursory customs check, Sagar made small talk with several agents it would seem he knew well. After which, they refueled and were airborne, sprinting to Mundha Pande Airport outside Moradabad at 585 miles an hour. Again in the cockpit for takeoff, Sagar now returned to the cabin and sat down next to Shikha on the plane's couch. He held his hand out to her and she grasped it like a lifeline. They were running again, but this time, for the first time, they ran toward something, not away.

Sagar and Shikha felt their resolve strengthen like hardening cement. Whatever might lay between them and Faria, surely it would yield. Encouraged by the promise of the book, Brigu's book, Shikha believed that in the hands of her sister its deeper meaning would be revealed. This was not coincidental, these possible events long lay dormant, as time and circumstance waited to align. Shikha recognized the looping pathways at play and wondered how many times the three of them had come close, only for the strands to fail to bind into a singular direction. If they could just reach Faria.

For her part, Shikha felt eager to offer her contribution, and while still holding Sagar's hand, she began to consider the import of her concluded research. While the building blocks were the same and the principle structures of life quite recognizable, her genetic material, her DNA was unlike any she had analyzed before. Other genomes she had sequenced in her career, E. Coli bacteria, Drosophila Melanogaster i.e., the fruit fly, mice, sheep and humans resembled a well-balanced but eternally simmering Brunswick stew of genetic material: unceasing cell division added helpful mutations over the eons. One continually came across reused and repurposed genetic information, as well as unused, discarded sections. Just as different recipes in might derive from the local flora and fauna and call alternatively for carrots, okra or even squirrel, one might also find an old potato in the bottom of the stew if the kettle is never fully emptied. Indeed, close to half a fruit fly's protein sequencing DNA is also represented in humans. Trial and error, and the necessity of existence itself, often results in the same answer, regardless of species or recipe.

In contrast, Shikha could only describe her DNA as, well, engineered. The large protein, enzyme and catalytic RNA molecule coding sequences were all present and familiar to her, yet they were organized in a more formalized pattern. All DNA is characterized by alternating sections, Introns and Exons: Exons become fully expressed as proteins whereas the Intron sequences, after translation to RNA and subsequent splicing, are not expressed. While Shikha had contributed to current research pointing to a more active and meaningful role for these "junk" Intron sections, she found her DNA was nearly devoid of them.

Systematically interspersed in their place were sequences that coded for DNA repair and cellular communication mechanisms. Several Shikha had immediately recognized. One controlled DNA methylation, a cause of mutations and therefore cancer. Too little methylation can lead to expression of harmful retroviral genes; too much leads to mutagenesis, DNA damage, and subsequently tumors. Recent publications indicated that effective interaction between cell nuclei and mitochondria, the body's vital source of chemical energy, was critical in maintaining cell health and minimizing the effects of aging. One of the sequences coding for the enzyme NAD, linked to mediating this interaction, was present again and again, almost as a theme is repeated in a fugue, and was embedded in her DNA. A third compound reappeared a third as often as the other two, a protein kinase which ensures a cell can pause division, repair DNA damage when it occurs and restart after repair has completed.

The pattern implied a persistent expression of genes that vigilantly maintained the integrity of her genetic code. It represented a systematic rather than reactive approach to maintaining cellular health. Many of the repeated sequences were not familiar to her and did not exist in common DNA databases. She had searched. Yet, even without full knowledge of what the remaining sequences coded for, Shikha could be certain of one thing. She, Faria and Sagar were able to withstand and repair DNA damage like no other organism, and it was by design.

Sagar could feel Shikha's mind churning away, scientifically fascinated with what it considered, but emotionally dissatisfied with the conclusions. Without her genetics background, he couldn't grasp the references filtering through to him. He stared at Shikha though and came to understand the underlying theme of her thoughts. Whereas the mechanical explanation of their existence left Shikha frustrated and wanting, to Sagar it was a welcome revelation.

His and the twins' extreme longevity was not just a random mutation. They were different because they were destined to be different, and while the reason for their design still eluded them, to Sagar it didn't matter. He suddenly felt like his life had been justified, had somehow been intentional. Perhaps, he thought, this was the true sense of religious Grace that Reverend Williams had tried to convey. Without a word spoken, Shikha felt Sagar's sentiments flush her body of doubt, like a child running headlong into the chill ocean waters of early spring; all that remained was the intense sensation of joy. Sagar embraced her, squeezing Shikha tightly. Their unrestrained emotions, their justification, did not go unnoticed by the Asuras most perceptive to their collective thoughts.

CHAPTER 25 - April 24, 1603

Abby and Tom rowed out into the river's main current, more confident in their craft and their abilities than on its maiden voyage. They both figured that Cikiyiyô Muksihs was watching them and while they wanted to impress him with their self reliance, they also knew if anything were to go wrong he would assist within minutes. Tom reflected on what Cikiyiyô Muksihs had taught them about the rare but extreme spring floods.

"We should have realized this. It's no wonder there aren't any permanent settlements along the river," Tom rattled on, mostly to himself. "It must mean in some years the territory upstream captures massive snowfalls which result in an outsized melting pattern. Perhaps northwards resides a mountainous region like the Alps. Really a fascinating cycle, I think." Tom paused for a moment, and added, "Abby, we must warn them, the congregation, that is." Abby remained silent, her mind lingered on shore. "Abby?" Tom repeated.

She skipped the schoolteacher's hydrological lecture and focused on his last statement. Her anger would never cool. "Tom, can you imagine their response if I were to go back and explain that the camp was in danger? They would again accuse me of witchcraft and burn me alive," she said. Tom had no response. "Perhaps you, Tom, or Sagar if he were here, could deliver the warning but even then, after their hard labor and no evidence for your claims, would they take action?"

"We still must try," Tom replied. His feeble response drew no retort. Until they approached the eastern shore, only the soft lapping of their oars on the water broke the silence. Abby rowed with a molten ferocity, which forced Tom to pull with all his strength lest the raft spin downstream. Facing west as they rowed, they heard the jubilant shouts of their families before they saw their faces. Turning to wave, Tom spotted Nate and Susan, Philip and Will tucked close to her, standing on the shore. It had just been one night but it felt like weeks since he had seen them. The twins stood to the right of his family, ready to assist as they neared. Faria waved back at him.

Tom and Abby coordinated to ease their craft into the shade of the overgrown shoreline where Nate stood waiting with a rope. He deftly anchored the log raft to an adjacent tree and helped them disembark through the mud. "The storm yesterday had us worried about you."

"We fared well enough, but did get a bit wet, yes," Tom replied easily. "The natives graciously allowed us to stay with them overnight, which renewed our spirits and dried our clothes. Still, I suspect we would have returned earlier if Abby had an equal match at the oars." Abby smiled at his comment, now realizing how challenging she had made the trip back for Tom. They all gathered around the dormant fire pit where Tom and Abby recounted the details of their adventure.

"So when do we leave to live with the natives?" Philip asked. The excitable boy drew a worried glance from his mother.

"That entirely depends on us, my boy. We have been welcomed, but our destiny is our own. Abby, what are your thoughts?" Tom replied. Her final exchange with Cikiyiyô Muksihs had not gone unnoticed by the schoolteacher.

Abby surprised him though. "This little camp may be crude, but it is also cozy. As long as the crops grow, the fishing is easy and the weather warm, I see no reason to leave. We must also bear in mind that we do not seek charity from the natives, but safety and counsel. Our own provisions must see us through the winter, not theirs. It is the only way to keep our destiny our own."

"So you think it safe for us, Abby?" Susan asked.

"It is far safer than where we were. The chief's son, Cikiyiyô Muksihs, indicated that the congregants' colony could be underwater in any given spring," replied Abby. The twins noted a flourish and hesitancy in her voice when she referred to Cikiyiyô Muksihs. "And I know Nathan and Tom keep a vigilant watch over our little camp but we have feeble means of defense in case of animal attack, or worse."

As if reading her thoughts, a high voice pierced the damp summer air from a small distance away, surprising them. "Miss Abby, The black bears in these lands are quite docile, unless you get between a mother and her young. I don't believe they or any of the other animals pose a danger. And on this side of the river, there are no native settlements within twenty miles. Not for a few years." It was Sagar who spoke. Leaning against a young maple tree, he very nearly smiled when they all pivoted to see him. His voice echoed with a lightness that brought relief to the twins, but it was Nathan and Tom who jumped to their feet to greet him. Each taking a hand, they shook his arms vigorously until finally evoking a laugh.

"Are you hungry? What can we offer you?" Tom said, shepherding the boy to the fire pit.

"Thank you, Mr. Tom, but no, I have eaten well enough the past few days," Sagar replied.

"How long were you listening?" Abby asked him, but it was Faria who responded, teasing that Sagar had been snooping about since daybreak like a little squirrel. Overnight, she sensed his steady approach, knowing he ran at great pace to reach them. As the others were learning Sagar's abilities, Faria took in stride his skills. Yet, she began to wonder why he tried to block some feelings from his mind.

Addressing all, Sagar said, "Forgive me for eavesdropping, but I did not wish to interrupt your reunion and your tale." He continued while facing Abby, "The congregants now follow their own path. I have left as well."

Abby looked up at the boy, recalling the cart ride from Rotterdam. On that windswept night seven months ago, she didn't realize her attempt to outrun her past and live a settled life among the congregants with George was in truth neither her dream nor her destiny. She now understood that you can no sooner outrun who you are than you can outrun the coming winter.

"So you'll be joining us?" Nathan blurted out, which drew encouraging smiles from all.

Abby added, "Please do, Sagar." Before Brigu collected him in

Istanbul, Sagar's existence alternated between one of extreme solitude, and living among rough men who valued him for his utility. The pattern wore on, decade after decade. Years of lonely survival in the wilderness or rough work in a port city: in a tavern, on the docks, aboard a local packet ship. He quickly learned to remain anonymous, unnoticed. Inevitably though, his unique abilities would emerge to the great advantage of his employer, but also drawing jealousy and suspicion. Sagar had a year, sometimes a bit longer until the question of age would also be whispered. He had been chased out of towns before and soon left of his own accord before the murmurs grew to shouts.

Only subtleties distinguished the captains, dockhands and tavern owners from Istanbul to Kolachi-jo-Goth to Mogadishu, like the differences between leaves from the same tree. It had been many years since Sagar had added a new pattern, a new experience to his catalogue of humanity; but this day he was welcomed for who he was, not for what he could do. While she did not say it in front of the odd assemblage that had become their family, late that night Faria reminded Sagar that yes, they all still had much to learn.

***

The storm that drenched Abby and Tom as they searched for the native village was the last rain for over a month. As summer intensified, the cool winds from the sea subsided, leaving a stifling, humid air on the camp like an unwelcome wool blanket. Tom, Nathan and Sagar made two additional trips to visit chief Quniyokat, where they were warmly received, excepting Cikiyiyô Muksihs's poorly veiled disappointment that Abby had not come as well. This delighted his mother. The twins and Susan's younger boys spent the days fishing and watering the crops. Bucket by bucket, they kept their acreage growing.

Apart from shepherding their small clan to meals, bedtime and weeding and watering duty in the field, Abby and Susan were free to continue delving into Abby's past. Most days they made little headway, content to recount what they had rebuilt from Tom's books and Abby's memories. One morning when Tom, Nate and Sagar were out exploring, the two women sat sharing stories of their upbringing. Susan always remained careful to underemphasize her privileged years but found it comforting to talk to Abby about the somewhat cold relationship with her father, whom she rarely saw. "Do you recall if your mother and father were, well, affectionate?" Susan asked.

"They were both kind enough, but as I think about it, my father was intentionally distant, as if observing me. I was the only child though, so perhaps that accounts for it," Abby said. "Still, I recall one winter's night I was sitting in front of the fire with my mother, eyes half closed. He must have thought I was asleep, my father, that is. I caught him watching me as if I were a strange animal. When he realized I took notice he smiled and gave me a wink. He tried to teach me what he knew of animals and such." She added, "He never hit me or was ill tempered, though."

Leading Abby in a different but familiar direction, Susan softly prodded, "So you are certain the symbols your mother would draw in the ashes matched those in the red book of Tom's? Would she explain their meaning, or incorporate other symbols, ones we haven't been able to find in the book?"

Abby said, "No, but, she would often draw the symbols around a little oil lantern. Did your family keep a flame lit even when a fire was unnecessary?"

"Not that I recall but the servants may have. Until Tom and I married, I must admit, I spent little time in the kitchen." Susan felt embarrassed at saying this but Abby wasn't really listening.

"There was this little lantern in the shape of a house, but the sides were bronze crosses, like the sort people living in the woods would put above their doorways. A Brigid's cross, I think it's called. My mother would always ensure it was lit from the hearth before we went to bed, despite the cost of the oil." Abby kept thinking, while the twins passed by on their way to the river with buckets. "Once, I tried to relight the hearth fire using a flint instead of the little lantern and my mother nearly threw me to the floor," Abby rambled but Susan listened intently, leafing through several books at once.

"Like this?" Susan said. She had come to an engraving within the heavy red book upon which they had relied. She pointed to a cross made from rushes or reeds with a square center where the reeds were bound together. Abby anxiously looked over her shoulder.

"Yes, that's exactly it, Susan. What does it say?" replied Abby. She would still rely on Susan to read passages of significant length. "My mother, hmm. She referred to the lantern as one of the keepers of the sacred flame. Sounds strange when I say it out loud. It's been in my mind, but I just realized it was there all this time."

"Here it refers to Saint Brigid," said Susan. She read to herself but conveyed details as she consumed the words on the page. "Saint Brigid... A patron saint of Ireland... cruciform of rushes first created during the conversion of a pagan chief to Christianity on his deathbed. How is this all related... Feast day February 1, also, I don't know this word, Imbolc. Wait." Susan became more focused now as she read on "The cross is believed in some locales to protect a house from fire. Here's more: At the monastery in Kildare, the sacred and eternal flame of Brigid was maintained by the nuns since pagan times, but rightfully extinguished by the order of King Henry VIII. Does this make sense to you, Abby? How could a flame commemorating a saint have been alight since pagan times yet kept by nuns? I find it rather confusing."

Abby watched the twins in the distance, standing at the river's edge. They had been watering the crops most of the morning. Before dipping each bucket into the river, they bowed slightly, arms raised. She thought of her mother. The little lantern with the sacred flame. From the hearth to the lantern, and back again day after day. Imbolc. That sounded familiar. "Does the book say when the flame at Kildare was put out?"

"No, but it must have been within the past eighty years," said Susan.

Abby whispered the words she recalled from her mother, "One of the keepers of the sacred flame." Abby moved closer to Susan, peering at the pages of the red tome. "Imbolc. Where did you see that word?" Abby said in a low tone.

"Here," pressing her finger to the page, "oh, and here again," replied Susan. The twins glided by with their watering buckets under a cloudless yet somehow white sky. Laden with moisture, the air subdued the chirps of songbirds in the distance. But Abby saw and heard nothing around her. She peered down a dark tunnel into the past leading to the witches' cave she visited with her mother as a young girl. Less clear than her solitary pilgrimages to the crones' home, she observed the memory as an outsider perched above the cave floor, even seeing her young self clinging to her mother's dress.

Abby's mother held the little house-shaped lantern high, its flame scattering light through the crosses on each side onto the broad cave walls. The withered denizens addressed her from the far side of the stone slab. "You ask much, nun with child, and while our powers have yet to fully wane, our exposure may be our ruin. Gaining you favor at the local manor is within our power, but what do you offer in return?"

"I would share with you the eternal flame of Brigid, unbroken through generations, guarded by my sisters in Kildare but now cast asunder by the King." Her mother's booming voice echoed through the cave, reaching every corner as if emanating from the rock itself. This surprised both her young daughter in the scene and Abby, watching from afar. Strangely, they jumped in unison. Abby couldn't recall her mother ever speaking with such force.

"A worthy trade, but flame rekindled is not flame eternal. Pray, tell us how this came to be?" inquired the nearest sister. Her gray eyes scoured the bold woman for any sign of treachery.

Abby's defiant mother stepped forward, placing the lantern on the stone slab. Still holding Abby's hand, she spoke more softly now, "Bringer of the early spring, protector of all that graze, the waters and sacred wells, one of the Tuatha Dé Danann, her servants have kept a flame which she brought forth alight through many ages. When threatened, the flame has been split thrice, honoring her triad, and kept safe until such time as they can be united. The lantern before you flickers with the same flame as that which Brigid herself hath lit. In protection of the flame, I have traveled to England with this child, the next keeper." She pointed to little Abby and added, "For if you are what you claim, you must know what she is."

Abby's mind receded to the present, to the white sky of the new world where Susan kneeled next to her. "Abby, dear, are you all right? You, I think you fainted," whispered Susan. Faria and Shikha hovered around Susan, looking on. "You just sat transfixed for minutes. I ran to get the twins in the hope they could revive you. When we returned, we found you slumped over."

With Faria's help, Abby sat up and wiped her brow with her kerchief. A slight breeze freshened the air with the breath of the sea, gently rustling the maple and oak leaves. Abby looked out over the vast river, now darkened by clouds. She turned to Faria, who still held her hand and said, "I think at long last we shall have some rain."

Abby's words forced a wide smile to appear on her adopted daughter's face. "The river has asked, and the sky will provide," Faria intoned. While relieved to hear Abby speak, Susan found her words confusing. She feared that revisiting Abby's memories had strained her to exhaustion.

"Are you sure you are well? Perhaps you should lie back down whilst I fetch you a bit of water," said Susan.

Abby breathed deeply. To no one in particular she said, "They weren't my parents. She loved me, but my, I don't know what to call her, my mother was a steward of something I couldn't comprehend until today. She was training me in those early years, but I failed to fit it all together. I was next. I was chosen."

Abby stood very slowly, as if the span of time from today back to the day of her vision bent her freckled shoulders. At full height, she looked to Faria and Shikha gazing up at her angelically, next to Susan, her unexpected and deepest confidant, just as heavy raindrops began to patter on the leaves above them. Spontaneously hugging all three, the weight of her vision dissipated into the air like steam from a kettle. In that embrace, Abby understood that the path from frightened redheaded child in the crone's cave to standing proudly among the trees of the new world had never been about her alone. She had unknowingly abandoned her charge as the next keeper of the sacred flame, yet that desperate action led her to the twins and in turn to this sandy shore. All their lives fell through time like tiny raindrops, feeding the unceasing river of destiny.

CHAPTER 26 - September 1603

The summer slipped by so easy and light that the first chill of autumn took Susan by surprise. When their small camp awoke to an early morning frost in late September, they began preparations for harvesting the barley. Tom had kept fastidious records of each day's weather, as well as observations on crop sizes and germination times. While his academic text on agriculture had induced the belief in Tom that all the turnips and parsnips should be pulled from the ground straightaway, a quick walk through the field and a glance at some of the other recommendations from his book convinced Abby that the author had never actually had dirt on his hands, much less owned a farm.

They all set to work on the barley, but without dedicated farm implements, the work progressed slowly. A single sickle was aided by various kitchen knives, but only Abby and Sagar had any proficiency in the field so the two of them continued to reap, while the others were left to separate the grain by whatever means they could contrive.

Abby lost herself in the familiar rhythmic action of cutting the barley stalks and had unconsciously begun to sing a tune. "You do have a lovely voice. What is it you sing, Miss Abby?" asked Shikha as she approached her to collect more cut grain.

"Sing? Was I singing, dear?" Abby thought for a moment and laughed. "We used to sing together on harvest days when I was younger. John Barleycorn. Here, this is how it goes," Abby said. She began dangerously conducting with the sickle but singing much louder, in turn drawing Susan and Faria over to her.

There were three men come out o' the west their fortunes for to try.
And these three men made a solemn vow, John Barleycorn must die.
They plowed,
they sowed,

they harrowed him in,
throwed clods upon his head,
Till these three men were satisfied John Barleycorn was dead.

"That's it." Soon enough she had them all singing along, helping to pass the time. Even Sagar joined in from the far side of the field. Five long days later, the barley sat snugly packed into barrels, ready for transport. Susan admired her calloused hands, wishing her parents and brothers in England could see what had become of her and her wayward family.

***

September ended with a last charge of summer heat, but the chill descended with purpose in October. Tom documented the extremes in his weather log and would often bring up the topic of temperature fluctuations as they gathered around the campfire each night. One crisp evening midway through the month, Abby reckoned that the turnips and parsnips were just about ready for harvest, noting that some plants should be preserved for next spring's seeds. The barrels full of barley and her presumption they would be planting again next year subtly boosted everyone's confidence in their winter survival prospects. Abby's words, however, reminded Tom of Cikiyiyô Muksihs' warning about the river's spring flood.

"We must warn the congregation before we depart. Our camp here would be underwater too," Tom added, after explaining what the chief's son had conveyed. To his surprise, his comments precipitated little direct response, but all eyes turned to Abby.

She waited for Susan, Nate or even Sagar to speak, but none were willing. "You are right, Tom," Abby replied. "I think you have a better chance of convincing someone if only you, or you and Nathan were to go. Captain Tanner and James should at least listen to reason." Susan exhaled sharply.

Addressing Sagar directly, Susan said, "Do you think they will be safe?" Fear rang in her voice; she referred to her husband and son, not the congregants. Susan hadn't considered that their response to a warning might be hostile.

Sagar always sat more distant from the fire, just outside the reach of its flickering light. He could often be found glancing over his shoulder into the darkness as the others chatted. He looked around the fire pit and replied to Susan, "If Mr. Tom and Nate are to return, they should go when the sun is highest, and there is little chance of confusion." Now looking to Tom, he said, "Make much noise, so that you don't surprise the guards. If the Gaithers have had their way, the stockade will be high and well manned." To which Sagar added after a brief pause, "I will follow you there."

Tom, always first to think the best of people, had learned to trust Sagar's intuition. He reckoned that Sagar had kept watch on the camp these past several months, although the boy never mentioned it. Nodding in acquiescence, he added, possibly for Susan and the younger boys' benefit, "I'm sure there's nothing to be concerned about, but all the same, Sagar, I thank you for the guidance. We shall leave tomorrow after breakfast, the three of us." The conversation soon ebbed and only Sagar lay awake, gazing up at the October sky.

After a cold morning meal, Tom, Nate and Sagar set out for the congregants' compound. Abby and the twins busied themselves pulling turnips and parsnips with the help of Philip and Will. Susan began packing up the camp. In the woods, Sagar led Tom and his son along the shoreline and after about an hour's walk, he whispered, "Just keep along this path and you will be at the gate in about a half-hour. I will be close." Before Tom had a chance to respond, Sagar darted into the forest, vanishing from sight. Nathan scrutinized his father for some reaction, but Tom just smiled and started walking.

As Sagar had suggested, Nathan and Tom spoke freely and louder than they might if just on a walk in the woods. At length, the stockade loomed in the distance. First visible as a contrast to the scattered and diffuse light of the forest, the high wall both darkened the forest floor and lightened the sky above it. Even in its early form, Cikiyiyô Muksihs had spotted the unnatural shape from across the river.

"Hallo!" Tom called out without warning, startling Nathan.

"Who's there? I wasn't told anyone was outside the fort," replied an invisible voice. Soon two figures stood above the wall peering over its highest point. The stockade ran at a height of ten feet, but where the path Tom and Nate trod ended, a larger gatehouse stood a good six feet higher.

"It's Tom Robbin here and my son Nathan. Is that Jacob Burns up there? We were in the same watch aboard ship, Jacob." Tom addressed the other man, until now silent.

With a stern look from the first guard, Jacob growled back at Tom, "And that makes us brothers? Did you two come begging for food?" which drew a laugh from his compatriot.

"No actually, we just ate a lovely breakfast," Tom said. "We wish to speak with Captain Tanner, if you please."

The guards roiled in laughter at his request. "That drunk? Now what'll you have to talk about with a shipless captain? I hear he hasn't left Mary's house in weeks," yelled Jacob.

Unfazed, Tom replied, "Then please fetch James, his son in law. We must speak with him."

His request stymied the guards, who turned their backs momentarily. Trying to stall Tom, they replied, "Is the dark boy with you?"

"You mean Sagar, who saved the first mate of the ship from drowning and ensured your safe passage to these lands? The lad who helped teach many of you how to smoke fish so you'd have something to eat in two months when the ground and river are frozen? That dark boy? No, he is not with us. Now for goodness' sake, Jacob, go get James," Tom yelled up at them in his most schoolmasterly tone.

They received no response, but the guards turned around again and Jacob disappeared. Within a minute, the wooden gate swung open, and James pensively approached. Both guards stood within the stockade's walls with guns ready. James led Tom and Nathan a small distance farther from the wall, and said, "Tom, young Nathan, I am so glad to see you, but you really shouldn't have risked coming back. These are dangerous times. Have you seen Sagar?"

Tom had many questions, but under the scrutiny of the

volatile guards, he knew he must deliver his message with haste. "Sagar is quite well and is living among us. James, we came to warn you. The congregation, this camp, your fort, are at risk from the river's spring flood. We have it on good authority . . ."

James interrupted him. "We've broken our backs making this camp secure, Tom, what do you mean, at risk? Even early this year, the river remained well below the camp."

"It was a strange year. The natives have said that the river level could be as much as fifteen feet higher during a wet winter. Look, James, this isn't like a river in England. North of here there must be a substantial mountain range which traps snow all winter, releasing it in torrents come the thaw. Have you wondered why the natives live inland and don't have any permanent settlements along the river?" James remained silent but listened intently. Tom continued, "We're not here to tell you to leave. We're not even saying that the camp should be abandoned, just that someone should be aware of the danger and to keep a close lookout come spring. It's up to you all what to do."

James breathed deeply and replied, "you trust these natives?" Tom nodded. "Even if it's true, I'm just not sure what can be done. Tom, you don't know what the congregation has become. We're servants, the Gaithers have their grip so tight."

"Come with us. We're going across the river in a few days," said Tom.

"If it were just me and Mary, perhaps we could. But the Captain's sick, and I still have some influence." James hesitated. "I fear without me here, many of the others would stand no chance. Herb Gaither would work them near to death." Even though the guards stood a good distance away, James added in a whisper, "I've been storing food for winter. Not just for Mary and me, but for the lot of us."

Tom understood, but had no response. Nathan, silent until now, unshouldered his pack, and handed it to James, who instinctively took it. Surprised by its weight, he had to grasp the satchel with both hands. "The guns Captain Tanner lent us are in it. There's also a bag of barley. It was Sagar's idea," said the young man, now as tall as

James. Tom put his arm on his son's shoulder and couldn't help but smile.

"Good luck to you, truly. God bless you and your families," James intoned. He looked like he wanted to say more, but just turned away and walked slowly back into the camp. The gate haltingly closed behind him.

Tom and Nathan began retracing their steps and a few minutes from the stockade they espied Sagar in the distance, waiting. He was not out of breath but Tom could tell he had been running. "We should depart for the western shore soon. After you left, the guards thought to follow, but decided instead to inform Herb Gaither of your visit. I might expect them to search for us tomorrow." They walked in silence for some time, oak leaves crunching under foot, until Sagar spoke again, "You did the honorable thing, Mr. Tom, and Nathan too."

Upon their return, they found the field picked clean of turnips and parsnips, the barrels of barley loaded onto the raft, and most of their belongings stacked neatly on the riverbank. The sun still sat high in the sky. "Tom, dear, were you able to warn the congregation?" Susan said, relieved at their safe return. She trotted up to the two of them, hugging each in turn.

"I spoke briefly with James, but not Captain Tanner," Tom replied. "We were right to leave. All of us." Abby stood with the twins at her side, knowing to whom he referred. "A tall stockade now rings the village and guards keep watch, weapons ready. James fears for their and many of the others' safety: not from what is outside the wall, but from what is within. He is caching food in the hope he can help others survive the winter."

Sagar had been walking a few steps behind Tom and Nate as they entered camp but when they stopped to greet Susan, he continued down to the river's edge. As the others talked he gazed west, not at the far shore of the river or the adjacent woods, but at the horizon and perhaps what lay beyond. Hearing Tom describe the day's events, Sagar shook his head and said to himself, "It has always been this way with men." Sagar trotted back to rejoin the others.

"Within that wall, Mr. Tom, no one will starve. I will make sure of it," Sagar said resolutely. He scrutinized their odd little clan: Faria and Shikha, acting the part of passive observers, no doubt reading his present thoughts; the young Robbin boys, eager for adventure and to meet the natives; Tom, unbounded curiosity feeding inner strength, if there were just more men like him; Susan, anchoring her family with practical compassion; and Abby, her nascent awareness, possibly the last of its kind, would emerge as a powerful force under the tutelage of Ayaks, the chief's wife.

Standing beside the twins, Sagar found all eyes upon him after his statement. In a melodic tone, he addressed the group, "It can often feel as if certain events have greater import than others. Departing from Amsterdam, contacting the natives, leaving the congregation and now crossing to the western shore. These actions seem bold and momentous. I have found though, that all actions, however small, resonate equally through time. Finding a book in an old chest, kindness shown to a dying sailor or a short conversation on the aft deck of a ship also serve destiny's design. It is the same with people. Some of us are born with purpose, some will perceive it as the years pass, and to others, there will be no revelation. The knowledge of one's place does not impart greater importance, indeed I have found it lessens it. One becomes bound to fate. Still, no one is adrift, we all contribute to the river of time. Yet some men, men like the Gaithers, seek to dominate the paths of others. They can cause ripples, sometimes waves, harsh enough at the time, but soon the water is smooth again."

Sagar took a step closer to the shore and said, "Whether by the sun's last rays, or the light of the full moon, we shall make our way across the river and camp on the western shore."

CHAPTER 27 - April 1, 2013

Sagar slept. He dreamed of the bite of swirling sands against his face, the high desert at dusk, and a city in the distance barely perceptible through the haze. He jolted awake when the plane touched down in Uttar Pradesh at Mundha Pande airport. Landing a private jet caused a pause in work at the airstrip, recently handed over to the Airports Authority of India for a significant upgrade. Upon their arrival, a long-bearded man edged away from the worksite, directing a cackle of triumph toward the northern mountains. To the airport laborers, he was simply one of the many holy men who wandered the hills and plains. He stood in the open space, yet was camouflaged from Shikha and Sagar by both the breadth of time and the cacophony of the laborers' thoughts around him. To the very few who still roamed the earth and recognized his timeless visage, he was known as Brigu or Bhrigu. Sagar had received his message. They had found their way back.

Used to landing in strange locations and provisioning for whatever might lie outside the plane door, Hehu collected several black duffel bags together and piled them at the base of the plane stairs. Shikha paced the tarmac, eager to begin their search for Faria. Shortly, a disheveled man on a moped appeared, curious but trying to act important as well. He began yelling at Hehu, who shrugged, but called out to Sagar. Appearing at the top of the jet's stairs, Sagar looked down and smiled at the official. He knew this type of man well and despite his appearance, Sagar bowed after approaching him and asked if it would be too much trouble if they could park the jet at the airport for a few days. Sagar produced several toys from his pockets, adding that they were gifts for the man's children and when he returned he would be happy to give his family a tour of the jet. The official looked Sagar up and down, and gazed at the plane for a moment. Giving his consent, he handed Sagar a crumpled form and sped away on the smoking scooter.

Waiting for the official to depart, the driver of a gleaming silver four-door Toyota Hilux pickup now descended upon the jet. Fearful another driver for hire would take this impossibly lucrative job, he skidded the truck to a halt and jumped out. Hehu began loading the bags into the truck's bed, as unhurried as the driver was excited, just enjoying the feel of the afternoon sun on his back. The pickup's driver, thinking he had been hired for transportation into the city, was surprised when Sagar bought the truck outright, offering him twice the vehicle's worth.

Shikha could still not hail her sister via text or using the local number she had, so the three of them, Sagar, Shikha and Hehu, set off for Rampur, a few miles away. Their route was easy enough and soon they reached the old fort and the library. Shikha hopped out of the truck, sped through the gardens and past a burbling fountain. She trotted up the wide steps into the Rampur Raza library and was greeted by an elderly man smiling widely. "You're back again!" he said, mistaking her for her sister. As she got closer, he squinted and became unsure for just a moment. Shikha forced a smile, ingesting her surroundings, slowing her pace and breath.

"I have lost track of myself again, my friend. What time did I leave yesterday?" she replied while staring into his aged eyes.

"An hour after Fajr, much earlier than usual," he intoned, referring to the Islamic dawn prayer.

"Yes, as you say it, it returns to me. Thank you and may your day be blessed by Allah," Shikha replied. She glided out, her movement unceasing. But as she passed the fountain, she halted, sitting on its tiled edge. Trying to reconcile what her eyes perceived and what her senses revealed, she saw gaps, vacancies but also a vision. Faria was alive but no longer in the city. Near the river. A small village.

Faria, stay where you are, I am coming, she thought, hoping her sister could still sense her feelings. Back in the truck, she instructed Sagar to head southwest where the meandering Kosi River flowed. He obliged, navigating the streets of Rampur until rutted pavement turned to hard-packed dirt. As they drove, Shikha sat rigid in the front seat, scanning the horizon and pointing at each crossroads. Within twenty minutes, they entered a village composed of low tan buildings, tidy but crude. Sagar stopped the truck when Shikha opened her door and bounded out. Following, he caught up with her as she entered the narrow streets. Hehu stayed in the Hilux, enveloping most of the back seat.

Shikha jogged along the main street, really more of a wide path, with Sagar at her side. A young boy caught sight of them and yelled out, "This way!" They followed. Their small guide reminded Shikha of Sagar in the rigging of the Spring Tide. He moved effortlessly, slipping through the crooked streets like water running through a canyon. His pace slowed and he led them into a mud-brick hut on the edge of the village. Waving aside a blanket serving as a door, they found Faria sitting on a mattress on the floor, awake but disoriented. Shikha ran to her. Their hands neared, pausing, almost afraid to touch for the first time in a century, until Faria fell into her sister's outstretched arms.

In that contact, Shikha knew Faria had not escaped an attack similar to what befell her on Long Island. Her sister had been at the library the day before, researching early Koran permutations, Bedouin mythology, really. She had become so engrossed in—she couldn't remember what—and suddenly felt a presence descend upon her. She didn't recall leaving the library specifically, but in a disoriented state, she sought safety. Recovering this morning, she found herself in the nearby village with a family she had known long ago.

"It's like certain memories have been wiped from my mind, Shi. There are black spots, vacancies. Look for yourself. But you have the book?" Faria said, responding somewhat disjointedly in words to her sister's thoughts. She looked up at Sagar.

Shikha tried to ignore their silent exchange. Long ago she grew weary of her ability to peer into both their minds, unrestricted. "Yes, we have it," she said, a bit too loudly. "It may be that Brigu was the author; he was, at least, its last owner before the book changed hands from Father Williams to Tom Robbin."

Faria didn't reply but subtly nodded. She still squinted through the light pouring into the small room, framing Sagar in the doorway. A desperate smile parted her lips. The lips he couldn't kiss. Having heard what happened to Faria in Rampur Raza, Sagar realized it was not his bravery that saved Shikha from the same fate, but his mere presence. The twins wondered the same.

"And Ramesh brought you to me?" Faria awoke from her thoughts and said, referring to the small boy still standing unmoved in the center of the room. "He can be as invisible as the stars under a full moon. I had him stationed at the far end of the village, for what I knew not," she continued. "I tutored his great aunt. Tough woman but kind on the inside... Are you perchance hungry? There is no greater food in all of northern India than that of Ramesh's mother," Faria rattled. Their arrival had refreshed her. Without being asked, the boy disappeared from the room. Sagar departed to fetch the truck and Hehu.

During the next few minutes, within their mental conversation, Faria ingested her sister's discoveries on their genetic origins. It was progress, definitive evidence, the first they had. Her reaction mirrored Sagar's, but in Faria's exhausted state, her outward response was more muted. "Shi, it is groundbreaking work. Surely you see this?" Faria said to her sister in a tired but passionate voice. Still sensing the relative disappointment in Shikha, she continued, "Your hypothesis had been that a few genetic mutations passed through our lineage, gave us such prolonged lives, correct?"

"Yes, that had been the most likely explanation," Shikha whispered.

"I need time to think, to reconcile the implications of your results with mine, but the notion we are genetically distinct from the rest of humanity presents so many lines of research for both of us, and," Faria paused, "it explains one thing." She need not verbalize what they both thought: through hundreds of years and dozens of relationships, neither of them nor Sagar had ever been able to have children.

They all shared an early supper, which lived up to Faria's billing. It would seem that Hehu was incapable of getting full. Eventually, he just got bored of eating. Once the low table had been cleared, Shikha revealed the tome they had gone to such lengths to procure. Faria began by turning Brigu's gift to Father Williams over and over in her hands, allowing its heft to drop her arms. The tactile feel of the book awoke their adoptive mother's consciousness. Abigail placidly peered on, validating its lineage but having no more knowledge of the book than when she and Susan reviewed it long ago. Faria finally allowed it to come to rest on the soft-grained wooden tabletop. Her reaction looked similar to that of David's. She first assessed the outer manufacture, next the various components, finally focusing on the content. She mentally catalogued the languages, lingering before beginning to translate when a harsh wind threw dust past the blanket door and onto the book's pages.

Shikha and Faria looked up at Sagar pensively, who was standing at a distance from them so as to not block the light falling on the table. He jumped out the doorway and disappeared into the light. A few minutes later, Sagar returned, grim faced but silent. Whatever had aroused their concern had passed. Still Sagar kept on guard, his back to the twins and facing outside with Hehu at his side.

Faria readdressed the text and became more excited with each passing page. She grasped Shikha's hand from time to time when reaching some critical passage. "The book seeks to tie the various deluge or flood myths into one narrative. This is the collected works of an extremely well-traveled individual who had access to un-plundered ancient sites spanning many millennia. Given the age, it stands on its own as a historic artifact, irrespective of whether these are original source documents or recopied pieces," she whispered. For a spell, Faria sat consumed with the text.

Minutes later she spoke again, still looking down, "I've directly translated Sumerian and Akkadian clay tablets as they emerged from the ground during excavations. The deluge myths they contained didn't end like this." She stood up and paced the room, trying to remember why she knew to ask Shikha to bring this book, and what had she been researching at the Rampur Raza library.

Faria stopped pacing and spoke, the emotion dropped from her voice, "We weren't ready for this when it belonged to Nathan and then Abby. But we are now." Sitting back down at the table she began to mark pages, inserting her fingers here and there. In rapid fire she turned from finger to finger. "Utnapishtim survived the flood on the Babylonian version of an ark, but this cuneiform tells of a second set of survivors, those closest to the gods who decamped to the mountains and were never seen or heard from again. Here, Satyavrata, the 7th Manu and the first king on earth who saved mankind from the deluge, depicted in resplendent blue, speaks of a race apart who tricked the gods. The Book of Daniel speaks of the Watchers, the Wakeful Ones . . . even the," she paused. "That's it! The Koran also refers to those who did not cleave to Noah's warnings, but hid from the flood in the high mountains. Rampur Raza must have earlier permutations of the official Koranic text, the versions resident in the minds and stories of the near east thousands of years before the Prophet Mohammed walked the deserts." A hot wind blew violently outside, swirling sand into the small room, but she and the others paid it no heed.

A second briefer section, which David had not reached, resided within the last pages of the tome. Flipping from pages written in Avestan to Vedic Sanskrit to Ogham to Elder Futhark, the tome traced the lineage of one of the most primitive yet universal human beliefs: elemental water as the mother of life: that is, the sacred Danu, the mother goddess. In Avestan, the word danu itself means river, while in the Sanskrit Rigveda, Danu emerges as mother of the Danavas and in turn, is associated with the waters of heaven. In Celtic mythology, Danu bore onto the earth those known as the Tuatha De Danaan, gods and heroes all. The flowing waters, the rivers Danube and Don took their name from their mother.

Faria had spent her adult years tracing these parallels of adopted and constructed belief, but there was also something deeper. Faria knew this at her core. Four hundred years ago, with the cool waters of the Connecticut River slipping around her small bare feet, Faria's soul resonated with the river's presence and its flow to the sea. It was not foreign to her: it was her, and she was it. It is, and shall ever be. There need be no additional human conventions, principles or hierarchies. The Israelites, at some distant time, realized this in their most basic understanding of the divine: YHWH, I AM.

With the sudden appearance of her sister and Sagar, Faria's loneliness, the anchor maintaining her mind in the now, had been hauled up. Layered memories collapsed upon her all at once. The white soil at the base of the mountains; Brigu's last commands to the three; Asha's dying words in Mari Indus on the sacred River Sarasvati near Rakhigarhi and now the book's revelations: all coalesced into a purpose and destination.

CHAPTER 28 - Winter 1603

After departing their temporary home near the river, Tom Robbin's family, along with Abby, the twins and Sagar were welcomed into the Pequot village; their careful planning and vigilant gardening ensured their arrival was no burden to the natives. Abby and Cikiyiyô Muksihs married upon the winter solstice, much to Ayaks' delight. In likely the first hybrid wedding ceremony of its kind, Susan was Abby's matron of honor, the twins her flower girls while the chief presided. The native settlement swelled to well over 200 people as all the inhabitants of the forest attended. Drawn to the ancient strength now consolidated yet still growing within the village, the woodland spirits also looked on.

Sagar, as became his custom, disappeared soon thereafter only to return for weeks on end in spring and summer. Where he went, nobody would ask. As the seasons passed, Tom always noted reluctance in the boy each year as the solstice approached. Despite missing his small wandering compatriot, for his part, Tom couldn't have been happier. By the first summer he had used half the paper brought from England in cataloging everything around him from native harvest and hunting practices to descriptions of trees and animals. Susan worked alongside him, sketching fine detailed images of the flora and fauna. Ink became a dear commodity until Kutomá Nipôwi and Nathan invented a local solution from soot and pine tar. It was serviceable and the more they made the finer the quality.

Tom also established a school of sorts. As best he could, he focused on a traditional education for his children in a unique setting: his and Susan's longhouse. Each morning he would lecture on mathematics, history and languages. For a few hours in the afternoon, he opened their home to the entire village: children, elders, anyone interested. Tom never became proficient in hunting or fishing, but each day he captivated a packed house with some natives traveling from adjacent communities to hear the thin white teacher.

In time, even Cikiyiyô Muksihs came to respect the man he once scoffed at as silly and delicate. To a young warrior, strength meant everything, but as his father reminded him, strength without flexibility was like the hard winter ice breaking up along the river's edge. Tom would openly admit what he did not know, but most interesting to the chief's son was the plurality, the openness of Tom's mind: he would lead those assembled in his longhouse in deductive exercises to discover answers themselves, such as why people aged, or why the seasons existed at all. When their collective conclusions did not align with the wisdom of Ayaks, of course, Tom was first to note that their answer was just one of many possible.

Ayaks seldom attended Tom's sessions, but on those rare occasions when she did, she publicly found his knowledge either comical or impractical, sometimes both. Privately though, she would quiz him on astronomy, the moon cycles and his religious beliefs. Tom's descriptions of Christianity, of the one God and His son the Christ confused Ayaks. He could never quite convey the notion of Grace in a way that aligned with the natives' beliefs. Abby knew why. She always attended these intimate discussions and as Ayaks aged, the fire-haired woman became her spiritual successor, blending with ease what she had learned from her surrogate mother, the twins and Ayaks into a cohesive spiritual view.

Ayaks believed the world was a single living organism born of and embodied by the mother goddess: the day and night her breathing; the seasons, her sleeping and reawakening; the rivers, her veins. The birds gliding above the earth, the creatures that dwelled on land and below the water's surface were all part of this creation, part of what Ayaks saw interchangeably as sacred yet accessible.

At first Abby came to view this mother goddess in tripartite: as giver of life, life itself, and the home of existence, but over time this description, the words themselves lost meaning to her and she simply felt at peace with all that was around her. No mediation or intercession was required to know God, no uncertainty of salvation, no predestined Grace: just the deep sense that every flower, every tree, every human was part of the creator and sanctified by its existence alone. Only failing to recognize this simple truth distanced humanity from its progenitor, as Abby had witnessed in England.

With Susan's steady aid, Abby recalled one more earlier episode from her childhood. Unlike the others, it did not strike her or Susan as dramatic or revelatory, but why some events linger and others dissipate, there is no telling. By late autumn in the year after her surrogate mother had ventured to the cave, life had changed for the little family. No longer did they dwell in a cellar room in town but instead they had been granted a tidy house on the edge of the manor fields. The stone cottage nestled against the forest where beyond and deeper still lay the witches' cave.

The woman who raised Abby as her child would wander endlessly through the trees without regard to season or weather, her young charge at her side. Whereas the villagers were wary of the dense, overgrown wood, in the most fierce of storms, she would turn to Abby and without a word slip on her wool overcoat, eyes glinting. The two of them would venture out into the wet and the rain to explore the forest. It was most alive, she would say, when the trees danced in the wind.

But on a wet autumn day, Abby's surrogate mother returned to the edge of the woods to find the manor farmhands clearing land. Her employer and his family had left to visit relatives in London and so she had been dismissed early. Abby recalled standing in the cold drizzle just watching the men hacking away at the trees, burning the grasses and smaller branches in a sooty, smoky pyre. At the time, Abby didn't understand why the black-haired woman that raised her wept, but she remembered reaching out her small hand in comfort, and the tight grip that took hold.

Abby understood now that her surrogate mother mourned as the Dryads had mourned the trees cut by the Congregants. During the encounter at camp, Abby had not overpowered the spirits who sought revenge, she appealed to their common kinship, a lineage thousands of years distant, which slumbered within her.

After this last recollection, Abby no longer sought answers in

Tom's books or in her past. She embraced the tutelage of Ayaks and found home in the village. For Abby and Susan both, survival from week to week and season to season left little room for reflection, but they stayed quite close and in rare spare moments, shared their joy in finding a life of meaning. Susan's energies remained focused on maintaining order within, and providing for her family. With Tom lecturing most days, provisioning for winter and daily foraging fell to her and Nathan. Abby, part of the chief's family, had less concern for basic necessities, but a heavier burden was upon her as Ayaks aged and the village began to depend on her spiritual guidance.

The quiet passage of many seasons shepherded chief Quniyokat into the next world and his son succeeded him in leading an extended tribe of the Pequots that spanned many villages. He sought Abby's counsel in all matters, and Shikha and Faria were never far from her side. In the broader native community the twins came to be viewed as an extension of the fiery haired woman; together they received supplicants in the same long house where Ayaks had.

CHAPTER 29 - Fall 1613

Sagar never established a permanent presence in the village as the Robbins or Abby had. He flitted through the village like leaves in the fall only to disappear for a week or a month. Winters would pass without any sight of him. In the natives' village, his strange habits earned him the name little black bear, hibernating in the winter. Always welcome at the new chief's table during feasts, few knew to where he disappeared when nature lay dormant.

Once Nathan suggested to Kutomá Nipôwi that they follow Sagar to learn his secret and know for sure why the boy didn't make the village his home. Nathan, grown to manhood but retaining the curiosity of a fifteen-year-old, hoped to quell village gossip. The chief's son-in-law, however, looked puzzled at the idea. Kutomá Nipôwi replied that Sagar didn't belong in the village, for he was one of the Makiaweesug, the little people. They trod their own path unless bound to someone for a specific purpose. Nathan retorted, and what of the twins then? Nodding, and in a tone which implied he felt he was stating the obvious, Kutomá Nipôwi claimed that the twins assisted Abigail. He folded his arms to conclude the discussion, whispering that it invited bad luck to talk of such things: any help from the Makiaweesug was a blessing not to be questioned.

Sagar made contact with James a few times a year, which helped him understand how best to aid the congregants. While Harold Gaither maintained tight control over who could pass beyond the stockade gates, even the clan Gaither had no choice but to grudgingly allow James some autonomy. Being the only blacksmith in camp and able to provide to those in need within the walled enclave, a reluctant James emerged as the people's quiet champion. Still, for both their safety, James and Sagar agreed to meet on the third and ninth new moons, well north of the compound where the Robbins and Abby had once camped and crossed the river. In September of 1613, Sagar arrived on the appointed day and waited for nightfall. James never came. Again, the next night he waited and yet for a third until a sliver of moonlight appeared. Something was amiss.

Sagar approached the congregants' compound at speed. Aware of the guard towers, he skirted the wall to where it came closest to the forest. Scaling the barrier in two leaps he dropped softly on the far side. All was quiet, especially next to the church, where a newly dug grave lay in wait for a coffin. Sagar made his way to James and Mary's house. Thick smoke poured from the chimney and light creeped out from underneath the door. Peering through a crack in the high wooden shutters, he glimpsed Mary and Captain Tanner sitting in front of a fire. James' body was laid out on a wooden table.

However conventional it felt, Sagar knocked on the door. He could tell by the sounds inside that Mary came to answer. "Who, who is there?" she said.

"It's Sagar, ma'am," he whispered back. Unsure if she heard him, Sagar began to repeat himself as the door opened just a sliver. Mary stood frozen for several seconds, but soon processed the scene before her and pulled the boy inside. Tanner turned from the fire and Sagar could see nine years of weathering in the man's face. A lifetime of labor had built his body into a fortress, now in decline like an abandoned medieval redoubt.

"What are you doing here? How did you know?" Mary said referring to her husband's death. "Are you ill? You're so thin, so small."

Selecting which questions to answer, Sagar spoke: "Two nights ago we were to meet, James and I. When he failed to appear I came looking for him. Ma'am, I am truly sorry for your loss. For my part at least, he was a very good friend. I am proud to have known him." Still oppressed with grief, Mary couldn't smile but Sagar knew she wanted to, comforted by the boy's sudden appearance and kind words. "May I ask, how did it happen?" Sagar added.

Unsure who would respond, Mary and Tanner looked to one another nervously.

"An accident at the forge, we believe," Mary whispered. Tanner scoffed.

"It was no accident. James was as careful a man as I ever knew," Tanner retorted, not angry at his daughter, but hot all the same.

"We have no proof of that, Father," Mary said. Turning to Sagar, she haltingly continued. "We found him at, at the forge two days ago, collapsed next to the bellows." She stopped, unable to go on.

Tanner stood and put his arms around Mary's shaking shoulders. "I'm sorry, dear. My suspicions mean little now. This is not just our loss, you see, it's the whole crew who have lost their mate." The aged man spoke quietly to his daughter, still a ship's captain from his beard to his bowed legs.

"You must leave," Sagar said.

"What, how? To live with you in the woods, son, we are not built for it. Across the river to the natives? No, again. We are just so different," Mary replied.

Sagar agreed with Mary. They would have no place among the natives, and even the integration of the Robbins and Abby into the Pequot tribe had required delicacy. Still, he thought there must be a way, a path he hadn't envisioned. Sagar sifted possibilities and events, past and future, watching them fall through his mind, combine and recombine in dull, faded colors. But a single hue began to dominate, glowing a brighter and brighter red until emerging in a shimmering, crystalline form.

"The comb," Sagar said. "Jorge's comb. Do you still have it?"

Mary looked down at him, puzzled. She nodded, adding, "Yes, but why?"

"Recall Jorge's words when he gave it to you," Sagar replied. On top of her grief, the past 20 minutes had spun Mary around so many times she felt dizzy. Sagar's appearance at the door, his cryptic words and now the abrupt memory of Jorge forced Mary to sit down. She tried in earnest to recall what Jorge had said before he died but she just couldn't. Tanner was no use either. They both looked to Sagar again, who intoned, "Wish upon the comb and love, salvation, even fortune shall be yours." The Captain and Mary let the words linger in the air, each wondering if the promise could be true, wondering if the gift of their old friend, dead these nine years, could deliver them.

Sagar spoke no more. Mary listened to the crackling fire, now burning low as it threw the shadow of her motionless husband against the wall of their home. Her face ruddy from two days of tears, she stood, legs wobbly, and approached a large sea chest on the far side of the room. Looking down, Mary took a breath and opened it. Her father turned and watched as she rummaged through the box. Before her arms reappeared, Sagar saw the faint red glow of the comb's ruby, encrusted in the handle. Mary cradled the gift and without returning to Sagar and her father, she whispered under her breath.

The simple words of a sea captain's daughter spoken in desperation did not crash idly against the walls of their home or to the packed dirt floor unheard. They vibrated through the air, into the forest, through the river and deep into the sea. Mary's request acted as an inviolable command, marshaling nature itself and her guardian spirits to a unified purpose. The incandescent light from within the red ruby slowly ebbed like the setting sun until it only reflected the firelight. Tanner and Mary noticed nothing, but Sagar shuddered as her words and the light ceased. Across the river in the Pequot camp, Abby shocked upright in bed and the twins turned restlessly in their sleep at the intensity of nature's response.

One hundred miles west, a small Dutch ship named the Onrust was about to run aground, her anchor having given way in the fast moving current of the Hellegat. Now obligated to heed Mary's command, the Grundylows of the brackish water silently edged the ship out into center of the channel, unbeknownst to its crew. Nature cannot conjure an object from the air, but she can alter the fates of men. Mary had pleaded for a ship to take her and her father back to Europe; that ship was captained by one Adriaen Block.

The river spirits of the treacherous passage later known as Hell Gate slipped Block's ship slow and easy around successive underwater rock ledges with the gingerness of a new mother carrying her baby. Into Long Island Sound the Onrust sailed, where the sea would quell the waves and tides, ensuring the vessel came to rest just outside the congregants' compound within a day and a half. The Onrust would be in need of a replacement yardarm for its lateen rigging, and someone who could navigate the waters leading East to the Atlantic. Captain Tanner was that man.

"Mary, dear, what did you say?" the aged Tanner asked.

"A ship. I asked for a ship," she said, looking only at the floor. "Father, there's nothing left here for you or me. It's time we return—me to England and you to the sea." Mary walked back to where Sagar stood, entreating, "Is this just nonsense? The raving of a dying Portuguese sailor and a boy trying to comfort a woman in mourning, or should I, dare I, have hope?"

Sagar stepped closer to her and into the firelight. He said to both Mary and his old captain, "I do not know the means of your deliverance, but if you wished for a ship and passage home, I am sure that ship will come. You would do well to pass the comb to whosoever captains the vessel as payment for your voyage."

In the early morning, James was laid to rest next to the colony's church, one of many who had lost their lives in the past nine years: some from sickness, a few from old age, but more small gravestones than large littered the plot. Sagar briefly looked on from a gap in the stockade before making his way back across the river to await the arrival of a ship, Mary's ship. Early the following day, Sagar swam out to meet a stout little vessel with a crudely repaired yardarm, anchored just out of sight of the broad river where beyond lay the colony. Buoyed by the sea, Sagar swam like a dolphin and within a half-hour, having exchanged pleasantries with Captain Block, learned of the curious accident that crippled his ship.

Under light wind and in calm water, a sliver of blue sky to the south grew gray, then black, approaching at great speed. The whirlwind passed across the Onrust's bow like a small tornado, Block explained, snapping the top yard but leaving the ship otherwise unharmed. Sagar, whom Block took as a native boy, suggested a suitable species of tree and location for a replacement. He offered to guide the ship into the wide but shoal-ridden river that lay beyond when the tides were favorable. Block heartily agreed and Sagar sped back to shore.

Running through the woods, each stride Sagar took landed firm and fleet, his path lined with bowing Dryads; even the sometimes troublesome Pishachas he encountered nodded in acquiescence to his quest. Usually Sagar would cross the river in a native canoe, but today he jumped headlong into the waters, riding a strong cross-current. The tides and river's flow offered no resistance to the boy. He found himself shepherded to the eastern shore and later back again by the kin of the creature who sought to pull him and Jorge into the ocean depths during the voyage across the Atlantic.

Sagar returned to the Onrust within five hours. Standing next to the helmsman, he piloted the ship to a safe anchorage on the river's eastern shore, well below the colony. As the ship slowed and backed onto its anchor, to their astonishment, the Dutch crew spotted two figures on the shoreline: a middle-aged woman and a stocky elderly man. Once on board, Mary was quick to offer the comb to Block, and while he hesitated to accept such a wondrous object, Mary's insistence overwhelmed him. Tanner and Block discovered they had one or two mutual acquaintances and soon were lost in tales of Fastnet gales and Europe's northern coast. His daughter at his side and his hands resting once again on a weathered oak railing, Tanner looked up from his conversation minutes later only to find Sagar gone.

Mary and Captain Tanner traveled with the Dutch crew in their exploration of the river through the winter of 1614. Having established a colony dozens of miles north of the sea, the expedition journeyed out the eastern opening of Long Island Sound into the wide Atlantic. With Tanner taking his turns at the helm and assisting in navigation, the Onrust and crew swept past the island now named for Captain Block before reaching Cape Cod. There, they transferred to the good ship Fortuyn, and subsequently traversed the shallow fishing grounds where Jorge lay, in time returning to Amsterdam. How the Onrust's replacement yardarm came to rest on the battered shore of a desolate whaling outpost of Spitsbergen, five hundred miles north of the Arctic Circle is another tale, a tale in which Captain Tanner also played no small part.

***

Many years later, after his mother and father had peacefully passed on, Nathan finally asked Sagar where he had spent those early years. Sagar sat in the warmth of Nathan's stone house, looking out the glass-paned windows at the silent snow falling under a moonlit glow. To Nathan, a lifetime had passed, but to Sagar only a drop of time. "I cared for the congregation, although they did not know it," he said. Sagar felt ashamed to look at Nathan. "I provided them game through the winters. In the spring, I kept their crops free from rabbits, squirrels and raccoons. In the summer, I watered their fields and in the fall harvested by light of the moon, leaving grain, turnips and later, squash, piled high."

"That third winter, do you remember it?" Sagar continued. Nathan nodded.. "Where the snow fell into April. Miles upriver, I surveyed the ice jams and when they were about to give way, through great difficulty, I reached James within the compound. He thought I was an apparition awakening him in the dead of night, but he heeded my words and saved many lives. I vaulted over the stockade to the fury of black powder explosions and shot chasing me into the woods."

Sagar's eyes narrowed, his gaze so intense it could have melted the delicate snowflakes lofting idly to the ground. "They had about nine hours to move people inland. Half the buildings in the compound were swept into Long Island Sound the next morning." Sagar's years had afforded him an understanding of men: their pettiness, their weaknesses, their fears. Their base motivations no longer surprised him. It was their destiny to thrive in the new lands. He merely assured it.

Sagar's eyes now clenched shut, he told Nathan of the congregants' struggles and success in the early decades of the seventeenth century. His reticence to assist the congregation grew, yet he could not abandon the mission that Brigu had placed upon him: protect the congregation. From the western bank, he observed them rebuild, farther inland this time. In troubled years, nets were repaired in the darkness of the spring, deer still miraculously appeared at the gate of their compound in the most brutal winter weather. Still, they began to find their footing. They learned the land, to fish, to hunt, when and what to plant.

Despite the death of James and the departure of Mary and the Captain, through the subsequent years, Sagar kept his vigil over the colony. He saw small skiffs first used for plying the river grow into fishing vessels which ventured further out into the Sound. In the generation born on this soil he recognized the faces of boys he once bunked with in the forecastle, their fathers now weathered by a hardscrabble life. The seeds of trade sprouted, some with the natives to the east, but largely with other pilgrims now in the new lands.

With trade came conflict. While sporadic Dutch settlements had failed upon the western bank, with Sagar's invisible help, the congregants survived and began to thrive, no longer fishing for sustenance, but for industry. Gunshots and arrows were exchanged on the few occasions that their fishing parties ventured west, either along the riverbank or the mainland's shore. This troubled Cikiyiyô Muksihs, who had grown in years and responsibility. His fire still burned white hot, but caring for an extended tribe had taught him to keep it buried deep, where it smoldered.

CHAPTER 30 - November 1637

Sagar retained silent watch upon the congregation into the 1630's and reported upon its growth back to Cikiyiyô Muksihs and his council. By 1630, Tom had limited his lectures to just once a week, with Nathan teaching the other days. To the end of his life, Tom's eyes had remained as bright as a young boy's but his body and mind deteriorated. Susan lived on just nine months after Tom passed away. She had seen her sons grow into leaders in the tribe and despite remaining close to Abby, she sought no aid when a slight cough progressed into difficulty breathing. Both Tom and Susan were buried across the small stream beyond the native village in the sacred grove reserved for venerated ancestors of the chief.

An incident in 1637 heightened hostilities. Three young men in their late teens ventured across the river to explore the western bank, armed with but one long gun. Late in the fall after the vibrancy of the maple's leaves had turned to browns and grays, the lads set out for the far shore. They made their way through the reeds lining the river, near where Sagar and Tom Robbin had first landed over 30 years prior. Led by the largest of the three, Harold Gaither Jr, whose face looked like bread dough, they gained elevation and stood surveying the river delta and the Sound below it. Still panting, Harold goaded his companions to explore farther west. Not ones to disagree with the son of the reigning patriarch of their village, they meekly acquiesced.

On the same day, the grown son of Kutomá Nipôwi, named Awáhsohs, and Nathan Robbin hunted mushrooms, the last of the season before winter's frost. Their path took them through dense hemlock groves, to the granite caves nearer the river. From one of these small caves emerged Awáhsohs, the chief's nephew, just below where the boys stood. Similar in build to his uncle but in nature to his father, his imposing and muscular frame looked almost comical carrying a basket of mushrooms. The boys caught sight of the native and stepped back from the edge of the rock outcropping. Awáhsohs unknowingly approached the boys, who now stood petrified. As he crested the top of the rock ledge, he caught a glimpse of the lads. Harold leveled the long gun at him and the native paused in his steps.

A few moments later, Nathan emerged from the cave and following his close friend, came upon the scene. Greeting the boys in English, the gun dropped but only slightly. "Hallo, I am Nathan Robbin. Where do you lads hail from?" He said.

"Across the river. I'm Harold Gaither," came the curt reply, with the assumption that the name carried some gravity.

"And what brings you to our side of the river, young Gaither?" Nathan said. He still spoke in a friendly tone but his thoughts refreshed with the obstinacy of the few privileged congregants. Among the traits absent in the Gaither line was an understanding of the subtlety of language. Taking the reply as a threat, the gun again rose, leveled at Nathan.

"Your side of the river? Ha! Our colony now has rights to the land upon which you trespass, granted by the Crown," barked Harold. Awáhsohs understood enough English to take these strong words as a challenge and catching its holder off guard, he batted the blunderbuss down. As he did so, Harold reflexively pulled the trigger. The shot missed both Nathan and Awáhsohs, but the native caught the brunt of the explosive report, burning his left arm and shoulder. Harold lost control of the weapon and it clattered to the rocky ground. Awáhsohs recovered the gun; in his anger and pain he swung it like a club at Harold, hitting him squarely in the arm and knocking him down. He dropped the weapon and the young men scattered, Harold clutching his injury and assisted by the other two.

Nathan tended to Awáhsohs' burns before they headed back to the village. Sagar happened to be present when they returned, meeting the shaken mushroom collectors at the village's edge. He listened to Nathan recount the experience to Cikiyiyô Muksihs and Abby with great concern. After living so many years in relative safety and solitude, they had already begun to fear colonial encroachment. The prior year, the chief had heard of larger conflicts at a council convened upon the death of the great Sachem Wopigwooit. Without a word, Sagar exchanged troubled glances with Cikiyiyô Muksihs and departed into the night.

Returning to the scene of the scuffle, he would remain planted to the spot for as long as needed, surveying the river for miles in both directions. The next day passed uneventfully, but Sagar knew better than to assume relief. No doubt the Gaithers had spent the day drumming up support for a raiding party, stirring the men of the colony into a fury and inciting fear in their wives. He had long foreseen this. Upon the morning of the third day, many boats set out from the far shore and Sagar discerned they did not contain fishing equipment. For just a moment he gazed out at the rising sun, knowing that destiny may pause in her pursuit but rarely veers from her intended path. At a speed which frightened the remaining leaves off the trees he passed, Sagar bolted for the village.

"Over a hundred armed men cross the river," Sagar told Abby, the twins and the chief. They all knew this force could not be directly countered. Nathan entered the longhouse when he heard of Sagar's hasty return. At worst, they had four hours. At best, the colonial raiders would not find them until near nightfall. Sagar and the twins exchanged thoughts underneath the desperate chatter of the others present. At all costs, they must protect Nathan's family and as many of the villagers as possible. Sagar spoke for the three of them, their plan fully formed. "Nathan, you must pack your family's belongings and lead those who cannot fight west, into the craggy hills. They will afford you safety. Chief, gather your warriors. We cannot defeat this threat, but we can harry it."

Sagar looked at the twins and the three of them closed in around Abby, the woman whose fiery hair was now tinged with silver but no less arresting than 30 years earlier. In a strange voice, seemingly channeled from another persona, he intoned, "Abigail De Danann, through whose veins flows the blood of Brigid, knower of her kin's script, Ogham, bringer of the early spring and keeper of the sacred flame: Your purpose is near-fulfilled. You have kept those who adopted you safe, but one act remains. Seek counsel with your true kin and return with haste."

The twins led Abigail from the wigwam, and Sagar had to physically block chief Cikiyiyô Muksihs from following his beloved. Regaining his composure, he and Sagar marshaled the native warriors while Nathan gathered the villagers and spread the word: they were departing within hours.

Between the river and the village lay miles of hilly and rugged wooden terrain, perfect for thwarting the formal advance of a military force. However, those who sought revenge against the natives, and perhaps to obliterate them from God's earth, were now seasoned woodsmen, most having been born in the new world. As Sagar knew only too well, they were adept at tracking animals, disguising themselves in the underbrush and moving in silence. An elaborate dance through the Connecticut hillside ensued, the colonists making headway, the natives dropping back, holding their ground, only to be outflanked by superior numbers. The colonists' principal advantage, their armaments, also made their position quite clear when they fired their bulky guns, whereas the natives could attack with little noise. Sagar reckoned they had slowed the advance to where the colonists might reach the village by early afternoon. He hoped this gave Nathan and Abby enough time. It would have to.

The twins knew the path to the grove of great hemlocks well and Abby followed them in a trancelike state. As they neared, Abby recalled her first encounter with this place so long ago, when her future husband had to lead her away from its mesmerizing power. In later years, she would learn something of what dwelled among the trees from Ayaks, her mother in law. A dark human form of legend, opaque and silent, that it was told led the natives across the frigid lands of the Northwest to their home along the bountiful eastern shores. Its purpose fulfilled, it lived on in solitude, power waning with each year. Abby was unsure if she believed the tales, but on this day, she could feel her body almost vibrating as the massive trees loomed in the distance, closer with each step. Something awaited them.

Filing through the trees, Shikha and Faria held Abby's hands, almost pulling her into the grove where an acute silence fell upon them like the softest blanket. Not so much a shape, but a feeling, a presence emerged from the largest of the trees and approached the three. The twins stepped backwards, leaving Abby alone. The darkness overwhelmed her, and just as she was about to fall, the most delicate hand, the color of harvested wheat, reached out from the blackness to support her. "Destiny be fulfilled, my daughter," rang a voice. In the instant of their touch, Abigail understood all. What she experienced as but a moment lasted nigh three hours. When the visage evaporated into the shadows again, Abigail pivoted and made for the village, the twins trailing behind her like a flowing cape.

After some trouble convincing the villagers of the need for hasty departure, Nathan saw off the first sortie of elders to the Western hills. They could carry little and traveled slowly but knew the way. Approaching gunfire soon overshadowed his sense of relief, as native warriors fell back into the outskirts of the village. Sagar appeared behind him, both comforting and startling Nathan. "Too few have departed. Spread the word. Tell the villagers: If they cannot run with it, leave it behind. It is early enough in the fall that we will still be able to provision for winter."

Without thinking, Nathan blurted out, "Sagar, can't you stop them? You must."

Sagar looked up at the desperate, aging man. He recalled the lad hanging in the rigging of the Spring Tide, standing up for the younger boys bullied in the forecastle. He couldn't expect Nathan to understand. "I cannot. The colonists are destined to thrive. If I were to intervene, not only would their survival be in jeopardy, it would set off a chain of events threatening your family and the natives who may yet live. The course is set, but have hope." Nathan looked back at him, mouth agape, until Sagar yelled, "Go! Now!" wakening him to his purpose. Nathan took a breath and set to evacuating the remaining villagers.

The first wave of colonists violated the village boundary, spraying shot into the fleeing natives, eagerly reloading. Elders and maidens fell where their ancestors had lived for hundreds, perhaps thousands of years. Nathan forced himself to ignore the massacre in the hopes of saving as many of his adoptive kin as possible. Viewing this horror from their defensive positions, the native warriors sensed their cause had been lost and were about to launch a suicidal direct assault. The warriors were now caught, knowing that in this desperate act they all would perish, leaving their families undefended and unprepared for the coming winter. Just as these forces were about to collide, Abby strode into the fray of battle, her adopted daughters, her spiritual guides and protectors resolutely at her side.

In the tongue of her own kind, that same language the sister hags had spoken when she ventured to their cave and asked their aid so long ago, Abigail began to chant. Spinning slowly, she inflamed the air around her, inciting a wicked wind which grew in momentum as Abby revolved. Her fiery locks, the color of a blacksmith's forge, red and white hot, trailed her body like the tail of a comet. The wind rose, higher, faster, enveloping the twins, who stood motionless, allowing their mother to feed off their energy, combining it with her own. She began to wield this vortex like a sword, arms raised high in the air, spinning it into a frenzy. When it reached to the tops of the hemlock trees, Abigail rained its full force crushing down upon the invading colonists. Propelling those closest to her back more than ten feet and rendering over 50 men unconscious, the remaining colonists knocked to the forest floor scattered, fleeing for the river.

Only one perished in Abby's attack. Her human body never designed to wield such force, Abby stood for some seconds while the routed colonists retreated. She then collapsed, falling back into Faria and Shikha's arms, her life gone. Several hours later the remaining invaders awoke from their stupor, finding the village abandoned and a mild autumn wind lightly rustling the fallen oak and maple leaves around them.

Abigail De Danann's physical form was hastened away by the natives and ultimately found rest in a stone tomb below New Haven. When the body expires under extreme duress, its spiritual form may be violently cast out, free to remain in this world, but also never to find peace. Abigail's last act so rent her body from her spirit, yet having united her strength with Shikha and Faria just at the moment of death, her soul found a welcome host within the twins: a direct transmigration that ensured Abigail's thoughts, her memories, her being would live on within her adopted daughters.

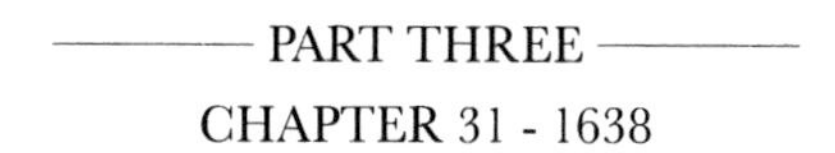

PART THREE

CHAPTER 31 - 1638

After the hostilities of the Pequot war ended in 1638, the twins and Sagar settled along with Nathan's family about nine miles west of the mighty Connecticut River where they had landed some 30 years before. At the time, the area was known as Hammonasset, but later became the town of Killingworth.

Through the 1640s and 50s, Sagar's reputation as a faultless and expedient messenger able to cover great distances had spread as far as Hartford to the north, throughout the Old Saybrook colony, and west to Stratford on the Housatonic River. Taken for a native youth, rumors simmered that he trekked hidden trails and river crossings and was advantaged by darker means of transit. However, pragmatic church and civic leaders were more than willing to put their beliefs and prejudices aside when they needed a letter or package discreetly conveyed within hours or a day.

As the southern coast's population swelled with English Puritans, Nathan sought correspondence with notable men of the time, and became a tireless advocate for native rights. He found an unlikely advocate for his cause in a Cambridge-educated minister now living within the New Haven Colony in Branford: Abraham Pierson. Pierson had moved from England to Massachusetts, to Long Island, and back across Long Island Sound to Branford. Dissatisfied with what he and his followers viewed as a waning of church hegemony over civic life, Pierson believed that only those belonging to the church were true citizens. It was on this point, through reasoned communications, where Nathan had tried to influence Pierson's thinking as it related to the native population, yet Sagar had played no small part either. On one of his trips to New Haven, Nathan asked the youth to deliver a letter to Pierson, and on this first visit Sagar ensured it soon became a regular occurrence for him to dwell for days at the Pierson household.

Arriving in the small village of Branford, Sagar had no trouble identifying the minister's house, next to the simple white church. Knocking on the door, a thin, energetic man greeted him. Sagar explained that he had a delivery for Reverend Pierson from Nathan Robbin, to which the man exclaimed, "Your English, it is quite advanced. How long have you known our language, who taught you, boy?" while ushering Sagar inside.

Sagar chose his words carefully, having much experience with men of Pierson's outlook. "I have lived with Mr. Nathan and his family for many years," he replied, hearing a young child, a boy of three or four he surmised, on the upper floor. A writing table sat just to the left of the fire over which were scattered many papers, and Sagar intentionally stared at the one on top entitled 'Some Helps for the Indians, showing them how to improve their natural reason, to know the true God and the true Christian Religion'.

Noticing Sagar's gaze, Pierson, now grinning, could hardly contain himself. "Oh, ho, so you read as well?"

Dryly, Sagar replied, "Mr. Nathan has many books. An entire library which I am free to read as I wish."

To which Pierson retorted, "I would very much like to hear about Mr. Robbin's library, but first, a question for you: In your readings, have you learned of the true God, and of Christ our Savior? There is one book which stands above all, our most Holy Bible." Sagar looked straight at the man he had just met, reading him like one of the dozen languages he knew, and edged nearer to the smoking fireplace. As the hearth warmed his body, he intoned to Pierson, "I have tried to learn something of the One God, yet it would seem as if He is no longer truly knowable by man. A great distance separates us from the Creator. Whereas I understand the rains, the sea's ebb and flow, or even the actions of men easily enough, how can I comprehend that which is infinite?"

Sagar waited for some time. His patience won out when Pierson said, "We come to understand God through our interaction with the world He created, but go on, boy, it would seem as if you speak the Word."

"Mr. Pierson, I am only an instrument of destiny. If it is so, that all paths were chosen before the foundation of the world, then what is the consequence of my actions?" Sagar said.

"It is so," Pierson replied stoically, "that Grace was given to us in Christ, the great mediator of that distance to which you spoke, before the ages began, yet . . ." A woman entered the room, chasing after a small boy. Momentarily distracted, Pierson turned to the woman and said, "How is young Abraham Jr? Such an active little chap." Recognizing the fear in his wife's face at seeing a dark youth standing at their hearth, he added, "I'd like you to meet a most fascinating native. This is young Sagar."

In less than an hour, Sagar had departed the Pierson's home, back on his way to New Haven. His brief conversation had engaged Abraham Pierson enough to secure him an invitation to return. Sagar subsequently would stay with the Piersons from time to time on his travels along the coast, discussing religion with the elder Abraham Pierson and assisting with translations of pamphlets into Pequot. He also grew to know young Abraham Jr well, teaching the boy how to recognize different animals' tracks and taking him fishing over the course of two summers. So different from his father, Abraham Jr was. Curious and intellectually flexible, he would follow his father into the ministry, but not follow in his father's mould.

In the third year he knew the Piersons, a comment made in jest by Abraham's wife, that soon enough young Abraham would be as big as Sagar who looked no different than when they first met him, garnered a dark glance from the elder minister, already wary of the close relationship his son had formed with the native. Sagar had known this day would come, as it always did, and he must disappear before a glance became open suspicion. That afternoon, Sagar and Abraham Jr would make one last hike down to Long Island Sound to fish, but instead of spending a windblown but clear autumn evening at the shore, about a quarter-mile from the Piersons' house, Sagar said goodbye to

Abraham Jr, telling the boy that he would not see him for a very long time, but to try to remember that Sagar would remain his friend. Someday, perhaps they would see one another again.

Many years later, and at Sagar's request, Nathan bequeathed his father's extensive library of books in their entirety to the Piersons, knowing that the catalogue would be passed on to young Abraham. The gift having been made under a singular condition: that the books were on perpetual loan to the Pierson family. They remained the property of three natives, twin girls Abraham never met, and the precocious young Sagar. Despite his prejudices, he was only too eager to accept the odd gift, noting that the conditions made no mention of the books passing to the natives' descendants. When Sagar delivered the chests of books to Pierson in New Ark, yet another waypoint in Abraham's quest to find his City on the Hill, the dark youth made sure to leave them at the doorstep during the night. Upon his death, Abraham gave them to his son, Abraham Jr, careful to outline their lineage.

These same books returned to within a mile of Nathan Robbin's grave when Abraham Pierson Jr became the minister of the Killingworth Congregational Church, where he would go on to found the Collegiate School, Yale University's precursor. So it came to pass, that the books Tom Robbin brought from England in the hold of the Spring Tide, that Abby and Susan used to research Abby's past, found their way into the permanent rare book collection at Yale's Beinecke library.

CHAPTER 32 - April 2, 2013

Rakhigarhi lay six hours to the east in Haryana. Asha's grandfather had come to believe Faria might find answers where the primordial River Sarasvati once supported a grand Harappan city, yet now only a small village stood. Faria, Shikha and Sagar would follow this clue, seeded long ago in the minds of the elders of Old Mari Indus by a man accompanied by a caravan of children. They would drive through the dusty night to the state of Haryana, Hehu in tow, against an angry wind seeking to propel them backwards.

In two hours they had reached Meerut. Sagar chose to turn north along Highway 82 rather than following the more direct route east, which would have taken them closer to Delhi. North to Karnal they sped, and back down to Rakhigarhi. By midnight, they had reached Jind and were following the Satluj-Yamuna canal running adjacent to Beed forest. The three of them spoke in low tones, exchanging words as much as thoughts. Hehu slept.

Faria had an acquaintance at the archeological site, but he was by no means a friend. Rakhigarhi's recent discovery in the 1960s had been forty years after Faria excavated at Mohenjo Daro in Pakistan, still the widely perceived epicenter of the Harappan and Indus River civilizations. This early culture spread across a thousand-mile arc from the Punjab and Haryana states of India, down the Indus River Valley, reaching as far west as the current Iranian Pakistani border. For over 1,500 years, spanning back past 3,500 BC, settlements clung to the Indus and other rivers, sharing construction techniques, religious beliefs and a still undeciphered pictographic language.

Faria explained one of the most curious aspects of the Indus civilization: evidence of its existence had been found 2,000 miles away in ancient Mesopotamia, where in the Akkadian period the Indus peoples were referred to as the Meluhha. Yet in India and Pakistan, even the earliest Vedic manuscripts and legends made no specific mention of these ancient predecessors. They only became known through direct archeological evidence. Imagine, she said, if the current inhabitants of Italy claimed no knowledge of, or shared history with, ancient Rome, despite the existence of Roman artifacts found as far away as central England.

"In the archaeological community an active debate still exists as to the extent to which the Indus civilization was a linear or direct predecessor to Hindu tradition; however, there is no doubt it wielded broad influence over the beliefs that arose and still exist across the subcontinent today," Faria whispered. Shikha couldn't help but laugh at her sister's formality of speech, so entrenched, as she herself was, in her specific scientific discipline.

"The most compelling evidence," Faria stopped talking, but her thoughts raced ahead and echoed in Shikha's and Sagar's brains. They only partially understood. The resonance between the three of them had grown so strong so quickly, that Sagar now found concentration difficult, yet he kept the Toyota tracking on the dark road. Shikha and Faria had given in to the collective consciousness like falling into a warm bed after a long, cold day.

Rakhigarhi was one of the earliest Indus settlements, her thoughts revealed. Local legend claimed it was built along the Sarasvati River, a waterway attested to 1,000 years later in the Rigveda, the oldest of Hindu scriptures. Sarasvati, the most easterly of the sacred rivers and one of the seven sisters in the Rigveda, had long since run dry. Seven sisters, seven pathways, seven attendants. Through Faria's mind flashed images of clay seals she had unearthed at Mohenjo Daro. A svelte human figure, bedecked by an arch of what could only be gracefully curving plant life. A tree or vines perhaps. Every seal, every clay tablet depicting seven attendants facing away from her. The Indus Valley female goddess, the mother goddess, enveloped in greenery and giving life to the earth through her seven sacred rivers.

Faria lost Sagar's attention when her thoughts spun into recollections of dates, excavations, and families she had lived with across the last century. He listened only to enjoy the meter of her mind, the connection itself, but not the words as such. Once they reached the outskirts of Rakhigarhi, he slowed the truck and pulled over, easing the vehicle into a fallow field. Hehu snored in the back seat. It had just passed one in the morning and Sagar closed his eyes too, but not to sleep, to concentrate. Something else lurked within their consciousness; he had sensed it for some time, since Faria began perusing Brigu's book on the outskirts of Rampur. When he had searched the village, nothing revealed itself; but a presence grew, first watching, next conjuring a bitter wind against their progress. Whatever Sagar first perceived striding the dusty streets outside where Faria took shelter, he knew it had kept pace but maintained its distance while they drove. There was no need to give chase, for it knew their path and destination.

With the truck parked and their minds weary from the intensity of the day's revelations, the Asura, a lower caste of supernatural being, crept physically and mentally closer, awakening the twins to its existence. Sagar opened his eyes just as Faria and Shikha's thoughts turned to a crescent of sensation descending upon them. It enveloped their consciousness from three sides, clouding their minds. Faria had experienced this while in Rampur Raza Library, but it had overcome her with such speed, she failed to recognize its purpose. Surrounded by her kin, she now could interrogate and interpret what she and the others felt. At the fore she sensed a mental blockade, a forced confusion seeking to oppress their senses.

The three flew from the vehicle and formed a defensive position behind the truck bed, back to back. A thousand yards away and closing fast, the warm night air to the East glowed an iridescent blue that gained in ferocity and crashed over them like an avalanche of color rolling down a wide mountain cirque. Unperturbed and with arms locked together, Faria and Shikha concentrated more acutely on the blue spirit's intentions while Sagar scanned for a point source of the disturbance, a body. The twins found what they sought in its reaction to their resolve. It recoiled after attempting to engage their minds, and the twins sensed frantic confusion. It had been sent to wipe their memories clean, not just the recent past but utterly. The twins captured one more sensation before Sagar spotted his prey and bolted after it. The Asura had performed this task many times for its masters, even on the three of them. For the first time ever, it had failed.

The blue crescent collapsed onto the dusty earth, dispersing. Sagar accelerated at his target, now moving in darkness. He neared the grisly creature scampering northward, ageless but aged, weary and now rancorous. Sagar caught its mind and intoned, "We only seek the truth. Ask your masters: is it not our fate to know?"

It rasped back at him, "You have no fate, Sagar Sur Sa, you are fate. Too long have you wandered and watched. I will return with such a host of my brethren that even the three of you will be undone." As the Asura sped away, Sagar slackened his pace and walked back to Faria and Shikha. The creature's threat found no purchase in their minds. They were no longer children shepherded across the world to do others' bidding, but had chosen lives beyond the reach of their creator's minions.

CHAPTER 33 - April 3, 2013

Hehu sat up. He squinted into the rising sun, shielding his eyes with his right hand. Late last night Sagar woke him, not an easy task, and dragged him into the truck bed so the twins could rest easier in the cab. As Hehu's eyes adjusted to the light he realized he was alone so he opened up one of the two black duffel bags, pulled out a camp stove and boiled water for coffee. While he waited for the water to boil he dispatched a tin of cashews, licking the salt off his fingers.

Hehu never thought much about himself. He existed as a bird upon the wind, gliding across the sea: precisely why Sagar found him such an amiable compatriot. As he sat on the tailgate of the pickup, Hehu breathed easy, sipping his coffee. He enjoyed the morning, observing his surroundings: the bushes, at first motionless, rustled awake by the early wind; the greying stalks of crops harvested long ago; the dusty haze above the horizon. If Sagar had returned in two hours or in two days, Hehu would have greeted him the same way, smiling and content. So about noon, when he espied three familiar figures in the distance to the west he began to set out snacks and make more coffee. He could see they were talking to one another; Sagar's arms waved as he made some point, but Hehu couldn't tell what he was saying.

Sagar walked ahead of the twins when they returned to the truck, his face gravely etched. "Want some coffee? There's cheese, dried fruit and a few, well, one can of cashews too," Hehu said. Sagar couldn't help but smile at the earnest young Maori. He was everything Sagar wasn't. No mental contention clouded Hehu's mind. He observed the world with a quiet stillness that Sagar envied.

"Thank you, no. I had something earlier. I hope I didn't disturb you too much last night," Sagar replied. Hehu shook his head no. The twins approached and began to partake of the picnic he had laid out, drinking down the warm coffee in gulps.

"This is wonderful, Hehu. I, we," Shikha said while chewing, motioning to Faria, "didn't eat prior to our walk. Many thanks." Sagar skirted around the truck, inspecting the ground at each step. He looked northeast, and seemed to almost smell the air. Inscrutable, he returned to the truck and reclined in the driver's seat. Faria walked over to him and said, "Are you ready?" He said he was. Hehu packed up the snacks, poured the coffee into a thermos and within a few minutes they had departed.

Sagar piloted the truck along the narrow road into Rakhigarhi where Faria instructed him to head to the far side of town. He weaved through the streets and turned on a hardscrabble access road. A manufactured office sitting idly adjacent to a dusty clearing was all that marked the archeological site. "Wait here," Faria said, hopping out of the truck and climbing the metal staircase to the trailer's door. It swung open before she knocked and a bespectacled man emerged, fidgeting with what looked like a potsherd.

"Faria, oh, is that you? I just received your note but could not be sure... I thought it might be some strange joke," he said, smiling, but even from the truck the others could sense the hesitancy in his voice.

"Sanjay, it has been a few years since the 2010 conference in Delhi, yes?" Faria replied, staring through his glasses. He looked back at her, trying to recollect something, but gave up and agreed.

"Oh, yes. You, um, presented on . . ." he stumbled, giving her a chance to chime in.

"Unconventional interpretations of the Proto-Shiva seal," she interjected. Sanjay still looked confused but nodded his head. "I have my sister and some friends of ours with me. Do you mind if I invite them in to your lab?"

"No, I guess not," he started, but when Faria's gaze met his, Sanjay more firmly replied, "Not at all, please, come in." He held the door open and the group filed past. The long narrow trailer had only one room, with tables along the walls and a single aisle down the middle. Nearest the door the tables were piled with woven baskets overflowing with dirt, while farther away the contents became more organized.

On the tables against the far wall sat wooden cases whose tops had been secured with tiny brass locks. "So what brings you to this backwater site?" Sanjay said once they were all inside.

Sagar and the twins understood their host's reticence: As an unknown, underfunded archeologist, Sanjay was working away like a lone prospector, trying to discover a rich vein of ancient history. He had no doubt heard of Faria, the tales, mostly true, she was as elemental to Indus Valley archaeology as the dirt they dug, but the two of them did not really know one another. Today, he saw her as a claim jumper. Faria stepped closer to him and introduced everyone. "This is my sister Shikha, Sagar, and our friend Hehu." She paused for effect. "Please forgive the abruptness of our visit. You see, Sagar represents a private benefactor interested in anonymously funding your research. The donor is notoriously secretive but quite generous." Shikha edged in front of Hehu to hide his look of confusion.

"My employer asks that you allow us to review your current research and findings, after which I am immediately empowered to provide you a grant of two-hundred-million rupees, to be paid out equally over the next five years," Sagar said.

Sanjay's eyes dilated and he felt short of breath. Sagar pulled a chair closer, which the researcher fell into like a load of sand falling out of a dump truck. He tried to speak a few times and could not, so Sagar continued, "What is asked of you is very little, but conditions do exist: you must share all your research with the archaeological community, but agree to brief your benefactor first; you must ensure that the workers on site are paid a handsome living wage and you hire with preference from the local community; and finally, you must teach an hour a week at the primary school in Rakhigarhi, spreading your knowledge of the ancient world."

Composing himself, Sanjay stood on shaky legs and putting his hands together, bowed slightly. "I am left overwhelmed by this blessing. We are terribly underfunded in our work and it is all I can do to help preserve the site. I have made little progress. He looked to each of those assembled. "If I have been cautious in my hospitality, I ask your pardon. You see, last fall a few of the boys from Rakhigarhi who help me dig unearthed some strange artifacts with motifs that I confess, I do not understand. Found at the same stratum as pieces dated from 3,400 BCE, they, well, let me show you. Follow me, please." He led them to the far wall, where he unlocked a densely packed case and lifted the lid. "Here, look at this," Sanjay said. He cradled a fully intact clay seal in his shaking hands and turned to Faria.

Used to imprint an insignia, writing or a scene into pottery, the clay seal was a common structure encountered from the period. It portrayed a man fending off two creatures, with Indus script adorning the top—Gilgamesh, fighting the lions on his quest to find everlasting life. Faria acknowledged the beauty and significance; she had seen at least one other quite similar to it at Mohenjo Daro. Sanjay gingerly laid it back in the case. "But now, look at this one." He cradled a broken tablet, placing it in Faria's hands.

Shikha looked not at the tablet but at her sister's face illuminated by the sun shining through the window. She felt her sister thinking, 'Tablet Ten of the epic. Reverently, Sanjay said to her, "What do you make of it?"

"It's Utnapishtim, the immortal survivor of the deluge who Gilgamesh sought out," Faria whispered, and Shikha sensed excitement growing within her sister. The tablet portrayed a small man inside a rectangle, surrounded by wavy lines. To his left and right stood larger figures, gods. Like the other artifact, she had seen the motif before but only at sites over a thousand miles to the west. On the far right of the tablet where it had sustained damage sat two small figures, standing on the top of a triangle. The damage may have been intentional, but she was not sure. She had not seen this scene. Anywhere. She traced her finger around the two figures.

"There's one more," Sanjay said, picking up a cylindrical item from the case. He paced to the other end of the dusty trailer and spread a thin layer of sand out on a table. Sanjay poured water into the sand a little at a time and mixed it with his chubby fingers until it clumped together. The others hesitantly followed him across the room to look on.

Placing the cylinder down in the sand he slowly spun it, rolling pin style, across the moist surface.

Its impression revealed a scene similar to the tablet Faria still held but in much more detail. In place of a stylized rectangle for Utnapishtim's ark there stood a well-defined watercraft, a symmetric lashed-reed boat with jagged lines below it representing water. A fish jumped close to the bow. Separated by two imposing figures and again on the right side stood a group of now five very small humans unmistakably on top of a mountain. The ancient pictographic text of the Indus River Valley civilization ran across the top of the image.

Over the twenty-four-hour period since they reunited, Abigail's memories, her beliefs, her perception had self-assembled from two dormant halves into a functioning awareness independent of but bound to Shikha and Faria. And Abby remembered this image.

"The Indus script remains untranslated, despite many attempts. We found this within a pottery graveyard, as it were. It was buried among piles of broken seals, pots and vessels, the only intact object," Sanjay said, breathing heavily. Shikha and Sagar recognized that Faria had a clear grasp of the symbols, perhaps as no other on earth could. She catalogued and ordered the characters pressed into the sand: x's, vertical wavy lines, anthropomorphic fish, and as Faria concentrated, Shikha could see the same images flashing in her own mind. To her, she saw in them chromosomes, cells and nuclei.

Not as close to their thought patterns but sensing their intensity, Sagar said, "These are striking finds, and I believe my employer would wish to hear of your promising work. If you will please excuse me, I will shortly return with confirmation of the arrangement we discussed earlier." The four of them left the trailer and began to walk around the site. Knowing that Sanjay was watching through the trailer's window, Sagar pulled out his cell phone and called his pilot to check in. All was well, and he had given five tours of the plane to the workmen at the airport, including a curious holy man who had never been so close to a plane, but scrutinized the inside as if he were an engineer. Hehu walked at some distance behind but once Sagar hung up, he approached, saying he was going to return to the truck if Sagar didn't need him. Sagar tossed him his phone and said, "Call your family. I know your father misses you." Hehu smiled and disappeared.

They had devised the plan for the financial grant on their hike early that morning and it had worked. Of course, Sagar would make good on his promise and fund Sanjay's research. Even if he made no formal scientific progress, Sanjay would now be able to provide for many in the village and if he could inspire one child during his primary school sessions, Sagar felt it worth the cost.

The three of them idly surveyed the expansive site while Faria explained Sanjay's finds. "The cylinder seal tells of a grand natural catastrophe and two sets of survivors. Those who descended as men and women: the progenitors of humanity, but it also depicts those who ascended back to their kind in the mountains, no longer free. The Harappan pictograms are not descriptive. Their blunt meanings are clear enough, but the nuances are lost with their culture." She kicked at a rock, watching it skip through the dusty ground before it stopped against a four-thousand-year-old mud-brick wall.

Faria continued. "This could be yet another local permutation of the Flood myth, one devised to explain a certain moral tenet. The Christian Bible tells that Noah's entire family emerged unharmed, worthy of salvation; yet in the Koran, one of Noah's sons perishes in the Flood, Allah decreeing the errant son unrighteous, so not of Noah's true kin. In the Gilgamesh epic, Utnapishtim, the model for the Hebrew's Noah, survives as a relic of the earlier age, almost as a cautionary figure begrudgingly imparting wisdom.

Abby's voice now rose within the twins, echoing into Sagar's mind: "The Flood. And God saw that the wickedness of man was great in the earth. And it repented the Lord that he had made man, and it grieved him at his heart. Girls," as she still called Shikha and Faria, "what is the Old Testament but a tale of growing distance from the Lord, Covenant to Covenant? As you say, Faria, there are many versions, many lessons, but there is a single truth: as much as the creator has withdrawn from humanity, humanity has become isolated from creation itself." As quickly as her thoughts emerged, Abby's consciousness descended into the twins again, like a great whale into the inky blackness of the sea.

The three of them stood now in waning daylight, shaded by the coolness of a crumbling wall. Faria began again, choosing her words as if plucking delicate flower petals: "This myth transcends cultures. It resides deep within humanity's collective unconsciousness. The clay seal, considered in the context of Shikha's genetic research, may depict the memories of an early humanity who, for a time, cohabited with a race of beings unlike themselves: an elder race, recalled to the heavens." Her words remained suspended in the air as if she had repeated them again and again until a strange wind scattered them into the dust. The breeze intensified, twisting piles of dry dirt into biting cyclones of sandpaper-coarse grit, circling around them.

Sagar's mind drifted. Faria's suspicions reflected so brightly within him, he no longer saw what was around him. Instead, he found his gaze pulled beyond the flat horizon to the high Himalayas. Unseen, yet he sensed what lay beyond, almost shivering from the alpine winds that blew. "So you believe it is the people of the mountains, this elder race that gave us our purpose years ago and who command the Asuras who now harry us?" Sagar said.

Faria stepped closer to be heard over the increasing winds. "Sagar, it is possible, even likely, that we are the elder race."

Shikha added, "Serving destiny, guiding humanity, for a distant creator."

Sagar cried, "To serve, only to have our memories cleansed: to be repurposed like the beams and spars of an old ship?" His voice bit the swirling air with frustration, but Sagar's intuition, the expansive thoughts of the twins and the power of this place told him she was right. He resisted still. "We are not human, no, but are we less than human? Do we not have the right to free will, or at least the right to believe in the illusion of choice, as humanity does?"

"Perhaps Brigu agreed. When he marked us to travel to the new world together, dearest Sagar Sur Sa, he gave us protection these past four hundred years. He gave us one other. Yes, destiny rolls over the millions who submit to her; but if challenged, even she must yield, to humanity and to us," Shikha said.

At their words, Sagar turned back to the twins and hugged them both. An intense vibration pulsed through him from the embrace and it quelled the fierce winds harrying them until all was quiet. As they returned to the trailer, Faria walked alongside Shikha, their shoulders so close that as their arms swayed, their hands would momentarily touch, sending another spark through Sagar's mind and body. They all knew they must follow the clue left to them in Mari Indus by Asha's Grandfather: they would dig here at Rakhigarhi.

CHAPTER 34 - April 4, 2013

An hour after dawn the next day, Faria had already marshaled thirty able laborers from the village and with Sanjay's direction, they began re-excavating the most prominent mound at Rakhigarhi. Disorganized, many excess laborers stood idle for hours at a time. No matter thought Faria, their lounging served its purpose too. Hehu and Sagar spent the morning driving back and forth to the closest city, Jind, the pickup loaded high with supplies for the dig. After three trips, Sagar disappeared into the trailer with a large plastic case. He emerged an hour later carrying a six-bladed remote aerial drone with an unusual looking device attached at its base: a multichannel spectrometer, able to capture visible, UV and infrared HD images. He waited until afternoon, when the temperature signature would be most consistent and began mapping the site from the air, foot by foot.

That evening, Sagar and Shikha poured over the captured, high resolution map of the area, while Faria guided Sanjay through an optimal excavation approach given the resources now available. Rather than importing skilled archeologists, Faria suggested that she and Sanjay could train villagers to perform the fine detail work required once the heavier excavations were underway. As Faria spoke to Sanjay, she also mentally consulted with Shikha.

Based on the resonance signature of the site imagery, Sagar and Shikha sensed promise from an un-excavated hill about a hundred yards southeast of the other mound sites. Sitting at a lower elevation, it had likely been overlooked by earlier teams who often equated height with prestige and sought to dig where artifacts would be most valuable. Faria recommended the heavy laborers be split into two work groups, one managed by Sanjay and one managed by her. Once Sanjay had chosen where his team would focus, Faria would do the same. Sanjay jumped at the notion, and called for his work crew to continue excavating the main mound closest to the trailer, just as Faria had expected.

The next several days passed with a familiar routine. Workers would arrive just after dawn and Hehu would have readied tables of food of a local variety but some more exotic to the work crew. After filling their bellies they would split up and dig, taking a break mid-morning for tea, and again at lunch when more victuals were made available. Sagar would disappear for hours, hiking through the lands around the town and exploring the mounds of Rakhigarhi.

Early one morning, a bearded local man, bedecked with a large topknot of black hair, walked onto the site and made directly for Hehu. He asked if he could bring his children to the dig the next day. Of course Hehu said yes, mesmerized by the intensity of the man's gaze. Word spread that families were welcome and by dawn, half the town had assembled. While they ran out of food within a few minutes, at least everyone had a bit of something to eat, and Brigu had orchestrated enough of a diversion to poke about unnoticed.

Faria spoke to the crowd in the local dialect, striking a generous bargain with them. The families of all workers were welcome for the morning meal so long as they prepared it themselves. Hehu requisitioned several stoves from Jind and under a large open tent, constructed a mess hall. Ingredients could be requested and Hehu would oblige by the next day. A week into the excavations, Faria began instructing some of the family members who now arrived for meals how to sieve dirt for small artifacts and uncover walls and floors using trowels and brushes rather than heavy shovels.

At breakfast, Sagar mentioned he had "something" to pick up in New Delhi, several hours drive away, and he'd be happy to purchase anything not available locally. Presented with a hastily drawn but extensive list, he left by nine in the morning, and try as they might to determine what his "something" was, he kept the secret until his return, after midnight the same day. Toyota pickup loaded to the gunwales and a delivery truck hired from New Delhi close behind him, Sagar screeched into the excavation site, jumped from the cab and began unpacking a large orange case.

He attached an electronic tablet pulled from the crate to a wheeled cart within the pickup bed and gruffly grappled the contraption to the ground. Hehu and Shikha , still awake, lounged in chairs arranged outside the mess hall, and had been enjoying the silence of the April night until Sagar's interruption. Hehu thought the device looked like an electric lawnmower but Faria recognized it as a ground-penetrating radar system. Sagar ignored them, focusing on calibrating the device. He disappeared into the office, returning with his laptop that held the site imagery he captured using the drone a few days earlier. Now acknowledging them, Sagar found Shikha and Hehu only too eager to help in his midnight endeavors.

They worked until sunup, focusing on the area where Faria's team had begun to dig, southeast of the main site. Hehu removed larger rocks from in front of the device, Sagar would inch it along the dusty ground, ensuring signal receipt, while Shikha consulted the aerial maps and guided him. Returning to their tents five hours later, Hehu and Shikha collapsed into bed while Sagar remained at the computer, reconciling the aerial data to the ground-penetrating radar signatures. He aimed to hand Faria a map of what lay yards below ground before she woke. To Sagar, their work was not a scientific exercise, not fodder for a peer-reviewed journal. He had never given up on Faria and he felt certain that if they could discover their origins, they could be united. A hundred yards away, mediating under a scrubby tree, Brigu listened to Sagar's thoughts, still those of a boy to him, and agreed.

Faria awoke late and filtering through her sister's unrestricted memories, straightaway she located Sagar still at work. As she approached, he closed his eyes, letting the subtle breeze she stirred slide by him as he inhaled her scent. He had overlaid the drone's visuals against below-ground image slices down 90 feet. The imagery seemed so incongruent that at first, both of them assumed the radar had been mis-calibrated or had malfunctioned. A few additional test passes assured them that the original data was indeed accurate. Where Faria and her team had begun digging lay a series of rectilinear walls, constructed of mud brick as in the previously explored mounds. They bore the hallmark characteristics of a growing city, added piecemeal and as necessary to extend a structure for habitation or to expand storage.

The questionable imagery came from strata below the mud-brick walls. Partially extending into the area de-marked for excavation by Faria but running farther southeast sat massive but precisely hewn megalithic stones. In the three-dimensional rendering Sagar constructed, they formed a path rather than a foundation. Still, some of the higher level mud-brick Harappan walls were built on top of the older but more evenly laid stone blocks, but just as often, diverged from their course.

Working in unison to the intonations of Hehu's Waiatas, or Maori songs, Faria's crew dug until dusk but could not penetrate to the top layers where the stone lay. Sagar and Shikha surveyed the broader area with radar, but as they moved south, the terrain and moisture in the soil prohibited them from identifying the full scale or nature of the megaliths. What they could perceive before the signal faded into noise was that the stones curved with the land, tracing a slow arc that must have predated the known Harappan site.

At supper, Sagar presented Sanjay with the legal documents for a non-profit corporation set up to fund his research. He also provided him with the details of a checking account at a New Delhi bank into which had been deposited forty-million rupees. For each of the next four years, on April 1 an additional forty-million rupees would be wired. It would seem as if Sagar did more than just shop when in New Delhi, Faria thought. Sanjay, for his part, had been living a dream for the past few days and with official documents in hand, left to call his parents in Lahore, making that dream a reality.

The twins and Sagar remained in the mess hall well into the black night; only a sliver of moon looked on. Puzzling over the site imagery, they had never anticipated the stone blocks. "Reminiscent in scale and dimension to those at Baalbek in Lebanon. But, they don't seem to align as a structure." Baalbek, Faria explained, contained thousand-ton rectangular blocks, the largest cut stones on earth, later used as the base of a Roman temple. Opinions differed as to how they were moved or who quarried them, but archaeologists generally agreed: they were not Roman, but much, much older. "Here, though," Faria continued, "the blocks run in a curvilinear path, unlike any ancient temple or complex I have seen. They don't stand in contrast to or stalwart against the landscape, rather, they run in concert with and trace the lines of the earth."

"Like a river," Shikha said.

Hehu peered over Faria's shoulder, saying, "They are big enough to be the veins of Papatūānuku, the earth mother." Hehu referred to the Maori earth goddess.

"Rivers are the veins of the earth, her lifeblood," Faria whispered. Tomorrow they would reach the stones and find out what lay beneath Rakhigarhi, she thought.

Sagar awoke before dawn the next day, hearing the faint sounds of digging. Knowing the workers from the village had yet to arrive, he pulled on his shirt and followed the crunch and clink of an axe and shovel. At Faria's site, he found Hehu digging away, singing in Maori. Working from memory, Hehu had lengthened the excavation in line with the path of the unseen stones below. A ninety-foot trench now sat exposed where the Harappan walls ended. Unnoticed, Sagar stood for several minutes watching his friend. Hehu sang of the earth mother Papatūānuku and the sky father Rangi in sweet embrace, but in darkness. Until their sons, yearning for the light between them, forced their parents apart for eternity, thus giving life to the natural world. Interrupting, Sagar asked, "Will they not be reunited, Hehu?"

Turning and looking up to Sagar, Hehu laughed. It was a hearty, deep bellow. "My grandmother sang that in time, they will be together once again, when the universe is ready for rebirth," Hehu said. "But my Grandfather, who lived in his own little house away from the family, said that the sky father had grown happy apart from his wife. Grandmama would usually throw something at him when he sang his version." Sagar laughed as well.

The dawn's first rays cast an orange glow over the vast plain. Sagar stared down the Sun, welcoming it, perhaps challenging it. Without turning back, he said, "Why do you dig so early? Is it not better to wait for the workers?" Hehu put down his pickaxe and climbed the several layers up to the surface.

Looking into the early light as his mentor did, yet shielding his eyes with his hand, Hehu said, "I saw the way the three of you stared at those images last night. Whatever lies beneath," now motioning to the large pit beside him, "it beckons to you."

Sagar turned to Hehu, putting his hand on the islander's meaty shoulder. "Breakfast. Then we dig together." They walked back to the mess hall, finding the villagers already assembling and the twins watching their approach.

By ten AM, Faria's work crew had uncovered the outline of three forty-foot-long stones, about nine feet wide. Sagar worked at one end of the excavation with Hehu at the other, both digging at such speed it took two sets of wheel barrow brigades to carry the dirt they shoveled to the surface, Hehu being stronger, but Sagar quicker. As the radar images had indicated, the line of stones traced a route south-east; a fourth and fifth monolith appeared at the edges of where they focused. After the tea break Sagar and Hehu widened the trenches around the stones, while Faria and Shikha led the fine detail team to clear and uncover the tops of the liths. Composed of the broader family relations of the heavy work crews, the detail team saw sons and daughters working alongside their parents and grandparents.

In the deep trench, Faria squatted low on an immense block of volcanic basalt. She ran her small hand along the stone, the pads of her fingers lingering upon its surface. The touch awakened hazy images in her mind, not her own memories but those of her ancestors. The blocks had lined the eastern shore of a great river, not to contain it, but to honor it, ebbing and flowing with its curves. The megalith she stood on had once been inscribed with characters but few remained visible after millennia of erosion. Shikha knelt down next to her sister and together they could recognize four lines of script carved into the hard stone. Faria's years traversing the sub continent gave her enough knowledge of geology to realize that this block was not from northern India. The nearest basalt she knew of lay much farther south and west, in the Deccan trap volcanic formation.

Hearing their thoughts, Sagar called out, "It continues on the side of the block, and looks much less weathered than on top," referring to the script. He had dug about a yard in a few spots, and saw the same characters, but those lying vertically still had traces of an ochre-colored pigment in the crevices.

Faria jumped down to Sagar and almost before landing, called to Hehu, "Focus here, let's try to get this side partially unearthed before dark." Hehu and his team had cleared the outline of a fourth block and had come up against the later Harappan wall, which they were wary to disturb. "Shi, here, and here again," Faria said, unable to take her eyes off the inscriptions. Shikha had followed her sister down from the top of the stone. "These are also represented in the Harappan script, but on this stone, they are more precisely cut, more elegant. These are reminiscent, some identical, to the earliest Vedic Sanskrit." Every foot of earth moved brought the twins more to inspect.

A few hours before dusk Sagar and Hehu had managed to excavate down four feet along the length of a single stone block, revealing two clear lines of script. The mound of dirt at ground level had grown into a hill in its own right. Unfortunately, the deeper they dug the longer it took to remove the dirt from the lowest levels and despite the earnest efforts of the village work crews, they were starting to fall behind the speed of Hehu and Sagar.

Faria stood and climbing back on top of one of the blocks, she looked around at the exhausted crew. Most had lived in the village their entire life, never knowing these giant stones slumbered nearby. They had been so focused on clearing the dirt that only now as they slowed did the workers realize the import of their excavation. That night, below the clouds of a looming storm, tales would be told in the village of the giant blocks, of the unknown language inscribed on them, and of the newcomers who had led the crew directly to where to dig. By morning, everyone in Rakhigarhi able to walk would be drawn to the site, the curious, cautious and incredulous. She addressed the team, calling out:

"Enough for today. Thank you all. Together, we have made tremendous progress." Faria knew they had employed brute-force archeology, crude but effective. As the team dispersed, Faria sought out Sanjay. She felt obligated to share their discovery with him and allay any fears remaining about their intentions.

Shikha and Sagar returned to the mess hall, having taking several panoramic pictures of the two lines of script. Despite the day's success, with each shovel of dirt, Sagar had grown increasingly uneasy. He sensed a presence lingering on the outskirts of the village, awaiting nightfall. The coolness of the air portended visitors from the mountains.

Faria found Sanjay still at work with his crew and called him over to her. With the influx of resources he had remained focused on his own dig, so excited to make real progress on a mound he had been wanting to excavate for over two years. "Sanjay, we have found something, different. Your benefactor and I only ask that you use discretion in revealing to the outside world what I am about to show you. There are those who may wish to see it reburied for another millennia. Come with me," Faria said. She led him toward her excavation and well before reaching the wide trench itself, he saw a newly formed hill: the long mound of dirt they had dug. He stopped walking.

"How, how deep have you gone?" Sanjay blurted. Faria slowed but did not stop walking.

"Come, Sanjay, there is much to explain," she intoned. He could not help but follow her.

35 - April 14, 2013

Faria returned alone to the mess hall about 20 minutes later, finding her sister at work on a laptop, assigning numbers and computing statistics on the symbols they found within the two lines of script. Shikha raised her eyebrow as Faria sat down. "Oh, Sanjay will be fine. He's still sitting in the hole." Shikha typed as her sister spoke.

"We need more data, additional lines, but still, I can adapt some pattern-recognition algorithms used in my genetic research to unwind this and decipher the script, if we assume these are letters; if not, we can use many-to-one hash and key values to represent," Shikha's words about the familiar and unfamiliar symbols trailed off as a new voice arose.

Abby returned to their minds, as curious as the twins, but less focused on the conclusion: "Girls, do you remember your hammocks? Ogham script is how I knew the design. Through your eyes, this looks like a version, but there is an elegance, as if Ogham were a child's attempt to replicate their parents' writing."

"Yes, it's too consistent, too continuous to be anything but a single language," Faria reflected across their consciousness, her view shared with all. She acknowledged that they needed more lines, more data, but in the sample set, she saw shared characteristics with several other languages: Harappan, Vedic Sanskrit, Avestan, Mycenaean, even Continental Celtic. She felt as someone might who had known modern Italian her entire life, confronting ancient Latin for the first time.

Shikha kept scrolling back and forth across the panorama images of the two lines of text. Zooming in and losing resolution she became frustrated; tapping her fingers on the rough wood table she said, "Does Sagar have floodlights? I bet he does." She jumped up and left Faria still staring at the screen. A few minutes later, Shikha walked by the mess hall with Hehu in tow carrying large tripods with halogen lights affixed to their tops and a gas generator. A light drizzle had begun to fall, unheard of for this time of year. "Are you coming with us?" she said to her sister. Back at the site they found not Sanjay but Sagar sitting alone on the unearthed block, awaiting their return but perhaps something else as well.

"It will not be an easy night," Sagar intoned. Hehu assumed he meant they would dig until dawn. Reading his drawn face, the twins knew better. Sagar Sur Sa looked not at them, but beyond, at the gathering host approaching the work site.

At ground level, the halogen lights deep in the earth cast a haunting glow skywards across the lip of the dig, a concentrated pure white sunrise. The misty drizzle crackled and spit as it landed onto the light's black casings. Faria had set them up on the far end of the stone block, close to its corner to accentuate the depth of the inscriptions. With their back to the light, Hehu and Sagar sought to unearth an additional line of text. It was there, sure enough. After the day's travails, Hehu still moved heavy loads, but at a slower pace. Sagar did not temper his efforts and dug with a quiet ferocity. Without the aid of the full crew, Faria instructed them to pile the dirt back on top of the stone block, allowing work to progress more quickly, and within two hours they perceived another full line of text.

The sharpness of the engravings implied that at least this side of the block had seen little weathering degradation. It must have been buried soon after the text had been inscribed, Faria thought. After entering the new line into her laptop's algorithm Shikha yelled out, referring to the translation, "I think I have a few words, and several possibles." Faria ran over to her sister and leveraging her knowledge of Sanskrit and Celtiberian corrected a few assumptions in Shikha's code, muttering to herself, "No, that is Pha, this is turned sideways, that's more a Ke, and that, hmm, that's not a D, it's an R." Her revisions changed the possible translation of a few words and brought meaning to three others.

On such scarce evidence, three lines of text, Faria would not draw any scientific conclusions. However, the circumstantial fact patterns leading them to this place and her visions from earlier today compelled her to believe that the inscription was indeed in the mother tongue, the progenitor of the entire Indo-European language family. Like from the single, stout trunk of an oak, in that text, she saw the living and dead branches of an expansive language set, spawned and grown through time and circumstance into dozens of extinct and modern languages as diverse as Punjabi, Kurdish, Welsh and Norwegian. What's more, as Faria reflected on the vast lineage, she visualized more connections, at first errant sparks, a letter or phrase, they soon built into a self-fueling fire that blazed in her mind. She thought she discerned the beginning of the message, but forced it from her present thoughts. Picking up the shovel at her feet, she said, "Keep digging. Everyone."

Into the rainy night they worked, the excavation growing narrower until Sagar and Faria stood nine feet below the top of the stone megalith in a trench only about a foot wide. Hehu and Shikha carried burlap bags of wet dirt up the side of the steep incline, depositing the soil on the top of the stone block. The rain began to cease, but in its place blew a chilling wind that buzzed as if threatening lightning with each gust. It drove Sagar on to dig ever faster, but Hehu grew pensive and turned in circles upon the stone lith, scrutinizing the air. "Sagar, is it us that angers the sky?" he asked.

"Be easy, my friend," Sagar replied. He stopped and leaned on his shovel. To the twins he said, "Hehu's work here is done for the night, isn't it, Faria?" Sagar kept his gaze fixed on an effervescent blue halo encroaching upon the massive pit from all sides.

"Yes, yes, we will begin to clean up. Hehu, you should return to the camp and rest. It is well past midnight, and in a few hours the workers will arrive," Faria said with haste. Hehu, however, would not be so easily dismissed. He stood planted on top of the basalt rock, now just half-buried in the earth.

"You think me afraid?" Hehu said. "I am. But my fear won't chase me from standing with my friends, with you all. If the children of the elements wish to practice their skills upon us this night, if Hine-whaitiri herself, the girl of thunder, should appear, I will tremble, for I am just a man. But I am a Maori man."

As Hehu spoke, the winds ebbed and for a moment all remained still. Sagar pulled him close while Shikha hopped up onto the megalithic stone, standing back to back with her sister. A frigid, cyclonic breeze began to rise, gusting as it circled the dig. When the arctic airmass descended into the excavation it struck the still sunwarmed but wet dirt, spawning a thick fog bank. The thousand-ton stone lith now looked as if were floating on a cloud, with four small beings riding it. The first Asura, the same they had encountered outside Rakhigarhi, swept by them and cackled deeply, brushing as much against their bodies as through their minds.

Coalescing from the ebbing winds, more creatures emerged, some grotesque, others lithe and beautiful, but all driven by a common purpose: to end Brigu's little experiment that had enabled Sagar and the twins to live freely. So few of the elder race remained, they were now too valuable to the gods and the Asuras to roam the earth unfettered. A more perfect precursor to humanity that still lived on from well before the great catastrophes, the twins' and Sagar's minds must be cleansed. Within days, the Asuras thought, the three would be thousands of miles apart, again serving humankind and destiny itself as the gods and Asuras once had, ages ago.

The rim of the pit now glowed a deep blue and thirteen bitter shapes ringed the perimeter, leaving no escape and offering no quarter. Yet, Sagar smiled upon his shaking Maori friend. "Your words strengthen me, young Hehu. Be not afraid, there is nobility in your actions. I only regret, if this is to be our end, that it has not come upon the sea, upon the great ocean of Kiwa. The waves never cease, forever may they roll on. I would have liked my bones to rest in the depths, ever serenaded by the churning sea." Hehu laughed and readied his pickaxe for whatever might come next. Still smiling, Sagar's eyes flashed red before he closed them, lowering his head to concentrate alongside his kin. Shikha and Faria did the same.

They began to push the Asuras away from one edge of the dig, surprising the spirits with their strength, but could make no permanent headway. As soon as they pressed forward, several would fly in from the opposite side of the pit. Each passing touch momentarily confused Sagar and the twins, allowing the remaining Asuras to inch closer. Hehu swung his axe at the creatures, again and again knocked to the rock by their parries until he rose no more. This was no stalemate, it was a slow containment.

In desperation, Sagar thought to break free on his own, charging the line and allowing the others to escape. But just before he bolted, Faria locked her arm to his. "Together, Sagar Sur Sa, one more press. We must try together." Faria held fast to Sagar's wrist, Shikha grasping the other. They internalized their defenses, letting the collective concentration build until the sand atop the basalt monolith began to dance. In a single movement, Faria, Shikha and Sagar channeled a pressure wave out across the perimeter at the circling Asuras. So ferocious was their unified burst of power that it cleaved the air, evacuating the pit before it came rushing back in with a momentous thunderclap heard miles away.

Their legs failed and the three slumped onto the rock's surface. All was black, but only for a moment. The icy blue vapor crept back to the edge of the pit and with it returned the most grizzly and determined of the god's minions. The spirits descended the walls of the dig, advancing upon three of the few remaining first race. Each sortie further weakened them until their resistance drifted away and the Asuras were free to roam their minds. But in breaking the twins' and Sagar's consciousness open, the Asuras set something altogether unexpected free. Now unbounded, what dwelled deep in Faria and Shikha emerged as the colors of a sunrise, orange and crimson, dispelling the cold spirits and settling warmly around Sagar, Hehu and the twins.

The first Asura to approach again met a slicing whip of red mist that coiled around it, placing the immobile spirit back on the edge of the pit. In that touch, it sensed a gravely ancient presence conjoined with the youth of humanity. The diffuse mist then converged into Abigail's familiar form, in the hues of barley fields awaiting the harvest. Now curious, the other spirits that had been driven back edged closer.

"Your mission diverges from nature's true design." Abby compelled the gathered spirits to listen. Her words required no medium for transmission; they invaded the perceptions and awareness of all present. "Surely you see this. Destiny never set a course of isolation between the gods, the spirits and mortals. Ages have passed and what have you done other than to increase this distance between humanity and nature, between creation and her creators. Look at what has become of humanity, of their home, and yours. Is this despite or because of your work? Let there be reconciliation." Her bare feet paced the stone monolith before she stopped at the closest point to the rim of the dig. "I will not stop your attack, but you must acknowledge your freedom to decide if it is righteous. Just as you have choice, so do these three. Let the lost resonance be rekindled. Allow the river of destiny to flow unimpeded. Let Sagar, Shikha and Faria and all their kind find their own ways."

Abigail De Danann, in whose veins the blood of gods and mortals had flowed, walked to the far end of the rock. One by one, the Asuras filed past her, bowing, before they dissipated into the now-warm night air. The stars returned to the sky, and after glancing at her daughters and Sagar, she chased after the infinite lights of the night.

Sagar haltingly stood and helped Faria to her feet. He clasped her hand and she rose, as near to him as spring is to summer in mid-June. Radiant under the stars, Faria's lips beckoned to him, but he hesitated, until she pulled him closer, her fingers running along the back of his neck, guiding him. Sparks danced and sputtered along their skin as their lips met and they remained locked as if no force could restrain or separate them.

With dawn's approach, the halogen lamps briefly railed against the might of the sun only to be swamped by its majesty. On the top of the stone block, in a bed of dirt, Hehu now slept unaware of the new day. Twenty feet below ground, in the coolness of the morning shade, Sagar squatted low and grabbed some loose sand, letting it sift back through callused and torn fingers while pressing his other hand to the words on the block of stone. Faria and Shikha finished brushing the dirt from the last characters of the fourth line of text and returned to where he crouched. They had completed their translation.

The monolithic stone blocks still reverberated with the faint song of the sacred River. First constructed, Faria explained, to honor the waters that once flowed a mere fifty yards away, their most ancient and weathered inscriptions gave thanks to the mother goddess and her seven daughters for the river's flow. Much later, just before primordial catastrophe laid waste to the land, the liths had again been inscribed, this time as a beacon and compass to humanity. These more crisply defined engravings were buried by torrents of water, mud and sand just days after the chisel had left its mark. As she glanced back at the long line of text, Faria murmured, "In the mountain pass leading to the great northern desert beyond, whosoever needs it, shall find aid from the children of the gods."

In time, the river's flow would return to shepherd the rains of the Himalayas to the people of the Harappan settlements before joining the sea. But the creators of the stone megaliths, they had not returned, except in very rare circumstances. Like the massive stone and its inscription, like the sacred river, like Abby and the descendants of Danu, the three of them were also of an earlier age. Underlying their existence, perhaps all existence, a powerful melody once uniting creation had faded into silence, but perhaps, it could be heard again, relearned if just more would listen.

Faria, Shikha and Sagar departed Rakhigarhi into the rising sun, leaving Sanjay with two able teams of workers and enough funding for the excavation to expand how he saw fit. Although Sanjay, the twins and Sagar did not know it, a shepherd of orphan children, indeed of humanity itself, remained to watch over the young archeologist's progress. The coming days would bring crowds and scrutiny to the site and Sanjay would need counsel and perhaps more. As he had since their emergence, Brigu observed humanity's cyclical path to enlightenment. As a leaf caught in the eddy of a curving river, progress toward the sea would sometimes stall until the smallest events aligned, pushing the leaf once more rushing downstream. The previous night's encounter did not stand alone in this river, but was put in motion hundreds of years beforehand, to idly wind its way to a stalled leaf, kicking into the stronger flow hundreds of years hence.

Of Hehu, he promised to remain at the dig, but when refueling two hours away from Rakhigarhi, Sagar poked at an all-too-lumpy sleeping bag in the bed of the pickup, from which the Maori emerged. "It is my choice and I am coming," is all he would say. "At least ride in the cab," was Sagar's response, laughing. Whatever adventure lay ahead for his mentor and the twins, Hehu refused to allow them to face it alone. They drove northeast into the foothills of the Himalayas, finding their path graced and guided by friendly Asuras. While thankful for the fellowship, they found the direction unnecessary. They now knew the way. By morning the village of Mana lay before them at ten thousand feet. Another 30 miles north and 8,000 feet higher loomed Mana Pass, where they would begin to search for their kin and their home.

Author's Note

The Spring Tide was born from a second and third reading of The Golden Bough in late 2012. While the modern scholar may discount some of Frazer's assumptions, his work still stands as an elegant and comprehensive treatise on what we know concerning myth, but also what we, perhaps, have forgotten.

The ancients intuitively understood that life should not be defined in terms of a single entity but on a collective scale, through the cycles of vegetation, of death and rebirth. Their myths, however crude modern humans view them as, sought to perpetuate this notion for future generations. Somehow, in the transliterated names, the adoption and redaction of thousands of years, we've lost this.

Life defies linearity. It turns back on itself, it retrenches, it cycles and cycles until it is released and reborn. A perception persists, rooted in the more base interpretations of Darwin's theory, that evolution implies a continual progression towards higher and higher ground. This notion took hold in Victorian times to give credence to the idea that humanity is poised at the pinnacle of an unceasing cultural progression, where an elect few stand ready to take the next step upwards. As recently as 30,000 years ago, what we consider modern humans coexisted and interbred with more than just one other sub-species. What if the Victorians' were right in their assumption, but wrong about who, or what, looks down from the evolutionary pinnacle? What if another species survives among us?

Acknowledgements

The author wishes to acknowledge the grace and patience with which his family kindly read iterations of this work. Their guidance and counsel was hopefully well received. Original cover art by Valerie Stitt.

CPSIA information can be obtained
at www.ICGtesting.com
Printed in the USA
LVOW08s1721020217
523021LV00003B/737/P